SEE
JANE
SNAP

OTHER TITLES BY BETHANY CRANDELL

The Jake Ryan Complex
Summer on the Short Bus

Text copyright © 2021 by Bethany Crandell

Published by Montlake, Seattle

www.apub.com

Amazon, the Amazon logo, and Montlake are trademarks of Amazon.com, Inc., or its affiliates.

ISBN-13: 9781542026888
ISBN-10: 1542026881

Cover design by Caroline Teagle Johnson

Printed in the United States of America

SEE JANE SNAP

BETHANY CRANDELL

 Montlake

To Dad
When I grow up . . .

CHAPTER 1

I am a strong, capable woman.

"I am a strong, capable woman."

I can do anything I set my mind to.

"I can do anything I set my mind to."

The world is mine for the taking.

"The world is mine for the taking."

I am no longer bound by the confines of my penis.

"I am no longer bou—*ugh*."

I snatch my phone from the center console and tap the screen, pausing the tutorial. I've listened to this YouTube video at least a thousand times and yet somehow am always startled by the transition from bra-burning, empowered female back to transgender woman, where we started. I'm sure there are better-suited self-helps out there, but I really like the sound of Dr. Deedee's voice; she's authoritative and confident. Probably because she's no longer bound by the confines of her penis . . .

I scrub the video back a bit with a drag of my finger and start again.

I am a strong, capable woman.

"I am a strong, capable woman . . ."

I repeat this exercise the entire drive and, by the time I reach the restaurant and squeeze my car into a narrow space between two identical Teslas, feel like I can conquer the world.

Yes, I can do this.

I've got this.

As we do every month, the Second-Wives Club of Mount Ivy General Hospital is meeting for lunch. It's not an *actual* club, of course, just a silly name we came up with over too many proseccos a year or so ago, and technically we're not *all* seconds. (Of the four of us, only Tamira and Heather are *actual* second wives, while Brielle is number four to Dr. Harold Dixon, plastic and reconstructive surgeon, and I'm the lone, nearly-extinct-to-this-world first wife.) But we thought it was cute, so we stuck with it.

We spend most of our time catching up on our families and idle hospital gossip, but because I also serve on the board of Mount Ivy General's special-events committee (yet another post I've been bequeathed), I loop the girls in on the latest activities whenever there's something to report. On today's agenda: the big Valentine's gala—held just three months from now—when we'll kick off the fundraising campaign for a new, state-of-the-art cardiology wing that will put Mount Ivy on the map, where it belongs. At least, that's the fluffy spin we're putting on it. Truth is, the hospital is terribly short on funds, and if they don't secure some big money very soon, all the specialty departments will be cut, starting with cardiology.

And since my husband, Dan, is the head of cardiology, and also the chief of the entire surgical department, it goes without saying that securing this new wing is very important to him.

Very important.

And not just to him and the countless doctors and nurses who report to him, but to our entire family.

I cut the engine and give myself a quick once-over in the rearview. Aside from the bruise-colored under-eye bags, I look pretty good. Better than I thought I would, considering I'm running on about three hours' sleep. I touch up my lipstick, blotting it against the mile-long CVS receipt that's rammed into the cup holder, then smooth wisps of my mousy, boring brown hair from my face.

Despite the empowering words still echoing inside me, my hands are a bit shaky. They've been doing that lately. A twinge of concern niggles at my spine, but I quickly dismiss it with the realization that it must be a quirky reaction to that new chamomile oil I've been using. (Just a dab on each temple before bed, to soothe out the stressors of the day.) I'll switch back to the lavender.

It's no surprise that my party is seated at the table in the far corner of the room that boasts lake views from all seats—the best table in the house, for the most respected wives in town—or that there's already a drink waiting for me. And it's got mint in it. A frustrated sigh settles in my chest. I don't like mint—

"There she is. Hey, girl!"

As always, Brielle's amplified greeting makes me smile. Even though she's been around almost a year now, her adorable southern drawl still catches me by surprise, and the fact that she calls me *girl*, when she could technically be my daughter (if I'd started as young as most of my classmates back in high school), is sort of endearing. Oh, to be twenty-five again . . .

I am strong.

I am capable.

I can conquer the world.

"Hi, everyone." There's an unfamiliar waver in my voice that gives me pause. I hope I'm not getting sick . . .

"Hi, hon." Tamira gives a little wave.

Heather doesn't offer a hello but instead raises her near-empty glass in greeting, liquor-soaked ice cubes tinkling against the crystal.

"Sorry I'm late. I had two PTA subcommittee meetings at school; both ran long." I drop down into the empty seat between Brielle and Heather, sighing as I hang my bag on the back of the chair. "It's been a busy morning."

"Tell me about it," Tamira says over one of her signature eye rolls. "I had a seven thirty with Olga." Olga, her massage therapist. "She claimed that was the only time she could get me in today. I mean, seriously? It threw off my entire morning."

"Aw, I hate when they only have those early-morning slots," Brielle adds sympathetically.

"Today we're enjoying Peachy Keens." Heather leans in, tapping my glass with the tip of her finger.

Heather Mills-Crosby, former soap opera actress married to Dr. Mitchell Crosby, general surgeon. (She was mostly an extra, but she did have a three-episode arc on *Days of Our Lives* a few years ago.) Along with her designer wardrobe and perpetual scowl, she has one of those affected accents—like Gwyneth or Madonna—that's especially notice-able after she's had a few drinks. Based on the way she's dragging out her vowels, I'm guessing the glass in her hand isn't her first. "It's peach whiskey, ginger beer, lime, and . . ." She glances down at the menu beside her. "Oh yeah, peach bitters, whatever the hell those are, and mint. It's delicious. You'll love it."

"Yeah, it looks great." I pick the glass up and take a drink. The hor-rible mint taste assaults my taste buds, bringing a grimace to my lips that I quickly force away. "Mmm. Yeah. That is tasty."

"Right?" She winks at me, then signals for our waitress with a crook of her finger.

"So, Tamira was just telling us about their next conference season," Brielle says, her doe-like eyes wide with excitement. Conference season: when our spouses are invited to speak at medical conferences, and we get to travel along with them, generally without kids, which is the big draw. "She said they might be going to Paris. Isn't that so exciting?"

"Wow. That—yeah." I nod encouragingly. "That would be amazing."

"Ugh, Paris is so cliché," Heather grumbles, and Tamira says, "I'm not even sure we can do it. Marcus has already committed to giving a talk at that orthopedics consortium down in Atlanta around the same time, so it may be a nonstarter."

"Atlanta? Yay!" Brielle gasps, then gives a happy little clap, offering a glimpse of her recent-past life as a Georgia Tech cheerleader. "I'll tell you everywhere you have to go. I swear, some of the best restaurants in the world are in Atlanta. *Oh!* And the live music is amazing—you have to go dancing!"

"We'll see," Tamira replies before taking a sip of her drink. "I'm too busy to give it a whole lot of attention right now."

"Here she comes," Heather mutters, turning her attention to the rosy-cheeked waitress who's just arrived. I glance at her name tag: MELODY. That's pretty.

"Yeah, I'll have another one of these," Heather says, rattling her empty in the air.

"Sure. Does anyone else want another round?"

"No," Tamira answers, "but we are ready to order."

My eyes snap wide. Oh . . . kay.

I quickly scour the menu while my friends rattle off their orders: a baby-kale salad with shrimp, pomegranate dressing on the side; a seared ahi salad, sesame-ginger dressing on the side; a nicoise salad with steak—cooked rare—and red wine vinaigrette on the side—

My gaze zeroes in on the pork belly burger, slathered in gouda with onion jam and roasted garlic aioli, with sweet potato fries—

"Jane," Tamira prompts. "What kind of salad do you want?"

I swallow through the pool of saliva welling in my mouth and raise my head.

"I'll have the, um . . . the pecan-crusted chicken with balsamic, on the side."

I hand off my menu to Melody, then, despite the awful taste, take another drink of my Peachy Keen. *Ugh.*

"So, do you know where y'all are headed next season?" Brielle asks Heather.

"Who the hell knows," she answers with a dramatic flip of her hand. "First, he said something about Annapolis; then it was Tampa;

now it's some neuropathy conference in Denver. I mean, Denver." Her scowl deepens over her lined lips. "Like my sinuses aren't jacked up enough as it is, he wants to drag me up into the mountains."

Denver.

Denver.

Without any effort on my part, my jaw muscles grow taut, my molars slamming together like opposing magnets.

How has it been two months already . . .

I quickly reach for my glass, breath catching when I see that my hand is shaking again.

Damn chamomile.

The cubes clink as I raise the glass to my lips and take another drink, longer this time. I wince as the minty-sweet burn trails down my throat.

"Oh my god, I know," Brielle goes on. "Denver's the worst. I always feel so light-headed when I'm there. How 'bout you, Jane?" She turns to me. "You're always so organized—you must have all your trips figured out already, huh?"

"Oh, um . . ." I clear my still-burning throat, jaw slowly easing back to a lax state. "You know, we're not really sure what we're doing yet. It's getting a lot harder to do these trips now that Avery's got so much going on."

"I swear, I don't know how you girls do it," Brielle says, shaking her head. "I feel like a headless hen whenever the boys are at our house—and they practically take care of themselves."

Brielle, fourth wife of fifty-three-year-old Harold, plastic and reconstructive surgeon, has inherited three teenage stepsons from her husband's first wife, Michelle. Tanner is nineteen, Quinn is seventeen, and Brandon just turned sixteen. The oldest is in college on the West Coast now, so his visits are few and far between, but the other two spend every other mediation-appointed weekend with their dad and Brielle. Poor kids. I can't imagine how difficult it would be to grow up with a rotating door of stepmothers. Not that growing up with a single mother was an envious road . . .

I take another drink.

I will never do that to Avery.

"Well, you know, I'd be totally lost without Carmen," Tamira admits over a flippant shrug. "There's no way I could get everything done if I had to deal with the boys all day."

Before Tamira married Marcus Bryant, orthopedic surgeon, she was Tamira Moores, second runner-up Miss Black America 2013, a title she earned while simultaneously working toward her master's in mathematics. Her plan had always been to teach, but once the infertility treatments kicked in, all her attention was, understandably, focused on getting pregnant. And by the time the twins finally arrived (Jaden and Isaiah, now four years old), she'd moved on to other ventures: she sits on the board of a nonprofit organization, Next Day Queens, that helps inner-city girls get into the pageant circuit. She claims it's not as fulfilling as teaching would have been, but to be honest, I think it's probably a better fit. I can't imagine someone with her intense disposition teaching students. Of course, I've never set foot in a college classroom, so what do I know?

"I don't know how any of you do any of it," Heather grouses, the word *any* stretching out over a mile. "Mitch's girls drive me fucking insane, and I only see them twice a year." She slurps back what's left of her drink, gaze darting between us and the kitchen door. She's ready for her refill. "They're little demon spawns, just like their mother," she continues, grating her fingers in the air like claws. "The oldest one actually got caught vaping in class the other day—"

Brielle gasps and Tamira says, *"What?"*

I shift in my chair.

"I know, right?" Heather goes on. "What the fuck is going on with this sixteen-year-old kid that she's vaping in the middle of English class?" I take another drink. "I swear, there's no way I could get through this whole stepmother nightmare without Dr. Jill and her magic pills." She raises her Kate Spade bag up at her side and gives it a shake, suggesting her magic pills are with her now.

Despite the subject matter, Brielle snorts and says, "Oh girl, you and me both. I'd be lost without Dr. Jill and the happy Zs."

"Happy Zs?" I ask.

"Zoloft," Brielle clarifies. "They're my saving grace."

"I hear that." Tamira raises her glass in solidarity. "The last time my prescription ran out, I about had a nervous breakdown. Of course, Marcus wouldn't call it in for me," she adds, which isn't surprising. Our husbands are very reluctant to abuse their scrip-writing privileges. "So, I had to send Dr. Jill a 9-1-1 text at two in the morning."

Now it's Heather's turn to snort. "God, I've sent her more than a few of those over the years. I swear, that woman is my fucking savior."

Dr. Jill is the most sought-after psychiatrist in town. Every woman I know sees her—every woman but me, that is. Dan knows her through the hospital and says that while she's nice and a good listener, she can't be trusted with confidential information. I'm not sure if that's actually the case or if it's just that the patients share the same information with each other that they share with her. Either way, I get enough emotional, motivational support from outside sources, like Dr. Deedee, to keep me going.

Not that I don't enjoy picking up a few tips along the way when I can . . .

"So, did you tell Dr. Jill about the whole vaping thing with your stepdaughter?" I ask Heather.

"Absolutely. She knows all our family's dirty little secrets."

"Mm-hmm," Tamira mutters.

"And . . . what'd she say?" I ask.

"Well—"

"Ooh! I bet I know exactly what she said." Brielle cuts Heather off over a giggle.

"Go for it." Heather smirks.

"Okay, she said that Mariah—it's Mariah, right?" Her eyes suddenly narrow. "She's the sixteen-year-old?"

"Yup," Heather groans.

Brielle smiles. "Okay, so *Mariah* isn't deliberately trying to be disruptive; she's just trying to figure out where she fits in the world—and who her people are. She's living her own truth, and that should be valued rather than criticized—"

Living her own truth?

"Am I close?" Brielle finishes.

Heather offers a rarely seen grin. "Ver-fucking-batim."

Brielle breaks out into laughter while patting her palms excitedly on the table. "I knew it! Oh my god, she'd be so proud of me—"

"Oh, finally," Heather mutters as Melody returns to the table with her new drink. Heather leans in closer to me, allowing the waitress room to swap them out.

"Your salads will be up in just a minute," Melody says.

"You know, I'll go ahead and take another one of these too." Tamira taps her still-half-full glass with her finger.

"Of course." Melody's smile *looks* very agreeable, but as a former waitress, I recognize it for what it really is. It's a smile that says, *I just asked you four minutes ago if you wanted another drink, and you said no.* A smile that says, *I know you think you're better than me because I'm the one doing the serving.* A smile that says, *Don't you dare feel sorry for me; I won't be stuck in this life forever—*

My phone suddenly chimes, indicating I have a new text message. Because this group is very casual—always sharing pictures and posts—I don't hesitate to pull it out while they continue with the conversation about Dr. Jill and her child-rearing wisdom.

I tap the screen and—*UGH.*

Frustration rattles through my bones as I stare down at my sister's typo-ridden message:

Moms parchment didn't go thru.

If they dive get it by tmrw they can't refill yet kids!

Translation: Mom's payment didn't go through. If they don't get it by tomorrow, they can't refill her meds.

Dammit. What is wrong with my bank? This is the third month in a row—

"Everything okay, sweetie?" Brielle gives my arm a gentle stroke, reclaiming my attention.

I blink hard. "Oh . . . yeah." I quickly swallow back my resentments while subtly turning off my phone. "Everything's fine. It was just . . . Avery. She had to give a speech in English class this morning and wanted to let me know how it went."

"Aww, that is so sweet." Brielle presses her hand against her heart. "You're such a good mama. No wonder you don't have to see Dr. Jill—you've got this parenting thing nailed down."

I force a smile as snippets of last night's conversation with my twelve-year-old start to reverberate through my mind:

I'm not saying I'm going to look at every single one of your messages, but I do want to see the kinds of things you're talking about with him—

It's my phone. I'm entitled to my privacy!

Yes, sweetie, of course you are, but it's my job to protect you—

Protect me from what? We're not doing anything—we're just friends!

I'm not talking about sex—

Oh my god! Don't say that word!

Honey, I just want to make sure you're okay—

Why do you always have to be in my business? Why can't you just trust me?

Sweetie, it's not that I don't trust you—

Then why do you want to look at my phone?

Because you've been getting into trouble with this kid. I just want to make sure—

It's because you don't have a life of your own! Get your own life already, and just leave me alone!

Leave me alone.

Not the three little words I desperately want her to say to me, despite the number of times I say them to her.

"I sure hope we get as lucky as you and Dan when it's our turn, which *hopefully* will be very soon . . ."

Brielle's leading comment pulls me back to the present, along with Tamira and Heather.

"Oh my god, are you trying?" Tamira asks.

Brielle's rich brown eyes narrow beneath a blooming smile. She nods quickly. "Yes! We started a couple months ago—"

"Oh, good Lord," Heather mutters and then takes a drink.

"Harold's been traveling a lot," Brielle goes on, "so we haven't had as many opportunities to make it happen, but we're definitely working on it."

"Oh girl, that's fantastic," Tamira says.

"It really is," I agree over a hearty nod of my own. Even though Avery and I aren't seeing eye to eye these days, being a parent *is* the greatest joy imaginable.

I take another drink.

Our conversation comes to a lull as Melody and another waitress deliver our food and Tamira's drink.

"So, what's the latest from the worker bees?" Brielle asks me, referring to the hospital's special-events department.

I finish the bite of salad in my mouth—still wishing it were a burger—and reach for the little notebook I keep stashed in my bag. Since I'm always serving on multiple committees—currently five: two for the hospital and three PTA related—I find that it keeps me the most organized.

I flip to the notes I took during last week's meeting.

"Okay, so they've decided to do a big dinner event to kick off the fundraising campaign for the new cardio wing. They're going to hold it the weekend before Valentine's Day and call it the Listen to Your Heart Gala—"

"Aww, that's so sweet," Brielle chirps.

"That's a depressing eighties song," Heather groans, and I can't help but smile because that's exactly what I thought when I heard it.

"They're thinking somewhere between two and three hundred guests," I go on. "Cocktail reception, three-course meal, dancing, probably a little auction, the usual stuff. And, of course, they want all of us spread out at different tables."

This is a tactic that has been very profitable during past fundraising events. The special-events team strategically seats us with potential donors who take particular interest in our husbands' fields of practice, the idea being that our husbands can engage them with insights on their work while we wives play the role of dutiful, smiling spouses to project a sort of picture-perfect image of where their money will be going.

"So long as I don't have to sit with that Marvin Gebhardt again," Tamira says while dipping her forkful of lettuce into the little dressing cup next to her plate. "He actually took his dentures out while we were eating—"

"No, he didn't!" Brielle cries.

"Oh, yes he did," Tamira assures her, punctuating the sincerity of her statement with a raise of her fork. "His top dentures. He popped them straight out of his mouth and smacked them down on the bread plate, then started scraping at them with the end of his spoon, like there was something stuck in them."

I make a sour face while Brielle says, "Eww, that's so gross."

"Isn't he worth like fifty million?" Heather asks.

"Mm-hmm." Tamira rolls her eyes.

"And how much did he give?"

Heather's follow-up question forces Tamira to sigh as she replies, "Two million."

Heather smirks. "Ah, the price we have to pay to keep the hospital afloat. They really should pay us for all the bullshit we do for them."

"Who are they targeting for the big bucks this year?" Brielle asks.

I shift in my chair, my jaw muscles starting to tighten again.

"Marcus said it was the Hoffstra's guy," Tamira says.

"Hoffstra's?" Brielle questions.

"It's a small drugstore chain in the Upper Midwest," I answer.

"Supposedly worth a couple hundred million and has a special interest in cardiothoracic medicine because the dad, who started the company like a hundred years ago, died of a rare heart condition," Tamira goes on, proving her husband's hospital intel runs deep.

"Oh, I think I know who you're talking about," Heather chimes in over the rim of her already near-empty glass. "He's super conservative, right? Totally into family values and not working on Sundays and all that shit?"

I shift again, my bra suddenly feeling about two cups too small.

"Yep, that's him," Tamira confirms.

"So, how much are they hoping to get out of him?" Brielle asks.

I swallow hard. "They're thinking he might be looking for a naming opportunity, which would be around twenty-five million."

"Dang," Tamira coos.

"Oh my god," Brielle gasps. "That would be amazing."

"Do they really think he'll give that much?" Heather inquires.

"They seem to think so," I reply.

"So, I imagine Dan will have to get pretty cozy with them, huh?" Tamira astutely wonders.

I reach for my glass. "Yeah," I say, then throw back another painful swallow. "They think Dan's the key to securing their contribution. They want him getting as familiar with them as possible. We're actually going to dinner with them tonight."

Brielle jumps back in, saying, "Oh, that's a great idea. Who better to sell them on the new heart wing than the best cardiothoracic surgeon on the planet!"

"Plus, you two are about as picture-perfect, wholesome family as you can get," Heather adds over a sloppy shrug. "Just don't tell them who you voted for during the last election."

I force a smile.

It's not the last election we're worried about . . .

From the corner of my eye, I see that my hand is starting to shudder again. I reach for the glass and drain what's left of the vile liquid.

I am a strong, capable woman.

I can do anything I set my mind to.

I am no longer bound by the confines of my—

"Oh! Look who's here!" Brielle's sudden shriek startles everyone at the table.

"Ohmygod," Tamira crows, now looking back over her shoulder.

"Speak of the she-devil," Heather adds.

I follow their gazes toward the hostess area, where a statuesque brunette is thumping away on her cell phone.

"That's Dr. Jill," Brielle coos. "Come on, let's go say hi."

Like lemmings on the beach, the three of them hurry through the crowded dining room to greet their illustrious savior, leaving me at the table by myself while thoughts of tonight's very important dinner start to swim through my head, suddenly making it harder to breathe.

Twenty-five million dollars.

What it will take to get this wing built.

To further secure Dan's position at the hospital.

To keep Mom safe.

To protect our livelihood—

I feel my body start to stiffen against the chair, my bones growing tense and rigid.

I am a strong, capable woman.

I can do anything I set my mind to—

Without thought, I lean over Heather's empty seat to where her bag hangs on the back of the chair. I cast a nervous glance over my shoulder, confirming my friends are still occupied, then pop open the snap, peel back the leather fold, and peek inside. The prescription bottle beams at me like a beacon in a storm, begging me to open it up and take one—just one. Not because I need it, or want it, but because . . . well . . . you just never know.

CHAPTER 2

My gut wrenches with disgust as I say my goodbyes and quickly head for the car, hijacked pill stashed deep inside my own purse.

What is wrong with me?

Why did I do that?

I've never stolen anything in my life, and certainly not someone's prescribed medication!

I fire up the engine and head out of the lot, Dr. Deedee's encouraging words once again filling the car.

I am a strong, capable woman.

I can do anything I set my mind to—

RIIIIIING!

The tutorial is suddenly cut off by the unnervingly loud sound of my phone. I glance at the dashboard display and see that it's my little sister calling. *Dammit.*

My grip instinctively tightens around the wheel.

Five counts in.

One long breath out.

Deep, cleansing breaths are the key to relaxation—

Right on cue, a different tutorial—this one courtesy of a Dr. Phil episode I saw years ago—starts to siphon through my mind. The same instruction I've relied upon for what seems a lifetime when it comes to dealing with my little sister.

One deep, five-count inhale through my nose—one, two, three, four, five—then a hard push through my mouth, like I'm blowing out birthday candles—

RIIIIIIIING!

My knuckles run white.

My molars clamp shut.

It's not working.

Why isn't this working?!

Come on, Jane. You can do this.

In through your nose, out through your mouth.

You're a strong, capable woman—

RIIIIIIIIIIIING!

Agh!

I smack the button on the display, accepting the call.

"What do you need, Julie?"

My greeting feels forced against my windpipe but sounds relatively pleasant to the ear.

"Hey, Janie! Did you get my text about Mom?"

Teeth clenched, I inhale a deep breath through my nose and start to nod as I reply, "Yes. I did. I just haven't had a chance to call the bank yet."

"Okay, yeah, that's cool. You just need to do it by the end of the day. That Marlene lady in the office said she'll be there until five, so you've got a little while yet."

"I'll get it done," I say firmly.

I always get it done.

"So, what's up for tomorrow? Avery and I were texting last night, and she said she has a soccer game in the morning?"

My hold on the wheel tightens, frustration quickly giving way to jealousy.

Despite the twenty-seven hours I endured birthing her, the food and designer clothing I provide her, the care I administer when she's sick, the countless hours I've spent taxiing her between activities and trying to wrap my brain around "new math," Avery would still rather send texts to my little sister than me. My sister, who can't hold a job, a boyfriend, or a conversation that doesn't include her asking me for money.

"It's an early game," I say. "Eight o'clock at Fletcher Field."

"Yeesh. That's brutal."

I sigh. Yep. And she has to be there at seven, and with the field nearly a half hour away, that means I have to get up at six to get her there on time. Welcome to my Saturday mornings.

"Well, I'll do my best to get there, but it sort of depends on how things go tonight," she goes on, her tone hinting of a giggle. "I started seeing this guy Blaze a couple weeks ago, and he said something about going to watch his friend's band tonight—"

"*Blaze?* His name is Blaze?"

"Yeah." She laughs. "Well, I mean, it's not his real name, but that's what everybody calls him."

"What's his real name?"

"I don't know."

I sigh again, and this time I catch a glimpse of my eyes rolling in the rearview's reflection. Of course she doesn't know his real name. That would imply she's had conversations with him that involve more than what they'll be drinking the next round.

God, I wish she'd be pickier about the men she dates . . .

"So, Mom was asking about you yesterday," she goes on.

"About *me*, or about the short, brown-haired woman who brushes her hair?"

Our mom was diagnosed with Alzheimer's a couple of years ago. At first, she just had trouble recalling little things—a word here or there, what time her favorite show came on—but over the last few months, bigger things have started to disappear from her memories, like people. Sometimes she recognizes me as her oldest straight away, calling me Janie Lou Bug just like she did when I was a child. But other days it's like there's a stranger living in her body, and she only knows me as the woman I am in that very moment: the woman who plays Uno with her; the woman who walks with her around the assisted-living facility; the woman who brushes her once-lustrous chestnut hair.

"You," she answers. "She asked for you by name, and Avery too."

"She did?" A grateful smile tugs on my lips. It's been a long time since she recognized Avery.

"Yup. I mean, she thinks she's in kindergarten or something, but still, she said, 'When do I get to see Avery Rose again?' You guys are coming down this weekend, aren't you?"

Mom's facility is in Cannon Park, a solid one-hour drive from where I live in Mount Ivy. I do my best to get down there a few times a month, but with my crazy schedule, sometimes it's hard to find the time. And getting Avery there is next to impossible.

"I'm not sure if I can," I say. "I've got a very important dinner with Dan tonight; then we've got Avery's game tomorrow morning, and I have the PTA rummage sale in the afternoon—"

"So maybe you can go on Sunday?"

I come to a slow stop at a red light, jaw clenched in restraint. Sunday will be the first day in nearly a month when I haven't had something on my docket. I'd planned to sleep in a little and maybe take a walk—

"Janie, she asked for you," Julie continues. "The doctors said we have to do our best to keep her memories alive. That it's good for her to see familiar faces as often as she can—"

"I know!" My interjection comes out with a lot more bite than intended. *Crap!* "Sorry," I quickly say, aware that Julie's enviable emerald eyes are splayed wide right now. I can't remember the last time I raised my voice at her. "I didn't mean to yell; it's just . . . I've got a lot going on, and . . ."

"No, it's okay. I get it."

"I'll try to come, okay?"

"Yeah. Okay."

The waver in her words suggests that she's fighting back tears—a sound that instantly transforms her from the thirty-one-year-old woman she is to the six-year-old child I had to soothe back to sleep after bad dreams woke her in the middle of the night.

I roll my lips over my teeth and clamp down, keeping my own emotions at bay.

I am a strong, confident woman.

I can do anything I set my mind to—

"So, how's everything with the new job?" I ask, shifting gears to something slightly less volatile. "Are they giving you lots of classes?"

Julie is a Pilates instructor, though not a very good one, based on the way she jumps from studio to studio.

"It's fine. The studio's really nice and all the equipment is good; it's just . . ."

She blows out a heavy, familiar-sounding sigh that prompts me to shake my head in disappointment—not at her, but at myself. I teed that one up perfectly.

"I swear the only reason they hired me is to cover the classes nobody else wants. They stuck me with the two o'clock in the afternoon slot; that's it. Two o'clock, Monday through Friday. Do you know how many people come to a Pilates class at two o'clock in the afternoon on a weekday? Two. Three if I'm lucky. It's bullshit, Janie. I can't survive on five measly classes a week."

. . . and there it is.

The subtle ask that will inevitably have me transferring another thousand dollars into her checking account.

All regret for my earlier aggression starts to drain from my body.

"Sounds like things are pretty tough," I say, almost robotically.

"Yeah. I mean, I'm okay. It's just getting tight with having to run the furnace at night now, and I'm burning through gas driving out to see Mom all the time. I go out there like four times a week, you know."

I inhale another deep breath through my nose, leg muscles tensing against the leather seat beneath me.

"Yeah, I know."

I know darn well that you visit Mom four times a week, because that was the arrangement we made when we put her in the facility. Dan and I would foot the bill, and you'd do the majority of the visits because you have the most time. It's also why we selected a home in Cannon Park in the first place—because it's closer to you!

Frustration mounting, I make an unnecessarily hard right turn onto Davenport and then see that the pick-up line outside Avery's school is already snaking through the parking lot and out to the street.

Dammit.

I'm later than I planned to be.

"I gotta go. I'm pulling into Ave's school, and I need to pay attention to what I'm doing."

"Oh . . . yeah, sure, okay. Do you, um . . . do you think—"

I sigh. "I'll put some money in your account."

"Really?"

I glare at the Bluetooth image of Julie's name on the dashboard screen while biting back a frustrated scream. "Yes, really."

"Oh, thanks, Janie. You're the best! I'd be lost without you guys."

I shake my head. Yeah, I know.

"And the bank thing for Mom?"

"I said I'd do it."

"Right. Okay. Thanks again. Tell Avery I'll see her tomorrow."

"Okay," I grumble, then disconnect from the call, mumbling, "Why? Why can't you just take care of yourself? Just once. Just one time."

I come to a slow stop at the entrance of the parking lot, just behind a minivan with those stick-figure family stickers on the back window—two parents, three girls, and two cats—while Dr. Deedee's soothing instructions once again waft through the speakers. But before

21

they have the opportunity to do me any good, I see Mrs. Garcia, the assistant principal, hustling down the school's front steps and through the parking lot, arms flailing over her head like she's trying to land an airplane . . . or capture someone's attention.

Our eyes lock.

Dread slithers up my spine.

Dammit.

What now?

Breath shallowing, I wave back to her, a forced smile slowly stretching across my cheeks.

No.

No, no, no.

Not today.

I mute Dr. Deedee and press the button, rolling down the passenger window just as Mrs. Garcia approaches.

"Hi there," I say as hopefully as possible.

"Hi, Mrs. Osborne." She lays her arms down on the open window frame and leans inside, her shoulder-length black hair framing her round face. "I'm sorry to track you down out here, but I wanted to make sure I talked to you before you saw Avery."

Her somber tone is enough to make my chest tighten, but it's that heartsick–puppy dog look in her brown eyes that makes me want to ball up in the fetal position.

I swallow hard, hands slowly falling away from the wheel. "Oh-kay. What's going on?"

She sighs. "Well, I caught her and that Caden Rodgers screwing around by the baseball field during fifth period."

"*During* fifth period?"

She nods and my stomach sinks.

Fifth period is Spanish class.

Dammit, Avery.

"What, um—what were they doing?"

"Well, I didn't see any plumes of smoke this time," she assures me with a raise of her hand, referring to the incident last week when she stumbled upon them smoking a strawberry shortcake–flavored puff bar, whatever the heck that is. "But they did leave behind a can of neon-green spray paint—at least, I think it was theirs," she quickly adds. "I'm not positive, because they heard me coming before I was able to round the backstop, but it was lying just a few feet from where they were hiding out, and there was fresh graffiti on the back of the dugout wall."

Graffiti?!

I wince, pained by the mere thought of my sweet little girl being so destructive. She's not that kind of kid—and I'm not that kind of parent! I didn't raise her to do things like that!

"Since there's no way to prove anything for sure, the most I could do is give them in-school suspension for cutting class, which would go on their permanent records," she goes on, brows furrowing compassionately above her eyes. "But I'm not inclined to do that, at least not with Avery. I thought you'd probably prefer to handle things yourself."

It's not the first time in recent memory that Mrs. Garcia has extended an offering like this, and given her motivation for doing so, I doubt it will be the last. After suffering a severe heart attack last year, Mrs. Garcia's husband was rushed to the hospital, where Dan performed a very complicated, life-saving procedure on him. (Something very tricky that has to do with restoring the size of the ventricles.) Since then, she's felt indebted to my husband—and by proxy, the rest of the family: a phenomenon that happens frequently in this affluent, smallish town. While my friends may have found a savior in Dr. Jill, countless others have found that same thing in Dan.

Dan.

A burst of hot breath suddenly tickles my lip as my jaw muscle instinctively starts to twitch.

Dr. Dan Osborne.

Cardiothoracic savior.

Everybody's hero—

"So, what do you think?" she asks, stealing me back to the moment.

"Um . . . y-yes." I'm nodding before a complete response even comes to my lips. "I think that dealing with it ourselves is probably for the best. Thanks so much for telling me. I'm—um, I'm not sure what's gotten into her lately . . ."

"She's in seventh grade, and that Caden Rodgers is pretty cute," she says with an easy flip of her hand. "It's a tough age to navigate. But she'll be okay." She gives the window frame a little pat, as if it were my arm. "She's a good kid, with a stable family life. She's got everything working in her favor. She's just hit a rough patch the last couple months—"

A stable family life.

A rough patch. For the last couple of months.

Oh god.

A terrifying thought suddenly explodes through my mind.

She doesn't know, does she?

The timing lines up with her acting out, but . . .

No.

No!

There's no way she knows.

She can't know!

Dear god, please don't let her know . . .

"—try not to worry," she goes on, oblivious to the true source of my pained expression. "She'll get through this just fine. Now, you have yourself a good weekend."

Despite my brimming fear, I manage a smile and say, "Thanks. You too."

Tears prick the backs of my eyes as I close the window and sink into the seat, chest tightening over every breath like my lungs are bound by a corset.

Shit.

Shit.shit.shit.

If Avery knows, she'll tell someone.

Just one slip of the tongue will ruin us. Will jeopardize Mom's care. Will destroy the very foundation of our lives!

My hands start to tremble against the steering wheel, prompting me to bolt upright in the seat, a desperate need to find calm suddenly stealing my thoughts. I unmute Dr. Deedee, hopeful that her words will bring me the same kind of resolve they usually do, but they don't. Not at all.

What is happening to me?!

I pinch my eyes tight, heart now thundering against my sternum as my hands instinctively start to strangle the steering wheel.

I can't breathe.

I can't breathe—

Panic attack!

The realization sucker punches me straight in the gut. My eyes splay wide, and I snatch my purse from the passenger seat. Zoloft! Zoloft will calm me down—*no! No, Jane!* Despite my brain's scrambly state, I'm still aware that taking a mood-altering pill for the first time when I'm driving, and surrounded by kids, is *not* a good idea. There's got to be another way—a safer way to calm my nerves—

A tutorial!

I grab my phone from the center console, open a browser, and thump out the words, How to stop a panic attack.

Finger shaking, I scroll to the bottom of the results page. Of course, the first few sites are always ads or straight out of a medical textbook—*I need practical application!* I stop at the last entry. I tap the link, swipe past the stock images of terrified-looking people, and go down to the list of strategies.

Come on, give me something. Give me something . . .

I scan it with desperate eyes:

Breathe.

UGH! That's what I'm trying to do!

Relax.

Screw you!

Take a series of deep breaths into a paper bag.

A paper bag?
I know darn well that there isn't a paper bag in my car, but desperation still prompts me to check the floor, and the back seat. No. No paper bags!
I don't have a paper bag!

Redirect your thoughts by using the rubber band
snap technique.

The rubber band—*huh?*
I quickly skim the instructions: Place a rubber band around your wrist. Whenever unwanted thoughts enter your mind, pull the rubber band and let it snap against your wrist. This action will snap you back from your scary thought and to the present moment.
A rubber band? Again, I turn my attention to the floor, then over my shoulder into the back seat in search of the—*aaagh!* I don't have one. I don't have a rubber ban—*wait!*
I pull open the ashtray and start pawing through the mountains of loose change and random trinkets and—*yes!* There it is. The extra hair tie I keep for Avery just in case hers breaks during practice or a game. It's thicker than a regular rubber band and still tight, as she's never used it, but it should work just the same. I slide it over my wrist and give it a tug. *Snap.* The elastic slaps the tender skin of my inner wrist but does little to pacify my budding anxiety.

Harder!

Pull it harder.

This time, I slide my pointer and middle fingers under the band and pull back as far as I can.

SNAP!

"Ouch!" I wince while inhaling a deep breath over gritted teeth.

This is stupid. It can't be helping—

Holy crap!

I got a deep breath.

That was a deep breath!

Do it again!

Eyes blinking in disbelief, I do it again.

SNAP!

OUCH!

Another pained—but deep—breath.

YES!

Again.

SNAP!

Again!

SNAP!

AGAIN!

SNAP! SNAP! SNAP—

The school bell suddenly blares, reclaiming my attention. Attention that for the last thirty seconds has not been focused on Avery and what she knows but instead on snapping the stupid hair band.

Relief swells in my chest, and I collapse against the seat, oxygen once again flooding my lungs.

It worked.

It actually worked . . .

The sound of middle schoolers permeates my surroundings—laughter, yelps, indecipherable chatter—as kids pour out of the building, streaming down the school's front steps like ants escaping a rainstorm. The line of pick-up parents slowly inches forward as kids climb into the waiting cars, while others head for home by foot or on bicycle, all of them loaded down with packs so heavy the kids look like they might topple over.

I keep my eyes fixed on the flagpole, Avery's designated waiting spot, as I creep through the lot. Since it's a private school and all the kids wear uniforms, picking her out of the crowd isn't always easy, but—yes, there she is. There's my girl.

An even deeper sense of relief settles inside me as I take in the beautiful sight of my daughter: blue eyes wide with childhood enthusiasm, dirty-blonde hair falling in wisps around her face, the french braid woven into her head ragged from the day's activities. As always, her red polo is untucked and hanging over the waistband of her plaid skirt. My little tomboy. And there's that smile. That wide, joyful smile that doesn't suggest anything in her homelife has been disrupted or unsteadied, rather that she is just trying to survive the seventh grade, like Mrs. Garcia said.

Avery suddenly turns in my direction, her gaze locking onto mine, her smile instantly morphing into that disgusted sneer I'm becoming all too familiar with.

My breath cinches up again.

Shit.

She knows.

She knows!

Panic floods my chest again, and I quickly reach down and give my band another hearty snap—*ouch!*—then another—*ouch!*—and another—*OUCH!* I'm still wincing when she opens the car door and climbs inside.

"Hi, honey," I manage.

She makes a grunting sound that could possibly pass as a greeting while slamming the door shut. She latches the seat belt into place and immediately turns her back to me, attention focused outside the passenger window.

Despite the fact that I've got nearly thirty years and as many pounds on her, I'm suddenly feeling really intimidated. Mrs. Garcia was wrong; this isn't just preteen angst.

Damn you, Dan!

She knows!

Nerves rattling, I heave the deepest breath I can manage and say, "How was your day?"

My question comes out wobbly and sort of thick, like I've been gargling mud. But she doesn't acknowledge the oddity, or even respond to it, so I clear my throat and ask again: "Ave, honey, how was your day—"

"Just go."

"Wh-what?"

"Just go!" She whips her head toward me, eyes unsettlingly wide. "I just want to get out of here!"

I jerk back, startled by her outburst. "Oh—okay. Yeah."

I shift the car into drive and slowly make my way through the parking lot toward the exit, hands cemented to the wheel, one eye cautiously fixed on her.

My nerves wrench when I take in her very loud body language. Her arms are folded tight across her chest—the same posture she carried as a two-year-old when I nixed her demands for more ice cream—and her jaw is clenched in that way she gets when she's really mad or—

I blink hard.

Or when she's bracing for something.

Like a punishment.

A relieved sigh feathers against my ribs, and my shoulders start to sag.

Oh, thank god.

This isn't about Dan.

She doesn't know!

This is about Mrs. Garcia. She knows she talked to me, and now she's posturing for that painful conversation we've had before. The one where I lecture her about the importance of making good choices and being responsible. The conversation that's delivered solely with the intent of helping her learn from her mistakes but only ends up driving her further away from me—

She's just trying to determine where she fits in the world.

She's searching to find her own truth.

The Dr. Jill wisdom my friends imparted on me starts wafting through my mind like an unfamiliar melody I desperately want to sing. Maybe a different approach is the key to getting through to Avery. Maybe if I allow her the freedom to discover who she is, without disapproval and judgment, she won't feel the need to act out so much.

I inhale a deep, hopeful breath and gingerly say, "Is this about what happened with Mrs. Garcia?"

The question no sooner leaves my lips than she turns toward me, screaming, "She's lying, Mom! We weren't even doing anything. Whatever she told you is a lie—"

"Whoa, whoa, whoa. Honey, relax," I say in my best Dr. Deedee voice. "I'm not mad; I just want to know what happened."

Now it's her turn to blink hard. Clearly, she wasn't prepared for that response. "Well . . . we were just eating lunch back there. That's all. We weren't doing anything bad."

"Okay," I say, nodding. "Are you supposed to be eating your lunch back there?"

She shrugs, the tension in her jaw slowly releasing. "I don't know. Nobody's ever said we can't."

"Okay. So, why did you guys decide to eat out there today?"

"We just felt like it."

I keep nodding. Not the most convincing explanation, but she's twelve . . . and I'm trying something new here.

Just go with it, Jane.

She's finding her own truth.
You need stability in this relationship.
Just go with it . . .

"And why didn't you go to class when the lunch period was over?"

"We didn't hear the bell. You can't hear it from all the way back there on the baseball field."

My gut is eager to point out the obviousness of why the ball field then wouldn't be a wise place to eat, but I refrain, committed to trying Dr. Jill's approach.

I need to get back onto solid ground with Avery . . . or at least some semblance of it.

"And you weren't doing anything you shouldn't have been—"

"No."

"You weren't spray-painting anything—"

"I said no!"

"Okay, sorry." I peel my right hand off the wheel and raise it up in a calming gesture. "I'm just trying to figure out what happened, that's all."

"She's got it out for Caden," she goes on, relaxing her posture as she turns to look at me. "Just because his older brother used to get in trouble all the time, she thinks he's going to be the same way. She practically stalks him, trying to catch him doing something—"

Something like vaping with you last week?

I quickly force the thought away.

That won't help anything.

"—there's no way she could've known we were out there unless she was following us. And she's not supposed to be out on the field, anyway. She's supposed to be in the office doing principal stuff—"

Again, I'd like to argue an obvious point—that being a vice principal involves a heck of a lot more than just sitting behind a desk—but the fact that Avery is even having this conversation with me right now stops me from doing so. This is the most we've talked in a month; there's no way I'm blowing that just to correct her.

"She's got it out for him, Mom. It's not fair. Somebody needs to report her to the police or something."

"Sweetie, Mrs. Garcia is a really nice lady. I don't think she's got it out for anybody—"

"Yes, she does! She's going to get him expelled because she doesn't want him there. She hates him! And she hates me, too, because I'm friends with him!"

"No, honey, she doesn't hate you. She's just trying to help—"

"I knew you'd take her side over mine." She flops back against the seat, scowling. "You never believe me."

Dammit.

The panic that consumed me moments ago is suddenly replaced by desperation—desperation to keep *this* relationship alive.

"I do believe you," I'm quick to say. "I'm not sure that she's got it out for Caden or you, but I do believe that you didn't do anything today. I'm sure it was just a big misunderstanding."

Her chin quivers slightly before she says, "You really believe me?"

"Yes. I do."

She turns to me and over a weak smile says, "Thanks."

"Of course, honey. I love you. I'll always believe you."

Her gaze drops away from me for a split second before she says, "I love you too."

My throat swells beneath the sound of those long-awaited words, any doubts I had about the sincerity of her testimony squashed by my own gratitude.

She loves me.

My daughter still loves me.

"Can we get a Starbucks on the way home?"

Her question catches me by surprise. "Oh, um . . ." I glance at the clock on the dash. I've got four stops to make before I have to start getting ready for dinner with the Hoffstras. I insisted that Dan make it an early reservation so Avery wouldn't be home late by herself tonight, which seemed like an infallible plan at the time, but now it's proving to be a hassle—

"Please . . ."

She stares at me with wide, hopeful eyes. Eyes I couldn't possibly say no to after what she just said to me.

"Okay. But just the drive-thru."

"Yeah, that's cool."

Smiling, she grabs her phone from her backpack and settles into her seat.

There she is.

That's the girl I know.

My happy, sweet girl—

My heart flops to the floorboard as I catch a glimpse of Avery's thumbs—her neon-green thumbs—pounding out a text message across the screen.

Neon freaking green.

Dammit, Avery.

CHAPTER 3

Every bone in my body is itching to call Avery out on her lie, but I don't do it.

I can't do it.

Her *I love you* felt too good, and as pathetic as it sounds, I need her acceptance more than I need her penance. Especially now, when I'm walking into the nicest steak house in town, psyching myself up to deliver an Oscar-worthy performance for the Hoffstras, the very people who can secure our livelihood and nearly everything I hold dear.

"You should've taken the pill," I mutter, scolding myself, again, for not indulging in the stolen Zoloft. I went back and forth a thousand times before I left the house, but in the end I determined tonight is not the right time for my inaugural drug run. Despite how I'm feeling, I have to go into this restaurant with a clear head and present myself as the happiest wife on the planet.

Shit.

I slide my fingers under the cuff of my silken ivory blouse and give the band—now an *actual* rubber band—a gentle tug. Not enough to hurt—just enough to remind me it's there.

It's there if, and when, I need it.

You can do this, Jane.

You are strong.

You are capable.

You can do anything you set your mind to.

With an affirming nod, I swing open the wooden door and step inside the busy reception area. Despite the crowd, Dan comes into view almost immediately. At six four, a full foot taller than me, with the build of a pro athlete, he stands out wherever he goes—like a Ken doll, sans the golden locks. (His Barbie blond has given way to a more refined silvery gray over the last few years.) Tonight, he's looking particularly dapper in that charcoal suit I bought him for our trip to Denver—

Denver.

A surge of unexpected anger suddenly swells through my chest, prompting me to ball my left hand into a tight fist and plunge my fingernails deep into my palm. *Ouch!* It hurts but somehow seems to dull the anger.

"Ah, here she is now." Dan greets me with one of his million-watt smiles and an outstretched arm. My stomach wrenches at the thought of touching him, but I know it's all part of the drill. *Happily married people touch each other.* Biting back my disgust, I sidle up beside him, inwardly cringing as his big hand presses against my shoulder.

"Phil, Dottie, this is my wife, Jane," he announces, like I'm a prize he won at the fair. "Jane, please meet Phil and Dottie Hoffstra."

Phil and Dottie Hoffstra look like any elderly couple you'd run into at Bob's Big Boy on Sunday afternoon—or, in this case, an overpriced steak house on a Friday night. Both have gleaming white hair—his thinning on top, hers that kind of style you can only achieve through a tight set and lots of back-combing—and each is dressed in their Sunday best: a tweed pantsuit for her, a navy suit with paisley-print bow tie for him. By all accounts, they're the grandparents next door, except that these grandparents literally hold my family's future in their hands, or more accurately, their pocketbooks.

You can do this, Jane.

Just put on a good show and then get the hell out of here!

Nerves rattling, I offer my hand in greeting. "Hello, it's so nice to meet you both."

"A pleasure," Mr. Hoffstra says. His dark eyes are kind, and despite his age, he's still got a very firm shake.

"Hello, dear." Mrs. Hoffstra opts for sandwiching my hand between both of hers rather than the traditional right-handed maneuver. "Very nice to meet you."

"If your whole party is here, I'll go ahead and seat you," the hostess gently cuts in.

"Yes, please," Dan says.

She leads us to a table in the center of the dining room, where Mr. Hoffstra pulls out the chair for his wife: a loving, chivalrous gesture that he undoubtedly perfected years ago. How nice of him. I settle into the seat across from Mrs. Hoffstra, while Dan takes the seat beside me, immediately throwing his arm over my shoulder to foster our own happily married image. My skin bristles at the contact, prompting me to ball my hands in my lap and once again bury my nails deep into the tender flesh of my palms.

You can do this, Jane.

It's just dinner.

Don't worry about Dan.

Just get through this dinner.

"Well, this is a pretty fancy place, isn't it?" Mr. Hoffstra says, taking in the white linens and crystal stemware adorning the table.

"They've got a rib eye that'll bring tears to your eyes," Dan says, chuckling in that unnervingly suave way of his. I shift beneath his hand. "You're a steak eater, aren't you, Phil?"

He snorts. "Born and raised in Michigan. Don't think they'd let me stay if I wasn't."

The background information the fundraising department passed on to us was limited to just a few details (not only are the Hoffstras über conservative, but they're also very private): As just stated, Phillip

Hoffstra, eighty-one, is a Michigan native and the only child of the late Earl Hoffstra (founder of Hoffstra's Drugs) and Kathleen, both born in 1917. Phil and his wife, Dorothy, have been married for sixty-one years and have a daughter named Melissa and a granddaughter in her early twenties. And that's it. That's all there is to know about them. Well, that and they have a net worth of close to $300 million that we need to tap into or else my entire world could collapse around me.

All of it.

Everything.

Everything I've worked so hard for.

The life so many of us depend on.

Decimated . . .

Gone.

My breath starts seizing up just like it did this afternoon at school. I quickly unfist my hands and transition my fingers up under the rubber band—*snap!*

"Good evening, my name is Chelsea," a stout brunette says as she appears at the end of the table. "I'll be taking care of you tonight. Can I get you started with something to drink? Perhaps one of our signature cocktails, or a bottle of wine for the table? We're currently featuring the Tradewinds vineyard out of Napa. Their pinot noir is especially popular and pairs nicely with filets and T-bones . . ."

I have no doubt that a glass (or bottle!) of wine would help smooth out my nervous edges, but I know better than to order first. Safer to wait—and hope that the Hoffstras are drinkers.

"I'd love an Arnold Palmer," Mrs. Hoffstra says, to which Mr. Hoffstra adds, "Count me in for one of those too."

My shoulders sag.

Arnold Palmers.

Iced tea, lemonade, and not one drop of liquor.

Dammit.

They're *those* kinds of conservatives . . .

"You know, it's been a long time since I had an Arnold Palmer," Dan joins in. "I'll take one of those too. Sweetie?" He turns to me. "What'll you have?"

Sweetie?

The word grates against my nerves like metal on concrete. In the eighteen years we've been married, he's never once called me *sweetie*. And how dare he call me that now, after what he's done—

My labored breath suddenly turns hot as my fingers instinctively fall away from the rubber band, reassuming their fisted position.

"Jane," Dan prods with a little squeeze to my shoulder that jars me back to the question. "What do you want to drink?"

I blink hard, chest heaving beneath my still-brimming rage.

"Oh. I'll, um . . . I'll have one too. An—an Arnold Palmer."

"Four Arnold Palmers it is," Chelsea confirms with a smile. "I'll be right back with those. And here are your menus when you're ready to take a look."

I sink my nails back into my palms, once again finding some calm beneath the pain.

Get it together, Jane.

You can do this.

You have to do this!

"Safe to assume you're ordering the rib eye?" Mr. Hoffstra says, glancing over the top of his menu at Dan.

"Absolutely. And you can't forget the loaded mashed potatoes."

"Steak and potatoes? You sure you're a heart doctor?"

Dan chuckles in that annoying way again. "It's called job security, Phil."

Both of the Hoffstras laugh, so I start laughing, too, even though it wasn't funny.

Nothing about Dan is funny.

Not a flipping thing.

Chelsea returns with the drinks, and we all place our orders: rib eyes for the men, crab cakes for Mrs. Hoffstra, a petite filet for me . . . not that I plan on eating much. With the way my stomach is wrenching, I'm surprised I'm able to sit upright.

"You know, this is our first time to Mount Ivy," Mr. Hoffstra says as we settle back into conversation, Chelsea en route to the kitchen with our orders. "We've driven through before—on our way down to St. Louis—but never actually stopped. It's a nice little city you've got here."

"Yeah, I think so," Dan replies, easing back into his seat.

"Do you mind if I ask what made you decide to settle here?" Mr. Hoffstra continues. "Seems to me you could be calling the shots at a big operation out in Boston or Minneapolis. Why settle in a small place like this where you had to start from scratch?"

Dan sighs and over an atypically modest grin says, "Well, you're right, Phil: I have had offers like that—plenty of them, actually—and when I first started out, I thought that was the right path for me. But then I really started thinking about the kind of program I wanted, the kind of legacy I wanted to leave behind, and I realized that the only way I was going to get that was to build it from the ground up. Old-fashioned sweat equity, if you will."

For weeks, the fundraisers have been coaching Dan on the best way to manage the Hoffstras. Aside from selling himself as an incomparable physician and an admirable husband and father, Dan was told to play up small-town values and the whole American-dream angle. It seems a bit forced to me, but based on the way Mr. Hoffstra is nodding, it's working.

"And besides that, there's a strong sense of community here," Dan hammers on. "Everybody's working toward the same goal—and not just at the hospital; it feels like the whole town is committed to making Mount Ivy the best it can be. We're like one big family, don't you agree, honey?"

Honey.

My nerves stand at attention.

There he goes again.

I burrow my nails in a little deeper and with a lot of conjured enthusiasm say, "Absolutely. We're like one big family. I couldn't be happier."

"Well, I can see why." Mrs. Hoffstra joins in, smiling. "It's very quaint. I peeked into a little antique shop right near our hotel. It had the cutest handmade gifts—oh! And we passed the loveliest church on our way in. It was Methodist, wasn't it?" She turns to her husband, who nods in confirmation. "Yes, the Methodist church right as you come into town. It has the most striking stained glass entryway. Is that where you attend services?"

Attend services?

Of course I've been to church before. On Christmas and . . . well, we went on Easter a few years ago. But attend?

Like . . . every Sunday?

I shift again, the chair suddenly feeling a lot stiffer than it did a moment ago.

"Well, we, um"—I swallow hard and as subtly as possible slide my fingers up under the rubber band and—*SNAP!*—"we tend to move around."

"Yes, unfortunately, I work most Sundays, so it makes it a little tricky to settle down in one specific place," Dan jumps in, his lie sounding completely believable. A skill he's recently proven himself very good at.

My top lip starts to twitch as another pang of anger nips at my nerves.

"Oh, I'm sure your schedule must make things very difficult," Mrs. Hoffstra says.

"Seems like Ken told us there was a Lutheran church around here," Mr. Hoffstra mutters absently, eyes narrowing in thought. "Isn't that what he said?" He turns to his wife.

"Goodness, I can't remember," she replies over an adorably helpless shrug.

"Is there a Lutheran church in town?" He turns to us.

"I honestly couldn't say," Dan answers with a slow shake of his head.

I shake my head, too, though it's not nearly as controlled a shake as Dan's was. It's more frantic bobble head than thoughtful response.

Keep it together, Jane.

You can do this.

"So, you mentioned that you've passed through on your way to St. Louis." Dan quickly reroutes the conversation away from our future of fire and brimstone to something—hopefully—less terrifying. "What brings you down there?"

"The Cardinals, of course."

"He's a huge fan," Mrs. Hoffstra adds, rolling her eyes.

I force myself to smile.

"The red birds, huh?" Dan says. "I'm more of a Yanks man myself."

Mr. Hoffstra grimaces, prompting Dan to laugh and then say, "Actually, basketball is my game. I played back in college."

My jaw muscles clench.

You and your basketball.

"Is that so?" Mr. Hoffstra nods with interest. "Where did you go to school?"

"Purdue."

"Ah, a Boilermaker," he says, approving of the team mascot with a hearty nod. "Good for you. Do you still play?"

"Every chance I get."

Yeah, you play, all right.

Every freaking chance you get—

OUCH!

I wince, startled by a sudden jolt of pain electrifying through my body.

41

I glance down at my hand, surprised to see that I've abandoned the rubber band and am once again ramming my nails into my palm—I didn't even realize I'd done that—

"But these days I think I spend most of my time on the soccer field," Dan goes on. "Our daughter plays on a club team, so that really keeps us hopping."

"Oh, you have a daughter?" Mrs. Hoffstra chimes in.

"Yes, Avery," Dan says. "She's twelve."

"Twelve? Oh my, that's a fun age, isn't it?" Mrs. Hoffstra turns to me, a reminiscent smile on her face.

Fun?

An image of said twelve-year-old's neon-green fingers suddenly comes to mind, forcing me to drill my nails even deeper into my palms. Over a strained laugh, I say, "Yes, twelve is a very fun age."

"I think she meant a very *busy* age." Dan jumps back in, taking hold of the conversation, like he always does. Because Dan's the most important person in the room. *It's always about Dan! I know what I meant, HONEY!* "She's got so many different activities it's hard to keep up with her. If she's not at school or soccer, she's at piano lessons, or sleeping over at a friend's house—"

The Hoffstras laugh because, by the way Dan tells it, he might as well be the one donning the chauffeur's cap.

As if he *ever* drives her anywhere.

My molars suddenly slam together.

As if he's the one scouring grass stains out of her uniforms until his fingers are raw.

My nostrils flare with heat.

As if *he's* the one staying up until two in the morning baking gluten-free cookies for the stupid bake sale—

I plunge my nails in deeper, so deep that my arms are starting to tremble beneath the pressure. Except this time, it's not my own pain motivating my movements; it's his. The pain I suddenly—desperately—want to inflict on Dan.

You don't do any of it, you lying dick!

"Do you have a picture of her?"

I hear Mrs. Hoffstra's question, but it sounds sort of muddled, like she's talking to me underwater—

Focus, Jane!

You're here for your future.

For Avery's future.

For Mom's future.

Not to kill Dan.

Even though he deserves it—

Focus on the Hoffstras!

I apply even more pressure and over a clenched jaw say, "I'm sorry?"

"Do you have a picture of your daughter?" she repeats with an encouraging nod.

A picture.

Of Avery.

"Uh . . . yeah—yes! Sure."

I slowly unclench my fists—palms throbbing from the assault—and dig my phone out from my bag. I ignore the three new texts from Julie (I called the damn bank!) and bring up my camera roll and start swiping through the images. Avery's not very cooperative when it comes to pictures these days. Each one has to be reviewed and put through a filter before I'm allowed to keep it, and god forbid I try to post it. Not that I have time for social media, but still . . . it would be nice to offer up something every now and then.

I land on a picture of her at last month's Halloween festival. She hated her class's fairy-tale costume theme, but I thought she looked absolutely precious in her Red Riding Hood cloak and gown. So sweet and innocent. Just the way she did on Halloweens past. When I'd spend weeks patterning and sewing her costume of choice, and then we'd trick-or-treat through the neighborhood until way past bedtime, until her jack-o-lantern candy bucket was overflowing and we had to use our coat pockets to keep up with the supply.

But that was before.

Before that sweet, innocent little girl started ditching class to do naughty things with bad boys, and then lie about it—

"Did you find a good one?"

Dan's prompt and subsequent nudge to the side steal me back to the present.

"Oh, um . . . yes. Here."

Blinking hard, I hand over my phone to Mrs. Hoffstra, mindful not to expose my wounded palm along the way. "That was at her school Halloween carnival. They had to dress up like a fairy-tale character."

A soft smile spreads across her wrinkled cheeks as she stares at the image, then holds the phone toward her husband for a look. "Isn't she pretty?"

"Mm-hmm," Mr. Hoffstra agrees with a hearty nod.

"She's definitely got your coloring"—she glances at Dan, referring to Avery's piercing blue eyes and fair complexion—"but she's got your smile, and I'm guessing your disposition," she adds. "Seems like little girls tend to take after their mothers."

I smile at her well-intended comment, but considering Avery lied straight to my face a few hours ago, I'm afraid she favors her father.

Thankfully, Mr. Hoffstra decides to reroute the conversation away from our personal lives and on to Brugada syndrome, the rare cardiac condition that took his father's life nearly thirty years ago. This offers my poor hand and wrist a short reprieve, requiring little more input from me than the occasional nod or a "That's interesting." But even better, it limits Dan's comments to those of a physician rather than a father, or a terrible husband.

With the way my blood is humming beneath my skin, I'm not sure my limbs can survive much more of Dan the Husband tonight.

After confirming we don't have time for dessert—the Hoffstras are tired from a busy day of travel, and Dan has to head back to the hospital to catch up on paperwork—Chelsea brings us the bill.

"I've got this." Mr. Hoffstra makes a move for the little leather folder, but Dan's faster than him and snatches it away before he even makes contact.

"Oh no you don't," Dan says firmly. "This one's all mine. My invitation, my treat."

"Fine, fine." Mr. Hoffstra raises his hands, chuckling. "But that just means next time is on me."

"Deal," Dan replies, grinning.

Despite the anger clouding my thoughts, I'm still lucid enough to know that Mr. Hoffstra's invitation is a good thing—they like us!—but the mere thought of having to play Ward and June again makes me want to crawl out of my skin.

You're almost done, Jane.

One dinner at a time.

You can do this.

Just a few more minutes.

The finish line is right in front of you—

"Excuse me, Dr. Osborne?" An older man suddenly approaches the table. My stomach wrenches when I observe the look in his eyes. It's the same starstruck look I've seen a thousand times. The look that used to fill me with pride but now just makes me want to scream.

Dan looks up from where he's signing the charge slip. "Yes?"

"I'm so sorry to interrupt," the man says sheepishly, eyeing the table with an apologetic smile. The Hoffstras look on with wide-eyed curiosity, while I swallow through the profanities tickling my tongue. "I'm sure you don't remember me, but my name's Carl Montgomery. You treated me last year . . ."

"Well, sure I do," Dan says, nodding over a manufactured, modest smile. He sets the pen down so he can shake the man's hand.

"Carl Montgomery. It's nice to see you, sir. How are you feeling these days?"

"I'm just great," he says, cheeks flushing at the gesture. "I'm sorry to bother you, but I just had to come over and tell you how grateful I am to you for what you did for me. I would have died if it wasn't for you."

"Oh my." Mrs. Hoffstra clutches her chest.

"No, no." Dan waves off the praise with a raise of his hand. "If memory serves, you were a pretty routine case. Just an . . . angioplasty and a stent implantation, am I right?"

"Yes!" Mr. Montgomery chirps, delighted by Dan's astute memory. "I can't believe you remember."

"Well, some things just stick," Dan says stoically. "And is that your wife?" He glances around Mr. Montgomery to a table in the corner, where a woman is looking on with a kind of moony-eyed reverence that makes my stomach turn.

"Yes, that's my wife, Janet. She said I should come over and say hi to you—to tell you how thankful we are for everything you did."

"Thank you so much!" Mrs. Montgomery calls out from her table. "We're so grateful!"

I swallow a disgusted sigh.

Save your praises, lady.

He doesn't deserve them!

Dr. Osborne doesn't just fix hearts . . . he breaks them!

"Isn't this something . . . ," an awestruck Mrs. Hoffstra mutters to her husband, who wastes no time nodding in agreement.

Aware of his captive audience, Dan turns to the Hoffstras. "You know, I should really go over and say hi. Would you excuse me for a minute?"

"Yes, yes, of course," Mrs. Hoffstra says.

"By all means," Mr. Hoffstra confirms.

With cultlike devotion in his eyes, Mr. Montgomery leads Dan across the room to meet his wife while the Hoffstras watch, captivated, as if Jesus himself has just walked away from the table to go heal a leper.

Liar!

A snarl tugs on my upper lip as another jolt of anger rips through my body, rattling my bones.

You are such a phony.

If these people knew the real you, they'd never treat you like their savior—

"You must be so proud of him," Mrs. Hoffstra says, oblivious to my distress. "It must feel so good to be married to such a wonderful man."

I dig my nails deeper into my palms and through gritted teeth say, "*Wonderful* doesn't even begin to describe him."

CHAPTER 4

"It must feel so good to be married to such a wonderful man," I mumble in a snarky tone as I climb up into the car, slamming the door shut behind me. "Yeah, it's *so* wonderful, Mrs. Hoffstra. It's about as wonderful as being old and gullible!"

I ram the keys into the ignition, cringing against the sound of my acidic words. That wasn't a fair thing to say. Mrs. Hoffstra and her husband are lovely people. Gracious and kind and beyond modest despite their substantial wealth. It's not their fault Dan's such a convincing liar.

Dan . . .

"*Aaagh!!*" I pound the steering wheel with my fists. "You are such an asshole!"

Asshole.

It's the first time I've said the word aloud, even though I've been thinking it every day for the last two months.

Every day since the truth came out in the seventh-floor suite of the Denver Marriott Gardens hotel.

Without thought, my grip tightens around the wheel as memories of that heart-wrenching night start playing through my mind: the receipt that was mistakenly emailed to our joint account, the bold-faced lie he told when I asked about it, the smug apology he delivered when he finally confessed, the implication that Mom might suffer if I said anything—

"Asshole. Asshole. Asshole!"

I yank the gearshift into reverse and quickly back out of the parking space. Scalding breaths steam from my nostrils as I screech through the parking lot, eager to get home . . . desperate to get away from all this—

I am no longer bound by the confines of my—

"Oh, shut up!" I grab my phone from my purse and slap at the screen, making contact with the "Pause" button to stop the car's Bluetooth feature. "I know, I know," I growl. "I am no longer bound by the confines of my penis. Well, you know what, Dr. Freaking Deedee? I am no longer bound by the confines of *any* penis—how about that?!"

My chest swells with a sense of empowerment. That's right . . . *ANY PENIS!*

I toss the phone into the center console and head for the exit.

Making a hard right out of the parking lot, I see Dan's sleek silver Mercedes sitting at the stoplight ahead of me, but he's in the left turn lane that leads to the highway rather than the lane that leads directly to the hospital.

My anti-penis mojo instantly fades, replaced by a bitter taste that's becoming all too familiar to my tongue.

Liar.

You said you were going to the hospital.

Where are you really going?

I tighten my hold on the wheel—wounded palms crying out in agony—and come to a creeping stop in the lane beside him, right in his blind spot so he can't see me. Not that he would notice, even if I were window to window with him. He may have laser focus in the operating room, but as a driver, he might as well be wearing a bag over his head. He never notices anything.

Because my SUV sits up higher than his sedan, I've got a decent view of the inside of his car through the passenger windows. Unfortunately, there's nothing in his back or passenger seat that hints of where he's headed, but thanks to the wide dashboard, I can see that he's talking on the phone. No names or phone numbers, though, just the words *DR. O'S CELL* illuminated across the display screen.

Who is he talking to?

I lean forward, craning my neck for a better look, so I'm able to see the side of his face—

My heart twists.

He's laughing.

He's laughing with whoever's on the other end of the line.

After what we just went through—

He's laughing?

A rumble of deep-seated fury rises up from my gut, forcing me to scream out my new favorite word—"Asshole!"—from the top of my lungs, but the insult only reverberates against my own ears, lost behind the layers of tinted glass surrounding me.

The light turns green and Dan punches the accelerator, zipping through the intersection and down the road to god knows where.

Follow him.

You deserve to know what he's doing—

No, Jane.

Don't do it.

Whatever he's doing . . . you don't need to see it—

He's a liar!

He can't keep getting away with this—

HONK!

The sound of a horn startles me, jostling my brain out of its argument. I glance at the rearview and find the car behind me flashing its lights, the driver gesticulating wildly toward the stoplight. As if I weren't aware it was green.

"Fuck you!" I grunt back to the stranger, slowly pressing my foot down on the accelerator.

Fuck you.

There's another sentiment I've been dying to express for the last two months; too bad I didn't get to deliver it to the party who actually deserves it. The party who's definitely *not* heading to the hospital like he said he was.

"Screw it."

I crank the wheel a hard left, tires squealing beneath the sudden change in direction, so now I'm following in Dan's wake.

His lying, laughing wake.

No more lying, asshole!

I hit the gas hard to make up for lost time, then slow my speed once he's within eyeshot—close enough to follow his movements but far enough that he can't tell it's me.

I keep my eyes fixed on his red taillights—two demonic little eyes taunting me with their knowledge—as we pass by the Costco in the center of town, beyond the post office and public works building, then the country club and surrounding golf course that hug the city limits.

Where are you going?

My grip on the wheel stays firm, my attention so focused on catching him in his latest lie that I don't realize how much time is passing or how far we've gone. That is, until I see a dilapidated sign off to the side of the road announcing our location nearly thirty miles from home: **Welcome to Morris Creek.**

"Morris Creek?" I mutter.

Morris Creek is a beat-up old country town that most Mount Ivy residents wouldn't even consider visiting, certainly no one I associate with. I've been here a couple of times before, but only with Dan to pick up food from his favorite BBQ place. Their St. Louis ribs are the only reason I can think anyone would drive all the way out here.

Is that what he's doing?

Getting BBQ?

We carry on down the road, passing by a mobile home park and a series of abandoned, junked-out cars, before he finally pulls into the run-down strip mall where the Bloated Pig (his BBQ joint) is.

Big Cal's Market sits like an anchor in the center of the mall (the letters *C* and *K* in its neon-yellow sign blackened with dead bulbs), with smaller stores on either side. There's the BBQ place, Mr. Wong's takeout, Lupe's Shoe Repair, a real estate office, a rent-to-own furniture store . . .

I slow down, allowing several other cars to pass me, before I turn into the lot. Despite the obviousness of our destination, something about this doesn't feel right. He just ate a sixty-dollar steak. Why would he need BBQ now?

My stomach shifts uneasily as Dan slowly makes his way down the length of the mall. He passes the Bloated Pig and the countless empty parking spots in front of it, then the shoe-repair place, then the market . . . never once even tapping his brakes.

I swallow hard.

He continues through the parking lot—passing every storefront—then finally turns right and disappears behind the side of the building.

What the heck?

Where is he going . . . ?

Suspicion mounting, I quickly determine that my Range Rover stands out too much here—even oblivious Dan would recognize the "Proud Mom of a Mount Ivy Panther" license plate rim in this environment—so I pull into a spot in the middle of the lot, right next to an old pickup with a "Perot '96" sticker peeling off its rear window, and take off after him on foot.

My heart beats hard and fast as I navigate my way across the broken asphalt and up to the corner of the building, coming to a stop in front of Fancy Nails nail salon, home of the ten-dollar fill, according to the hand-painted sign on the window.

I press my back up against the building and slowly peek my head around the corner for a better look. *Huh?* It's just an empty lot: a blanket of aged asphalt illuminated by a lone, naked bulb attached to the side of the building. But Dan's nowhere to be seen. I don't see his car anywhere—

Wait.

A faint light in the distance catches my attention.

I narrow my eyes.

It's a blue light that's flashing off and on like it's pulsing. It's coming from the back of the mall.

What is that?

Despite the obvious danger of the situation—single woman / dark parking lot / no witnesses—I press on, hunched over and creeping through the shadows like a cartoon villain in pursuit of hidden treasure, except it's not treasure I'm after: it's the liar who isn't where he said he'd be.

My heart slams hard against my ribs as I slowly make my way toward the back of the building, navigating around weeds and random pieces of trash, the blue light getting brighter—pulsing more intensely—with every step. And now I can hear the *thump thump thump* of music too. That low hum of bass, like dance music.

Dance music?

What the hell is going on?

I'm just approaching the corner of the building when I notice a shimmering sign hammered to an old telephone pole across the lot from me. I glance over each shoulder, confirming I'm as alone as I feel, then take a step closer for a better look—

My stomach drops: THE BONE YARD.

The Bone Yard.

I know that name.

I've seen it before.

In Denver.

On the charge receipt—

My teeth slam together, jaw muscles turning to concrete, as another flood of rage starts erupting through my veins.

He's here.

Right now—

I have to see this.

I need to see this!

I sink back into the shadows of the building, aware that what I'm about to do is monumentally stupid and will provide me nothing but heartache, but for some reason I have to do it.

I have to witness this.

I have to see firsthand what's become of our life!

I crouch down and nervously peek around the corner. The light pulses wildly back here, casting spastic flashes of blue to splay across the asphalt and the two dozen or so cars parked in the lot. I cast another glance over each shoulder, then scurry into the parking area before coming to a hunched-down stop behind a dark minivan. I peer around the front fender to take inventory of my surroundings. From here I can see the building head-on. There are three loading docks, each with a steel roll-up door and a ramp leading up to it. The first two doors are shut tight, probably padlocked until morning, when the deliveries come in, but the third door, the one at the far end of the building, is wide open, the silhouettes of its partying patrons illuminated by the wild blue light, the thump-thumping music pulsing in time to their movements.

Asshole. You don't even like to dance.

Fury grates my spine as I turn my attention back to the cars in the lot: a pickup truck, another minivan, a Jeep, Prius, Prius, Prius—

There it is.

There's Dan's Mercedes.

He's parked near the dumpster in the far corner of the lot, just below the parking lamp.

It's dim, but there's enough light that I can see his silhouette and—

Oh god.

My heart wrenches, an unexpected whimper escaping my lips.

There's someone in the seat beside him—

In *my* seat.

You know who it is, Jane.

You don't need to see this—

Despite my screaming gut, I creep around the parked cars before finally coming to a stop behind a big SUV, not more than a stone's throw from them. I peek my head around the bumper—

No.

No, no. no.

I shake my head frantically.

I shouldn't have looked.

I didn't need to see this.

I don't want to see this!

But . . . shit.

I can't look away.

I can't look away!

Wide eyed and breathless, I watch as my husband strokes the cheek of the handsome man sitting in my seat: Julian, the radiologist. Dan introduced me to him at last year's Christmas party as the new guy he'd been playing hoops with on the weekends. Of course, I didn't think anything of it at the time. Dan's been playing basketball every weekend since we met nearly twenty years ago. He was an all-American in high school and played on a scholarship in college. After medicine, basketball is his greatest passion, so adding another guy to his roster of *ball buddies* didn't strike me as concerning in any way. But I know better now. Being one of Dan's ball buddies isn't just a reference to the time they spend together on the court.

The rage that was just propelling my movements gives way to suffocating betrayal. I've pictured this scene thousands of times since he confessed the truth, but witnessing it firsthand—

Seeing him in the act—

Watching him touch someone else—

I thought it would feel strange to see him with another man, but it doesn't even play a part. The pain is the same, no matter who sits in that seat. Julian's just a person . . . the person my husband loves instead of me—

Dan suddenly leans in and kisses him, prompting my stomach to wrench, a swell of bile surging up my throat. Those aren't *my* lips, Dan! *You vowed you'd only kiss my lips!* I quickly turn away, fist pressed to my mouth in hopes of stifling the sour stream, but it's no use. The acrid liquid burbles into my mouth like remnants of a leaky pipe, forcing me to spit and sputter my dinner all over the car's oversize tire.

Dammit, Jane!

Why did you look?

Why did you follow him here?

Why the fuck did you want to see this?!

I hear a car door slam, then another. Wincing against the taste, I swipe the spittle from my mouth and peek back around the car. Dan and Julian are walking toward the Bone Yard hand in hand.

Hot tears swell in my eyes as I watch them climb up the ramp of the loading dock, then disappear into the sea of male bodies, blue light, and pulsating music.

Asshole.

How could you do this . . . ?

My chest shudders with broken, wounded breaths, and I pinch my eyes shut tight, trying to unsee what I just saw.

Wishing I'd never followed the damn car.

Wishing I'd never believed him when he said he loved me.

Wishing I'd never committed my life to a cheater and a liar.

Liar!

Anger quickly seeps its way back into my bloodstream, once again dictating all my thoughts, stirring up a rage so deep my body starts to shake.

I hate you.

I HATE YOU!

Just like at the restaurant, I burrow my fingernails into my palms and stalk back toward my car, spitting and hacking against the burn still lingering on my tongue.

Asshole.

Asshole.

Asshole.

I'm just feet from the car when my phone chimes with a new text message. I snatch it out of my bag. It's from Avery. Sweet, lying little Avery:

YOU NEED TO BRING THE ORANGES TMRW

I reel back.

What?

Why do I need to bring the oranges? Jennifer Sutton is the team mom this year; it's her job to bring the oranges to the game!

I quickly pull up Avery's name from my contact list and call her.

The phone rings three times before she finally picks up.

"What?" she grunts.

"What do you mean I have to bring the oranges? Why can't Mrs. Sutton do it?" Given the circumstances, the pinched quality in my tone isn't surprising.

"I don't know."

"So, she's expecting *me* to do it?"

"I guess."

"Well, what exactly did she say to you?"

"She just said that she couldn't do it and asked me to ask if you could."

"She *asked* you?"

"Yeah."

"When?"

"I don't know. Like . . . Monday or something—"

"*Monday?*"

"Yeah."

My jaw muscles grow taut. "Avery, you can't just spring stuff like that on me. You have to tell me right away. I've been to the market three times this week—and now I have to go again. I really don't want to do this tonight—"

"So, do it tomorrow."

So, do it tomorrow?

Her flippant response sets my already-feverish blood to boiling. "Excuse me?" I bite back.

She blows out a sigh. One of those heavy, teenage girl sighs that can only be delivered along with a monumental eye roll.

"*What?* God," she goes on, "I'm just saying you don't have to do it tonight. Just go in the morning. Or don't do it at all—I don't care. Nobody eats the oranges anyway."

Nobody eats the oranges anyway?!

So, the thousands of oranges I've cut up over the last seven years were totally pointless?

Just a waste of my precious time?

Because nobody eats the oranges anyway?!

My hands start to tremble as I swallow back the fresh surge of rage that's rising up from my feet, and the slurry of four-letter words following in its wake.

"I'm sorry, okay?" she continues, sounding anything but sorry. "I'll tell you earlier next time—"

"Yeah, you're damn right you will." My tone is abrasive and must sound as unfamiliar to Avery's ears as it does my own. But right now, I really don't care. *I don't care!* "Okay, so I guess I'm going to get the oranges nobody's going to eat. I'll be home when I get there."

Huffing like a bull, I stalk back across the parking lot toward the market, mumbling hateful words about stupid, lazy Jennifer Sutton under my breath the whole way.

"I knew I couldn't trust you to take over team mom duties," I snarl through gritted teeth as I rip a plastic bag from the spool stationed in the middle of the produce section. "I told you it was hard work, but you said you were up for it. You said your divorce gave you perspective on what was important." I yank another bag from the spool. The metal stand shakes beneath the volatile movement. "Guess we know how important the fucking oranges are, don't we? Don't we, *Jennifer*?"

I load up the bags—not even bothering to check if the oranges are ripe or damaged—then storm up to the fifteen-items-or-less line, where there are two people ahead of me.

Why is there no fucking self-checkout?!

Snippets of Dan and Julian's make-out session flash through my mind, forcing my limbs to grow restless. I start rocking from one foot to the other—a little dance that's meant to settle my nerves but sadly isn't working.

The woman in front of me casts an annoyed glance over her shoulder.

"Can I help you?" I snip, cringing against the bitchiness in my voice and the gritty texture in my mouth. My tongue feels like sandpaper. Sandpaper laced with puke.

She scowls, then turns back around.

I drop the basket of oranges onto the floor and fish out the canister of Altoids from my bag. I pop the lid and see the blue pill I stole from Heather; it stands out like a little beacon against its white wintergreen neighbors. A beacon meant to provide me some peace—some control!—in this shitstorm that my life has become.

I tuck the pill in my front pants pocket, eager to take it once I'm back in the car, and pop a mint in my mouth.

The line moves forward, so I shove the basket with my foot while searching the small refrigerator beside me for something to wash the pill down. Unlike every other grocery store in America, there's no soda or water, just alcohol. Tiny little bottles of wine and liquor like you'd find on an airplane.

Ordinarily I wouldn't drink before a thirty-mile drive, but a little something extra to settle my nerves before I get home and have to deal with Avery will do me some good. Besides, it'll probably take at least that long for the pill to kick in anyway.

The line moves forward again, so I quickly grab a bottle of white zin, then kick the basket forward with another nudge of my foot.

Come on, let's go.

The woman in front of me slowly starts to unload her items onto the conveyer belt: cans of cat food.

One can, two cans, three cans . . .

My jaw clenches at her sloth-like movements.

Hurry up!

. . . four cans, five cans, six cans . . .

Just dump them the hell out!

I blow out an annoyed groan. The cashier—a young woman, no more than eighteen or so—glances at me but doesn't say anything.

. . . seven cans, eight, nine, ten . . .

I shift impatiently.

Come on, lady! I can't take pills without liquid.

I can't open the wine inside the damn store!

. . . eleven, twelve, thirteen, fourteen . . .

Thank god.

I pat my pocket.

Soon, little one. Very soon—

. . . fifteen, sixteen, seventeen, eighteen . . .

Wait.

What?!

. . . nineteen, twenty, twenty-one . . .

OHMYGOD!

My veins start to palpitate beneath a sudden surge of hot, angry blood.

What the hell?

It's fifteen items or less.

Fifteen fucking items!

I grind my molars together, biting against the scream that's rising in my throat.

. . . twenty-two, twenty-three, twenty-four . . .

My entire body grows tense, all my nerves and muscles turning rod tight. I plunge my nails into my palms.

She's not the enemy, Jane.

You're not really mad at her.

You're mad at Dan.

And Avery.

And fucking Jennifer Sutton—

I pinch my eyes shut and drop my head, refusing to watch.

I'm going to lose my mind.

I'm going to kill her—

Beep. Beep. Beep.

Thankfully the cashier starts scanning, which means the cat lady must be done.

But now I'm counting the beeps.

One, two, three . . .

Hurry . . .

Beep. Beep. Beep.

Seven, eight, nine . . .

Oh my god!

I plunge my nails in even deeper. So deep I swear I can feel the skin start to break.

Beep. Beep. Beep.

Sixteen, seventeen, eighteen . . .

My teeth are about to crack.

Beep. Beep. Beep.

Twenty-two, twenty-three, twenty-four . . .

Oh, for fuck's sake! You better finish checking her out, or I'm going to shove that cat food straight up her—

"Ma'am, I can help you now."

The cashier's call startles me.

I open my eyes.

"Ma'am?" she prompts.

Chest heaving, I slowly unclench my fist and raise my head just in time to see the cat lady leaving the store, her shopping cart loaded down with three full bags of cat food.

Three bags.

Bitch.

Blood still running hot, I unload my basket onto the belt. The cashier gives me a nervous glance but wisely doesn't say anything. She weighs and scans the oranges, then pauses when she gets to the wine.

"Can I see your ID?"

As much as I'd like to think she's complimenting me on my youthful appearance, I know that's not the case. Grocery stores around here card everyone. I hand over my license—which she barely glances at—then she returns it to me with a forced smile and says, "That'll be eleven dollars and fourteen cents."

I swipe my credit card through the little machine, and while it processes, I glance down at my driver's license. My blood instantly grows feverish as I read my name: Jane Louise Osborne. Osborne. I thought that was a name I could trust, a name that would provide me the life I always longed for.

Bastard.

With my grocery bags looped over my arms, I exit the store, tossing my driver's license into the trash barrel just outside the door, and head for the car, where my sanity waits beneath a stolen pill and a tiny bottle of wine—*oh, hell no!*

My eyes splay wide, my teeth once again cementing together at the infuriating scene unfolding in front of me. Evil cat lady has just climbed into her little hatchback, abandoning her grocery cart in the empty space beside her, even though there's a cart corral just ten feet away.

Ten feet!

"You better not be doing that," I mutter over gritted teeth. "You better not be that lazy . . ."

Her engine starts up, and the taillights come to life.

My pulse spikes.

She's going to leave it there.

She's just going to leave it.

My eyes narrow, fury swelling as I approach the car.

The white reverse lights come on.

Don't you leave that cart.

Don't you fucking do it!

The car slowly starts to back out of the spot—

CRACK!

Something deep down inside me breaks, like a levee has just given way after a big storm. Seething, I reach inside the bag and grab an orange. I chuck it at her car and scream, "Put your fucking cart away!" The orange smacks the rear window, then rolls down to the ground with a thud.

Damn, that felt good.

She slams on the brakes. "What the hell are you doing?" she yells out her window.

Given the circumstances, her question is probably fair, but all my rational thoughts are gone—buried beneath the jarring hum that's now pulsating through my body, my veins infested by wasps and hornets searching for a way out. But there's no way out—no way that doesn't involve me beating the shit out of her car with fruit!

I grab another orange and throw it. This one hits her back bumper.

Yes.

"Stop it!" she screams.

Another one. It hits her tire.

YES!

"Stop doing that!"

"You need to put your cart away!" I growl, my tone now bordering on demonic, suggesting my head is about to start spinning. "You can't just leave your cart wherever you feel like it!"

I throw another orange. This one nails the roof.

I quickly reload, ready to fire again, but she must recognize the crazy in my eyes because she ducks her head back inside, then throws the car into drive and peels away toward the exit. Despite the distance, I still throw the orange, not with the intent to hit her but just because it feels really good.

So.

Fucking.

Good.

Winded, I stand in the parking lot, bags dangling from my hands like I'm Billy the Kid—ready for a showdown—and watch as she turns out of the lot and disappears down the highway.

"Holy shit . . . ," I mutter, blinking hard as my blood slowly comes back down to a simmer, clearer thoughts returning to my brain. "What the hell did I just do?"

My knees go wobbly as a hurricane of emotions starts swirling inside me. I just verbally assaulted a perfect stranger. I threw oranges at her, for ditching her cart.

Dumbstruck and ashamed, I stagger to my car and climb inside. I toss the remaining oranges into the passenger seat, then promptly twist open the bottle of wine. I take a drink to wet my palate, then fish the little pill out from my pocket. It's so small—not much bigger than a pea—but will undoubtedly provide me the calm and restraint I so obviously need. It better.

I place it on my tongue and wash it down with a nice, long drink.

There we go.

Come on, baby.

Work your magic . . .

CHAPTER 5

Thirty minutes later. Still in the grocery store parking lot...

"I am no lawn-ger bound by the confines of my peeeeenisssssss!" I collapse against the steering wheel, cackling. "You are so funny, Dr. Deedee. Deedee. Duh, duh, Deedee. Duh, duh, Deedee . . ." I sway against the seat, snapping my fingers in time to the rhythm of my awesome new song. I just made it up—right now. It just . . . came to me. "Duh, duh, Deedee. Duh, duh, Deedee—ooh, that feels good . . ."

I close my eyes and squirm down deeper into my seat. I put the seat warmer on high, and it's . . . *oh yeah.* I sink my top teeth into my bottom lip, savoring the warmth against my butt. "Mmm . . . I like that." I drag my palms down the front of my thighs, moaning—

Knock. Knock. Knock.

My eyes spring wide, and I quickly turn toward my window.

"Well, hellooooo!" I cry out. There's a man standing right next to my car. And he's precious, all dimples and broad, muscly shoulders. My lady parts suddenly start to tingle.

I groan.

That feels nice . . .

"I'm a police officer," he says, flashing a shiny gold badge up to the window. He's not wearing a uniform, just a well-fitting T-shirt. *Really* well fitting. "How are you doing tonight, ma'am?"

"Ahmaaazing," I answer, shifting against the seat. "How are you, Occif—foff—fofficer Poncherello?"

The overhead parking lamp provides enough light that I can see his dark eyes narrow a little bit. *Mmm . . .* that must be his sexy smolder. It looks just like Erik Estra—Ester—Estah—whatever that actor's name was who played Ponch. I miss *CHiPS*. That was a good show. And Ponch was . . . *damn.*

I lick my lips.

"Can you roll your window down please, ma'am?"

Oooh! He wants to get up close and personal.

FUN!

I press the button on my left side. The passenger window goes down. I snort. The passenger window is going down instead of my window—

"This one." He raps on my window again with his knuckle.

"I know, I know," I snicker. This car has *so* many buttons . . .

I press a different one and my window drops.

"Are you feeling okay tonight, ma'am?"

"Ohmygod, I feel *so* good right now, Occif—off—fofficer." I inhale a deep, delicious breath as another surge of warmth tickles my butt. "I put the seat warmers on, and it's just . . . *mmm* . . . yeah, it's so good."

"Have you been drinking tonight?"

Another snort. "I wish! All I got was an Arnold Palmer." I make a gagging sound. "Have you ever had an Arnold Palmer, Off—ffoficer?" I shake my head, chuckling. That is a hard word to get right. "They're *soooo* boring. Just lemonade and iced tea. I mean, *blaaach*, right?!"

"What's that there?" He points to the half-drunk bottle of wine sitting in the center console.

"Oh! That's my zin." I start to laugh as a new song takes shape in my head. "That's my zin, that's my zin, that's my zinny, zinny, zin . . ." Wriggling along to the beat, I pick the bottle up and hand it over to him. "It's not very good, but you can have what's left."

He holds the bottle up to the light to examine it. Probably checking the vintner.

"Trust me, dude. It's pretty bad. I gottit in the check-out line. I wuhzz behind that crazy cat lady."

"This is all the alcohol you've had to drink tonight?"

I nod.

"What else do you have in that bag?" He motions to the oranges on the seat beside me.

"*Ugh . . .*" I blow out a heavy sigh. "Those are the oranges for my daughter's game. I had to pick them up 'cause freaking Jennifer couldn't do it."

"Jennifer?"

"Stupid Jennifer Sutton." I roll my eyes. "She's just reeediculous. She said she wanted to be team mom this year but . . . come on!" I smack the steering wheel. "If you can't even bring the oranges, how are you going to do everything else that comes with being team mom, you know?"

His eyes do that sexy narrowing thing again, making my girlie parts spasm with excitement.

Oh, yeah. I see you, Poncherello.

I see you.

"We received a complaint that a woman was attacking people with oranges in the parking lot tonight. Do you know anything about that?"

My shoulders start to sag. "Yeah. That was totally me."

"That was you?"

"Mm-hmm."

His dark eyebrows scrunch up like little caterpillars, like he's surprised that I admitted it so easily. But hey, I'm no liar.

That's what Dan does, not me!

"Ma'am, I'm going to need to see your license and registration."

"Ooh . . . well, thasss gonna be a little bit tricky," I snicker. Not only did I throw my license away, but I also tore up my registration slip and the three oil-change receipts that were stashed in my glove compartment. Anything that had the name Osborne got torn up. Torn up. Torn up. Torn up, torn up, torn up—

"You don't have any identification?" he asks, interrupting my shimmy-shaking new song.

My bottom lip rolls out into a pout. "Nope. I'm sorry."

"Do you know your name?"

"Uh . . . yeah. It's Jane."

"Jane what?"

"Jane . . . Holliday."

Technically it's not a lie. I was a Holliday long before I was an Osborne. And I've decided I'm going back to it. First thing tomorrow, I'm going down to the courthouse to change it—or . . . do I go to the DMV for that?

DMV.

Dee Emm Veeee . . .

Dee Emm Veeee . . .

I snap my fingers. There's a song in there somewhere—

"Jane Holliday?" he repeats.

"Yup. That's me. Jane Holliday. Holliday. Hollahhhhdaaay!"

"*You're* Jane Holliday?"

"Reporting for duty." I smile proudly and raise my hand to my temple in salute, but smack myself in the eye in the process. I laugh. *Whoopsie!*

"Jane Holliday who went to South Glenn High?"

I gasp. "Oh shit! How'd you know that?"

He stares at me for a hard beat—like he's studying me—and then flashes me a little Poncherello smirk. "That's classified."

I smack the window frame. "Shut up! I'm classified?"

He nods.

Holy shit.

"So, tell me, Jane. Do you live around here?"

"Pfft! No way!" I sputter, spraying spit across the steering wheel. I burst out laughing again. It's raining inside my car! It's raining spit!

"I'm going to need you to step out of the car."

"Really?" My eyes grow wide and I gasp. "Why? Am I being arrested? Are you gonna put me in handcuffs?" I growl at him while pawing my hand through the air like a sexy little cougar.

"Not unless you give me a reason to."

"Oh, I'll give you a reason . . ."

I pull on the door handle, but it won't open. "Uh-oh," I laugh, then try it again. Nope. Still won't open—

"You need to unlock it," he says. "Press the button."

"Okay, okay. I got it. I swear it's like freaking mission control in here." I swipe at the row of buttons beside me. I press one, and this time the rear passenger window starts to drop. I snicker. "Whoopsie. Houston, we have a problem." I press another button and then try the handle again. "Eureka!"

Officer Dimples backs out of the way while I plop my feet down onto the ground. *Whoa!* That's not quite right. I'm sort of wibbly. And wobbly. Like I'm standing on Jell-O. *Whoa!* Is the ground made of Jell-O?!

"You okay, Jane?"

He grabs my wrist to stabilize me.

"I am now," I moan, my tortured skin electrifying beneath his touch.

He's so strong and warm and . . . cop-ish.

"Let's get you down on the ground."

"Mmm . . . yeah, let's get me down on the ground . . . ," I purr back, eager to put the squishy Jell-O to work. I grab on tight to his meaty arms and let him maneuver me down to a cross-legged position beside my car.

I start to giggle. "I'm sitting criss-cross applesauce. Just like kindergarten."

Grinning a little, he squats down in front of me, hands braced against his knees to give me a nice shot of all the muscles running down his forearms.

I shift against the squishy asphalt.

He's such a tease.

"What are you on?" he asks.

"Huh?"

"What are you on?"

"Uh . . . the ground."

He sighs. "What kind of drugs are you on?"

I scoff. "I'm not. I don't do drugs!"

"No?"

"No way." I wave off the suggestion with a super-fast swat through the air. So fast I could prah-babably do it professionally. "I'm a mom—I'm the freaking PTA predis—pred—pre—"

"President?"

"Yes! Exactly. I'm the PTA predisent. I don't do drugs. No way."

"So, you didn't take anything tonight?"

"No—well, I mean, I took one of Heather's happy Zs but—*oh shit!* Is that why you're here? Did she report me? 'Cause I only took one, I swear." I raise both hands in the air, surrendering. "I've never stolen anything before that—"

"What's a happy Z?"

"Zoloft!"

"You took a Zoloft that didn't belong to you?"

I drop my head, and my hands. "Yeah. That's bad, huh? Stealing is bad."

"Yeah, it is—"

Flashing red and blue lights suddenly appear out of nowhere—except that they're attached to a police car. A real-life police car! "Look!" I point while scrambling up to my squishy feet.

A man gets out and starts walking toward us. It's way too dark to tell for sure what he looks like, but I can tell he's tall and skinny. Like a string bean.

"How's it going? You must be Detective Chavez," String Bean says. "I'm Officer Gunnerson."

"Good to meet you," Ponch—er, Chavez says back to him. They shake hands. "Sorry to jump in here, but I was in town working a case, and your dispatch said you were short-staffed, so I figured I'd lend a hand."

"Yeah, that's great," String Bean says. "We're always low on manpower up here." He turns and looks at me. "So, is this the assailant?"

Assailant.

Ass. Ass. Ass—

"Ass-ailant!" I scream and then start laughing. Who comes up with these words?

"Yep, that's her," I hear my muscly cutie-pie say back to him. "She claims she's had very little to drink, and that she's only taken one Zoloft, that was stolen—"

"That's right, I stole it!" I confess loudly. "And Detective Poncherell-oh was just about to take me into cuts—custody, weren't you? You needah frisk me, don't you?" Girlie parts sizzling, I do a quick about-face, spreading my legs wide and pressing my hands against the side of my car. "Come on, frisk me," I order, pushing my butt out as far as I can. Muscly guys love butts. "You better make sure I don't have any concealed weapons on me."

"Do you?" Chavez asks, and there's a little wobble in his voice like maybe he's scared. Or . . . laughing.

I snort. "No! But you should still check."

I give my tail feathers a sexy shake, and—*whoa!* I lose my balance and crash face-first against the back passenger window. I start to laugh again. Ohmygod. I just smashed my face on the window—

"That's not Zoloft," String Bean says.

"Yeah, no shit. She's lit up like a Christmas tree."

I snort. Don't lick the Christmas tree; you'll get sap in your mouth—*ooh!* I wonder if the window tastes like sap. I press my tongue against it and start to laugh. It's so cold—

"Did you get any ID?"

"No, but I sort of know her. We went to high school together."

High school?

Huh?

Ponch—er, freakin' Chavez—went to high school with me?

I try and look over my shoulder, to see if I rebem—rebember him, but the glass tastes too good to leave. It's so slick and cold and . . . *mmm* . . .

I'm gonna lick this window all night long.

All night long.

All night looooong . . . all night, all night . . .

My all-time favorite Lionel Richie song starts to play in my head. "All night long . . . ," I mutter against the glass, swaying to the familiar music.

"So, what are you thinking here?" Chavez asks. "You gonna run the plates and find an address for her?"

"Yeah. But I'll get her down to the station first and let her sleep it off in the drunk tank. So long as she's not behind the wheel, she's not a threat to anyone but herself at this point."

"Unless she gets ahold of those oranges."

String Bean laughs. "True."

"Do you need to take any statements?"

"Just the cashier's," String Bean says. "I already spoke to the victim."

The victim.

I snort, causing a foggy spot to appear on the glass in front of me.

Cat Food Lady is the victim.

"Well, if you want, I can do the transport so you can talk to the witness," Chavez offers. "No sense keeping you out here any longer than you need to be."

"You sure you don't mind?"

"Nah. It's on my way."

"Well, all right then." String Bean's voice lifts. "Thanks a lot, sir. I appreciate it."

"Sure. Happy to help."

"Good night, Occifer String Bean." I wave to him, my tongue still pressed firmly against the glass.

He ignores me.

String Bean is a mean bean.

I snort again. That totally rhymed.

"Okay, Jane. I'm going to take you down to the police station now."

Sexy Chavez puts his hand on my shoulder.

"Ohmygod, yes!" I cry out against the glass.

His hand is made of thousands of little needles, each one pricking me in just the right spot.

More. More. GIVE ME MORE!

I quickly turn and plant a hungry kiss square on his lips . . . or is that his cheek—

"Whoa, whoa, whoa. None of that." He pushes me away with a firm hand. "You have to keep your hands to yourself."

I swipe at my slick mouth and start to laugh. "Um, thasss not gonna be possible. Have you seen yourself?"

The corner of his mouth twitches. "I need you to put your hands behind your back, Jane."

I gasp hopefully. "Handcuffs?"

"Yep. Turn around."

Grinning, I tuck my hands behind my back and turn around.

My body shudders as he grips my wrist with his hand. Skin-to-skin contact. *YES!* He wraps the cold metal around my wrist and snaps it shut, grazing the rubber band welts in the process.

"Oh god," I whimper.

"You okay?"

"Mm-hmm. *So* okay."

"Oh man." He chuckles. "I don't know what you're on, but you're gonna feel like hammered shit in the morning. Come on."

He keeps one hand on my shoulder and ushers me to the car while spouting off a bunch of stuff about my rights and remaining silent or whatever, but all I can focus on is how warm his hand is. It's like he's made of fire; he's practically melting my skin off! Not like Dan. Dan's always so cold—like a Popsicle. A big lying, cheating Popsicle.

Fuckin' Dan—

"My husband's gay, you know!" I blurt out.

"Oh yeah?"

"Yep. And I'm not ah-sposed to tell anyone, but y'know what . . . I feel like telling someone." He opens the back door and helps me inside. "So, I'm telling *you*, Detective Sexy Pants," I say, looking directly up into his pretty eyes. "He would rather have a penis over a vagina; can you even believe that? My husband would rather have a ding-dong over a nay-nay. A dick over a chick—" I sputter out a laugh. Dick. Chick. Another rhyme—I'm a genius!

"I'm really sorry to hear that," he says.

"Yeah, it totally sucks! I mean—not for the other gay dudes. Do your thing, man! I don't care. I'm no homo—homomo-mophobe, but *my* husband should not be gay—*ohmygod!*" I gasp. "Have you ever sat back here?" I drag my fingertips along the seat cushion behind me. "This is like velvet. Is this velvet?"

His lip twitches again. "Doubtful."

"Well, it should be." I shift to my side and press my cheek against the world's softest seat. "This is the most comfortable seat I've ever sat in." I nuzzle my cheek deeper. Like a little kitty cat. Meow. My eyelids are starting to feel *really* heavy. "Hey—hey, Chavez." I glance up at him.

"Yeah?"

"Isssit okay if I just lay down here for a minute? Just for like . . . a minute?"

"Yeah, that's okay. In fact, it's a really good idea."

CHAPTER 6

Methylenedioxymethamphetamine (MDMA) is a synthetic drug that alters mood and perception. It is chemically similar to hallucinogens and stimulants, producing feelings of increased energy, emotional warmth, physical pleasure, and sexual arousal, as well as distorting time and sensory perception. It was initially popular in the nightclub "rave" scene and is more commonly referred to as Molly or Ecstasy—

"I just—I don't understand . . ." I scrub a bruised palm across my aching forehead, still trying to make sense of the toxicology report in front of me, but I can't. No matter how long I stare at the words, or how many times I'm assured this test is accurate and reliable, it just doesn't make sense. "I'm telling you," I say, again, "I didn't take ecstasy; I took Zoloft. I swear it was Zoloft."

At least, I thought it was . . .

The haggard quality of my voice makes me wince but has little effect on the discharging officer stationed behind the glass panel in front of me. She gives me a tired look, then over a sigh repeats what she's already said: "Ma'am, it doesn't make a lick of difference to me what you did or didn't take. All I care is that you sign the report confirming you've read the findings. So, go ahead now . . ."

She taps one of her long red fingernails against the glass like she's actually touching the signature line at the bottom of the report. My already-burbling stomach wrenches as I glance down at it. Technically, it's not an admission of anything, but signing it still feels like I'm confessing to something I didn't do.

Ecstasy?

Seriously, Heather?

"Oh, for god's sake, Jane, just sign it so we can get the hell out of here," Dan growls under his breath.

I glance up at him, wishing he would be a little more sympathetic, given the obvious misunderstanding—I would *never* intentionally take ecstasy!—but as I take in the Bulls cap that's pulled down low over his eyes and the fleece jacket he's got zipped up to his chin, I know there's no compassion for me here. All he's worried about is being recognized, that someone might see the almighty Dr. Osborne bailing his wife out of jail on a Saturday morning.

As always, it's all about Dan.

Even though the cops obviously know who I am—they found Dan, after all—it's my maiden name that's listed on the bottom of the page. I must have offered that as my name last night. Considering my hatred for Dan and everything he's affiliated with, it makes sense. I sign it as it's written—*Jane L. Holliday*—then shove the report back through the little window to the officer. She rips off the bottom copy, adds it to the pile of other paperwork I've already signed, staples it all together, and then shoves the whole stack back to me.

"You have a nice day, ma'am."

I add the papers to the plastic bag of personal effects already draped over my arm and follow Dan down the hall into the lobby. Just like the steel bed I woke up on this morning, the stark white walls and upholstered guest chairs don't look the least bit familiar to me. Try as I might, I can't remember a thing about coming here last night.

My shoulders start to slump, a blanket of embarrassment settling over me.

What did I do?

How could I have been so out of control?

Dan wastes no time sliding his sunglasses into place as he pushes through the front door and steps outside. I squint hard against the morning sun and quickly dig into the plastic bag to retrieve my purse. I need my sunglasses. Where are they . . . *dammit.* They must be in my car—

"Come on, let's go!" Dan snaps over his shoulder, not even bothering to slow his hurried stride.

Asshole.

A twinge of that same anger I felt last night nips at my spine, but it's fleeting. I'm too tired too—*god*, I'm too sore to care. Everything hurts: my head, my wrists, my palms, my eyeballs . . .

Grimacing, I throw my purse over my shoulder and set off across the parking lot, shielding my eyes with my hand. A murky memory suddenly comes to mind. *Did I salute someone last night?*

Dan's already in the car, engine running, when I climb inside. The sour taste that's been lingering on my taste buds for the last fifteen hours starts to pool inside my mouth as I settle into the passenger seat, the memories of what happened *here* last night still very much intact.

Stifling a swear, I lock my seat belt into place.

"What the hell were you thinking, Jane! Following me to the Bone Yard? Are you out of your ever-loving mind?" Dan starts yelling the second we pull out of the parking lot, enraged gaze shifting between me and the road ahead. It didn't take much for him to deduce why I'd been in Morris Creek, especially when the cops told him where we could find my car. And when he asked me directly—in the few minutes we had alone—I confessed without hesitation. I may be a lot of things, but I'm no liar. "You could have exposed me," he goes on, voice raised to levels I've never heard before. "Is that what you want? Are you *trying* to ruin my career? Because I'm not the only one who's going to suffer if the Hoffstras don't give us that money and I end up losing my job. You do realize that, right?"

"Yes, of course I know that. I was just—"

"You were just *what*? Trying to make a fool out of yourself in the middle of a parking lot? Trying to get thrown in jail?"

He levels me with a stern look that's meant to make me feel like a child.

It works.

Tears prick my eyes, forcing me to drop my head.

"You realize how monumentally stupid that was, don't you?" he goes on, hammering home a point I'm already very aware of. A point that's been reverberating through my mind like jackhammers since I came to in a jail cell five hours ago. "We're trying to fly below the radar—present the perfect image—and here you are getting high and attacking people with fruit. *Fuck!*" He pounds his fist against the steering wheel. "What the hell were you thinking?"

My chin quivers. A hot tear slides down my cheek. The paternal-like disappointment in his voice is infuriating, but what's worse is I know it's deserved. He's right. That was a monumentally stupid thing to do. I knew I shouldn't follow him. I knew nothing good would come of it. But I still went. And as much as I'd like to argue that I never would have been out there had he just gone to the hospital like he said he was going to, he's not the one who caused the spectacle; I am.

Despite his lies and infidelities, Dan has never come close to exposing our truth to the world, but I did.

A mountain of shame settles in my lungs, forcing my chest to shudder with every breath. *I did this. I'm the one who lost control.* My stomach starts churning again, prompting a surge of bile to rise in my throat. I quickly press my hand against my lips, swallowing it back.

He blows out a heavy sigh. "What's wrong?"

"I . . . I don't feel good. I think I'm going to throw up."

"No surprise there," he says, tone softening a smidge. "Most people get sick coming off ecstasy. I saw it all the time in my ER rotation." It's subtle, but I'd swear he's easing up on the gas, which helps a little, given the curves of this windy road. I'd almost believe he's doing it for my benefit, except that I know how much he loves this car, and the thought of me retching all over the precious leather interior is probably what's motivating him. That and his boyfriend's ass. He wouldn't want Julian sitting on a puke-stained seat. "Considering how sensitive you are to medications in general, it'll probably get a lot worse before it gets better."

A sneer pulls on my lip. Save the bedside manner for your ball buddy, Dr. Dickhead.

"Where did you even get the ecstasy, anyway?"

"Heather."

He scoffs. "I should've figured. She's a walking disaster—"

"No, she's not." I quickly uncover my mouth to defend my friend, though I have to admit I'm more than a little alarmed to know she had an entire bottle of ecstasy in her purse. *Is that normal? Do people just walk around with a bottle of that stuff?* "And I didn't know it was ecstasy. I thought it was Zoloft."

"Zoloft? Why would she give you a Zoloft?"

I level him with a nasty glare that definitively answers his question. Fear fills his eyes. "You didn't tell her, did you?"

"No! Of course not."

"So, what, you just asked her if you could have one, and she gave you the wrong pill?"

Another surge of guilt slams into me, forcing me to drop my head again. "No. I took it out of her bag when she wasn't looking."

"You stole it?"

I pinch my eyes shut, wincing against the disappointment in his tone. It's nearly identical to the sound of the voice in my head. That nasty little voice that's been berating me for the last five hours. The one that tells me I'm a terrible mother and a horrible friend for behaving the way I did. That same voice that says I don't deserve even a smidge of the life I'm trying so hard to hang on to—

"Well, you're accumulating quite the rap sheet, aren't you?" he goes on. "Attacking perfect strangers with fruit. DUI. Narcotics theft—"

"They're not charging me with any of that," I spit out defensively, then quickly return my hand to my mouth as another surge of nausea starts burbling up. I cough against the acrid burn, and thankfully it stays at bay.

"Yeah, only because that cop pulled some strings. I hope you realize how lucky we are. There's no way we could have kept that from leaking had they actually charged you. Everyone in Mount Ivy would have known what you did."

"I know."

Before Dan picked me up, I was told that Chris Chavez, a boy I sort of knew during my brief and wonderful stint at South Glenn High School, was the officer who took me into custody last night. (Sadly, I have no recollection of seeing him.) Apparently, he's a detective down in Chicago, and made arrangements for me to participate in a first-time-offender's program in lieu of getting charged with any of my crimes. With my schedule, I have no idea how I'm going to make the sixty-mile trek down to the city twice a week, but somehow, I'll figure out how to make it work.

I have to.

Because once again, *my* family's livelihood depends on me hiding the truth.

"How'd everything go with Avery?" I ask.

I was told that the police got ahold of Dan last night—just an hour after they took me into custody—but rather than have him bail me out then, I instructed them to have him pick me up later this morning, after Avery's game. Despite my whacked-out state, it seems I had enough wherewithal to know I didn't want her seeing me in that condition.

"Fine," he says. "She was already in bed when I got home last night."

"Well, what'd you tell her this morning? Where did you say I went last night? Because I'd been texting her right before—well, before everything happened . . ."

"I told her your mom got sick, so you drove down and ended up staying over."

"Did she believe you?"

He shrugs effortlessly. "Yeah."

I swallow a pained laugh. Of course she believed him. Why wouldn't she? Dan's an exceptional liar.

"And how was the game? Was she upset that I wasn't there? Did it affect how she played or anything?"

He turns to me, eyebrows cinched up beneath the rims of his sunglasses, like I just asked if he kills puppies for fun. "No. She was fine. She scored a goal and got two assists—she played great. They won four to one."

She played great. And they won.

That's good.

And she didn't even care that I wasn't there.

I swallow hard.

"So . . . did, um—did my sister show up?"

"No. Was she supposed to?"

"She said she was going to try . . ." Biting back the nausea actively creeping up my throat, I fish my phone out of my bag. I have to power it back on, and when I do, I find a text from Julie sent at 2:18 this morning.

No way I'm comma make the game.

Tell Avery I'm Soddy—be there next firm.

Translation: No way I'm going to make the game. Tell Avery I'm sorry. I'll be there next time.

I'm sorry. I'll be there next time . . .

My heart twists at the painfully familiar words.

Julie's signed off with them a hundred times before, and every time I fire back a disapproving text in response. Something about how a promise is a promise and that you always honor it, especially when a child is involved. But as I sit here now—on the verge of throwing up, thanks to my drug-induced stupor—I realize I can't say anything. Because after last night, I'm just as unreliable as she is. I'm just like my sister.

Which means I'm also like my mother.

Dammit.

CHAPTER 7

Dan wasn't kidding.

It gets a lot, *lot* worse before it gets better.

Somehow, I manage to make the drive home without throwing up, but the second I walk into my bedroom, the floodgates open and all hell breaks loose. And it isn't just vomit; it's coming out the other end too. Fast and furious, stripping my insides like I've been gargling Drano rather than sipping ginger ale. I stay in the bathroom for hours, woefully transitioning from kneeling in front of the toilet to sitting upon it, the entire time taunted by torturous memories of what got me here in the first place: Dan and Julian kissing in the car, oranges smacking windows, the blue pill—*AGH!* That stupid, tiny little pill that was supposed to help me feel better but instead nearly ruined my life!

It's five in the evening by the time things settle down and I dare climb into the shower to rinse myself off. I sit, cradled in the fetal position on the stone floor, until the water runs cold, then work my way into a fresh pair of pajamas and crawl into bed. Thankfully, Avery went straight from the game to her friend's for a sleepover, so she hasn't seen me, but Dan has decided to make an appearance.

"There's some Motrin and Gatorade on the nightstand," he says, his tone no longer angry but still heavy with disapproval. "I'm going to the hospital. I won't be home tonight."

In my condition, there's no way to determine whether he's trying to be an ass by telling me where he's going or if we've graduated to some twisted, secret-code communication system now that I know the truth (hospital = gay bar), but I don't care either way. I just want him to leave so I can go to sleep and wake up feeling like myself again.

Whoever that is . . .

~

Beep. Beep. Beep. Beep—

My eyes snap wide and I bolt upright, smacking the obnoxious alarm screaming from the nightstand beside me. *What on earth?* I haven't used a real alarm clock in years. Where did that come from? Disoriented, I lean forward for a better look. The red numbers are blurry—sleep still clouding my vision—but they're bright enough that I can make out the time: 7:15.

Why would an alarm be set for 7:15 on a Sunday—

It's a beautiful day in this neighborhood, a beautiful day for a neighbor—

My phone, also sitting on the nightstand, suddenly erupts with my *usual* wake-up call. The *Mister Rogers' Neighborhood* theme song that always starts my day off right. Or at least on a hopeful note. I grab the phone to silence the alarm and see a new text message from Dan, sent at 4:45 this morning.

Early surgery.

Text me when you get up so I know you're awake.

You have to be in Chicago at 10!

Wait.

Early surgery?

But . . . he never has surgeries on Sundays.

They're only scheduled on weekdays.

And Chicago?

Why would I have to be in Chicago today—

Ohmygod.

A swell of panic suddenly floods my chest. I quickly tap on the screen and pull up the calendar.

It's Monday.

It's freaking Monday!

I slept through all of Sunday.

Shit!

Avery has to be to school soon.

Shit.shit.shit.

I hop out of bed and race down the hall, teetering down the front stairway like a drunk at closing time.

Am I still stoned?

No. No, I can't be.

This has to be a sleep hangover.

I stumble through the foyer and into the kitchen, where the smell of freshly brewed coffee lingers in the air. My stomach doesn't turn, so I guess that's a good sign.

Avery looks up from the sectional in the adjoining family room, where she's working her way through a bowl of cereal while she watches TV. "Whoa, are you still sick?"

"Wh-what?"

"Dad said you caught whatever Grandma had. He said that's why you slept all day."

I blink hard.

Dan covered for me.

Yet another lie, but this one was to protect Avery from the truth.

To protect me from *her* disapproval.

"Uh . . . y-yeah. I, um, I did catch what Grandma had. But I'm better now."

"Are you sure?" She takes another bite of cereal, eyes narrowed skeptically. "'Cause you sort of look like crap."

I rake my fingers through my hair, forcing a laugh despite the insult. "Yeah, I'm sure. So . . . you'll be ready to leave for school in fifteen?"

"Yeah. Will *you*?"

"Mm-hmm. Yep, I just, um . . . I just need to get dressed and—"

Whoa.

My bladder suddenly drops to the floor, weighed down like a water balloon dangling from the faucet. *Pee. I have to pee!*

"—yep. Fifteen minutes," I say urgently. "I'll be good to go."

I hustle back upstairs, my footing already more stable than it was on the trip down, and head straight to my bathroom. I yank off my pajama pants and plop down on the toilet—

Aaahhh . . .

It comes as no surprise that my urine is the color of apple juice—there can't be an ounce of hydration left in my body—but what is surprising is how clean the bathroom is. The tile floor is streak-free; the heap of soiled towels I threw in the hamper are gone. It even smells good in here—more like Bath & Body Works than a porta potty.

I blow out a heavy, grateful breath. Dan's always been a neat freak, so I know that his tidying was more about easing his own OCD than helping me, but I still appreciate it. The reflection in the mirror, however, isn't nearly as pretty a sight. Avery was right: I look like crap.

The natural waves that I usually blow out straight hang limp across my shoulders, like overcooked noodles stuck to the bottom of the pot, and the rings circling my eyes are so dark you'd think I just went a couple of rounds with Mike Tyson.

I *look* like a drug addict, which is just great, considering I'll be attending my first-offenders group for possession of an illegal substance in just a couple of hours.

"Thanks a lot, Dan," I grumble. If he went to all the trouble of setting the alarm, he could have at least given me some time to get ready.

I splash some cold water on my face, scrubbing away the eye crusties with a washcloth, then attack the dried puke that's spackled to my teeth and tongue with my toothbrush and a big rinse of mouthwash. I'm not usually one for concealer, but today it's a must. I smooth a healthy dollop across my entire face, then roll on a quick coat of mascara, wincing at the angry red lines splintering across my eyeballs. There's not much I can do with my hair at this point, so I dampen my brush, drag it through the brown mess a few times, and finally tie it back in a low ponytail.

I hustle back into the bedroom, grab some undies and a bra from the top drawer, then a pair of black leggings and a gray sweatshirt from the second, and get dressed. My stomach growls as I slide my feet into my running shoes, reminding me I haven't eaten in thirty-six hours.

Thirty-six hours . . .

I shake my head, baffled.

How is that even possible?

How can people do drugs and still carry on with life?

I head for the door, making a quick pit stop in the bathroom for one final look in the mirror.

Ugh.

Now I'm a drug-addict soccer mom . . . perfect.

Avery's rinsing her bowl at the kitchen sink when I make my way back downstairs. I grab a travel mug from the cupboard just behind her and can't help but notice that her nail beds are still outlined with neon-green paint. A twinge of anger starts to rise in my chest—the urge to call her out on her crime tickling my taste buds—but I swallow it away over a heavy sigh. Who am I to call anybody out on bad behavior?

I pour myself a cup of coffee, grab a package of Pop-Tarts from the pantry, then head for the front door, saying, "All right, let's go."

Thankfully, Dan got rid of the oranges, but the car itself feels uncomfortable as I settle into the driver's seat, like all the shameful acts I committed—and still can't remember—are buried beneath the leather and gadgetry, waiting to reveal themselves like little ghosts when I least expect them.

Dammit, Jane.

You were so stupid.

So, so stupid.

Another pang of guilt snakes up my spine as I back down the driveway and hit the road.

As usual, Avery tunes the radio to her playlist, while my thoughts wander to the day ahead. After I drop Avery at school, I'll have exactly two hours to get down to Chicago for the ten-o'clock meeting. My chest starts to tighten. Ordinarily, two hours would be more than enough to make it to the city, but I have no clue where I'm going. No idea where to park or where to go once I get there. The only information provided on the discharge paperwork was the name of the program, the Women's First Offenders Group, and an address in southwest Chicago. The address of the police-mandated program I *have* to attend or else be faced with a fine, possible jail time, and my very own rap sheet.

Disgusted with myself, I tear into the silver Pop-Tart package with my teeth, then start breaking off chunks and shoveling them into my mouth. Avery casts me a sideways glance but thankfully doesn't say anything.

We're just pulling up to school when I say, "I'm really sorry I wasn't at your game. You know I would've been there if I could."

"Yeah, I know."

There's not an ounce of disappointment in her response, which makes me feel good. At least she knows that's where I wanted to be.

We say our goodbyes—mine an "I love you, have a great day," hers a grunted-out "Later"—and I'm just about to pull away from the curb when Claudia Ruiz, associate PTA president, appears outside the passenger window, and I'm suddenly reminded of yet another shameful ramification to my pill-popping escapade: the PTA rummage sale. *Crap!* It was Saturday afternoon, an event *I* spearheaded and have been organizing for the past month, with all the proceeds going to the eighth-grade Washington, DC, trip, and I wasn't there.

I wasn't there for the biggest freaking fundraiser of the year because I was too busy shitting out vital organs in my bathroom!

My stomach wrenches around the Pop-Tarts as I roll the window down.

"Hey, Claudia."

"Oooh, honey." She sucks in a deep breath over her teeth. "You're still not feeling well, huh? Dan said you got hit pretty hard with the ole flu bug."

The flu.

Right.

I start to nod, disgusted but also unnervingly grateful for my husband's ability to sell a lie. "Yeah. It must've been the flu."

"He said you got it from your mom?" Her expression sours. "Did a lot of people at the nursing home have it?"

"Yeah . . . it, um . . . well, a bunch of the residents got sick. Everybody's fine now, but it was sort of concerning at first, you know, because they're all so . . . old."

To my ears the lie is obvious, but thankfully she doesn't seem to notice my bumbling, because she just carries on, saying, "Well, I'm just so glad that no one else at your house caught it. You did the right thing by isolating yourself. Now is not the time of year you want to be getting sick, what with the holidays coming up."

Right, the holidays . . .

I can use my mug shot for our Christmas card.

"So how did the sale go?" I ask.

"Fantastic! We brought in close to three thousand dollars; can you believe that?"

My eyes widen. "No. That's—wow! That's great."

Our goal was only two thousand. Looks like people ponied up.

"Yeah, everything ran like clockwork. The food vendors got there right on time and had everything ready to go when the sale started, and all the parents who signed up actually showed, except that Jennifer Sutton." She rolls her eyes. "You know how she is." I nod. Yes, I definitely do. "But other than that, it was perfect."

I sigh, relieved. "I'm so glad to hear that. But I feel terrible about leaving you with all the work—"

"Oh, please." She waves away my apology. "You were sick; you can't help that. Besides, you did all the heavy lifting ahead of time. Everything was organized, right down to the second. All I had to do was stand there and collect all the money," she says with a laugh. "I swear, Jane, even when you're sick, no one can take charge of a situation like you."

I force a smile.

Flinging f-bombs and oranges at perfect strangers on a Friday night? Yes, Claudia, I know how to take charge of a situation, all right.

CHAPTER 8

Thanks to a surprising amount of traffic and several directional missteps (really, Siri?), I don't get into the city until just after ten.

Late on my first day . . . great.

The three-story police station is a newer building—all red bricks and glass embellishments, with tidy landscaping hugging its perimeter—but it's located in the middle of a rougher-looking neighborhood. Not body-chalk-outlines-on-the-sidewalk rough, but one of those areas where there are more bars on the windows than curtains, and the corner liquor stores appear to be well attended despite the early hour.

I grip the wheel a little tighter as I turn into the fenced-in visitors' parking lot down the block from the station. I stupidly take a quick look at myself in the rearview—still a vision of day-old dog poop—then grab my bag and start speed-walking toward the station.

"Hey, pretty lady, can you thpare a dollar?" a toothless man—dirty and reeking of body odor—calls out from where he sits behind a loaded-down shopping cart just to the right of the intersection I need to cross. He's holding a hand-scribbled sign that says, PIGEONS KILLED MY FAMILY. NEED MONEY FOR A BB GUN.

I tuck my bag in a little closer and press the crosswalk button. "Sorry, not today."

"Thath okay. God bleth you anyway."

I smile a little. With the way my day is going, I need all the blethings I can get.

There's a security checkpoint at the station's front entrance that delays me another five minutes, so by the time I reload my keys and phone into my purse and get to the information desk to ask for directions to my classroom, it's already ten after ten.

Crap.

"You're gonna go right up these stairs here and then down the hall to your right, room 225. Officer Bates is your instructor. She'll be really glad to see you." Officer Moore, according to her name badge, is smirking like she knows the punchline to a joke, but no one's told me the setup.

My chest tightens as a scary image of Kathy Bates in *Misery* suddenly comes to mind. "Officer Bates? Room 225?"

"Mm-hmm." She nods, smirk deepening across her cherubic cheeks.

"Okay. Thanks."

Nerves ratcheting, I hoof it up the U-shaped stairway to the second floor. As instructed, I turn right, passing by four doors before I arrive at number 225. A small dry-erase board to the right of the closed door says WOMEN'S OFFENDERS GROUP in red marker.

Offender.

I'm an offender.

My stomach rolls, another pang of guilt slicing at my soul.

Dammit, Jane.

I pinch my eyes shut and inhale a deep breath through my nose.

"You can do this," I mutter on the exhale while gently grazing the recovering skin on my wrist. I was so out of it this morning that I forgot to grab a rubber band. "You are strong. You are smart. You are capable of anything you set your mind to . . ."

For the first time, Dr. Deedee's words aren't doing me a lick of good, so I change up my mantra to something a bit more motivating:

"You don't have a choice, stupid. If you don't do this, you and your family will lose everything!"

I give my head a resolved nod, then reach for the handle and open the door.

"Can I help you?" A stout, middle-aged woman poured into a police uniform turns toward me, hand pressed against her ample hip, head cocked like I've just interrupted something very important.

I swallow hard.

"Hi. Sorry, I'm . . . Jane Osb—Holliday," I quickly correct myself. Dan and I determined it would be safer to use my maiden name if given the option. "I'm supposed to be in this class—er, this group."

I step forward, handing her the enrollment paperwork the discharge officer sent me home with Saturday morning. She studies it with a narrowed gaze while I cast a nervous smile to the handful of women sitting in folding chairs in a semicircle around us. At first glance, I'd say my gutter-rat look fits right in.

"Jane *Holliday*." She spits out my name like the words hurt her tongue. "Arrested in Morris Creek Friday night for possession of an illegal substance and assault . . ."

I gasp, my cheeks igniting with heat at the sound of those horrifying, shameful words. *Arrested.*

Jane Holliday was arrested.

And she just announced it to everyone in this room!

"You are aware that we start at ten, Holliday?" she continues, unmoved by my obvious humiliation. "It says it right here on the paperwork." She points to the page. "Mondays and Fridays at ten a.m."

I raise my hand to my forehead and give my brow a little scratch, a feeble attempt to shield myself from my audience.

Please don't let anyone from Mount Ivy be here.

Please, god . . .

"Yes, I know. I'm—I'm sorry. There was a lot of traffic, and then Siri—well . . ." She reels back, her pinched expression morphing into an offended one. She doesn't want excuses. "It won't happen again," I quickly say.

"I sure hope not, because that would suggest to the rest of the group that you think your time is more valuable than theirs. Is that what you think, Holliday? Do you think you're more important than these ladies?"

"No." I shake my head.

"Good. Because we don't operate that way here. Everybody's on equal footing. Nobody's more important than anybody else, understand?"

"Yes. Absolutely." I tighten my grip on my purse straps, wishing they were a piece of rubber about to strike my skin. Now I get the joke. Officer Bates isn't an author-maiming wacko; she's a drill instructor with a penchant for punctuality, and an obvious dislike for me. "I won't be late again," I assure her.

"Go ahead and sit," she grumbles.

Head hanging like a scolded third grader, I scurry to the empty chair on the end, right next to a black woman about my age, who mumbles, "Hang in there, girl," under her breath when I sit down.

"All right, as I was saying," Officer Bates goes on, glaring at me while she assumes an uncomfortable-looking, cross-armed stance. She really should get a larger uniform. Her shirt sleeves are Saran Wrapped to her arms, not leaving much room for her to move. That can't feel good. "Not only am I a law enforcement officer, but I'm also a certified drug-abuse and mental-health counselor. I've been a member of the Chicago Police Department for twenty-two years and have been administering this program, and others like it, for the last ten."

She punctuates her résumé by making intentional eye contact with every one of us. I blink hard beneath her heated gaze, while the woman beside me sighs.

"Every one of you is here today because you were charged with a class C or D misdemeanor," she continues. "But rather than formally charge you, you're being given the opportunity to erase that mistake and start fresh; all you have to do is complete this course. And believe me when I say it's not going to be easy." She's pacing in front of us now, like a bear walking its enclosure at the zoo. Her steel-toed boots squeak beneath her intentionally slow and lumbering steps. "Over the next four weeks, we're going to dig deep into what earned you the seat you're sitting in right now. We're going to figure out what your triggers are and how you can take control of them so you can make better decisions in the future. Decisions that won't land you on probation, or in a jail cell, 'cause that's where you'll end up next time—"

"Hun-uh. No jail for me," a woman down the way says, prompting another to say, "I'll do anything to keep it off my record."

"I hear that," the woman beside me mutters.

Despite my nervousness, I nod.

Me too.

I'll do anything.

"At times it'll probably be a little uncomfortable, but trust me when I say that you *will* leave this class a stronger, healthier person than you are right now. But you only get one shot, so don't screw it up."

Under different, less terrifying, circumstances, I might feel the teensiest bit motivated right now. I want to be a stronger person . . .

"First thing we're going to do is level the playing field," Bates continues while plopping down into the folding chair in front of us. "Everybody needs to stand and tell the group their name and what they were charged with. No details, just the basics. We'll start down here."

She points to the opposite end of the half circle from where I'm sitting, which I think is good because it means I don't have to go first. Or do I even need to go at all? She already announced to everyone what *I* did . . .

"I'm Maya," a young girl—no more than twenty—stands and announces in a disinterested voice. "I got caught with heroin."

Heroin? My eyes spring wide.

She's so young!

"Donna. Assault," the next woman, at least my age with what sounds like a pack-a-day habit graveling her voice, says.

"Lina. Crank. And assault."

"Angel. Assault and possession of meth."

I shift against the metal chair.

Is this really where I'm supposed to be?

One accidental ecstasy and a few rogue oranges earn me a seat in a roomful of drug addicts and criminals?

"Birdy," the plump little blonde two seats down from me says in a surprisingly thick southern drawl. Less polished than Brielle's accent, but just as cute. "Indecent exposure."

A woman—Lina, I think—snorts out a laugh.

"It's a long story," Birdy admits over a shrug as she plops back down in the chair.

My next-door neighbor stands. "Iris. Petty theft."

And then all eyes turn toward me.

Jane, THE OFFENDER, whose stupid actions nearly cost her everything.

Humiliation barrels into me, burying my breath deep inside my lungs.

I blink hard.

I don't want to do this.

I don't want to be here—

"Come on, Holliday . . . ," Officer Bates grunts impatiently.

"Uh . . . I, uh . . ." I drag my thumb across my wrist, desperately wishing I had something to snap or tug, but there's nothing there. It's just me. Just me and my quickly unwinding nerves—

"You got this, girl," Iris mutters in a low voice from beside me.

She sounds nothing like Dr. Deedee, but for some reason her words have the same effect. Air slowly starts seeping back into my lungs.

Okay.

I can do this.

With my right hand still pressed longingly over my left wrist, I slowly stand and say, "I'm . . . Jane. Possession and assault."

"Possession of what?" that Lina lady asks.

I cast a wary glance toward Officer Bates, silently begging her to intervene and protect at least *some* of my privacy, but she doesn't say a word.

Shit.

Shifting beneath the women's curious stares, I swallow hard and say, "Ecstasy."

The horrible word no sooner leaves my lips than a surprisingly familiar male voice from the doorway says, "Okay if I come in?"

Everyone's attention, including mine, immediately shifts to the door, the spotlight thankfully turning away from me and onto—*ohmygod.*

My breath catches again.

My eyes snap wide.

It's him.

That's . . . Chris Chavez.

My arresting officer—

The guy from high school—

The guy I—

Oh no . . .

Broken memories from Saturday night suddenly start playing through my mind like grainy images on a children's View-Master: Officer Sexy Pants. Deep-set dimples and muscular arms. Ponch, from *CHiPs.* Windows—*licking windows!*

A flood of embarrassment erupts from the soles of my feet, traveling all the way up to the tip of my tangled head. I quickly drop my attention to my lap.

"Well, hello there . . . ," someone mumbles as she takes in the sight of him.

"Mmm . . . ," someone else groans.

"Of course, of course. Come in. Let me introduce you." Officer Bates calls him over, a surprising lilt in her voice. "Ladies, this is Detective Chavez. He's one of the officers who helped design this program, effectively keeping all of *you* out of jail."

"Gracias, Detectivo," someone purrs from the other side of the room.

"To what do we owe the honor of your visit?" Bates asks while glaring in the vicinity of the comment.

"I just happened to be in the building and thought I'd stop by, see how you're all doing."

I brave a quick glance up and find him standing right next to Officer Bates, surveying the lot of us. Given his muscle-hugging black thermal and well-worn jeans, I'm not surprised he's earning catcalls from some of the ladies. But what is surprising is that I didn't recognize him when I saw him Saturday night. Now that I have a name to put with the face, it's so obvious. He looks just like he did back in high school, sans the laugh lines and the dusting of gray along his temples. Those are the same mile-deep dimples I used to pass in the hallway, and that's the same warm smile I saw from across the room in . . . biology? Or was it Spanish class? The fact that I couldn't recognize him—especially after he'd, apparently, recognized me—is just—

Crap.

His deep-brown gaze lands on me, prompting my cheeks to ignite with heat. A mortified breath gets tangled up in my lungs, all the blood in my veins turning to concrete. I can't move. I can't breathe. All I can do is sit here looking like a turd on a doorstep . . . and feeling like the world's biggest fool.

Hey, classmate, I turned out pretty good, didn't I?

The corner of his lip starts to twitch before he finally breaks his eye-lock and turns back to Officer Bates. "This looks like a pretty good group you've got here."

"We'll see," Bates answers skeptically. "I was just telling them that this isn't going to be a walk in the park."

"That's for sure. They call this one the ball buster." Chavez thumbs toward Bates, prompting my classmates to laugh.

"Oh, stop it. I'm not that bad," she grouses back.

"Nah, I'm just kidding. You're great," Chavez says, and her cheeks flash a delicate pink at the attention. "You're *all* great," he goes on, turning back to us. "Which is why you're here. Each of your arresting officers saw something in you that led them to believe you deserved a second chance. So, I hope you'll all take advantage of it and take this program seriously."

"Oh, they will," Bates insists, firing a stern look around the room.

"All right then. I'll let you get back to it," Chavez says. "Ladies, I wish you all the best of luck."

His gaze quickly sweeps across the room but freezes when it lands on me.

I swallow hard.

The same lip twitch I saw a moment ago deepens into a smirk, those damn dimples on full display. He gives a little nod and then heads out of the room.

The tension that cemented my joints in place slowly eases away, but there's still a sea of humiliation lying in its wake.

Bates finishes our session by distributing "journals"—which are actually just the two-dollar composition books you find at the drugstore—to each one of us, with the strict instruction that we're to write down a response to whatever prompt she provides us at the end of each class, so she can review it during the next class. Our first prompt has already been written down for us:

IF I COULD CHANGE ONE THING ABOUT MY LIFE, IT WOULD BE . . .

I swallow a sigh.

That's a tough one.

"Don't overthink it," Bates says. "It's just an exercise that's meant to help you explore your feelings. But you need to do it. I will be checking. Failure to complete a writing assignment will get you expelled from the program; is that understood?"

Head nods and murmured yeses fill the room.

"All right then. I've signed off on all your attendance cards. You'll need to get them time-stamped at the front desk on your way out. I'll see you again at ten o'clock on Friday. That's ten o'clock *in the morning*, Holliday," she adds snidely.

I force a smile. "Right. Ten o'clock."

We file out of the room and down the stairs, lining up in front of the time clock—nearly identical to the one I used to punch back in my waitressing days—that sits on the corner of the information desk.

The lobby is busier than it was an hour ago, and though I can't imagine why anyone from Mount Ivy would be here, I still keep my head low and my attention fixed on the floor.

"Seems like you made an impression on someone," that Iris woman says from behind me as we slowly shuffle forward.

It takes me a moment to realize she's talking to me.

"Huh?" I glance back at her. "Oh, yeah, I know. She's definitely got a thing for punctuality, doesn't she?"

Her dark eyes narrow, and she shakes her head. "I wasn't talking about Bates. I was talking about him."

I follow the point of her red-tipped finger over my shoulder toward the far corner of the lobby. Chavez is talking to a uniformed officer at the base of another flight of stairs, and even though he appears to be deep in conversation, his attention keeps shifting to me. Our gazes meet, prompting my breath to hitch against my ribs. He stares at me for a long beat before the same grin I saw upstairs emerges again, sending a fresh surge of humiliation to rise in my chest.

Inside the classroom was one thing, but please don't acknowledge all my stupidity out here!

I quickly turn away, dragging a self-conscious hand across my brow.

"Looks to me that he likes what he sees."

The teasing quality in her voice suggests that she's trying to make friends with me. But I'm not here to make friends. And she couldn't be more wrong about what she's witnessing.

"No, it's definitely nothing like that," I mutter.

He doesn't like what he *sees*; he's amused by what he *saw* . . .

CHAPTER 9

I'm not sure I'd call it a *perk*, but Cannon Park, where Mom and Julie live, is only a twenty-minute drive from the police station. I decide to make the detour and pay Mom a visit. Who knows, maybe a little maternal do-gooding will act as penance for my evil ways.

Carol, my favorite nurse, is on duty at the front desk.

"Well, hi there," she says warmly, not even acknowledging my bottom-of-the-toilet appearance. "Aren't you a nice surprise on a Monday."

"Hi, Carol. I was just in the city for some . . . business and thought I'd pop in."

Business. Is that what I'm calling it?

"Well, she'll be so happy to see you; probably think it's her birthday, with all the visitors."

"*All* the visitors?"

"Your sister's here too."

I push out a smile. "Julie's here too? Great."

"Yep. She's with her now."

She hands me an orange VISITOR tag that I slap against my chest while asking, "How is she?"

Her smile sags, and her head tips in that thoughtful way that answers the question before her lips even form the words.

Mom's not *Mom* today.

"Gotcha," I say.

"But she *is* in really good spirits, so it should still be a nice visit."

I head down the hallway to room 119. Besides being just around the corner from the nurses' station, this suite is private—equivalent to a one-bedroom apartment with its separate kitchen and living room—and looks out on a beautiful rose garden. Mom groused about it at first, saying it was too "fancy" for her tastes, but I can tell she really likes it, which makes me happy. All I've ever wanted was to provide a safe and stable environment for my family, and thanks to Dan's generous paycheck, we can.

We just have to keep it that way . . .

The door is halfway open, so I can hear Mom and Julie giggling before I even enter the room. Like so many other traits, they share the same laugh. Where mine is sort of chuckle-y and a bit restrained, theirs is more . . . childlike. Carefree. Like in that moment, the only thing their bodies know how to do is laugh. Along with their green eyes and measurable thigh gaps—I've always been a little envious of that.

I smooth back my hair and give my cheeks a quick pinch for color, then push through the door saying, "Knock, knock."

"Janie!" my sister calls out from where she's sitting beside Mom on the love seat. "Look, Mom. It's Janie Lou Bug!"

Mom smiles at me, but there's not an ounce of recognition in her eyes.

I swallow a little whimper. These days are never easy.

"Hello," she says. "What did you say your name was?"

"Jane, Mom. I'm Jane. I'm your oldest daughter."

She nods slowly. Not out of recognition, but like she's hoping the movement will help the name stick to her brain. "Jane. Okay. Jane and . . ." She turns toward Julie.

"Julie," my sister says. Probably for the hundredth time. "She's Jane, I'm Julie."

"Jane and Julie. Jane and Julie," she repeats. "Well, I can't say I remember you, but those sure are pretty names."

"Pretty names for pretty girls," Julie says. "That's what you always used to say."

"Did I?" Mom asks.

I smile.

Julie laughs. "Yes. You did."

"If you say so." Mom shrugs and starts to laugh herself.

Carol was right. She *is* in good spirits today.

I set my bag down on the small dinette table and make my way over to them.

"Is it okay if I give you a hug, Mom?" I ask.

"Yes, sure."

As we've been instructed, I don't squeeze too hard or too long—our goal is to make her feel loved, not uncomfortable—but I can tell she's a bit thinner than she was when I was last here a few weeks ago. I'll need to follow up with Carol on my way out to make sure she's eating enough.

Julie and I exchange a quick hug, and then I pull a chair from the dining table and sit down across from them.

"So, what are you doing here?" Julie asks. "You never come on Mondays."

"I had to come into the city for some PTA business, so thought I'd stop by."

The lie stings my tongue but still comes out relatively smooth.

Great.

Now *I'm* getting good at it.

"So, are you feeling better?" Julie asks, surveying me with a raised brow. "Dan called and told me how sick you were. Dan is her husband," she clarifies for Mom. "He's a doctor."

"Oh, good for you," Mom says.

Good for you.

She probably doesn't remember saying those words before, either, but she has said them to me—with regard to Dan—plenty of times, and usually with a sour undertone. Despite his generosity to her over the

103

years, Mom's never been over the moon about Dan. He's always been a bit too "highfalutin" for her tastes.

I can't even imagine what she'd think of him now, if she knew the truth . . .

I smile at Mom, then turn to Julie and say, "Yeah, I got hit pretty hard. So, Dan called you?"

At this point, I'm not at all surprised to hear that Dan's lies have made their way to Julie, but the fact that *he* called her just reiterates the severity of the situation. In all the years we've been together, Dan and Julie have never had more than a handful of conversations I wasn't party to. Not for lack of effort on Julie's part, but because Dan doesn't think a lot of her. Mostly because her survival depends on regular contributions from his paychecks, though her endless string of deadbeat boyfriends and minimum-wage jobs hasn't helped his opinion of her either. Like me, Dan values security and stability.

Stability.

Without thought, I drag my fingertips along my wrist, wishing there was a band there to snap.

"He called me yesterday morning," Julie answers as she uncrosses her long, Pilates-toned legs and leans forward, grabbing a handful of Skittles from the bowl on the coffee table in front of her. A chill creeps across my skin. Used to be that Mom's sweet tooth was quenched by all things chocolate, plain M&M's being her go-to, but now she's all about fruity, tart-y treats: Skittles, Smarties, jelly beans . . . It was one of the first indications that something was wrong with her. Turns out dementia doesn't just steal away precious memories; it's also been known to hijack taste buds. The doctors assured us it was a fairly common phenomenon, but witnessing the woman who used to inhale chocolate like it was pure oxygen suddenly start smacking on Starburst didn't feel *common* at all. It was scary!

And five years later it still is.

"I tried to get ahold of you all day Saturday, but you never returned my calls or texts," Julie goes on, tossing a few of the candies into her mouth. "I figured you were just pissed about me missing Ave's game, but then Dan called and told me that you had been throwing up all night. Said you got food poisoning?"

Food poisoning?

What happened to the flu?

My gut wrenches as another lie is unwittingly added to my résumé. A lie I have no choice but to substantiate.

Thanks a lot, Dan!

This would be a whole lot easier if you could stick to *one* story!

I swallow hard, scouring my brain for a believable response. "Yeah, I, um . . . well, Dan and I went out for dinner with some people Friday night, and I guess I just got a bad piece of meat or something."

"Oh, I'm so sorry to hear that." Mom presses a sympathetic palm to her chest.

Like the Skittles, the tenderness in her voice is a reminder that she's not in her correct state of mind. That's not to say she's a mean person—she's not—it's just that she's not particularly maternal. Never has been. Where other moms would tend to a scraped knee with a hug and a healing kiss to the Band-Aid, my mom—if she wasn't working the late shift or out with one of her boyfriends—would tell me to be more careful and not to get any blood on the carpet.

"Did your husband get sick too?" Mom asks.

"Oh, um, no. He was fine."

"How was Avery's game? Was she pissed I wasn't there?"

I have no doubt that Avery *was* upset that her walks-on-water auntie wasn't in attendance, but I'm not about to admit that to Julie. Not when Avery couldn't have cared less that *I* missed her game.

I shrug. "No. She seemed fine."

"Who's Avery?" Mom asks.

My heart twists at that question like it does every time she asks it. "She's your granddaughter," I say. "She's twelve. See, that's her over there." I point to the framed school picture sitting on the credenza on the other side of the room. The one that sits beside a faded Polaroid image of my father, the love of her life. He passed away when I was fifteen, but he walked out on us when I was only four, so my memories of him are about as limited as Mom's are of Avery right now. Frustratingly, though, her brain (and heart) hangs on to him as if he were still in the picture, even when she's in her right state of mind.

"Oh my, she's a cutie, isn't she?"

I nod. Yes, she is.

Even with green fingers.

"Why didn't you go to her game?" Mom turns to Julie.

As sinister as it is, I can't help but feel a little grateful that she's the one having to defend her actions now. We'll see how our *sweet* mother takes this news.

"My boyfriend and I got invited to go backstage at that concert," Julie says, chuckling in a way that suggests she's probably already told her this story. "And while we were there, the water main under the building broke and the whole place flooded, and the fire department had to come and rescue us—"

"Oh, yes, that's right!" Mom throws her head back, laughing. "You showed me the picture of you by the big fireman." She motions toward Julie's phone, sitting on the love seat between them.

"Yes, exactly," Julie chortles while reaching for her phone. "Janie, you have to see this picture. It's so funny!" She swipes at the screen, searching for the picture, while her laughter starts to ramp up. "The firefighters made us wear these huge life preservers, even though there was only like a foot and a half of water—here! Look at that." She slides the phone across the tabletop. I glance down at the image. It's Julie—dripping wet, though still looking like the boho beauty she is—a neon-orange life preserver wrapped around her neck, a very burly firefighter standing beguiled at her side.

A heavy sigh settles in my chest, and even though I already know the answer, I still find myself asking, "Is that Blaze?"

"Pfft. No, that's Jamal. Blaze turned out to be a total loser."

I fight the urge to roll my eyes.

The guy named Blaze turned out to be a loser? Shocking.

"He started crying when the fire truck showed up," she goes on over a growing laugh. "Can you believe that? He was like a two-year-old, crying in the corner. Apparently, he's got some weird fear of sirens or something."

"What?" Mom questions behind her own laugh.

"I know, isn't that crazy?" Julie says. "I mean, I've dated guys with issues and, you know, like wild fetishes and stuff, but never one that's freaked out by sirens."

"I went out with a guy who liked to pee on me in the shower," Mom admits.

I cringe while Julie snorts and says, "Shut up! He was into golden showers? Are you serious?"

"Yes. I mean, I think that's right . . ."

"I'm sure it is!" Julie squeals excitedly.

Despite the disappointment flicking my heartstrings, I can't help but nod in agreement.

As much as I'd prefer she remember more important things—like, oh, I don't know, *my name!*—over nasty little tidbits from her sordid, post-abandonment dating past (another trait she clearly passed on to Julie!), I'm still grateful for it. It means there are still pieces of *her* in there.

"Oooh! I've got another one," Julie goes on, settling into the corner of the love seat, inside leg bent at the knee so she can get extra comfy. "I went out with this guy who was totally into cartoon characters. He asked me to wear a Tweety Bird mask every time we did it."

Mom snorts. "Stop it! You're kidding."

"No!" Julie crows back. "I'm totally serious. It was one of those old-school Halloween masks. You remember the plastic ones that had the elastic string around the back, and they came with a one-piece costume? They were made of plastic or vinyl or something. They were impossible to move in. You know, the kind you got at Woolworths."

Mom's shrug implies the reference is lost on her, but it's not on me. I know exactly the kind of costumes she's talking about, and they weren't just hard to move in; they were hard to breathe in. (Mom treated me to my first store-bought Halloween costume the year I turned eight. She claimed it was because I was doing so well in school, but looking back, it was clearly meant to cushion me for the life-altering blow that she'd gotten herself pregnant with Julie. So much for casual dating with no strings attached!) As excited as I was to be Jem, of *Jem and the Holograms*, it was practically a near-death experience trying to breathe through the teensy little slit of a mouth hole. I had to raise that mask up and gulp air between every door we knocked on just so I wouldn't pass out.

"Anyway," Julie goes on, laughing harder now, completely unfazed by Mom's unawareness. "Yeah, he'd ask me to wear the Tweety one pretty much every time we did it. And then when we were done, he'd tell me to go clean my feathers in the shower!"

"Oh! That's funny," Mom cries. "What else? Were there others?"

"Are you kidding?" Julie wails. "I could go on for days!"

I swallow a disappointed sigh.

I wish I could say that this unsettling conversation is another indication that Mom isn't in her right mind, but I can't. This chummy locker-room talk is very reflective of the kind of relationship Mom and Julie have—or had, before she got sick. They've always been more like girlfriends than mother and daughter, unlike Mom and me, who have never dipped a toe into friend territory. The role of *mother*, however, has swayed back and forth between us more times than I can count. But once again, the fact that Mom's brain is hanging on to this connection is actually a good thing, even though it's more than a little disheartening. There are certain topics moms and daughters do *not* need to explore.

"What about you?" Mom turns to me. "Do you have any kinky stories in your closet?"

My eyes spring wide, and my heart starts to race. Even though there's no way she can possibly know what kinds of stories are hiding in the *closets* at my house, I can't help but feel incredibly self-conscious right now.

"I, uh—"

"Pfft! Not even," Julie cuts me off with a flippant wave. "Janie's only had sex with one guy her entire life, and he's so straitlaced he probably doesn't even take his suit off when they do it. No offense," she adds as an afterthought.

I raise my hands, assuring her no offense has been taken.

By all appearances Dan *is* very straitlaced (his laces being the only *straight* thing about him!), though I have no doubt the guys at the Bone Yard have slightly different insights into that perspective.

I shift against a little pang of anger.

"You've only been with *one* man?" Mom asks, eyes wide in disbelief. "What are you, religious or something?"

"No, not particularly."

"So, you were just saving yourself for Mr. Right, is that it?"

I shrug. "Yeah, something like that."

"Janie's got the perfect husband and the perfect life," Julie joins in, winking at me while she tosses the rest of the Skittles into her mouth. "I want to be her when I grow up."

Her comment is meant as a compliment, and two months ago I would have taken it that way, but now? No. I wouldn't wish my *perfect* life on anyone. Even my train wreck of a little sister.

∼

News of my weekend illness spreads through Mount Ivy like wildfire and seems to grow more dire with every passing day. What started out as a little flu bug on Saturday evolves into near appendicitis by Thursday night's Rotary meeting. Anita Riggs, of "Riggs Realty, where everything I touch turns to sold!" even showed up with a bouquet of get-well lilies and a box of Godivas for when I was feeling strong enough to eat.

Thankfully, I was armed with a snug-fitting rubber band and managed to *snap* my way through that stressful situation without breaking, but it's getting harder and harder to keep up with all the lies. How Dan has managed to live this way—undetected and mentally sound—for as long as he has is nothing short of impressive.

I should probably erect a statue in his honor.

A great big penis statue with his face etched into the balls.

Speaking of my loyal husband, he hasn't brought up the incident even once, but he is very intent on making sure I get down to Chicago for my "meeting" (how we're referring to it in case Avery's within earshot) on time. He went so far as to push back this morning's coronary bypass surgery just so he could take Avery to school and I could get on the road earlier.

Of course, Avery looked miserable when I said my goodbyes—she'd always prefer to ride in smug silence with me than her father—but I didn't really have a choice. With my criminal record on the line, and the Mount Ivy gossip mill eager for another frenzied round of the telephone game, I couldn't run the risk of being late again.

It's only 9:27 when I pull into the parking space in the police station lot, which is perfect because I still need to respond to our first writing prompt. I cut the engine, turn the ignition back so Dr. Deedee can stream through the speakers, and pick up the notebook. I stare down at the prompt:

IF I COULD CHANGE ONE THING ABOUT MY LIFE, IT WOULD BE . . .

The answer is obvious, but I'm not about to write it down in a book, or anywhere else for that matter. That would be about as foolish as actually telling someone! No. Despite Bates's assurance that she doesn't care what we write down, I have to be very careful how I respond to anything inside this "journal." If I were to be honest, and it ended up in the wrong hands—

A blanket of goose bumps suddenly erupts across my skin, sending a chill snaking up my spine.

My god.

The damage would be devastating.

I quickly scribble out something vanilla enough not to be damning but still containing enough truth that I don't feel like I'm lying, again:

I want a better relationship with Avery.

I close the notebook, then dive into the box of Godivas I left in the car last night. A little celebration for my punctuality and completion of my first assignment. *Good job, Jane!*

At quarter to ten, I head for the building. The same homeless man I saw on Monday is still camped out near the crosswalk. Today his sign says, **WIFE WAS KIDNAPPED. 98¢ SHORT ON RANSOM.**

I can't help but laugh.

"Good morning, pretty lady. Got thum thpare change?"

"I'm sorry, I don't," I reply without any real thought. Not only do I never carry cash—if it's not plastic, it's not in my wallet—but Dan has a strict rule when it comes to helping the homeless: never give them money because you don't know where they'll spend it.

"Thath okay." He offers up a wide, toothless grin. "God bleth you anyway."

I'm not sure if it's the sincerity behind his gummy smile or the nauseating thought that *any* part of Dan is rubbing off on me, but one of the two prompts me to say, "Actually—wait. I have something in my car you can have. Hang on . . ."

I hustle back to the parking lot, grab the box of chocolates (nine of the dozen still intact), and hurry back to him.

"I'm not sure if you like chocolate, but here." I cautiously hand him the box. "They're really good."

And thankfully all truffles, so you'll be able to gum them down pretty easily.

"Wow. Tho fanthy," he says, eyeing the gold box with reverence. He raises his gaze to mine. "Thank you, pretty lady."

My chest swells. "You're welcome. I hope you like them."

The security line to get into the police station is easily twelve people deep, but it's moving quickly, so I'm feeling good about things. Not only do I look a heck of a lot better than the last time I was here, but I've still got eight minutes to get to my class, *and* I practiced a random act of kindness; I could be my own bumper sticker today—

"Somebody's trying to avoid the wrath of Officer Bates, huh?"

I glance over my shoulder and find that Iris woman, whom I sat next to on Monday, standing behind me.

Iris, arrested for petty theft.

On instinct, I tighten my grip on my purse straps.

"I'm sorry?"

"You're on time," she says, motioning to her watch.

"Oh . . . yeah." I force out a little laugh. "I'm pretty sure she'd have me tarred and feathered if I wasn't."

She grins. "Probably."

I turn back around, shuffling forward as the line continues to move. She continues with her probing. "Do you have a long drive in?"

"Um . . . yeah." I cast a quick look back but don't make eye contact. That should give her the hint that I'm not really looking to chat. "It's just over an hour."

"An hour? Where are you coming from?"

"Mount—er . . . Morris Creek."

Morris Creek?

Seriously, Jane?

Yes, it's better than revealing the truth, but saying you're from Morris Creek is like returning to the scene of the crime.

Dumbass.

"Morris Creek? That's gotta be close to a hundred miles. It only takes you an hour to get all the way down here?"

My breathing grows shallow beneath her barrage of questions. Questions I'm definitely not prepared to answer.

Please, just leave me alone.

"Yeah, I, um . . ." I drop my head, avoiding her speculative gaze, which I can see from the corner of my eye. "I tend to speed a little bit."

She makes a snorting sound. "I guess so."

We shuffle forward again.

Only two people ahead of me now.

Come on, hurry up.

"So, how did it work out that you ended up all the way down here?" she questions. Again. "Aren't there some other programs closer to home?"

I clear my throat, buying myself some time as I mentally dig through all my lies for one that will sound legitimate. One that won't reveal that my arresting officer was a guy I sort of knew from high school. A guy who could easily dismantle my life with one well-worded Facebook post. (I didn't actually check, but we've got to have *some* friend in common.) My heart starts to beat a little faster. As subtly as possible, I slide my finger up under the cuff of my sweater and give it a little tug.

Snap!

"Yeah, I guess they, um . . . they don't offer a program like this up there," I reply, nerves thankfully settling a twinge. "I think it's more of a big-city kind of thing."

I brave a look up and find her nodding. But it's not a nod of under-standing; it's one of those really slow nods that suggests she knows I'm lying.

Shit.

"Uh-huh. Right," she says.

"Ma'am. Come on through, please."

Thankfully, the officer calls me to the security checkpoint, permit-ting me to turn my back on Iris.

I unload my purse, phone, and keys onto the table, then quickly walk through the metal detector, hoping to put a little bit of distance between me and my interrogator.

"Looks like your boyfriend's here again."

Boyfriend?

Definitely not another question but still a comment I wasn't prepared for.

Confused, I turn toward her and follow her gaze across the lobby—*oh.*

My breath catches.

It's him.

Detective Chavez.

He's talking to a couple of uniformed officers near the elevators—

He suddenly turns my way, dark eyes instantly locking onto mine as if he could feel me looking at him. Embarrassment floods my chest as the same amused grin he wore on Monday quickly slides back into place.

Officer Sexy Pants.

Another onslaught of broken memories flits through my mind, snapshots of what happened just a week ago tonight: him banging on my window, me searching for buttons—so many buttons!—the wine. I gave him the wine, and then I—

Ohmygod.

I kissed him!

His grin seems to grow, as if he's tuned into my thoughts, like he's reliving the mortifying experience along with me. My humiliation deepens, but with it comes a twinge of annoyance.

Okay, I get it.

I made a complete ass of myself.

It was funny.

But the joke's over!

Move on!

And please, god, don't tell anyone!

"You okay?" Iris asks, astutely reading my body language.

I peel my gaze away from him while giving my head a righting shake. "Yeah, I, um . . . I just don't want to be late."

She casts a skeptical glance toward Chavez, then turns back to me and over a shrug says, "Whatever you say."

CHAPTER 10

The chairs have been rearranged from Monday's half-circle formation into a tight circle with all chairs facing inward so that when seated, we'll be looking at each other.

I swallow hard and give my band a preemptive snap.

That's a whole lot of face-to-face lying . . .

"Glad you finally decided to show up, Holliday."

Despite the fact that Iris and I walked in together, and that it's only 9:57, Officer Bates once again makes a point of putting *me* in my place.

"Good morning," I mutter back to her, shifting beneath the straps of my bag.

"Take a seat," Bates grumbles.

There are only two empty seats in the circle, and thankfully they're not together. Not that I don't *want* to sit beside Iris. I mean, I'm sure she's a perfectly lovely woman—aside from her petty theft arrest—but I'm not looking to buddy up with anyone while I'm here. Especially someone who asks so many questions . . . and who already knows I'm a liar.

Iris takes the seat between Donna, the smoker arrested for assault, and . . . Lina? Yeah, Lina. That mouthy woman who was arrested for assault and possession of crank, which I *think* is slang for cocaine, but I'm honestly not sure.

I take the last empty seat on the opposite side of the circle from Iris, right between Maya, the way-too-young heroin user with enviable black curls draping down her back, and Birdy, the southern girl arrested for indecent exposure. As I look at her now, wearing a delicate, peasant-style top, her freckled cheeks flushing the prettiest shade of pink thanks to the warm air blowing down from the vents above, I can't begin to imagine how she earned that arrest. *Indecent exposure?* She looks so sweet and innocent. There must be an interesting story there—not that I intend to find out what it is.

"Mornin'," she says to me, her thin smile traveling all the way up to her pale-blue eyes.

"Good morning."

She surprises me by leaning in a little closer and, in just above a whisper, saying, "What'd you do, run over her dog or somethin'?" She says the word *dog* like it's spelled with an *a* and a couple of extra *w*'s: *dawwg.* She glances toward Officer Bates. "She doesn't seem to like you a whole lot."

"No, she doesn't," I whisper back to her and, despite my annoyance with Officer Bates's greeting, find myself smiling. Her accent is so adorably thick and backwoods it's a bit of a struggle to understand her.

"Well, hopefully she eases up on ya a little bit."

I nod. That would be nice.

"All right, ladies. Now that everyone's finally here, we can get started. Pull out your journals and open them up to your first prompt."

We all heed Bates's terse instruction, flipping the covers on our notebooks so the first page is exposed. I can't help but notice that my southern neighbor has written down a lot more than I have. She's filled up the entire first page, and by the rippling of the lined paper, it appears she even wrote on the back. I steal a quick glance over at Maya's and see that she's also written a lot more than me. Two full paragraphs.

Uh-oh.

"Fine. Good. Okay . . ." Bates is circling us from behind, glancing over our shoulders to confirm that we've done the work. "Nice," she says when she comes up behind Birdy, and then she stops dead in her tracks when she's behind me. I hear her sigh.

"Seriously, Holliday? You can't come up with more than a sentence?"

All eyes in the circle shift toward me. My breath catches, and on instinct, I press my notebook against my chest to protect it, even though there's nothing damaging there. I glance back at her. "Sorry. I, um . . . I didn't realize we needed to do more than that."

"Well, you do," she grunts over a tired look. "A lot more."

"Okay. Sorry. I'll do more next time."

Birdy casts me a sympathetic glance while Bates finishes her rounds, then settles up against her podium. "All right, so the prompt was, 'If I could change one thing about my life, it would be' what?" she reminds us, her gaze sweeping across the room. "By show of hands, how many of you responded to that prompt by including someone else in your answer? Your significant other, your kid, your friends . . ."

"I talked about my mom," Angel (assault and meth), sitting on the other side of Birdy, says while waving her hand carelessly through the air.

Other hands start to rise. First Donna's, then Lina's, Iris's, Birdy's . . .

Beside me, Maya raises up her right hand because her left is pressed up against her mouth. She's been nibbling her nails since I got here.

I tentatively raise my hand.

"Exactly," Bates says over a slow nod. "That's the thing about women. We view our world through our relationships, and when given the opportunity to change something in our world, nine times out of ten it won't be limited to us—it will involve someone else. Angel, what did you say about your mom? What would you like to change about her?"

She shrugs. "I want her to get off her ass and get a job."

Donna snorts and Maya giggles over her fingers.

"So, your mom isn't working?" Bates follows up.

Angel shakes her head, the four-inch gold hoops in her ears swaying with the movement. "She hasn't worked in almost two years."

"Why not?" Lina asks.

Angel reels back. "Excuse me?"

"Go ahead and answer," Bates jumps in, then glances around the circle, saying, "This is what this group is all about, ladies. I told you we were going to dig deep to find out what got you here, and you do that by communicating. So, go for it." She raises her palms as if conceding authority. "Ask questions. Talk about things. So long as you keep it respectful, it's always beneficial."

My stomach turns, and I instinctively tighten my hold on the notebook.

There's no way discussing *my* life with perfect strangers—criminals!— will ever be beneficial.

Angel sighs, then turns back to Lina. "Because she'd rather cash her disability check than go to physical therapy and get better."

"Shit, everybody'd rather collect than go to work," Lina fires back, unimpressed.

"Your mom has an injury?" Iris asks.

"Yeah, something with her back. It's called . . ." Her shimmery lips purse in thought. "I don't know . . . socratic or scio—"

"Sciatica?" Iris follows.

Angel nods, pointing an affirming finger at Iris. "Yeah, that's it. Her sciatic nerve. She used to work at the Home Depot and was lifting some bags of concrete, and it just went out on her."

"That can be a really hard injury to recover from," Iris says.

"Yeah, I've heard that sciatic thing hurts real bad," Birdy chimes in, and even though the topic isn't funny, and her comment isn't meant to be, Maya still giggles and Lina snorts and says, "Damn, girl. Where the hell are you from?"

"Pine Bluff, Arkansas," Birdy answers easily, like she gets that question a lot.

"What are you doing in Chicago?" Donna with the Marlboro voice asks.

"I moved up here to be with my boyfriend, Wade. That's who I wrote about." She motions to her journal.

"What would you like to change about him?" Bates takes over again.

"Oh, um . . ." Birdy turns to Angel, as if seeking permission to shift the conversation her way.

Angel raises her palms without hesitation, like she's just dropped a bomb on a doorstep and is grateful to be rid of it. "That's all you, girl," she says.

"Okay, well, um . . . well, Wade's real sweet most of the time. Like, he's always leaving little notes around the house and bringin' me flowers and stuff, bless him. But then there's other times when he's like . . ." Her blonde brows furrow in thought. "I don't know, it's like his panties get all twisted, and he gets upset real easy about stuff. It's just hard to deal with. I think it's on account of his childhood," she goes on, her thoughts sounding more absent now. "His daddy got put in jail when he was little, so his mama remarried this guy, Larry, who's a good-enough guy, but, you know, he had other kids already, so he never paid much attention to Wade. So, I think maybe he's got some issues with all a that, you know? 'Cause his real daddy wasn't around—"

"Focus, girl," Angel cuts in over a tired groan and a snap of her fingers.

Birdy blushes. "Right. Sorry. I guess I just worry that when he gets in one of his grumblin' moods, he's gonna, I don't know, do somethin' stupid."

"Like kill you?" Lina asks bluntly.

"Lord, no." She presses her hand against her chest. "He'd never do nothin' like that. He loves me too much—and Rosebud, that's our little girl." She turns to me and smiles, as if somehow aware we're both mothers. "He'd never do nothin' to hurt me or Rosie. I just don't want him hurtin' himself somehow."

"Do you think he's suicidal?" Bates asks.

Birdy shakes her head. "No, ma'am. But sometimes when he gets in one of his frets, he just starts talkin' about how sad he is, and how he can't imagine livin' without me, and . . . I don't know." Her shoulders slump. "Sometimes it's like he's two different people. One minute he's perfectly happy and all sweetie pie, and the next he's just a sad, mopey little puppy."

"Has he ever been treated for bipolar disorder?" Iris asks.

"Bipolar?" Birdy's brow furrows. "I don't know what that is."

"It's a mental illness that causes people to have drastic mood changes," Iris explains.

"That's called PMS," Lina grunts.

Maya sputters out a laugh, sending pieces of chewed-up fingernails flying onto the floor.

I cringe and as subtly as possible shift my legs away from her.

"No, that's called menopause," Donna chimes in, and everyone starts to laugh.

Everyone except me, and Iris. I can't help but notice she's still wearing a concerned expression. It reminds me of the face Dan makes when he's worried about a patient, when he wants to fix them but isn't quite sure how.

"No. He ain't never been tested for nothin' like that. He don't have mental problems," Birdy says over a firm shake of the head. "He's just real sensitive and gets worked up sometimes, that's all."

I can tell by the look on Iris's face that she doesn't necessarily agree with Birdy's less-than-technical explanation. And a week ago I probably wouldn't have either. But now I know better. Perfectly sane, rational people can get really worked up, and do *really* stupid things, if pushed to their limits. It doesn't mean they've got a mental disorder; it just means their lives are falling apart.

And that they're married to a liar—

"What about you, Holliday? Who did you write about?"

I probably shouldn't be surprised that Bates redirects the interrogation to me, but it still catches me off guard.

"Oh, uh . . ." I fumble with my notebook, pulse spiking nervously.

Rationally, I know that I can talk about Avery without exposing our secret, but with all their gazes zeroing in on me, I can't help but feel a little anxious.

I don't want to do this. I don't want to share any part of my life with these women.

An unwelcome and familiar tightness returns to my chest. I quickly lay my journal down on my thighs and slide my finger up under the rubber band—desperate to stop the panic before it takes hold—but stop short of snapping when I glance across the circle and lock eyes with Iris. There it is. That same sense of calm I felt when she spoke to me the other day. I blink hard, taken aback by the sensation.

"Whenever you're ready, Holliday," Bates prods impatiently.

Gaze fixed intently on Iris's, I say, "I wrote about my daughter."

My voice comes out in little more than a whisper, but it's loud enough that Iris gives me a subtle nod—like somehow she knows she's anchoring me and too swift a movement will break the connection—and for Birdy to say, "Aww. You've got a little girl too? How old is she?"

"Tw-twelve. She's twelve."

"Oh, that must be a real fun age," Birdy coos.

"What's her name?" Angel asks.

"Avery."

In my periphery I see her nod while Birdy says, "Ooh. That's real pretty."

I bravely pull my gaze away from Iris and turn to her. "Thanks. She's named after my husband's aunt. She was his favorite person growing up."

"Oh! That's just like me!" Birdy squawks excitedly. Lina reels back, scowling at the outburst. "I was named after my mama's favorite person too—well, sort of. She never actually met him, but she's been moony eyed over Mr. Burt Reynolds practically her whole life. Ever since she saw *Smokey and the Bandit* when she was a kid."

"Wait." I blink hard, startled. "I'm sorry. Are you named after Burt Reynolds the actor? Like, your name is Burty? With a *t*? Not Birdy like a . . . bird?"

She smiles pridefully. "Yes, ma'am: B-U-R-T-Y. Burty Reynolds Bedford."

My jaw starts to sag while Donna snort laughs and says, "Your parents named you after Burt Reynolds?"

At her age, there's no way Maya can possibly know who Burt Reynolds is, but she snickers just the same.

"I know it's sorta funny, but I really like it," Bird—er, Burty—says, unapologetically.

"As well you should," Iris affirms, despite the smile tugging on her lips.

"Who the fuck is Burt Reynolds?" Lina scoffs.

"Hell if I know," Angel mumbles.

"He's that old actor who looks sort of like Tom Selleck but not nearly as hot," Donna clarifies.

Lina raises her palms and mutters, "Who the fuck is Tom Selleck?"

"So, what is it you want to change about *Avery*?" Bates cuts in, turning the tables back on me.

It takes a second to reconcile the fact that my nerves are much calmer than they were a moment ago. Calm enough that I think I can answer the question without having to rely on Iris, or my rubber band, to do it.

"I'd just like us to get along better," I say. "We seem to be fighting all the time lately."

"That's 'cause she's a walking hormone," Donna grouses, the scent of musty cigarettes lingering on her words. "I've got two girls, and both of them were hell on wheels at that age—"

"Twelve goin' on twenty-five," Lina mutters.

"Exactly," Donna grunts back.

I shift in my seat. "Yeah, I know a lot of moms who are dealing with those kinds of issues, but that's not what's going on with Avery. She's really modest and doesn't seem to be interested in boys right now." Unless they're armed with cans of spray paint. "It's more like . . . I don't know." I drop my head slightly, vulnerability niggling at my spine. "She's just acting out a lot."

"What, she doesn't like being dropped off at school in Mommy's Range Rover?" Lina questions snidely.

Her comment brings a flush of heat to my cheeks. I don't care that she knows what kind of car I drive—clearly she saw me pull into the parking lot—but I hate that she pointed it out to the group. Not because of what they'll think of me, but because driving around in a $100,000 car (that Dan insisted I get) doesn't fit in with my Morris Creek backstory.

People from Mount Ivy drive expensive cars, not people from Morris Creek!

"So, what *is* Avery doing?" Iris jumps in.

Still annoyed by Lina, I swallow hard and turn to her. "She, um . . . she's just getting into some trouble at school."

"What kind of trouble?" Angel asks.

I shrug. "Nothing too serious," I lie. "Her grades have dropped a little. She misses some assignments here and there—"

Donna and Iris nod while Lina mumbles, "Like every other kid in the world—"

"—she's cut a few classes," I go on, strangely motivated to up the ante, just to shut Lina up. "She got detention once. And, um . . . well, she got caught vaping a couple weeks ago."

"Oooh . . ." Iris sucks in a deep breath over her teeth.

"Nah, that's nothin'," Maya offers beneath a heavy-lidded grin. "I vape all the time. It's no big deal."

"You're not twelve," Iris fires back.

"I've heard vaping's real dangerous," Burty says.

"It is," Iris agrees.

"I do it sometimes," Angel adds, shrugging. "But just when I'm at a club or whatever."

"It's way better for the environment than smoking," Maya goes on, apparently interested enough in the conversation to drop her tasty fingernails away from her mouth. "And they smell way better than cigarettes. No offense." She glances across the circle at Donna.

"None taken," she grunts back, a little too easily to be believed.

"So, what did you do to her when she got caught?" Iris asks.

Once again, their collective gazes zero back in on me, my already-hot seat now threatening to burn me.

"Well, we tried taking her phone away, and her other devices," I explain. "But that didn't really work, so, um . . ." From the corner of my eye, I see Bates fold her arms over her chest, like she's amused by my bumbling. I swallow hard. "So now we're trying something different—"

"You're locking the princess in her tower?" Lina snorts.

I raise my chin a bit higher and defensively say, "No. We're . . . letting her live her own truth."

Iris's brow furrows, and Donna says, "Huh?"

"What the fuck does that mean?" Lina grunts.

My breath shallows.

Yeah, Jane, what the fuck does that mean?

"It, um . . . it means that we're allowing her space to find her own place in the world," I reply, my tone void of all confidence. This sounded a *lot* better when Heather said it. "You know . . . letting her make her own mistakes so she can figure out who she is . . ."

Silence fills the room, just long enough for a swell of bile to stir in my gut, before Angel bursts out laughing and Lina says, "What the actual fuck?"

"You're not punishing her?" Donna questions. "You're just gonna let her do whatever the hell she wants, no matter how stupid or dangerous it is?"

I swallow hard, suddenly wishing I'd sneaked in a few appointments with Dr. Jill myself, so I would know how to defend her advice. Advice that sounded really good last week when surrounded by my friends, but now . . . doesn't.

"It's—it's just a tactic we're trying," I say weakly. "A lot of people I know use it with their kids."

"Yeah, rich people," Angel mutters under her breath.

My chest starts to tighten.

"Wait, I think I've heard about this," Maya jumps back in. "It's called, like, hands-off parenting or some shit—"

"Nah, I got it!" Lina leans forward in her chair, ruby-lined lips rising into a smirk. "You're one of those hipster parents who thinks every kid should get a trophy just for showin' up, right?"

"Ugh. I hate those parents," Angel mutters.

"That's not what a hipster is," Maya mumbles, fingers once again sandwiched beneath her teeth. "They wear corduroy pants and have beards and shit—"

"Well, is it working?" Iris steps back in.

My throat is quickly growing thick, swelling beneath their obvious judgment. This journal entry was supposed to be easy, but instead it's turning into my crucifixion. And freaking Bates is just sitting here letting it happen!

On instinct, I slide my finger up under the cuff of my sweater and start to pluck at the rubber band. Not hard snaps—nothing that anyone would notice—just a quick succession to temper some of the stress that's building in my bones. *Snap. Snap. Snap. Snap.* I thrust my chin forward and, mustering up all the confidence I can, say, "Yeah, actually, it's been working great."

Iris's gaze falls to where my fingers are working beneath the thin layer of black cashmere. "Glad to hear it," she says.

Her tone is encouraging, but the glint in her eyes as she returns her attention to my face confirms what I suspected downstairs: she knows I'm lying. And based on the skeptical looks everyone else is wearing, they're probably not far behind.

"All right, who else wrote about one of their kids?" Bates asks, thankfully, *finally*, steering the conversation away from me.

"I did," Donna grunts with a raise of her hand. "I wrote about my oldest, Harmony."

"How old is she?" Angel asks.

"Twenty-seven. Stupid kid." Donna shakes her head. "She just started working down at the Rear End out on Route 9—"

"The Rear End? Isn't that a strip club?" Lina scoffs.

"A *gentleman's club*," Donna corrects over a heavy sigh.

"Oh shit," Maya mutters.

"I swear that girl is trying to send me to an early grave." Donna proceeds to elaborate on her daughter's poor career choice while I sink down into my chair feeling like I've just been dragged over the coals. How am I going to survive six more classes with these women? They're horrible!

The moment class ends, I take off down the stairs, ignoring Burty's "Have a good weekend!" comment that trails behind me on the way. She's sweet enough, but I've got to get out of here before I start looking for oranges. The lobby is still teeming with activity, and before I even raise my head to confirm, I can feel that I'm being watched. And I know by who.

UGH!

I ram my attendance card into the time stamper, then cast a quick glance to my left as I head for the exit—

I knew it!

Freaking Chavez.

He's standing in the same spot by the elevators staring at me, again. Stalking me with that stupid grin and lucid memories of what I did a week ago. Memories he clearly wants to taunt me with.

Not today, buddy!

I can't handle any more scrutinizing today!

Pulse hammering, I storm out of the building and hightail it across the street toward the parking lot, desperate to put this maddening world of criminals and drug addicts and annoying detectives—a world I don't belong in!—behind me.

"Thee you thoon, pretty lady," the homeless guy calls out to me as I blow by him.

"Yeah, whatever," I growl through my gritted teeth.

"Jane!"

My stomach drops to the dirty concrete at the sound of my name.

It's Chavez.

Now he's following me?!

Uh-uh.

NO!

Outside the police station, I'm a free woman.

I don't have to take your ridicule out here!

I keep my head down, pretending I don't hear him, and press on, hurrying my steps.

"Hey, Jane!" he calls out again, and now I can tell that he's getting closer.

Dammit!

Just leave me alone!

I weave my way through the parking lot and quickly climb into my car. Breathing hard, I jam the keys into the ignition and turn the engine over—

"Hey, Jane! Hello!" Flashbacks of last Friday night slam into me as Chavez calls to me from right outside my driver's window. "Are you okay?" he says, surveying me through the tinted glass with a scrunched brow.

My jaw muscles tense as I slam the button to unroll the window.

"I see you found the right button today," he taunts, that maddening grin of his instantly reappearing, bringing with it the urge to ram my fingernails into my palms.

Not today!

"Didn't you hear me calling you—"

"Yeah, I heard you." I cut him off with a demonic-sounding growl. "I just don't want to talk to you. I'm not in the mood for any of your shit!"

He reels back, dark eyes snapping wide. "Huh?"

"Look, I know I was a great big idiot last week, okay? I get it. Believe me, I get it! I know all the window-licking and Poncherello, Sexy Pants stuff was really freaking funny, but it's over, okay! I don't need you mocking me with that stupid grin every time I walk by."

"Wait. What? No." He blinks hard. "That's not—"

"I can't handle any more judgment today," I snarl over whatever bullshit comment he was about to make. "Not from those horrible women up there and most definitely not from you! Now get away from my car so I can get out of here!"

"But I just wanted to see how you—"

I pound my fist against the button, raising the window and silencing his impending insults. *Not today!* He quickly backs out of the way as I reverse out of the spot and head for home.

Home.

Where everyone knows I'm a good mom.

Or at least try to be.

Where my friends support me and accept me for who I am.

The parts they know, anyway . . .

CHAPTER 11

It's Sunday afternoon. Dan took Avery down to Chicago to watch a Bulls home game, which means I've got the whole house to myself. And because all my committees are on hiatus for the upcoming holiday (somehow, it's already Thanksgiving week; I'd swear it was just Labor Day!), the only thing on my to-do list is to work out the Thanksgiving menu. Normally, I'd relish this rarely offered alone time, but today it's proving to be a little frustrating. No matter how hard I try to focus on finding the right maple bourbon apple pie recipe, all I can think about is what happened on Friday, with the women in my group . . . with Chavez in the parking lot . . . I didn't handle it well. Not so much the women but with him.

Now that I've had some time to cool down, it's dawned on me that lashing out at him was about the stupidest thing I could have done. He knows things about me—things that could destroy me and my family—and if I'm not careful, he could stop being the cop who's amused by me and instead be the cop who wants to make me pay for my crimes outside the classroom. As much as I hate the thought of spending three more weeks with those women, I *have* to keep my position in that class, which means I'm going to have to figure out a way to tolerate their scrutiny. And even though it sickens me, the only way I can see doing that is by lying to them. About everything.

Starting tomorrow, every journal entry will be a complete fabrication. A one- to two-paragraph snapshot of a life that has absolutely nothing to do with me. A life that can't possibly cause me any pain when it's put under the microscope, because it doesn't actually belong to me.

And as for Chavez . . . I'll just have to offer him the sincerest apology I can, then pray that he keeps my *real* life under wraps while continuing to think I'm the world's biggest mess. Loser. Idiot. Failure. Fill in the _____.

~

"Good morning," Dan says to me as I make my way into the kitchen Monday morning.

He's just returned from a run. His cheeks are flushed from the brisk air, and there's a heady, manly scent lingering around him. I used to get turned on when I'd wake up and find him like this, but now . . .

Ugh.

"Morning," I mutter back. I head straight for the coffeepot, filling my travel mug to the brim. "What time did you guys get home last night?" I ask, heading toward the fridge for the creamer. With Avery out of school for the week, I'm not too concerned about bedtimes, but I'd still like to have an idea what kind of mood I'll be dealing with when she finally wakes up.

"Close to midnight." He backs up against the counter, allowing me room to navigate.

"Good game?"

"Nah. Not really. A couple of Miami's starters were on the DL, so it wasn't much of a matchup. We had fun, though. Stopped for banana splits on the way home."

"That's nice." I give my coffee a quick stir before I twist the lid into place. "I'm sure Avery had fun."

"Yeah, we both did. It was a good time."

My heart wrenches a little. It's been a long time since Avery and I had fun together.

"So, you're headed down to your meeting?"

"Yep." I grab an English muffin from the pantry and drop it into the toaster.

"How's that going?"

"Fine." There's no point in telling him the truth, not when I've already worked out a game plan to make things better, and it involves being an adept liar. Practice makes perfect, right?

"Nobody's asking any questions about why you're there?"

"Not specifically, but the entire class is about open communication, so stuff comes up sometimes."

"Like what kind of stuff?" The sudden rise in his voice grates against my nerves. I grab the peanut butter from the cupboard, a scowl tugging on my lips. "You're not saying anything, are you? Because even something that seems benign could be potentially damaging."

I turn and level him with a hard look. "No, Dan. I'm not saying anything potentially damaging."

"I'm not suggesting you're doing it intentionally," he says, raising his hands defensively. "I just know how you women can get when you're talking. Sometimes you get carried away, and things come out—"

"*You* women?"

He sighs. "Sorry. That came out wrong. It's just that I've seen you and the second wives in action before. In two hours, you hear more hospital gossip than I hear in a year—"

"Yeah, hospital gossip. Nothing *potentially damaging*." I snatch my muffin out of the toaster, dropping it onto a paper towel before it burns me. "I don't have many of those kinds of conversations with the second wives."

"You don't?"

Growing more irritated, I slather a glob of peanut butter onto the muffin. "No. I mean, sometimes we get into parenting stuff or really general conversations about relationships, but we never get into anything super deep."

The statement comes out with firm confidence, though I'm not entirely sure it's true.

We talk about deep things sometimes, don't we?

"Well, whatever. Just be careful, okay?" he continues. "You know how much is riding on this."

"Yeah, I'm *very* aware," I assure him while taking a bite of the muffin.

Fatherly warning delivered, he blows out a heavy sigh, then says, "Are you really going to need all of those?" He's looking at the collection of serving bowls and platters I have stacked in the corner for Thursday's upcoming feast. "You said it was just us and your mom and your sister."

"It isshh just ush," I answer over another bite. The peanut butter is sticking to the roof of my mouth, making it difficult to talk. I take a drink of coffee to wash it down. "But just because the guest count is smaller doesn't mean the menu changes. I still have to make all the same things."

Normally, Dan's parents fly in from Scottsdale to spend the holiday with us, but this year Dan surprised them with a six-months-early anniversary cruise through the Panama Canal. (Apparently fifty-three years is a bigger milestone than fifty, when we gave them a gift card to their favorite restaurant.) Of course, they didn't question the strange timing—even wealthy people like free trips—and I didn't have to. It's hard enough to manage Dan's lie in our regular life, but adding his parents into the mix would be next to impossible.

He grabs a bottle of water from the fridge and starts heading toward the stairs. "Well, don't go overboard," he says over his shoulder. "You know I've got plans for dinner Thursday night, so I'm not going to be eating a whole lot here."

Once again, I'm wise enough to know what his dinner plans are—or, rather, who they're with—without asking, but that doesn't take the sting out of hearing about them. Last I heard, Thanksgiving was about spending time with your family—*with your child!*—but apparently that's not the case when Dan's involved.

"Yeah, I know," I grumble as I shove the rest of the muffin into my mouth.

I know . . .

~

"Girl, you are seriously jacked if you only like hanging out with your girlfriend when you're stoned," Lina scoffs at Maya, who was stupid enough to share her *honest* response with the class.

I stare down at my 100 percent, grade-A bullshit response and grin:

WHAT IS YOUR FAVORITE THING TO DO?

Go to the movies by myself, especially horror movies. I love all the blood and gore. Decapitations are the best! No one in my family likes them, so I treat myself whenever I can.

Not only do I cringe at the first sight of blood and guts, but I haven't been to a movie by myself in at least fifteen years.

"I didn't say it was *only* when I was high." Maya pauses from her incessant nail-biting long enough to counter the accusation.

"*What?*" Lina bolts upright in her chair, palms raised, black-lined eyes bulging. "You just said that. Didn't she just say that?" She turns to the women on either side of her, looking for confirmation.

"You did," Angel confirms over a drawn-out nod.

"Yeah, honey, you did," Donna agrees.

"Ya did," Burty reluctantly confirms.

Maya sighs. "Okay, well, maybe I said that, but I didn't really mean it. I like my girlfriend when I'm not high; it's just . . ." She raises her hand back up to her mouth and starts working on her thumbnail again. "I don't know. She's kind of boring when I'm sober."

"Then what the hell are you doing with her?" Lina questions. "Why are you hanging out with someone you don't actually like?"

And *this* is why I will never answer another journal entry honestly. Because a truthful response like Maya's—"My favorite thing to do is play *Mario Kart* with my girlfriend"—will quickly evolve into an interrogation about her personal life, and I'm not about to dive into anything remotely personal with any of these women ever again.

As soon as class is dismissed, I head down to the lobby to seek out Chavez so I can deliver my apology. I assumed he'd be in the lobby stalking me as usual first thing this morning, but he wasn't here. And he's not now. I guess my outburst on Friday left an impression on him too.

I punch my attendance card at the front desk, hoping that Officer Moore will be here to offer me some directions, but instead am greeted by a familiar and unwelcoming face: Officer Bates.

Crap.

She moves faster than I would've thought she could . . .

"What do you want, Holliday? Class is over for the day."

"Yes, I know. I was just . . . well, I was hoping you could point me in the direction of Detective Chavez?"

"What do you want to see Chavez for?"

Not only does her response come out with a defensive tone, but it's registering about a thousand decibels louder than I'd like. I drop my head, lean in a bit closer, and reposition myself so my back is facing the time clock, where my classmates are currently punching their cards just a few feet away.

"It's a personal matter," I answer, my voice strained and intentionally low.

"A *personal* matter?" She cocks her head. "With Detective Chavez?"

I nod quickly.

Yes, a freaking personal matter!

She stares at me for a long beat before she blows out a sigh and says, "Hang on."

With a slug's urgency, she pushes out of her chair and slowly disappears into the open doorway behind her.

"Everything okay, Jane?" Burty presses a hand against my shoulder, demanding my attention.

Shit.

I inhale a quick breath through my nose, then turn to face her. And Iris. Iris is staring at me too.

Double shit.

"What do ya need to see that detective for?" Burty asks. "You didn't get into any more trouble, did ya?" The concern on her face is so genuine I can't help but smile a little.

I shake my head. "No. I'm not in trouble; I just, um . . ." I swallow hard. "I just have to talk to him about something. It's . . ." I toss a flippant hand in the air. "It's not a big deal."

Iris's eyes narrow in that knowing way of hers—just like they did during class when I professed my love for creepy dolls with big, blinking eyes—but thankfully she doesn't say anything.

"Oh good. I'm glad it's nothin' to fret over," Burty says over a relieved breath. "We're gonna get some pie at the diner around the corner, if you wanna come? You could meet us when you're done."

Sweet as her invitation is, I have no interest in spending any time in a seedy diner with two women I barely know.

"Sorry, I can't. I need to get home. I've got a lot to get ready, with Thanksgiving and everything."

"Oh, right." Burty forces a smile over her now-pouting lower lip.

She looks like Avery.

"Maybe next time?" Iris suggests, undoubtedly aware that my response is going to be a lie. Which it is.

"Yeah," I say. "Maybe next time."

"I hope you have a real nice Thanksgiving, Jane." Burty suddenly throws her arms around me and gives me a hug. A really tight hug that forces my ribs to compress against my lungs.

I sputter over the sudden loss of breath and say, "You too, Burty."

I give her a reciprocating pat on the back that I hope signifies the end of our spontaneous lovefest, but instead it prompts her to squeeze even tighter, so now our torsos are completely smashed together and her soft blonde curls are pressing into my face. The sweet tang of her strawberry-scented shampoo floods my nose.

"I'm so glad to know ya," she goes on.

I glance up at Iris, who's wearing a smirk despite my obvious distress, and again say, "You too, Burty. You too."

They disappear through security and out the front door. My other classmates do the same, thankfully the rest of them oblivious to or unconcerned with my presence.

Officer Bates finally returns, looking more perturbed by my presence than she did a few minutes ago. "He says you can go back," she grumbles. "But don't think this is special treatment, Holliday," she's quick to add. "He's got lots of women that come through here wanting to talk to him. He's not doing *you* any special favors."

Again, I'm not clear why Bates feels the need to single me out, but I'm not about to inquire. I simply accept her instruction with a "Thanks for your help" and get on my way.

Chavez's office is located in an entirely different building—a three-minute walk from this main building—and requires a special visitor's badge and passing through two more security checks to get into. I had no idea stalking me required so much effort.

I'm buzzed inside by a uniformed officer who looks about sixteen years old, then am told I can find Chavez down the hall behind the second door. My heart beats unnervingly hard as I head down the long linoleum-covered hallway, silently reciting my apology along the way:

I'm sorry I snapped at you.

I was having a particularly stressful day and lost my cool.
I am so grateful for the opportunity to be in this class.
Please forgive me . . .
. . . and please don't destroy my life.
I pause just outside the door.
You can do this, Jane.
You can do anything you set your mind to.
I give my rubber band a few plucks for good measure, give my hair a little fluff, and then step inside.

The room is relatively small and split into four workspaces that are divided by four-foot walls, a narrow walkway running down the middle of them. Like cubicles but without an ounce of privacy. The space on my immediate left sits vacant—just an empty desk and chair filling its ten square feet—while the one on my right is occupied by a woman who's got a phone pressed to her ear and is talking loudly. I have no idea what language she's speaking, but it sounds like she's trying to clear a hairball from her throat. She's too engrossed in her call to even notice I'm here.

There's no one in the cubicle behind her, though based on the cluttered desk and cup of coffee steaming next to the computer, its occupant has just stepped away for a minute. And then, in the back-left corner, sits Chavez.

He's also on the phone but, unlike his colleague, is very aware of my presence.

My breath catches nervously as he locks eyes with me and waves me over, that amused grin, as always, tugging on the corners of his lips.

You can do this, Jane.
He can make fun of you all he wants, so long as he doesn't blow up your life!

"Yeah, I know," he says into the phone while motioning for me to sit in the guest chair on the opposite side of the desk from him. "Yeah, it's definitely a long shot, but it's worth looking into. She was his last known contact, so—yeah. Yeah. Right, I know . . ."

While Chavez finishes up his call, I hug my bag against my chest and cautiously eye my surroundings. On the desktop in front of me sits an orange Hooters coffee mug that's loaded down with pens and pencils, a stack of hot-pink Post-its beside that. There's an open file spread out in front of him, a stack of handwritten notes piled up on top of it. His writing is very neat—all capitals.

On the credenza behind him are stacks of file folders and notebooks, a thirsty-looking plant, and three framed photos. One is of Chavez standing on top of a rock, a stunning mountainous view behind him; the other is of a darling little boy with enormous brown eyes and dimples deep enough to get lost in—the mini version of Chavez—and the last picture is . . . oh my. There's a grinning, glassy-eyed Chavez and another guy (looking equally drunk), each weighed down by countless layers of Mardi Gras beads, beers raised as if toasting the photographer. And in the background are several very voluptuous, scantily clad women who look more than a little eager for their opportunity to earn some of the beads the guys are wearing. It seems Officer Sexy Pants enjoys himself a party.

"All right, well, call me if you find anything. Yeah, okay. Okay. Thanks."

Chavez drops the phone into the cradle with a heavy sigh, then turns to me. My chest tightens, and my gaze immediately zeroes in on those dimples. Those forever-deep dimples that are just begging to explode into laughter over what a complete fool he thinks I am.

I shift in the seat.

Do it, Jane.

Just get it over with.

Just say what you have to say and get the hell out of here.

His lips start to part like he's going to say something—

Do it, Jane!

Do it before he starts talking and you lose your nerve—

"I'm so sorry for the way I acted on Friday. I was stressed and upset and I just lost my cool and I'm so sorry—" The words are erupting out of my mouth like vomit, fast and furious, without a pause between them. "Please don't kick me out of the class. I'll do anything. I'm so sorry but please—"

"*What?* No, Jane—"

"I can't have a record," I go on, too consumed by my own desperation to hear what he was trying to say. I plant my palms on the edge of the desk and lean forward, bracing myself against the barrage of pleas. "It'll destroy my whole life. You have to understand that I was just stressed, that's all it was—"

"Jane—"

"And I took it out on you. And I swear, I didn't mean to," I carry on, shaking my head emphatically. "I just—I lost my mind for a minute, but I swear it won't happen again. Please don't kick me out of the class. I need this class—"

"*Jane.*" He leans across the desk and firmly presses his palms against the tops of my hands. I'm not sure if it's the heat of his touch or the fact that his hands are perfectly controlled while mine are trembling, but one of the two instantly steals my words, leaving only winded breaths coming from my mouth. He locks his eyes onto mine and in a firm voice says, "I'm not going to kick you out of the class. And I'm not mad about what happened on Friday."

Heart hammering against my sternum, I blink hard. "Wh—huh?"

He shakes his head, an earnest expression settling in his eyes despite the smirk still sprouting across his cheeks. "I'm not mad about Friday," he repeats. "If anything, I'm the one who owes you an apology."

My jaw sags. "What? *Why?* What do you have to apologize for?"

"For making you feel uncomfortable, like I was mocking you somehow . . ."

His eyes fall from mine for a quick beat before he slowly pulls his hands away and settles back into his seat. "I never meant to make you feel that way. I just wanted to see how you were doing, that's all."

Nothing in his tone or demeanor suggests he's lying, but . . .

"Then why do you always look like . . . that?" I motion to his face.

"Ah hell," he sighs, then drops his head and gives it a little shake. "This stupid mouth has gotten me into more trouble . . ." My gaze instinctively shifts back to the image of him and his buddy partying it up in New Orleans. I'd venture to say his stupid mouth has served him pretty well . . .

"This," he says, reclaiming my attention as he taps his dimpled cheek with his finger, "has nothing to do with what I think about you. I mean—it does. I'm always happy to see you; it's just that this smirk is sort of my default expression."

I've heard of resting bitch face—even seen it in action with my Zoloft-, er, ecstasy-hoarding pal, Heather—but resting *smirk* face?

"I know it sounds like bullshit," he continues, clearly tuned into my doubt. "But it's true. I used to get into trouble all the time as a kid because my mom thought I was laughing at her when she was trying to be serious punishing me or whatever. And my teachers—*man*. They used to get so mad at me. Do you remember our sophomore year when someone pulled the fire alarm during that antidrug assembly, and the sprinklers came on in the gym and got the entire school soaked?"

I shrug; my high school memories—especially those from my brief stint at South Glenn High—are a bit muddy. As much as I would have liked to have been enjoying the teenage antics that other kids were enjoying, I was too busy trying to keep my world from spinning off its axis: a difficult task when your mom insists on shaking it like a snow globe whenever things start to feel the slightest bit settled.

"Well, I took the hit for that," he goes on. "The principal figured out that it was someone on the soccer team, but because I couldn't keep a straight face when she questioned me, she figured I had to have been the one to do it, even though I told her I didn't."

"It wasn't you?"

He scoffs. "No. It was Brian Metcalfe. That dick. I got suspended for a day and missed two games."

I sigh, unexpectedly relieved and beyond grateful to learn this information. "Okay, well . . . wow. That's actually really good to hear. I've been worried this whole time—since that night in Morris Creek—that you've been thinking I was a raging lunatic or something."

"Well . . ."

His smirk deepens into something different from what I've seen before. Something playful and . . . charming?

"So, you *do* think I'm a raging lunatic?"

He chuckles. "No, but it was pretty funny. Not how messed up you were," he quickly clarifies. "That wasn't cool. Mistaking ecstasy for Zoloft is definitely *not* funny, but attacking a woman with oranges because she didn't put her cart away . . ." He shakes his head, now very clearly amused. "Well, I've been a cop for almost twenty years, and that's the first time I've ever heard of that."

I drop my head, cheeks flushing with deserved embarrassment. "Yeah, well, that definitely wasn't my best moment."

"Nah, it's okay. I mean, given everything you're going through, a little breakdown seems pretty justified."

My brows cinch, and I raise my head. "Everything I'm going through?"

"Well, yeah. With your husband," he says, voice lowering a bit. "I'm sure it's not easy with him being . . . you know . . ."

My chest tightens beneath his leading statement.

"Him being . . . ?"

His eyes narrow. "Gay."

I gasp, quickly covering my mouth with my hands.

He knows?

How does he know?!

Who told him?

Terror electrifies through my bones. I quickly turn over my shoulder to see who else is in the room with us.

Someone must be watching me.

Reporting me.

Is it her?

Is it the hairball hacker?

"You told me right after I put you in handcuffs."

Another gasp as I fling my attention back to him. *"I did?"*

He nods.

"I told you that? I—I did?" I pat my chest, hard. "I told you that?"

"I guess you don't remember, huh?"

A petrified wail rises in my chest, suddenly making it hard to breathe. I shake my head, chin quivering nervously.

"Oh. Well, you know what, I'm sure it was just the drugs talking. People say all kinds of crazy stuff when they're strung out. Forget I said anything."

My own fuzzy memories from that night assure me that what he's saying is true—people *definitely* say (and do!) crazy stuff when they're strung out—but with regard to this . . .

With regard to Dan . . .

Shit.

That's definitely not the case.

I know it, and Chavez does too.

I drop my head, suddenly terrified by the decision in front of me.

He's just provided me the perfect "out." Freedom from the blanket of fear I've been hiding under for the last ten days, served up on a silver platter, with a shiny gold ribbon slapped on top. It's the best gift I've ever been given. Yet for some inexplicable reason, I'm not sure I can accept it.

I don't think I can lie to Chavez.

Or maybe I don't want to. I'm already drowning in so many lies that the idea of telling someone the truth—grabbing a lifeline—sounds so liberating and . . .

Shit.

So dangerous.

My throat swells with a deep-seated ache as I slowly raise my head to look at him. His smirk is softer now, more sympathetic than amused. Tears prick the backs of my eyes, but I don't say anything. I can't.

He gives me an understanding nod, then reaches for the box of Kleenex on the corner of his desk.

"I'm not going to say anything, if that's what you're worried about," he assures me as I tug a tissue from the box. I quickly dab at my eyes. "What happens between you and him—whatever brought you to that parking lot that night—that's your business. I was just there to get the orange-throwing lunatic off the streets."

Despite my mood, I laugh. "Yeah. You don't want her running loose around the city."

"No way. We have to protect our citizens, and our citrus supply."

I press the tissue across my sniffly nose and then inhale a shuddery, yet surprisingly deep, breath.

"Maybe it would help to talk to someone," he offers. "A therapist or—"

I'm shaking my head before he can even finish the thought. "That's not an option."

"Oh. Okay . . . then, I guess it's a good thing you're in the class with Bates. She's pretty good at helping people work through stuff."

I snort. "That'll never happen. She hates me, and that whole class is just . . ." I blow out a heavy sigh and collapse against the seat, shaking my head. "That's why I was so upset on Friday. The discussion got a little heated and stressful, and . . . *shit*." I offer him a pleading look. "I am *really* sorry for treating you like that. I'm normally a very calm, kind person. I guess I'm just not managing my stress very well these days."

He shrugs off my apology. "I totally get it. Some days it feels like my middle name is *stress*." He motions to the files on his desk and the ones behind him, as if to suggest that everything surrounding him is stressful. Given his profession, I have no doubt that's true. "You just need to figure out a way to get rid of that stress without the use of oranges, or rubber bands."

My eyes snap wide, and I instantly reach for my wrist. "What? How did you know that?"

"I'm a detective, remember? It's my job to solve mysteries."

I level him with a tired look that prompts his grin to soften again, though this time it doesn't appear to be motivated by sympathy but rather sincerity. Already I'm learning how to differentiate.

"I felt the welts when I was putting the cuffs on," he says. "At first, I didn't think much of it, but once I got you to the station and got a good look at them, well . . . I thought maybe you had . . . that you tried . . ." His dark brows furrow, and he slowly averts his eyes away from me. Like he doesn't want to say what he's thinking.

That I had what?

What would I have tried to—

Oh god.

My heart twists. I shake my head. "No. God, no. I would never do that. I have a daughter. I would never leave her—"

"No, no, I know." He returns his attention to me, hands raised in a calming gesture. "I figured that out once I saw the rubber band. It was pushed up high on your forearm, so I didn't see it at first. But I know now it's just one of those techniques people use to ward off stress and panic attacks. I looked it up online when I got home that night."

"You looked it up when you got home?"

"Yeah. I wanted to make sure you were okay."

His response is so easy—so automatic—I can't help but feel a little flattered. And then I catch another glimpse of that Mardi Gras picture. *Relax, Jane.* Good-time guys are always masters of flattery.

"Hey, Chavez, Chief wants to meet with—oh! Sorry. Didn't realize you had company." I follow Chavez's gaze over my shoulder to the doorway, where an older bald man is leaning into the room. He smiles. "Excuse me, ma'am."

I smile at him.

"What's up?" Chavez asks him.

"Chief wants to meet with us about the Belleview case—says he's got a lead on a next of kin."

"Great. I'll be right there." Chavez returns his attention to me. "Sorry about that. Duty always calls at the worst time."

"No, it's fine. I need to get going anyway." Suddenly feeling self-conscious, I quickly stand and secure my purse over my shoulder. Chavez stands up too. "Thanks for talking with me," I say. "It helped a lot."

"Yeah, of course. Any time."

My inclination is to offer him a parting handshake, but that feels a little too formal, considering what's just transpired. I give him a smile instead, then turn and head for the door—

"Hey, Jane," he calls after me.

I turn back.

"If you're ever interested, there's this place I go when I'm really stressed that I think you might like. No pressure," he quickly adds, a soft blush now accentuating his smirk, "but I'd be glad to meet you there sometime. It might help."

Under different circumstances, I might feel like a tenth grader who's just been asked to the dance by the school's most charismatic ladies' man, but I know better. The little flutter in my chest has nothing to do with hormones or hopeful expectations, but rather how uneasy I'm feeling. While spilling the proverbial gay-beans offered me a twinge of relief, more than anything it's leaving me feeling incredibly exposed and even a little . . . reckless. Like I'm about to rip off a Band-Aid I can't put back on.

"It was just a thought." He jumps back in, astutely reading my hesitation. "It's not a big deal. I'm sure you'll find something else that helps—"

"No, wait," I cut him off with a shake of the head while quickly reorganizing my thoughts. Chavez knows the truth, and he's not going to say anything. He's assured me of that, and I trust him. If he says he has something that might help me, then I should at least consider it; otherwise I'll probably end up on suicide watch, with the way I've been snapping my wrist lately. "I think maybe I'd like to try something different."

"Yeah?" He actually smiles this time. Not a smirk, but a full smile, so I can see his teeth. They're very straight and very white. "Okay, great. Here, let me give you my number."

He grabs a pen from the Hooters mug, scribbles his number down on a Post-it, and offers it with his left hand. Given his desk accessories, I'm not surprised to see there's no wedding band. "Call me anytime," he says.

"Okay. Thanks."

I tuck the note in my purse but don't bother to look at it until I get to the car. And when I do, I can't help but flash a big, toothy grin myself. There, below his home *and* cell phone numbers, he's written the name *Officer Poncherello*.

Very funny.

CHAPTER 12

It's three thirty in the afternoon. The dining table is centerfold-worthy, decked out in crystal stemware and our rarely seen wedding china. Soft candlelight pours from the autumn-themed centerpiece onto the wooden tabletop beneath it. The air is thick with the smells of Thanksgiving: oven-roasted turkey, baked apples and brown sugar, overly buttered potatoes. A relaxing fire crackles in the adjoining living room, and I've just poured a glass of pinot—pleasantly dry, with just the right amount of spice. By all appearances, Norman Rockwell could have painted this scene. It is truly a day to give thanks.

Unfortunately, the atmosphere isn't fitting the mood.

The turkey took about two hours longer to cook than anticipated (it always does!), so Dan's grumbling about, annoyed by the delayed schedule. He's got places to go and men to do—er, see—after all.

Avery's mad because I won't let her spend the night at my sister's, a post–turkey dinner tradition they've maintained for the last six years. (If she'd just confessed that she'd gotten detention last week instead of trying to hide the slip in the bottom of her backpack, it wouldn't be an issue!) And Julie's tap-dancing around directly asking me for money, even though it's obvious she needs to. Her rent is due in six days, and she can't cover it.

The only one not causing any trouble is my mom, and that's because she's not here. My chest crimps sadly. Apparently, she refused to get into the car with a "perfect stranger" (Julie) to be carted off to "Lord knows where" (my house) to eat dinner with a bunch of other "strangers" (me, Dan, and Avery), so she stayed at the nursing home. I'll visit later this weekend, assuming she's agreeable to strangers by then.

I'm not sure there's an actual description for my mood. I'm landing somewhere between annoyed, disappointed, frustrated, and restless. Like I've got an itch I can't seem to scratch.

I press the wineglass up to my lips and take a long drink.

Thanksgiving should *not* feel like this.

"Come on, Danny boy, there's gotta be someone you can set me up with. I'll even take a proctologist, so long as he's cute."

It's not the first time Julie's tried baiting Dan for a hookup with one of his colleagues. I guess this means last week's firefighter didn't pan out.

"No," he grumbles over a forkful of stuffing. "Nobody at the hospital is available."

"What's a proctologist?" Avery questions. "That's what my friend Jasmine's dad does."

"A butt doctor," Julie answers, smirking.

"Ew, gross!"

"It's an essential medical position," Dan chastises them. "Though far from a surgeon."

I roll my eyes and take another drink.

"You're seriously telling me there are no single men in the entire hospital?" Julie asks.

"Nope." Dan shakes his head, holding firm.

Julie casts me a wry grin. I shrug and stab a piece of turkey with my fork.

"Well, what about one of the guys you play basketball with?" Julie hammers on, pausing to load her fork with sweet potatoes. "One of them has to be single."

"Sorry," he grumbles.

"They wouldn't be interested in you anyway," I mutter under my breath.

"Jane—"

At least I *thought* that was under my breath.

From the head of the table to my left, Dan blasts me with a stern look that sends a shudder up my spine.

Whoops.

"Why wouldn't they be interested in me?" Julie asks, confirming that I was a *lot* louder than I realized. Thankfully, she doesn't pick up on Dan's reaction.

I quickly shake my head. "Oh—um. Well, I didn't mean *you* specifically; it's just that all those guys are in committed relationships, right, Dan?"

His gaze is lasered in on me, lines of restraint splintering across his forehead like cracks on a windshield. Clearly my lies aren't up to par today. I reach for my glass and take another long drink, washing down the lump that's quickly building in my throat.

"Yeah, that's right," he finally replies, thankfully rerouting his attention to Julie. "None of them are in the market either."

She sighs dramatically. "Fine. I guess I'll just get some cats and start watching *Wheel of Fortune.*"

"Oh, stop it," I grouse.

"Oh, yes! Auntie, please get a cat!" pet-starved Avery jumps in. "Please, please, please."

"Aw, honey. I would if I could, but they're not allowed at my apartment."

"You know, if you're that desperate, I'm pretty sure the guy who pumps my gas is single," Dan offers over a sardonic grin and a mouthful of potatoes. "He said something about needing a good woman to clean the grease out of his jeans. Of course, that means you'll have to up your laundering game."

He says this knowing full well that our dryer is currently tumbling a load of Julie's laundry. The second of the day.

"Very funny." She scowls back at him.

I take another drink.

Christmas is going to be freaking fantastic!

"All right, time for me to get going."

Twenty minutes into the meal it took me fourteen days to plan and prepare, Dan pushes himself away from the table, laying his napkin next to his still relatively full plate. So much for stuffing yourself on Thanksgiving.

"Where are you going?" Avery asks.

I turn to Dan, a smug expression on my face.

Yes, Dan. Please tell your daughter where you're going . . .

"Work. I've got patients I need to check on," he says easily. So easily it makes my skin bristle.

"But it's Thanksgiving," Avery counters. "Can't you skip and stay home? The Bulls are playing later. I wanted to watch the game with you."

"Sorry, kiddo. I can't."

Her shoulders sag, and she fires me a nasty look.

Me!

She fires *me* a nasty look.

What did I do?

"How about you record the game, and we'll watch it together this weekend?" he goes on, sliding his empty chair into place under the table. "We can make banana splits."

She shrugs. "Yeah, okay."

"Tell you what—why don't you go out and start the car for me," he adds, falling victim to her warranted disappointment.

Her eyes brighten. "Really?"

"And if you promise to be really careful, I'll even let you back it out of the driveway."

"Oh my gosh! Yes, yes, yes! I'll get my shoes!"

She springs from the table and thunders upstairs to her bedroom, all her grievances instantly forgotten.

Once again, Dan is the hero.

Oh, happy day.

"Well, I guess somebody knows the key to Avery's heart," Julie says.

Dan smirks with pride while I take another drink.

Asshole.

"Okay, don't wait up," he says to me. "It'll probably be a late one."

"I figured," I say through a forced smile.

He gives Julie a cursory "Good to see you" with a sterile, one-armed hug, then saunters around the table and offers me something very similar. No emotion. No sentiment. No lung-crushing exuberance that steals my breath and fills my lungs with the sweet smell of drugstore shampoo. Just an obligatory physical act meant to convince our audience that we're still a happily married couple.

"So, what's the deal with these meetings in the city?" Julie asks as soon as Dan and Avery have left the house.

My eyes grow wide, and I swallow a surprised gasp.

How does she know?

"Meetings?"

"Avery said you're going to some meeting in Chicago. She said Dan's been driving her to school."

"Oh, right. Yeah. It's just a couple times a week. They're no big deal. I'm just meeting with some of the . . . um . . . the fundraising ladies from the hospital." It's the first time I've had to lie straight to Julie's face, and it's proving to be a bit difficult. I quickly stand and start gathering dishes. "Remember I told you about that big event in February? The Listen to Your Heart Gala . . ."

"Vaguely," she mutters, following me into the kitchen with the basket of rolls and two dirty water glasses.

"The hospital's holding this huge event because they're running on a deficit and will have to cut all their specialty departments unless they can secure enough money to keep them going. Since the cardiology group is the most prominent, they think that's key to getting the funding, but if they don't, they'll be getting rid of almost everybody. It'll just be a regular old community hospital, and everyone will have to drive into Chicago to see a specialist."

"Oh shit," she says over a grimace.

Yeah. Oh shit, indeed!

"There's an older couple—the Hoffstras, the people we went to dinner with a couple of weeks ago—who *seem* like they're on board to make a big contribution, but apparently there are a couple of other hospitals in similar situations they're talking with, so right now there's no guarantee that they're going to give any money to Mount Ivy."

"Damn, that's scary, Janie."

I nod. Don't I know it.

"So, why are you meeting all the way down in Chicago?" she asks.

Great question, Julie.

Why the hell are we meeting all the way down in Chicago?

Scouring my brain for a plausible response, I quickly make my way back into the dining room, Julie following close behind.

"We're, um . . . we're working with a consultant who has an office down there," I offer with a hearty nod, hoping the movement will add credence to my story. "She's got a ton of experience and knows a lot of the donors we're hitting up, so . . ."

"Oh, thank god." She blows out a relieved breath. "Here I was worried something bad was going on."

"Something bad?"

"Yeah, I thought maybe you were seeing a divorce attorney or something."

Divorce?!

A surprised and terrified gasp ripples through my body, prompting the gravy boat I just picked up to bobble in my hand. A puddle of gravy splashes over the lip and onto my fingers.

"Wh-why would you think I'd be seeing a divorce attorney?"

She shrugs. "Well, I didn't really. But Avery said that Dan is hardly around anymore and that you seem sad all the time, so I just thought maybe something was going on with you two."

My heart twists with the very sadness Avery has apparently tuned into.

I had no idea she picked up on any of my moods.

Or that sadness was even one of them.

Is it?

"You guys are okay, right?" Julie asks, concern furrowing her brow. "There's no trouble in paradise, is there?"

I shift uncomfortably, my turtleneck suddenly feeling about two sizes smaller than it did a second ago. "No. We're fine. It's just . . . you know how his schedule is." I toss a flippant hand through the air for added effect, sending a glob of gravy flying across the table. *Whoops!* I feel my cheeks flush with heat, but I carry on like nothing happened. "There's just always something going on. But, yeah, we're just fine. No trouble in paradise."

She glances down at the puddle of gravy on the table. "Good. Glad to hear it."

I grab the mashed potatoes and quickly head back into the kitchen. "So, things didn't work out with the firefighter, huh?"

My sister's always-sordid love life is about the last thing on my mind right now, but that conversation was way too close for comfort. Dan was right: I'm totally off my lying game today! Thankfully, Julie doesn't seem any the wiser for the sudden swing in conversation.

"Nah," she groans, following behind me with the untouched apple pie in her hands. "He was really cute, but he was kind of a dick."

"Really? How so?" I grab a dish towel and wipe the rest of the gravy from my hand.

"He's super self-centered," she explains while grabbing a fork from one of the plates and digging into the pie. I'm too full to even consider joining her, but it looks really good. And by the way she's lapping the metal tines, it must taste that way too. "We went out for dinner, and I swear all he talked about was his job. I mean, I'm all for saving people from fires," she assures me while diving in for another forkful, "but he didn't ask one thing about me the entire time. It was just three hours of him blabbering on about all the training he does, how he's being promoted to lieutenant, blah, blah, blah. It was one of the worst dates of my life."

Three hours with a man who's obsessed with his career and doesn't give a damn about you or what you want? A fresh swell of annoyance rises in my chest. Try eighteen years . . .

Avery bounds back into the house out of breath, her cheeks as pink as the cranberries on the table.

"How'd it go, Lightning McQueen?" Julie asks.

"It was so fun," she huffs over a sated grin. "He let me drive all the way to the end of the street!"

"Wow. So cool," Julie replies. "That's a long way!"

It's actually *not* a long way—two hundred yards at best—but in her mind it must've felt like a mile.

"Were you nervous?" I ask.

She turns to me, and right on cue her smile starts to fade. "No. I was with Dad."

To my ears, her tone is as acidic as it always is, but my heart hears something very different. It hears the sound of a little girl who is well aware that things in her world aren't quite as peachy as her parents would like people—*her*—to believe they are.

"Still, you had to have been a little freaked out, pressing the pedals all by yourself, right?" Julie jumps in, restoring a bit of Avery's enthusiasm.

"Yeah, that was kinda scary. I had to scoot the seat all the way up just so I could reach them."

"Could you even see over the steering wheel?" Julie asks.

Avery shakes her head. "Not really. Dad had to keep one hand on the wheel so I wouldn't crash into anything."

She starts to laugh. One of those deep, guttural laughs that only a child can make when they're absolutely overcome with joy. My mouth pulls up into the contented smile I've been waiting for all day—*finally, something to be thankful for!*—but the celebration is short lived as the truth of where that laugh is originating settles in on me. Avery is only happy because she's sharing this moment with Julie. It has nothing to do with me, as much as I'd like it to.

I swallow against the ache building in my throat and say, "I've been thinking, and I guess it's okay if you stay over at Auntie's tonight."

"Really?" Avery's eyes grow wide.

"Yes. But you have to promise never to hide a detention slip from me again, got it—"

Ooof!

Before I can even get the words out, Avery is hugging me. I wrap my arms tight around her and press a kiss on the top of her head. The women in class would probably tell me she's hugging me for the wrong reasons—that she's grateful only because I'm giving her what she wants, even though she doesn't deserve it—but I don't care. I needed this hug. And Avery needs a happy Thanksgiving.

"Thanks, Mom. I won't lie about detention again, I swear."

"You better not."

"Well, hurry up and get your stuff, dude," Julie instructs excitedly. "We've got movies to watch!"

"Okay, okay!" Avery releases me and takes off to go pack her things.

"Why the change of heart?" Julie asks.

I offer up a shrug that I hope looks effortless. "It's Thanksgiving. If you can't stay up all night watching Harry Potter with your favorite person, when can you?"

There's a waver in my voice that prompts me to drop my head and start wrestling with the dish towel in my hands.

"Hey, you okay?"

She's suddenly at my side, hand pressing gently against my shoulder.

I nod.

"You sure?"

My already-aching throat starts to swell beneath the concern weighing down her questions. I can't remember the last time Julie was worried about me. It's always the other way around. Always.

"'Cause you know you can talk to me about anything," she goes on.

A twinge of temptation flickers in my chest—a momentary urge to unload my burden on her—but it disappears faster than a whisper in the wind.

As much as I resent it, Julie, and more importantly, Mom, both depend on me and the stability that my life—my marriage—provides them, almost as much as Avery does. I'm not about to ruin her Thanksgiving by informing her that it's on very shaky ground.

I slowly raise my head to look at her. The worry filling her green eyes confirms my decision. *She can't know the truth.*

I clear my throat and muster up the best big-sister smile I can and say, "Nothing's wrong; I'm just emotional. Too much of this," I joke, tapping the wine bottle that's sitting on the counter beside me. "I'm so grateful to have you around, Jules. And that kid up there adores you . . ." I knuckle back the tear welling in my eye while motioning toward the stairs.

Her worry gives way to a relieved smile. "Yeah, well, the feeling's pretty mutual."

I smile again, a genuine one this time.

"You know, you could come with us," she offers. "We could have a little slumber party. Do our nails, braid each other's hair, gorge on ice cream . . ."

Delicious as the thought is, I don't hesitate in shaking my head. "Nah. This night is just for you guys."

"You sure? It would be so much fun."

"I know it would," I say. "But, really, it's fine. You guys go and have a good time."

Her shoulders sag beneath her flowing tunic top. "But it's Thanksgiving. I hate the thought of you being here all by yourself."

A twinge of anger pricks at my nerves.

I do too.

But I wouldn't be alone if my husband weren't a lying, cheating asshole.

I swallow against the knot of frustration building in my throat. "Are you kidding? A night alone is exactly what I need after the week I've had."

"Yeah?"

"Yes," I say with authority. "Now get out of here and take my kid with you. Ply her with sugar and sweets, and don't let her go to sleep until dawn."

"Yes, sir." She laughs, while giving me a mock salute. "Any chance I can take this to my house too?" She points to the apple pie, then flirtatiously bats her eyes at me.

"So *that's* how you get all those free drinks."

She grins.

"Yes, you can take the pie. And I'll transfer some money into your account too. Just in case you need it."

Normally, I wait for Julie to ask for money, but . . . it's Thanksgiving.

"Aw, thanks, Janie." She throws her arms around me and gives me a hug. "You're the best, you know that?"

I force a little smile.

Yeah, I'm the best, all right.

Too bad no one else in my family thinks so.

~

I sip my way through another splash of wine while I clear the table and start on the cleanup. The washing machine's busy with all the linens, the china's soaking in the sink—too delicate to run through the dishwasher—and now I'm tackling the leftovers.

A dozen empty plastic containers sit in a line across the countertop. I load the first two with stuffing, seal the lids, then move on to the turkey. Since I'm the only one who eats the dark meat, I load up a small container with that, then fill a bigger container with white meat for Avery and Dan. The potatoes are next. They're Dan's favorite, which is why I always make a double batch.

Freaking Dan.

"You're getting plenty of potatoes tonight, aren't you?" I growl while burying the serving spoon deep inside the bowl. I scoop up a big dollop and then slap it down into the container. "Must be nice to have *two* Thanksgiving dinners . . ."

I reload the spoon, my gaze catching on a familiar image of Dan that's magnetized to the refrigerator. It's the picture of him after he finished running his first marathon last spring. Dripping with sweat, a prideful smile stretching across his chiseled jaw. I remember how proud I was of him that day. How impressed I was that all his training had paid off. Hours and hours of training so he could cross that item off his bucket list. Because it's always been about Dan's lists. Dan's goals. Dan's desires . . .

A jolt of anger suddenly electrifies my bones, prompting me to pull the spoon back and launch it—catapult style—directly at the picture. The potatoes smack against the fridge, covering the left portion of Dan's stupid, selfish face, while bits of potato sail through the air, landing on the quartz countertop and hardwood floor like fluffy white grenades.

Despite my anger, I burst out laughing and load the spoon up again. *Smack!* Another direct hit, this time covering the rest of the picture.

"How does that feel, *Dan?*" I taunt the potato-covered image while reloading the spoon for another attack. "The all-powerful Dr. Osborne likes his potatoes, doesn't he?" *Smack!* Reload. "'Cause it's all about what

Dan wants, isn't it?" *Smack!* Reload. "It's all about Dan." *Smack!* Reload. "Dan, Dan, Dan . . ."

By the time I reach the bottom of the serving dish, the refrigerator is spackled in a thick coat of potatoes, and I'm seriously considering moving on to the green bean casserole when it dawns on me that Julie and Avery could walk in at any moment. It's not likely, but on occasion Avery forgets something and they have to turn around and come back for it. Explaining away a meeting in the city is one thing, but justifying the mess in front of me would be another. As therapeutic as hurling food is (potatoes *or* oranges), I have to find another way to work through my frustrations. Somewhere I'm allowed to make a mess. Somewhere I can't get myself into any trouble.

A nervous flutter rolls through my chest as I glance toward the breakfast nook, where my purse is hanging on the back of the chair.

I probably can't get into trouble if I'm with a cop . . .

I set the empty bowl down on the counter, wipe my hands on the dish towel, and head for my bag, where Chavez's Post-it note is tucked into the interior pocket, right next to my lipstick.

He said I could call anytime, but he didn't mean Thanksgiving, did he? Surely, he's having dinner somewhere. With his family or one of the *many* women who visit him at the station. I'll just text him. Then he can get back in touch with me when he's ready. Which probably won't be until tomorrow or maybe even next week. With the long holiday weekend, there's no telling what people are up to.

I thump out a message that I hope doesn't sound as desperate as I feel:

Hi. It's Jane Holliday. Hope you're having a nice Thanksgiving. If you're still willing, I'd like to take you up on your offer. Let me know when is a good time for you. Thanks.

I set the phone down and start cleaning up my nightmare of a kitchen. Much to my surprise, my phone chimes with a new text before I even pull the sponge from the sink. It's from Chavez:

Are you free tonight?

Foolishly, my heart starts to beat a little faster.
"Calm down, girl," I mutter. That's likely his default text response to all women.

Yes. We just finished dinner.

His reply comes lightning fast.

Great.

Meet me at 1122 Bancroft Drive

I'll meet you at the gate.

Bring a bat if you have one.

My eyes snap wide.
Bring a bat?
Good Lord, what have I gotten myself into?

CHAPTER 13

The address Chavez sent is just a few blocks from the police station in the city. Traffic is light, so I'm able to make the trip in just under an hour. The dashboard clock reads 6:28, but it might as well be midnight for how dark and desolate the streets are. I guess everyone's at home spending time with their families. What a novel concept.

I keep a firm grip on the wheel as I make my way through the neighborhood and finally come upon the address. It's a huge lot—spanning the size of an entire city block—with a tall chain-link fence guarding its perimeter. Strips of black plastic are woven in and out of the links, making it impossible to see what's hiding behind it, but given the barbed coils wound around the fence's lip, it must be important.

I hug the curb until I arrive at a dimly lit driveway, where the chain-link fence turns into a gate. It stands just as tall as the fence and is lined with the same barbed-wire crown, but it isn't shaded with the plastic, so I'm able to see through it. My pulse spikes nervously as I take in the scene in front of me: a nearly empty parking lot lit up by one yellowing overhead lamp and a small shed sitting at the far end of the lot in front of yet another veiled fence, a faint light emitting from its one lonely window.

"What the hell are you doing here?" I mutter, eyes wide with uncertainty. This is the second time in as many weeks I've found myself searching for a man in a dark parking lot. It's like I'm trying to earn my own Lifetime movie.

A light suddenly ignites from inside a pickup truck parked in the lot. A figure hops out, and even though it's dark, I can tell by the broad, stocky silhouette that it's Chavez. A relieved breath settles in my chest. Okay. Everything's okay. He's here . . .

He heads toward the gate, that damn smirk emerging through the darkness like the North Star, as he enters the spray of light pouring out from my headlights.

"Come on in," he calls out as he swings the gate open.

I smile nervously and give a little wave as I pass by.

I park my car next to his, then quickly hop down onto the gravelly lot.

"Any trouble finding me?"

"Nope. It was easy," I say. "Sorry it took so long—it's a bit of a drive for me."

"No worries." He comes to a stop at my car's rear bumper, while I instinctively hug myself against the crisp night air. "Did you bring a bat?"

"I did, but I'm not sure it's the kind you had in mind." I open the back door and pull out Avery's old Wiffle ball bat that I dug out from the storage space above the garage. It's yellow, made of cheap plastic, with a tip that's roughly the size of my thigh, and if memory serves, it makes a sort of whistling sound when you swing it. "Will this work?" I ask, raising the bat up for inspection.

He strides over, his smirk giving way to a chuckle as he takes the bat from my hands. "Uh . . . no. But that's okay. I came prepared."

He tosses my bat back into the car, then heads over to his truck, where he pulls out a backpack and two aluminum bats from the cab. He straps the pack over his shoulders, then hands me one of the bats and says, "Now we're ready for battle."

I laugh nervously, squeezing the cold metal against my palm.

We're going to battle?

We make our way across the lot to the little shed, where an older man, dressed in oil-stained mechanic coveralls, greets us from beneath the cover of his thick, bristly beard.

"What the hell are you doin' here on Thanksgiving, Chavez?" he grunts through the narrow window, proving his facial hair isn't the only bristly thing about him.

Chavez laughs. "How you doin', Jessie? Everything good?"

"Good as it can be," he huffs back.

"Okay if we go a few rounds?" Chavez asks, raising his bat.

The man shifts his attention to me, sizing me up with his narrowed gaze. I swallow hard and tighten my grip on the bat.

"Yeah, all right," he snuffs. "But she's gotta stick close to you. She can't go roamin' all over the place like that last chick you brought in here."

That last chick.

Of course I'm not the only woman he's brought here. Ladies' men like Officer Poncherello are always on the move.

"Understood," Chavez agrees with a nod.

"Head to the back forty," Jessie instructs. "We just got a couple of cruisers in from the South Side that are still in pretty good shape."

"Sounds good. Thanks a lot, man."

Jessie signs off with another grunt, then presses a button on the wall inside his shed that prompts the gate in front of us to unlock and slowly slide open.

My eyes grow wide as I take in the sea of abandoned cars hiding in the shadows in front of us.

"Is this a junkyard?" I ask.

"Sort of. It's where they take vehicles after they've been investigated. Like if they were involved in a fatal accident or a serious crime, the CSI team does their thing with them first, and then they bring them over here before they're eventually shipped off to a salvage yard. We call it Smash Land."

"Smash Land," I mutter absently, my eyes growing wider as the reality of what I'm about to do starts to settle in.

We're going to smash things . . .

"Come on." He gives my jacket a little tug. "We're going this way."

The lot is illuminated by a few overhead lamps, so we're able to safely navigate our way, though with the carpet of glass crunching under our feet, it feels anything but secure. My heart starts to pound a little faster.

We're going to smash things!

"So, you have a good Thanksgiving?" Chavez asks as we round a bashed-in minivan and head toward the back corner of the lot.

"Yeah. It was gre—" I cut off my canned response with a sigh as I'm suddenly reminded that I don't have to lie to Chavez. He's the one person I can actually tell the truth. "No, actually it was pretty horrible. My entire family wanted to be somewhere other than at home with me. How was yours?"

He shrugs. "My dad ate too much and fell asleep in his recliner with his hand down his pants, my mom and aunt tormented my sister about her love life, and my nephew cried because he wasn't allowed to watch the Snoopy special until after dinner. It was pretty magical."

I chuckle, delighted by the enviable visual, and also the fact that he was with his family and not one of his *many* women. Though I'm not sure why I even care . . .

"Well, it sounds perfect," I say, reclaiming my thoughts with a little shake of my head. "I'm sorry I interrupted it."

"I'm not."

I glance up at him. "No?"

He shakes his head, the dimple in his cheek deepening beneath his growing grin. "Not at all. In fact, I was sort of hoping you'd call."

My breath catches with unexpected hopefulness. "You were?"

"Yeah. I've been dying to get back out here and beat something up."

"Oh, right. Of course," I say sheepishly.

Get your head on straight, Jane.

He's here to work out aggressions—and so are you!

"Ah, look at those beauties," he says.

We come to a stop in front of a pair of black-and-white police cars. One is tire-less, with a severely impacted rear bumper that accordions the trunk all the way through the back seat, and the other is missing both passenger doors, revealing a completely charred interior. The seats have a crispy sort of look to them—the singed vinyl peeling away in sheets like scorched skin after a bad sunburn—and the dashboard bears a striking resemblance to a melted crayon.

"What happened to these cars?"

"No idea," he answers while peeling off the pack and setting it on the ground.

"I thought you were a detective."

He smirks at my little jab. "I'm off duty."

"Oh, right," I say, smirking back.

With his bat in his left hand, he sidles up beside me and gives me a little nudge with his right shoulder. "You're up, slugger."

I swallow hard, excitement and uncertainty colliding in one massive knot in my throat. "Are you sure?" I tighten my grip on the bat while casting a nervous glance over my shoulder. "This doesn't seem right."

"Trust me, it's very right. Go ahead," he urges. "Just give it a whack."

"Where?"

"Anywhere," he says, amused by my nervousness. "Like this."

He steps up to the tire-less car, raises the bat back behind his shoulder, and swings through—

"Huuugh!" he grunts as the bat smashes into the front passenger door. I reel back, startled by the sound, and by the huge dent he's left behind. "Just avoid the windows, since I forgot the goggles," he adds over a satisfied grin.

"Okay. Right. No windows."

My heart adopts a faster beat as I step up to the burned-out car.

Just whack it, Jane.

Just whack it!

I raise the bat—which is a lot heavier than the one I brought—and give it a little swing.

Thunk.

It smacks against the front fender, not even leaving a scratch.

"Ah, come on. I know you've got more in you than that," he taunts. "Put some meat behind that swing."

My cheeks flush at his playful banter.

I raise the bat and give it another try.

"Ugh!" I grunt.

BANG!

I hit the same spot, but this time I leave a dent. Not a big one, but it's still there. About the size of a golf ball.

Pride swells in my chest and I grin.

"There she is!" Chavez crows. "There's the little orange thrower."

The little orange thrower.

I laugh at the nickname, but the reference instantly transports me back to the night I earned that moniker, to the feelings that brought me to that maddening place in time.

An image of Dan and Julian making out in his car suddenly appears on the cruiser's hood. My lip pulls up into a sneer, and I raise the bat. With every ounce of strength in my body, I slam it down against the steel—

BANG!

My body shudders against the impact—like kickback from a rifle—causing me to stumble backward.

"Whoa, you okay?" Chavez is quick to stabilize me with a hand to the small of my back.

His fingers graze the narrow space of exposed skin that lies between the waistband of my jeans and the hem of my jacket. Unexpected flutters fill my chest, my nerves frustratingly delighted by the warmth of his touch, but I don't have time to process what that means or why it's happening. All I can focus on is the euphoria that's thrumming through my veins. The exquisite release I feel from smashing that car.

"Yeah, I'm good," I say, quickly righting myself and raising the bat again.

I'm *very* good.

~

Bang!

Agggh!

Crash!

Ugggh!

Boom!

Smash!

Over and over, I attack the burned-out car with my bat—slugging and swinging, grunting and yelping out my rage—while Chavez works over the tire-less car beside me, pausing every few minutes to admire my handiwork.

"Damn, girl," he says when I finally drop my bat, too winded to continue. "I think you killed it."

I'm hinged forward at the waist and panting, palms pressed against my knees in search of breath. I glance over at my car and grin. "Yeah, I . . . did good . . . didn't I?" It looks like they pulled it off the set of *The Walking Dead*.

"Feel like you worked off some stress?"

I nod over a breathless laugh. "Oh my god, yes. That was amazing. Except I'm pretty sure my arms are going to fall off."

He chuckles. "Yeah, you're gonna be sore tomorrow. And the next day. And probably the day after that . . ."

I laugh again. "However long it lasts, it was worth it."

"Good, I'm glad. I've got some water here, if you want any."

"Yes, please. Water would be good."

Who knew beating the shit out of a car would be such a good workout?

I join him where he's unloading his pack at the base of a tower of old tires. Along with a bottle of water, he pulls out a small Tupperware container and two plastic forks. He unscrews the cap from the water bottle and offers it to me while he leans up against the tires with the container.

I take a long pull, savoring the rush of cold against my heated lungs.

"I've also got some pie here, in case you worked up an appetite." He peels back the cover, offering me a glimpse. "It's blackberry," he clarifies, aware that it looks more like a pile of gloppy, purple slop than a piece of pie. "It tastes a lot better than it looks."

"You sure?"

"Yes, I'm sure." He levels me with a playful glare. "Here."

He hands me a fork and pushes the container closer.

I scoop out a small portion and with deliberate caution raise it to my mouth while he watches expectantly.

"Okay, you're right," I mutter over the surprisingly tasty bite. "That's actually pretty good."

He grins.

"Did your mom make that?" I ask.

"No, I did."

"*You* did?"

"Yeah, *I* did. Does that surprise you?"

That image of him draped in Mardi Gras beads comes to mind, quickly followed by the bright-orange Hooters mug sitting on his desk.

"Yeah, actually it does," I concede over a little shrug.

"Why?"

"I don't know." I scoop out another helping and pop it into my mouth. "I guess because you've got this whole . . . vibe about you." I motion up and down the length of him with my fork.

"Vibe?" He looks like he's about ready to laugh.

Fighting my own amusement, I say, "Yeah, you're like this macho ladies' man who likes to party and bring women down to the station so they can check out your cool detective stuff."

He snorts. "What are you talking about? I don't bring women down to the station so they can check out my *cool* detective stuff. I work in cold cases. I don't have any cool detective stuff."

"Not according to Officer Bates. She said that women are practically lining up outside the station to visit you."

Despite the limited light, I see a blush emerge across his tan cheeks.

"I'm right, huh?" I tease, giving his arm a playful nudge with my knuckle. "Come on, admit it. I'm right."

He shakes his head, chuckling. "Sorry to disappoint you. But no. I'm not a macho 'ladies' man'"—he air quotes the words for effect—"and I don't parade women into the office. Other than my family, you're the only non-cop who's ever visited me at work."

I reel back. "Really?"

"Yeah."

"Then why would Bates say that?"

His blush deepens as he returns his gaze to me. "I don't know," he moans. "Probably because . . . she likes me."

My eyes snap wide and I gasp. "She likes you?"

I suddenly feel like I'm back in high school exchanging gossip in the hallway.

"Yeah. I think so," he admits over a heavy sigh. "She . . . *ugh*." He rakes his fingers through his crown of thick black hair, looking positively tortured by the words leaving his mouth. "She's been asking me to do things with her for quite a while now—ever since I got divorced—and . . . yeah. She was probably feeling a little threatened by you or something."

I blink hard, not sure which piece of surprising information to respond to first.

"You were married?" is what I end up going with.

"Six years."

"Wow. What—um, what happened? If you're comfortable saying," I quickly add, aware that I may have overstepped my bounds.

He shrugs. "Nah, I don't mind. It's actually a pretty typical story for a cop. She hated the danger and the hours and the fact that I couldn't tell her what I was up to—especially when I was working undercover"— a husband who doesn't talk about his job all the time? If only!—"and then when I got shot, she pretty much called it quits—"

"You were shot?"

My outburst makes him laugh. "Yep. Right here." He presses a palm to his chest. "The bullet went straight through my sternum and out the other side."

"Oh my god." I instinctively press my hand on top of his, saying, "Are you okay?"

His gaze darts down to his chest for a quick beat—long enough for me to realize how warm the coupling of our hands is—and then he returns it to me, saying, "Well, yeah. I am now. It's been almost eight years."

"Right, of course." I blow out a chagrined sigh while slowly pulling my hand away. "I just meant—"

"No, I know what you meant." He smiles kindly. "I was in the hospital for a while and had to do PT for a few months because my back was pretty messed up. I've got a pin in it now, which makes it hard to do certain things, but all in all I got off pretty easy. Thankfully, I had a really good doctor; otherwise it could have ended very differently."

Aware of the importance of a good doctor, I say, "Yeah. You could have been killed."

"I know," he says, his voice suddenly taking on a somber tone. He drops his head slightly. "My partner *was* killed that night. He took two shots straight to the heart."

I gasp, clutching my own chest in horror.

"We were working undercover with some drug dealers, and things went south and . . ." He extinguishes a pained sigh while shaking his head. "It was pretty bad."

"I'm so sorry," I say, resisting the urge to reach out and touch him again. "You two must've been really close, huh?"

"Real close. I was supposed to be the best man at his wedding, but he was killed just a week before, so it never happened."

I wince. "That's awful. His poor fiancée. She must have been devastated."

"She was. We all were. Jay was such a good guy—honest, loyal, funny as hell. Shit . . ." He shakes his head, a grin reemerging as his thoughts undoubtedly wander back to memories of his friend. "The last time we hung out was for his bachelor party. God, that was crazy. We went down to New Orleans and dragged him to this strip bar—"

"Wait, is that the picture that's on your desk? Where you guys are wearing all the beads?"

"You saw it?"

I nod.

Yeah, I saw it, all right.

And the bevy of scantily clad women—er, strippers—surrounding you.

"Man, that was a wild night," he goes on, oblivious to my budding annoyance with the opposite sex. If they're not ogling their *ball buddies*, then they're eyeing some other buddies of the double-D variety! "That was a drag strip club, but he didn't know it. We kept buying him lap dances, and he just kept saying, 'You guys, Rochelle's gonna kill me! She's gonna kill me!' and then, when we told him they were actually dudes, he got so embarrassed that he took off running into the street. He almost got trampled by one of those wandering street bands."

I blink hard. "So, wait. The strip bar you were at was a *drag* bar? All the strippers were men?"

"Yep. All of them. And you couldn't even tell. They looked *just* like women. Except for this one guy. Oh man." He shakes his head, chuckling. "I swear, his Adam's apple was the size of a grapefruit. It was so obvious, but Jay still didn't clue in. Poor guy, he was so loaded."

Once again, I'm surprised to find myself relieved by yet another Officer Poncherello assumption I got wrong.

"Sounds like it was a pretty great night."

Laugh dwindling, he says, "Yeah. It was. It was the best night. At first, I wasn't going to put the picture up because I thought it might make me depressed, but it actually makes me feel better—like he's still around, you know?" I nod. I don't remember a thing about my father, but I'd know his face anywhere, thanks to the collection of pictures Mom kept of him. "I've also got his Cubs cap in a drawer at home, and I keep his old coffee mug on my desk at work. It's ugly, but it reminds me of him, so . . . yeah." He shrugs. "I guess it's just my little coping mechanism."

I swallow hard. The hideous Hooters mug is a coping mechanism, not a proclamation of his favorite place to get wings. And stare at boobs.

"And your wife left you during all of that?" I ask.

"Not right away, but within a few months."

"Unbelievable," I mutter.

"And the cherry on top of it all was that when I was finally healthy enough to come back to work, I was transferred out of vice, which I loved, and into a desk job—cold cases," he clarifies, "which is where I am now. Needless to say, it was *not* the best time in my life."

"No, I imagine it wasn't."

"That's actually when I started coming here," he goes on, motioning to our surroundings. "I was seeing a therapist, which actually helped a lot, but I was still so mad that I had to find a way to work out my aggressions without getting myself into trouble. Turns out beating the hell out of a car does the trick." His familiar grin slowly reemerges, prompting me to nod in agreement. Yes, it does. "And it's all good now," he goes on. "The desk job is surprisingly interesting, and because it's more of a nine to five, it allows me time to do other stuff: rock climbing, traveling, baking . . ." He winks at me, sending an unanticipated flutter to erupt in my chest. "I feel like I'm learning how to take advantage of my life now, you know?" I nod again. He got a second chance at life. It makes sense that he'd want to make the most of it. "And things are even pretty good with my ex now. I mean, it's not like we're friends or anything, but I don't hate her anymore. And looking back, it was just a matter of time before we got divorced anyway."

"Really?"

"Yeah. We grew apart way before the shooting. We were basically just going through the motions. Playing the part . . ."

His comment hits surprisingly close to home, forcing my chest to tighten with unease. I raise the water bottle to my lips and take another drink, then quickly change the subject to something less familiar.

"So, based on what Jessie said," I say, thumbing back toward the check-in shed, "you still come here quite a bit?"

"Not as often as I used to, but yeah. Every now and then. I brought my sister with me the last time I came."

His sister?

His sister is the *chick* he brought with him last time?

Okay, make that *three* assumptions I got wrong . . .

"So, anger is a family trait then?" I tease, another flood of unexpected relief driving my question.

He snorts. "Oh yeah. That girl's got a *lot* of anger to work through. Her husband—the dick—bailed on her a year ago, right after their son's third birthday. No warning, just a note that said, 'Sorry, I can't do this anymore.'"

I gasp. Dan may be a horrible husband, but at least he's a good father. Abandoning your child is inexcusable; I know!

"It got pretty ugly for a while there," he goes on, "especially when she had to move back in with my parents. But she's a tough girl. She'll get through it okay. Actually, you probably remember her from school, Stacy Chavez? She was a year older than us . . ."

My eyes narrow in consideration, but no one comes to mind.

"She was junior class president?" he offers. "Ran track and was on the yearbook committee . . . looks just like me but shorter . . ."

"Sorry."

He tips his head, a tender smirk riding his lips. "You don't remember much about high school, do you?"

"Not really. That was, um . . . that was a really hard time in my life. Not like what you went through—" On instinct, I lay my hand against his arm in reassurance but just as quickly pull it back, the warmth radiating through his jacket too much to process. "I just had a lot of . . . stuff going on back then."

"Stuff?"

Considering what he's just shared with me, and that he already knows the most personal thing about me—or about Dan—it's a little ridiculous that I'm hesitant to answer his question. But I am. I don't like this part of my life.

I drop my gaze a bit. "My mom was kind of a mess back then," I admit. "She dated around a lot—always looking for someone to replace my dad, I think. He walked out on us when I was four," I add over a callous shrug. I got over his abandonment years ago. "But she was never happy with any of them, until Gary . . ."

My lips pull up in a reminiscent grin as I think back on the sixteen months Gary was in our lives. Such a kind, thoughtful man; he treated Mom like gold and loved Julie and me like we were his own. I remember how excited I was when we moved in with him, and not because we got separate bedrooms for the first time, but because Gary's zip code afforded me the luxury of attending a good school: South Glenn High.

A lump of long-forgotten disappointment starts to swell in my throat.

She never even acknowledged what she did.

How devastating that was to me.

She just showed up at school—her car packed with all our stuff—signed me out of English class, and then drove the three of us back to the barely-getting-by life we'd finally escaped—

"What happened to Gary?" he asks, pulling me back to the present.

"Oh, uh . . ." I right my frustrated thoughts with a quick shake of the head. "She broke up with him. She'd heard through the grapevine that my dad had died, and, I don't know . . ." I sigh, returning my gaze to his. "I guess it just brought back all the unresolved feelings she still had for him, and she decided she could never be serious with anyone else again. So, she pulled my sister and me out of school, and we left town."

His gaze softens sympathetically, but thankfully he doesn't press for more details. Instead he just says, "Yeah, it was weird. One day you were at school, and the next day you were gone. You just disappeared."

Disappeared?

More like I was kidnapped out of the perfect, stable life I'd come to love.

"You noticed?" I ask.

Another adorable flush crosses his cheeks. "Well, yeah. You did sit two tables away from me in chemistry . . ."

The fact that he remembers what class we had together is nothing short of mind-boggling—I can barely remember what classes I took in high school—but that he remembers where we sat is just crazy.

"What are you, a ginkgo addict or something?" I tease while helping myself to another bite of his messy pie. "Your memory is insane. How do you remember that stuff?"

He stares at me for a beat before he shrugs and says, "It's hard to forget anything about your high school crush."

My eyes snap wide, and my breath catches in surprise.

"What?" I sputter, working hard not to launch blackberry bits all over him.

His grin tugs up higher on one side as he leans in deeper against the tires. "Oh yeah. I had it bad for you, Jane Holliday."

"You did?"

He nods, and a ridiculous explosion of schoolgirl tingles erupts in my chest.

"But . . . um." I swallow hard, my breath feeling strangely short beneath my words. "You never said anything. You never even talked to me. Did you?"

He chuckles at my black hole of a memory. "No. Believe it or not, I was way too shy back then to talk to girls. But I was planning to build up enough courage to ask you to the Valentine's dance."

The Valentine's dance.

The event alone doesn't stick out as anything significant, but the timing sure does. It was February 13 when Mom piled me, Julie, and all our stuff into the car and drove us away from the perfect *family* life I'd come to love with Gary.

"So, would you have?"

"I'm sorry, what?" I bring myself back to the present with a quick shake of the head.

"Would you have said yes? If I had asked you?"

"Oh . . . um . . ." His question prompts the silly, teenage euphoria already thrumming through my veins to ignite like wildfire behind my cheeks. I drop my head slightly, allowing my hair to shade some of the flush. "Yeah. I would have said yes."

"Good to know," he says over an adorable grin, then proceeds to load up his fork with another dollop of pie. He raises it toward his mouth, stopping just before he eats it to say, "Maybe someday I'll ask you to another dance, Jane Holliday. After you're divorced, of course."

The flirtatious compliment isn't lost on me, but that's not what prompts my breath to catch.

It's that word: *DIVORCE.*

CHAPTER 14

Of course the idea of divorce had crossed my mind before Chavez so naively (and adorably) mentioned it at the impound lot a few days ago. That devastating night in Denver, it even came up in conversation, but only for a moment. Once Dan explained the fragility of the situation at the hospital and emphasized the devastating financial impact an untimely separation could have on not only us but also Mom and Julie, I had no choice but to push it out of my mind.

But now it's back, erupting in my thoughts like one of those moles in a whack-'em arcade game just waiting for me to smash it with the mallet. DIVORCE.DIVORCE.DIVORCE.

And that's rational, right?

My husband is gay, after all, and has been cheating on me for most of our marriage. That's not the kind of marriage I signed up for. That's not the kind of marriage *any* woman signs up for! Of course it makes sense that I'd be thinking about getting a divorce—

But then Mom would have to move somewhere cheaper; she'll end up at a dodgy, state-run facility with underpaid staff who treat her like every other patient rather than the special mother—and grandmother—she is. And Avery will grow up in a broken home filled with uncertainty and instability. Everything I've tried so hard to give her will just . . . disappear. Just like *I* disappeared from South Glenn High. Back when I had a chance to become something more than I am now—when I had opportunities, and hope. Before I had to rely on a handsome cardiothoracic resident I met while waiting tables to offer me something bigger—something better—than I had. Something I deserved—

"Aggggh!" Frustration nips at my spine, forcing me to raise the yellow Wiffle bat in the air and strike the shrubs that line our back walk. Pain radiates through my aching shoulder muscles (three days later, I'm still popping Advil), a handful of leaves falling to the flagstone pavers at my feet. It's a much less impressive result than Chavez's aluminum bat would have provided and, unfortunately, much less satisfying too.

This isn't working!

As terrified as I am to share my situation with anyone, it's become painfully obvious that I can't work this out on my own. (If not for the sake of my aching muscles, then at least for the safety of my landscaping.) Chavez is a great listener and provides surprisingly sound advice, but our . . . relationship took a bit of a turn the other night. A turn I have no idea how to navigate right now, but one that assures me he can't be my therapist.

What I need is the sound, honest wisdom only a woman with life experience can provide. A woman whose blunt observations and matter-of-fact opinions have always rubbed me the wrong way but now might be just what I need to hear. A woman who knows all the players but no longer has access to the game.

~

Gina is the nurse manning the front desk today. She's not as friendly as Carol (who unfortunately doesn't work on Sundays), but she still informs me that Mom "seems to be having a good day." It's not the assured response I was hoping for, but it's enough to calm my nerves a bit. I need her to be fully present to provide me the kind of advice I'm looking for.

I make my way down the hall, inhaling motivating breaths the entire way, then give her door a hearty rap with my knuckle.

"Who's there?" she calls out almost immediately, which is a good sign. When she's *Mom*, she's quick to react to visitors.

I push the door open and lean inside. "It's me, Mom."

Her distance vision isn't what it used to be, so I'm not surprised to see her squinting from where she sits on the love seat, but it's obvious she recognizes my voice.

"Oh, Janie. Hi. Come in." She waves me over with a smile while scrambling off the love seat and hurrying across the room to greet me.

My heart twists at her agility. She still moves like a teenager, so graceful and free. If only her brain were so generous.

"Good to see you, kid."

"You too, Mom."

She throws her arms around me and gives me a hug. It's not particularly tight—her hugs never are—but thanks to my time at Smash Land, it still hurts.

"What's wrong with you?" She pulls back, surveying me with a narrowed gaze. "Why did you just whimper?"

"Oh, it's . . . nothing." I instinctively raise my left hand to my right shoulder. "I just worked out really hard the other day, and I'm still sore, that's all."

"Well, there's some aspirin around here somewhere," she says, already looking disinterested with my pain. As always, her bedside manner could use a little work. "You want something to drink?"

"Sure. Whatever you've got is fine."

I set my bag down on the little dinette table, then make my way over to the love seat while she clanks around in the kitchen. An episode of *The Love Boat*, her favorite show, is playing on the TV.

"Who's the guest star on this episode?" I call out to her.

I'm not really interested in the answer to that question, but it's a good way to determine how *herself* she is today. It's likely she's seen this episode ten times before. If she can remember some of the details of the show, odds are she'll remember some of the details of her own life too.

"Tom Hanks," she calls back to me over a budding laugh. "He's playing an old college buddy to . . . oh, you know. The guy with the animal name—"

"Gopher?"

"Yes! Gopher," she chuckles. "Tom Hanks is trying to score with the cruise director, and Gopher can't stand it, so he's pretending to be her boyfriend to keep him away."

"Oh, right." I nod. "I remember this one."

Because we lived on Mom's meager waitressing paycheck, our entertainment was limited to whatever channels our TV antenna could pick up, the one that came in the clearest being an all-reruns channel. So, while other kids my age were indulging in the delicacies of cable shows—*Tales from the Crypt, Fraggle Rock, Remote Control*—I was learning life lessons from people who wore bell-bottoms and had really bad haircuts. Not that the Bradford kids weren't entertaining, but sometimes eight was *way* more than enough.

"Here." Mom returns to the room and hands me my drink. My stomach twists. It's V8 juice. Yet another of her newly acquired tastes.

I force down a polite sip, then set it on the coffee table.

"So, what's going on?" she asks as she settles back into her spot beside me.

"Nothing much. I just thought I'd come by and see how you were doing." And tell you that my husband is secretly gay and ask if you think I should divorce him. "I missed you at Thanksgiving."

She sighs. "Julie said I was being pretty bitchy. Sorry."

My mom's never been one for apologies, but ever since she was diagnosed, she'll offer them up on occasion. Though I think it has more to do with her own frustration for not remembering than actually feeling bad for any mistreatment of us.

I give her arm a little pat. "That's okay. You didn't miss much."

"How's . . . Avery?" Her gaze drifts to the picture on the credenza. "Is she still playing soccer?"

I nod quickly, delighted she remembers. "All the time. She had a game yesterday, and she scored the winning goal."

"Good for her." She pumps her fist in support. Gina was right. She *does* seem to be having a pretty good day. "And you're still doing the whole PTA thing?"

"Yes. I'm the president."

I've told her this before. More than a few times.

"Well, good for you. I'm sure you're doing a great job."

My cheeks flush beneath one of her rarely delivered compliments. "I try."

"They can't ask for more than that, can they?"

I grin and shake my head. "No, they can't."

She grabs her own glass of V8 from the end table and takes a long drink, gaze shifting back toward the TV.

"This was his first TV acting job. Did you know that?" Mom asks, referring to a very young Tom Hanks on the screen. "He did this, and then not too long after he started on *Bosom Buddies*. That was a good show." She laughs. "You remember that one, don't you?"

"I do," I answer, my voice cracking with a sudden burst of nervousness.

Shit.

Mom is definitely on her game today. Which is good. That's what I wanted. But that means I actually have to tell her what's going on. I have to say it out loud, then hear her response. And Lord knows she's going to have a lot to say—

You can do this, Jane.

You need help working through this.

You can't smash cars for the rest of your life.

I inhale a shaky breath through my nose.

I am a strong, capable woman.

I can do anything I set my mind to—

"Dan's gay," I blurt out before I lose my nerve. She rips her gaze away from the TV and fires it directly onto me. "He's been cheating on me with men for almost our entire marriage. And now he has to bring in a ton of money for the hospital, or they'll shut down all the specialty departments, but the people who have the money are super conservative and will only give their money to someone who fits the picture-perfect family mold, so I can't tell anyone. And I don't know what to do because I'm just living a big lie now. I don't even know who I am anymore. I feel like I'm dying inside—"

Dying inside?

The words sound a little dramatic against my ears, but . . . *shit.* They're true! That's exactly how it feels. Like someone's laced my veins with acid, and little by little I'm slowly being eaten alive. All the things that make me who I am are disintegrating, one cell at a time.

"I don't know what to do!" I go on, emotions starting to strangle my words. I push myself off the love seat and start pacing the floor, Mom's wide eyes tracking every step while she remains uncharacteristically quiet. "I love my life—I mean, not the cheating-husband part, but the rest of it is good. You're here in this great facility where the people care about you, and I get to pick Avery up from school every day and go to all her games and be on the PTA. How can I run the risk of losing that?" I throw my hands up, the question hanging in the air for a nanosecond before I continue. "She's my entire world! Everything I've done—every decision I've made—was so that *she* could have the life she has. But *ugh!*" I blow out a pained grunt, fisting my hands in front of me. "I can't keep living like this. I'm so mad all the time. I just want to hit things! I want to punch people and scream and just . . . *aaaagh!*" I shake my fists, teeth clenched in frustration, and anger, and—"I don't know what to do!" I turn to her, chest heaving beneath my frantic breaths. "Do I get divorced? Do I stay with him? What should I do?"

She blinks hard, understandably startled.

Alzheimer's patients sometimes have a hard time keeping up with conversations—even on good days—and I just dumped a mountain of words on her. That, and I asked her for advice. It's been a lifetime since I did that . . .

"Mom," I say, making my way back to the love seat. "I know I don't ask for your help very often, but I need you to tell me what to do. I'm going crazy trying to figure it out by myself. I need your help. Please, tell me what to do about Dan."

She adopts one of those broken smiles that assures me she's empathizing with my pain. A smile I've never seen her offer before but one I'm beyond grateful for now. She reaches for my hand and, with a thoughtfully tipped head, says, "I'm sorry, dear. Who is Dan?"

Who is Dan?

My heart flops to the floor.

No.

No!

Not now.

Not after what I just told you!

Not when I need you the most!

My chin starts to quiver, and through a quickly tensing jaw I say, "My husband, Dan. The doctor. The tall doctor with blond hair and blue eyes . . ."

"Oh. Right." She's nodding like she's made the connection, but it's obvious she hasn't. She doesn't have a clue who Dan is. And based on past experience, I know that she doesn't remember who I am or what I've just shared with her either. That's the thing about Alzheimer's: it doesn't operate on a set schedule, no matter how crucial the timing.

A fresh surge of anger swells through my pores, forcing me to stand up and head for the door before I start screaming at her and her fucking unfair disease.

"Are you sure you can't stay awhile longer?" she calls out to me, completely oblivious to the last three minutes of her life. "*The Love*

Boat's on. It's a good one. Tom Hanks is the guest star. And I've got lots of goodies to snack on."

She springs off the love seat and hustles into the kitchen, where she pulls a Costco-size bag of Skittles from the cupboard. She offers it to me with an encouraging smile.

Tears prick my eyes, and I give my head a little shake. "No thanks. I prefer chocolate."

CHAPTER 15

MONDAY

10:00 am "Meeting" in the city

1:30 pm Phone call with fundraising team (Listen to Your Heart Gala)

3:15 pm Avery pick-up

3:30 pm Avery practice—Mann Field

5:45 pm Avery piano

7:00 pm PTA meeting—Multipurpose Room (gluten-free holiday bake sale)

I stare down at my schedule and scowl. It's bad enough that it's another busy day, but I'm also running on very little sleep, which is going to make accomplishing each one of these tasks that much harder. Thanks to yesterday's disappointing visit with Mom, I tossed and turned all night, racking my brain for someone else to confide in, but I kept coming up frustratingly short.

Obviously, all the second wives are off the table. Even if their husbands weren't Dan's colleagues, not one of them can keep a secret to save her life. Except for Heather, though I'd venture to say those ecstasy tablets won't buy me her confidence as much as they would a severe tongue-lashing for dipping into her stash. And while Julie *seems* like the obvious choice, given her nonexistent relationships with anyone in Dan's circle, she relies way too much on my marriage to be impartial. Besides that, her own disastrous love life assures me she wouldn't offer very sound advice anyway.

By three o'clock this morning, the only thing I'd determined was that not only is my entire world crumbling, but I don't have one person I can ask to help me pick up the pieces.

I pick up a large coffee (with a double shot!) on my way into the city, along with what I hope is a gum-able breakfast sandwich for my homeless friend at the crosswalk. His funny signs and chipper greetings always bring a smile to my face; I could use one of those today. The pit stop makes me tight on time, so I hightail it through the parking lot and toward the street, my shoulders slumping when I see that the corner near the crosswalk is empty. Darn it.

My mood continues to spiral down the toilet when I make my way through security and, despite a whole lot of unsubtle searching, don't see Chavez anywhere in the lobby—not that he said he'd be here; I guess I just assumed, or maybe I hoped . . .

Get it together, Jane!

You're not here for a prom date.

Get your ass upstairs before you're late!

With a righting headshake, I hoof it up the stairs and into the classroom with just a minute to spare. I take my usual seat opposite Iris and next to Burty—or where Burty *should* be sitting. She's not here yet.

"Good morning, ladies. I hope you all had a good break," Bates barks out as she starts circling the group to review our journal entries.

Since we didn't meet the day after Thanksgiving, we had to do two entries in preparation for today's class. The first one I bullshitted per usual:

PROMPT: WHAT ARE YOU MOST LOOKING FORWARD TO THIS THANKSGIVING?
ANSWER:

Baking! I've always loved to bake, especially Thanksgiving pies. And my daughter loves it too. We'll spend the whole day baking together. We're like Martha and mini Martha. We should have our own show!

But the second one I actually answered honestly. Mostly because it was the only good thing that happened to me over the break, but also because I thought it might serve as a little jab to Bates, to get back at her for the way she treats me. At three thirty this morning, it felt like a pretty solid plan, but as I lay the notebook out for inspection, I'm not so sure that was the best move.

She comes to an obvious stop behind me, heavy breaths falling over my shoulder like shrapnel looking for a place to land.

PROMPT: WHAT WAS THE BEST PART OF YOUR LONG WEEKEND?
ANSWER:

Spending Thanksgiving night with Chavez. He swings his bat hard and bakes a damn fine pie.

I shift against the metal chair, angling my head a bit so my hair falls away from my face to obscure her view—

"Uppph . . ."

The sound she makes is somewhere between a whimper and a growl and follows her as she carries on around the circle, her boots slamming against the floor much harder than usual.

I quickly slap my notebook shut while hanging my head in regret. *Dumb move, Jane.*

Very dumb.

"So, I guess Burt Reynolds is a no-show," Bates grumbles as she finishes her rounds. "Anybody heard from her?"

I raise my head, not surprised to find Donna, Lina, and Angel shrugging and shaking their heads with disinterest, and Maya's too busy eating her nubby thumbnail to even hear the question, but it's the expression on Iris's face that gives me pause. She looks . . . worried.

"She's sick," Iris answers Bates. "She caught something over the weekend. Thought she'd be well enough to come in today, but apparently she's still under the weather."

Bates sighs while Lina mutters, "I reckon she done ate some bad turkey," in a rude, Gomer Pyle–sounding southern accent.

Angel stifles a laugh while Donna rolls her eyes and mumbles, "Bad turkey's no joke."

"Well, she can't come back without a doctor's note," Bates continues, easily buying into Iris's story. But I'm not. Something's off here. As a well-versed liar myself, I can feel it. "That's the rule. You miss class, you have to have a doctor's excuse or you're out."

"Yeah, she knows," Iris says. She offers Bates an affirming smile, then slowly shifts her attention to me. Her dark gaze locks onto mine the way it has countless times before, but today it doesn't offer me even an ounce of peace. It just makes my nerves stand on end.

My eyes narrow, and I slowly raise my palms, silently questioning what's got her so upset.

She gives her head a slow shake while worry lines splinter out from the corners of her eyes. My chest grows painfully tight. I know those lines well. I've seen them a thousand times in my own reflection, anytime I'm worried about Avery.

I glance at Burty's empty seat, then turn back to Iris. I give her a little nod. I have no idea what I'm committing myself to, but whatever it is—whatever she knows about Burty—I want in.

~

". . . he's holding her baby hostage. Says he's got her locked in the bedroom. Didn't even let her out to feed her breakfast—"

Iris called Burty the second Bates released us from class, and now she's relaying to me what Burty's saying to her as we race across the street and toward the parking lot to my car.

"He locked her in the bedroom?" I growl over winded breaths. "What the hell is wrong with him!"

"It's okay, honey." Iris is talking to Burty again, her tone so much calmer than mine. "We're coming to get you. Jane's going to drive us. We'll be there in just a few minutes. Just try to stay calm—"

Heart racing, I unlock the car doors with a smack to the key fob, then climb into the driver's seat while Iris hops in on the passenger side. She didn't ask if I wanted to drive, just told me I was going to. Which is fine. I want to help.

"—your little girl's going to be okay," she goes on while I start the engine and peel out of the parking space. *Where am I going? I don't know where I'm going!* "She'll be okay. You just stay as calm as you can so you don't upset her, okay? We're on our way, Burty. We'll be there soon."

The second she ends the call, I scream, "Where am I going?"

"Hang a right at the station, then left on Baltimore. We'll take that for a couple of miles, then turn right on Quigley."

Hands strangling the wheel, I follow her instructions and barrel out of the lot and down the street.

"Watch your speed. There are cops everywhere around here," Iris reminds me as I blow by the police station.

"Right. Sorry." I ease off the gas a smidge. "I can't believe he's doing this." I cast her a horrified look. "How can he lock a child in the bedroom? That's abuse!"

She shakes her head, the same worry in my voice evident on her face. "I don't know. He's clearly got some mental health issues."

"Should we call the police? Or . . . CPS or someone?" I ask.

"Let's just get there and then figure out what to do. He's unstable. We don't want to escalate the situation unnecessarily," she says, not even a waver in her tone. "Once we get a lay of the land, we'll have a better idea how to proceed."

I have zero doubt that Iris is as upset as I am, but you'd never know it by her levelheaded comments and even tone.

"How are you so calm right now?"

"I was an army field nurse for six years and then worked in the ER for twelve," she says, prompting my jaw to sag in disbelief. Iris, charged with petty theft, is a nurse? I mean, it makes sense, given some of the comments she's made during class, but how on earth does a nurse end up being charged with petty theft? "Believe me, I've dealt with way worse drama than a crazy, cheating boyfriend."

I gasp. "Is that what happened? He cheated on her?"

"Yep. Or at least that's what she thought was going on when we talked about it last week. She said he'd been acting weirder than usual—having more of his 'emotional spells' or whatever she calls them—and he was getting harder to be around because he cries all the time. At first, she thought he was just homesick or dealing with his daddy issues or whatever, but then she saw a sexy text from some girl, and she started getting suspicious—"

"Poor Burty," I groan, empathizing with her plight.

Cheaters be damned!

"I told her she needed to confront him to find out for sure."

"Did she?"

She shrugs. "I don't know. Last time I heard from her was yesterday morning. She sent me a text that said . . ." She pulls the message up on her phone and starts reading it to me: "'He's too fitful to ask. I'll do it later tonight. I'll let you know what he says . . .'"

Her voice trails off, leaving me wide eyed and wondering.

"So, did she text you back?"

She shakes her head. "I texted her a couple times last night but never heard anything. I was hoping maybe they were up late talking, sorting through stuff—you know how that goes." I nod, even though I don't know how that goes. Dan and I haven't stayed up late sorting through anything. Mostly he's just told me how it's going to be, and I've complied. "I just figured I'd wake up this morning and there'd be something from her, but there wasn't. And then, when she didn't show up for class . . . *damn*." She blows out a painful-sounding sigh. "I'd have driven over to check on her, but I had to drop my car off at the shop this weekend. I should've just taken an Uber or a cab. I knew something wasn't right. I just knew it."

Iris may be field ready on the outside, but her mom guilt isn't so easily camouflaged. She must have one of her own at home.

"Hey." I reach across the center console and grab her arm, and her attention. "You did everything right. You listened to her problems. You gave her good advice. You followed up with her. There wasn't anything else you could do."

"There's always more you can do."

"Well, I think you did a lot. I mean, you guys just met a couple of weeks ago. The fact that you're *this* invested in her is pretty incredible. I've been friends with people for five years who wouldn't help me as much as you've helped Burty."

She offers me a weak smile and then, in a sarcastic tone, says, "You need some new friends."

I force out a little laugh because she's obviously trying to lighten our mood, but the sentiment isn't lost on me. She's right. I probably do need new friends.

"Okay, you're going to hang a right up here." She motions to the four-way stop in front of us.

I turn down a street that's lined with old, brown-bricked duplexes, the roots of towering oak trees erupting through the sidewalks in front of them.

"She's that one on the left"—she points across me—"with the old Camaro in the driveway."

I pull to a stop against the curb across the street from the house in question, heart jackhammering against my sternum. The street is so quiet right now. Other than the elderly woman walking her dog at the end of the block and the plumber unloading some equipment in the driveway over my shoulder, it's like a suburban ghost town. You'd never know something horrible is taking place behind those walls.

"So, what's the plan?" I ask, eyeing the old house with trepidation. "Are we going in Van Damme–style? Kick the door down? Or maybe go through a window?"

She levels me with a hard look. "We're going to knock on the door."

My cheeks flush over a sheepish grin. Right. Of course we'll knock. My first hostage situation has my adrenaline kicking a little harder than usual.

Stride for stride, we make our way across the street and up the front walk toward the house. Fallen leaves crunch beneath our feet, but otherwise everything seems very calm and quiet—

"Waaaaaaah!"

A horrific wailing sound suddenly emerges from behind the front door of the duplex's right side.

I gasp. "Who was that? Was that the baby?"

"I don't think so." Iris shakes her head, eyes wide with uncertainty. "That didn't sound like a child—"

"Noooo! No, please!"

Another horrific cry, but this one is distinctly male.

"That's gotta be him," Iris says. "Burty says he cries all the time."

The wailing continues like the soundtrack to a B horror movie as we scramble up the concrete steps and across the porch to the front door. Iris pounds on it with a heavy fist. "Burty?" she calls out. "Burty, honey. Are you in there?"

The crying stops for a split second before Burty's familiar voice responds, "I'm here! I'm here—come in!"

Iris grabs the handle and pushes the door open just as the male voice cries out, "Who's here? Who's that?" His pained wails—thick with the same southern drawl as Burty's—echo off the aged hardwood floor.

"Burty, where are you?" Iris calls as she steps across the threshold and into the house.

I follow close behind her, surveying my new surroundings with wide, nervous eyes. The living room that we're standing in is small, filled with mismatched furniture that's too big for the space, but it's tidy. Other than the two suitcases sitting next to the door, there's no clutter anywhere. No dirty dishes. No magazines. Not even a child's toy in sight—

"We're back here! Through the kitchen!" Burty calls out.

"Who's here?" he cries out again.

Iris takes the lead, quickly guiding us through the living room and into the narrow galley kitchen on our right—

"Sweet baby Jesus," she gasps, coming to a grinding halt that forces me to smash into her.

I stumble back a few steps while saying, "What? What's wrong—"
Oh my god.

My eyes snap wide as I find my footing and take in the scene in front of me.

"He's crazy! He's got my little girl locked in the bedroom! He threatened to tie her to a tree and make her sleep outside!"

Burty is screaming from where she's standing at the far end of the dining room in front of us, pointing to a closed door opposite her. Her cherubic cheeks are a fiery-red color—not their usual delicate pink—her golden curls a tangled mess against her shoulders, like she's been raking her hands through them all night. But it's not her that's stolen our attention.

It's him.

The heavyset, twentysomething guy she's pointing at.

The man with swollen, bloodshot eyes and tears streaming down his face. The man with a mullet and a distinct farmer's tan despite the long-sleeved weather. The man who is completely and utterly naked, with the exception of the gigantic elephant head that's projecting straight out from his—

I blink hard.

Is that—

Sweet baby Jesus, indeed!

All his man business is covered by an elephant's head. A crocheted elephant's head with a long trunk to house his penis, floppy ears attached to each side, and a sort of cuplike sack to hold his . . . sack. All held in place by one flimsy piece of gray yarn that's tied tight around his ample waist.

"Who the hell are these people?" His plea reclaims my attention, bringing me back to the task at hand.

"We're just here to help," Iris says calmly, hands raised to solidify her statement.

"We don't need yer help!" He turns toward us, his shockingly long trunk now facing us head-on. I gasp. It's got eyes too. The plastic kind with unattached black pupils, like you buy at the craft store and glue onto Popsicle sticks or felt or . . . crocheted elephant penises, apparently. *What the hell is going on here?!* "We're workin' it out between us."

"Like hell we are!" Burty growls back at him. "We're not workin' out a dern thing! You're a lyin', stinkin' cheater, Wade Grundy!"

"I said I was sorry!" he pleads over an onslaught of tears. "I didn't mean for it to happen. It was an accident—"

"It was an accident? So, what, you were just droppin' off a shipment of willy warmers and your ding-dong fell into her honeypot? Is that what happened? Just one of those awful post office accidents you're always hearin' about?"

Iris suddenly grabs my hand and gives it a hard squeeze. I'm not sure if it's meant to acknowledge Burty's astuteness to Wade's infidelity, or that she also heard the phrase *willy warmers* and is now feeling as squeamish as I am. Either scenario works.

"Tell me, Wade," she goes on. "Which warmer did you wear for her?"

"No. No, no, no," he blubbers while violently shaking his head. "I'm not gonna answer that—"

"Tell me—"

"No."

"Tell me!"

"The giraffe," he cries out. "It was the giraffe, okay?"

A nauseating visual of a very long giraffe neck anchored by an orange sack suddenly comes to mind, forcing me to drop my head before I gag. Or scream. How can we be talking about penis socks when there is a child who hasn't eaten all day locked in a bedroom!

"I swear it didn't mean nothin'," he goes on.

"Well, it means somethin' now! You know the giraffe's my favorite. Damn you, Wade! Now you gone and ruined giraffes for me forever!"

I blink hard. She's not the only one.

"Come on, baby," he says, desperation dragging down his words. "I'll make it right. You know I will. Just let me make it right—"

"You can't make this right!" she yells. "You cheated on me! There's no way I'm stayin' with you, Wade. I'm takin' my girl and gettin' the hell away from you!"

She makes a move toward him, but he's quick to scream out, "No!" and assume a jumping-jack position, blocking the doorway with his hands and feet in all four corners. The big elephant sways like a pendulum with the movement. "You can't leave, Burt! I won't let you leave—"

A high-pitched cry suddenly shoots out from behind the door Wade is guarding, prompting the hairs on my neck to rise. I've never heard a child cry like that before. My pulse spikes.

"She's cryin', Wade! The poor thing is starved! I need to feed her!" She makes another move for the door, but he's quick to respond with a bolstered-up chest, like he's ready for a fight.

"No! She only eats if you stay—"

"That's enough!" Iris cuts in, stepping forward with a shocking amount of confidence. The entire house falls silent, but my heart is beating so hard I can hear it in my ears. "Look, I know you're upset, but that little girl has nothing to do with your fight. You can't punish her for your mistakes. You can't starve her—"

"She ain't starvin'!" he barks back at Iris, then turns toward Burty with heat in his eyes. "She ate a huge bowl a food last night—you saw 'er yourself!"

"That was last night!" Burty screams. "It's almost lunchtime!"

"Listen to me!" Iris takes a brave step forward, finger pointed toward his face. "You're going to open that door and let that child out of there, do you understand me?"

He reels back, clearly surprised by her instruction.

"Come on, Wade," Burty pleads softly, taking advantage of his bewilderment. He turns toward her, chin quivering with emotion. "Please just let me give her somethin' to eat. She's hungry."

He blinks hard, and his shoulders start to sag like he's finally going to concede. A hopeful breath fills my lungs. This is it. The moment of truth. *Do the right thing, Wade. Do the right thing—*

"Nuh-uh." He shakes his head. "She only eats if you stay—"

Another ear-shattering cry erupts from behind the door, and much like it did in the parking lot a few weeks ago, something inside me snaps. I grab the first thing I see—a roll of paper towels—and raise them. Just like I did with my oranges. Just like with Chavez's bat.

"Step away from the door," I growl.

"No!" He quickly counters my threat by stepping forward himself, chest puffed up to accentuate his substantial size. He's got at least a foot and more than a hundred pounds on me, not to mention an elephant, but weirdly I'm not intimidated.

"Yes," Iris joins in with an equally demonic-sounding voice. She grabs a plastic flyswatter that's hanging by a magnet on the refrigerator door and starts smacking it into her open palm. "You are going to step away from that door, and you're going to do it right now."

"No, I'm not," he grunts while swiping back spittle from his nose. "She either gits both of us or neither."

Iris glances at me, and I give her a hearty nod in return.

"On three?" I say.

"One . . ."

"Two . . . ," I say.

"Three!" we scream in unison and lurch forward, swinging with all our might.

Wade bats away my first hit with a swipe of his hand, but Iris makes contact on his right arm, forcing him to turn his attention toward her, which leaves his entire left side exposed to me.

"Aaagh!" I go in hard, walloping him in the head, then start attacking his waist and lower back as he returns his attention to me.

"Stop hittin' me, you crazy bitches!" he screams, windmilling his arms through the air. He lands a blow across my cheek, sending a jolt of pain screaming through my veins. It knocks me back a step but only accelerates my drive to stop him.

I tighten my grip on the paper towels and come in harder, screaming, "You lying cheater! She's too good for you! She's too good for you!"

Bethany Crandell

I'm going straight for his face now, prompting him to raise his hands defensively, while Iris heads around back and starts whipping his bare butt.

"Owww!" He drops his hands to try to restrain Iris, but she's quick and skirts away before he can make contact. Once again, he's left himself vulnerable to my attack. I go in for the kill, raising the paper towels up high above my head, then smacking the elephant straight across the trunk.

"*Ugh!*" He drops to his knees, and Iris cries out, "Burty, go! Go get your girl!"

Burty skirts by us and into the room while Iris and I hammer on, pummeling Wade's back and head while he writhes uncomfortably on the floor.

"Got her!" Burty calls, bolting out of the room. She's moving too fast for me to get a close look, but I can see that she's carrying someone small, wrapped in a blanket in her arms. Thank god, the baby's safe!

"Go to the car!" I scream, raising the towels for another blow. I whack him hard on the head. The paper towel roll is starting to bend, but surprisingly the towels are still intact. It's a good thing Burty splurges for the two-ply. If not, there'd be a big mess in here by now. "Iris, get the suitcases!" I pause from my attack long enough to grab my keys from my pocket and toss them to her. "Honk when you're in the car, and I'll come out!"

She passes off the flyswatter to me, then hustles to gather the bags while calling out, "Keep hittin' him! Don't let him get up!"

My left arm's nowhere near as strong as my right, but I manage to get in a few good whacks on his leg and thigh while continuing to pummel his shoulder and the side of his head with the paper towels.

"Owww! Stop! Please stop!" he cries out from his fetal position on the floor, one hand protecting his elephant, the other his face. "I'm sorry. I'm so sorry!"

198

In all fairness, his cries sound genuine, and those tears are as real as any I've ever seen, but it's not like I'm hitting him with a brick—it's a flyswatter and a roll of Bounty, for god's sake. Any pain he's experiencing is very temporary. Unlike the pain he inflicted on Burty and sweet little Rosebud. That pain will last a lifetime.

I keep smacking until I hear the horn, then take off running through the house and across the street to my car. The back windows are tinted, so I can't see Burty and Rosebud, but I can see that Iris is in the front seat and has wisely already got the engine running.

"Everybody here?" I ask over winded breaths as I hop into the driver's seat and slam the door shut.

"Yeah, we're all here," Burty says nervously from the back seat. "But you better move it—he's comin'!"

I turn to my left and see a very haggard and angry-looking Wade staggering out of the house.

Shit.

"Go, go, go," Iris demands.

I ram the car into drive and hammer my foot on the gas, peeling out into the street just as Wade steps off the curb crying, "Burty! Burty, please!"

Heart racing, I glance in the side mirror and can't help but snort when I see him chasing after us, that big gray elephant flip-flopping like a piñata after a hearty blow.

When all this is said and done, I've *got* to ask Burty about that.

"Holy crap! You guys were amazin'," a breathless Burty says. "Y'all were like ninjas or somethin'."

"I don't know about ninjas, but oh my god! That was intense," I laugh, adrenaline still hammering through my veins. "I can't believe we took him down with paper towels and a flyswatter." I turn to Iris, expecting to see her laughing along with me, but she's not. She's just staring at me with a blank look in her eyes.

"What?" I ask.

She motions toward the back seat with a quick tip of the head.

My eyes narrow. I glance over my shoulder—

"Oh my god!" I shriek, my eyes snapping wide. Burty's got something in her arms all right, but it's not a baby.

"What's wrong?" Burty asks. "You're not allergic to dogs, are ya?"

Dog? *That's* a dog?

I blink hard, taking in the unsightly creature in front of me. In its better days, it probably passed for a terrier of some sort. But with more skin showing than fur, and those gigantic bulbous eyes taking up nearly its entire face, I'm thinking something in the troll family is probably more accurate.

"Jane?" Burty follows up, waiting for my answer.

"Uh . . . no. I'm not allergic." I quickly return my attention to the road. "I just wasn't expecting—"

"Yeah, I know," Burty mutters. "She's not the prettiest girl at the prom, but she's such a little love. Aren't ya, my little Rosie girl? Huh? You're Mama's little muffin, aren't ya? Yes, you are. You're my sweet little baby muffin girl."

"Can you believe this?" Iris mutters quietly, tone hinting of the same amusement I'm starting to feel myself.

Lip twitching, I turn to her and whisper, "It's a dog. We just beat the shit out of that guy over a fucking dog."

"A fucking *ugly* dog," she adds, biting back her own laugh.

Tears well in my eyes, and I quickly cover my mouth with my left hand while keeping my right on the wheel.

"You mind if I feed her in the car?" Burty, unaware of our budding hysterics, asks. "She's a little bit messy on account of her not havin' all her teeth."

I snort through my veil of fingers, quickly trying to cover it up as a cough. "Sure," I manage. "Whatever you need to do is fine."

I roll my lips down tight over my teeth and clamp down, willing myself not to burst out laughing. In my periphery I see that Iris has turned her body completely away from me so she's facing the window, trying to do the same.

With my eyes focused on the road, I hear Burty fumble around in the back seat, then the distinct sound of a metal tab being peeled off a can. A putrid smell fills the car, prompting me to gag. Yet another innate response I'm forced to stifle.

"Here you go, baby girl," Burty says in a loving voice. "Here's some yummy breakfast for you." My stomach turns as the dog attempts to eat the food. Without any teeth, there's a whole lot of licking and slushing going on. "There you go, sweetie," Burty continues. "Mean ole Daddy didn't give you any food, did he? It's okay now. Mama's here. Mama's here, and it's gonna be okay . . ."

Still facing away from me, Iris reaches across the console and grabs my arm, giving it a gentle squeeze. My heart swells with a burst of unexpected joy. It certainly wasn't the rescue mission we thought it was, but damn if it still doesn't feel good.

CHAPTER 16

I drop everyone off at Iris's cute little house on the Lower West Side (she generously offered to put up Burty and Rosebud until they can find other arrangements), then make my way back up to Mount Ivy. With all the day's excitement, I completely forgot about the conference call with the hospital fundraisers, but it was just an overview of what would be discussed at this Saturday's big committee luncheon anyway. *If* they even noticed I was absent from the call, they won't be upset; those ladies love me. And besides that, who could possibly argue that assisting in a dangerous hostage-rescue mission didn't trump a silly conference call?

I've got about an hour to kill before Avery gets out of school, so I hit the McDonald's drive-through and then camp out in the school parking lot until the bell rings. With my fries stationed in the center console's cup holder, I pull open my phone and start a new search—the first one in a long time that doesn't include the phrase *self-help* in its criteria.

"Oh my god!" I sputter over a fry as I take in the bevy of willie warmers (also known as cock socks, peter heaters, and woody hoodies) on the screen in front of me. Along with elephants, giraffes, and every other animal on the planet, there are also hot dogs (with condiments!), tuxedos, Minions . . . there's even a fully decorated Christmas tree. (What lucky lady wouldn't want to wake up next to *that* package Christmas morning?) I have no idea how sweet little Burty is involved in this industry, but given the number of Etsy retailers selling them, it seems like a pretty lucrative venture—

My phone rings, the screen indicating it's Avery's school calling. *Shit.*

My stomach sinks, and all the woody-hoodie amusement instantly drains from my body.

Dread building, I tap the screen.

"Hello?"

"Mrs. Osborne?"

"Yes."

"Hi, it's Ron English."

I swallow hard. Ron English. The principal.

"Yes. Hi, Mr. English. How are you?"

"I'm well, thanks, but Avery's not having such a good day."

"She's not?"

"No. Unfortunately, there was an incident with her and another student this afternoon. She's safe and healthy," he quickly adds, "but she's gotten herself into some trouble. Would you or your husband be able to come down to my office to discuss?"

"You need me to come in? This isn't something we can discuss over the phone?" Or through my car window, like Mrs. Garcia does?

"No, it's not. What Avery did warrants suspension from school. We're required to have an in-person meeting with the parents in cases like this."

Suspension?

My stomach twists, the french fries no longer sitting well.

"What, um—what did she do?"

"We can discuss that when you get here."

"Right. Okay. I'm on my way."

A furious and terrified wail rises in my lungs as I disconnect from the call. I fist my hands, burying my nails deep into my palms to keep from screaming, but the words echo inside my head just the same: *Why, Avery? Why are you doing this?*

~

Ron English is in his late fifties. He has wide-set eyes and one of those smiles that never reveals his teeth. He's the kind of man who wears T-shirts with the school mascot on them rather than suits and has goofy pictures of himself and his grandkids displayed on his desk. He's authoritative but not demanding, and carries himself with a kind of quiet confidence that suggests he's seen, heard, and done it all and that none of it fazes him—like a military vet, sans the hazard pay. Even now, as he recounts Avery's infractions, he's not at all rattled. I, on the other hand, am not faring so well.

I swallow through the boulder-size knot in my throat while blinking against the tears pricking my eyes.

". . . as far as pranks go, it was relatively harmless," Mr. English goes on. "Though a dozen rolls of wet paper towels certainly create a big mess."

I nod in agreement. Yes, I have no doubt that a dozen rolls of wet paper towels would create a big mess when balled up and used like grenades to decorate the faculty bathroom.

A *very* big mess!

Dammit, Avery.

"It doesn't appear there was any damage to the plumbing," he goes on. "But if there is, we'll be asking you and Caden's parents to pay for the repairs."

Freaking Caden Rodgers.

"Yes, of course." I sniffle. "We'll pay for any damage she caused."

"The suspension is just for one day," he continues, "and she'll be expected to stay up with her classwork so she can hit the ground running again on Wednesday—"

I continue nodding, my anger and desperation quickly threatening to make an appearance.

"All right then, all that's left is to get your signature on this form." He slides a piece of official-looking paper and a pen across the desk toward me. "It states that we met and discussed the incident and that you're in agreement with the resulting disciplinary action."

I scribble my name on the page, then slide it back to him.

Oh, yes. I am definitely in agreement with the resulting disciplinary action. I just wish I knew what motivated her to do anything that would earn her a disciplinary action in the first place.

"I'll have my assistant email you a copy of the form for your files." He stands and offers me his hand. "Thanks for coming in today."

"Thank you. And, again, I'm so sorry."

He sighs over a warm smile. "For what it's worth, I think Avery is a really good kid; she just seems to be having a hard time right now. Have there been any big changes in her life recently? Anything that might be causing her to act out?"

I shake my head. "Not that I can think of."

"And everything's okay at home?" He gives his cheek a little tap with his finger. It's one of those subtle gestures meant to call something to one's attention without actually telling them what it is—like when you touch your tooth to indicate a piece of lettuce is where it shouldn't be—but his hint is totally lost on me.

Confused, I raise my hand to my cheek and feel a little scratch across my skin. From where Wade hit me. *Crap.* I completely forgot.

I quickly shake my head. "Oh, no. This is nothing. It's—no. Everything's fine at home."

"You're sure?"

"Yes," I say emphatically. I appreciate his concern, but it's totally unwarranted. Dan may lie to me, but he'd never hit me. He's not *that* kind of asshole. "This is nothing to be worried about, I assure you."

"Okay." He easily accepts my response. "I just wanted to be sure. Sometimes kids respond to difficult situations with irrational behavior," he explains, and I can't help but nod. Kids aren't the only ones. "Thanks again for coming in. We look forward to seeing Avery back at school on Wednesday."

My limbs are shaking as I make my way out of the office. Anna, Mr. English's secretary, whom I know from PTA meetings, offers me a smile that I'm sure is meant to be kind and supportive but right now feels judgmental. I drop my head and make my way out into the hall, where Avery is waiting for me. She's sitting on one end of a long wooden bench—head hanging low, arms folded tight across her chest—and on the other end is a dark-haired boy who's mirroring her posture. This must be Caden.

Anger swells in my chest, forcing my teeth to slam together. "Let's go," I growl.

I hear the soles of her worn-out sneakers smacking the floor behind me, but I'm not about to slow my stride so we can walk together. I'm too mad to be that close to her right now. I'm not sure what I'd say, anyway. Probably something I'd regret. The silent treatment is definitely a better choice until I can clear my head a bit.

"Mom?" she calls out, but I continue to ignore her, pushing my way through the front door and storming down the front steps and into the parking lot. Fighting the flurry of four-letter words tickling my tongue, I climb into the car, wrap my hands tight around the steering wheel, and inhale a hot breath through my nose—

"Aren't you even going to ask me what happened?"

"*What happened?*" I whip my head toward her, enraged by her bold question. "Are you kidding me?" She blanches, startled by my aggression. "I know what happened, Avery. You vandalized the teachers' bathroom!"

"No, we didn't!" she cries. "It was just a prank. It was just paper towels!"

"Just a prank? Do you have any idea how much damage paper towels can do?" I scream back at her, not unaware of the irony of my question. "You could have ruined all the plumbing. It could cost thousands and thousands of dollars to repair that!"

"Well, I didn't know that!" she screams back at me. "All we wanted to do was play a prank. We weren't trying to break anything."

"Yeah, well, you're lucky you didn't! But prank or not, that was a stupid thing to do. What were you thinking?"

"We were thinking it would be funny!" she counters with way too much attitude.

I jerk back. "*Funny?* Okay. We'll see how funny it is tomorrow, when you're stuck in your bedroom all day with no TV, no phone, no iPad—"

"What am I supposed to do?"

"I don't know. Stare out the window? Count your toes? I don't really give a shit—"

The swear catches both of us by surprise, stinging my ears and prompting her eyes to snap wide. I rarely swear around Avery, and certainly never *at* her. My throat swells tight, breath shallowing in regret. In rage.

"You don't give a shit about anything anymore," she snips.

"*Excuse me?* I don't give a shit about anything? What's that supposed to mean?"

She levels me with a wicked look but doesn't answer the question.

"Tell me," I press. "What do you mean, I don't give a shit about anything anymore? You think I don't care about you ditching class, or spray-painting dugouts, or huffing fake cigarettes with some stupid boy?"

Her jaw twitches in obvious restraint before she rips her gaze away from me, grumbling, "Forget I said anything."

My instincts are to do exactly as she says because I can tell we're venturing into uncharted territory right now. Territory I'm not sure I'm ready to explore. But a little voice inside me—a voice that annoyingly sounds a lot like Officer Bates—is urging me to press on.

"No. I'm not going to forget it. Tell me what you meant."

She shakes her head.

"Avery, tell me," I demand, pressing my hand against her thigh. "I want to know."

She stays statue still for a long beat before she turns back to me, her big blue eyes glistening with tears.

My heart wrenches, my anger quickly giving way to concern.

"Honey, what? What is it?"

Gaze locked tight on mine, her sweet little chin starts to quiver, and she says, "Don't you even care that Daddy's cheating on you?"

Her question sucker punches me square in the gut.

"What? Honey, no. It's . . . your dad . . . he's not . . ." The lie dangles from my tongue like a worm on the hook—just waiting for her to take a nibble—but the desperation in her eyes won't allow me to cast the line any further, because she already knows the truth.

Dear god.

She knows the truth.

My ribs collapse against my lungs, smothering all the breath in my body.

She knows.

She knows!

I scrub a nervous hand across my forehead, my vision now blurring with tears. I drop my head, though I can still feel her gaze locked in on me, waiting for an answer. Waiting for me to tell her that she's right. That her dad—the man she holds up on the highest pedestal—is a cheater and a liar.

I pinch my eyes shut, agonized by the rawness of this moment. I knew it would happen at some point, but I never imagined it like this. Somehow, I thought I'd be prepared. That I'd be calm and rational and able to deliver the devastating news with a sense of stability and reassurance. The way a mother *should* deliver this kind of news. Instead I'm a terrified mess, sitting here in the school parking lot without a clue how to respond to her, a cup of french fries growing cold between us.

I swallow against the ache building in my throat and, while slowly reopening my eyes, admit that what she's saying is true. "Yes, honey. Of course I care."

"Then why aren't you doing anything?" she pleads, her precious voice quaking with emotion. "Why don't you tell him to stop?"

Though naive, her question is still legitimate, and pierces my soul like a dagger. I knuckle back a tear and say, "It's . . . it's not that easy. It's very complicated—"

"How is that complicated? You just tell him not to do it."

Humility swells inside me, prompting me to drop my head again.

If only it *were* that easy . . .

"Do you know who she is?"

She.

Oh, Avery . . .

I turn toward her. The betrayal in her eyes, so reminiscent of my own, nearly breaks me.

"How did you even find out about this?" I ask, intentionally evading her question.

"I heard him talking to her on the phone in the garage." She sniffs while scrubbing away a tear with the heel of her palm. "He told her he loved her, and he couldn't wait to see her." She hangs her head. "I knew it wasn't you because you were in the kitchen making dinner. He didn't know I was there."

My heart wrenches at her obvious pain, while a fresh surge of anger starts seeping through my veins.

Damn you, Dan!

Look what you're doing to her!

Look what you've done to our daughter!

"So, do you?" she goes on. "Do you know who she is?"

The mom of one of Avery's closest friends recently got divorced and remarried the dad of another close friend (a scandal that kept the PTA humming for more than a few months), so it makes sense that she'd be hyperfocused on the players involved. I shake my head while gently swiping back a strand of tear-soaked hair from her cheek. "No, honey. I don't know who it is."

I hate the idea of lying to her, but revealing Dan's truth to Avery isn't my job; that's all on him.

"How long have you known?" I ask.

"Awhile," she says over another sniffle. "Since you guys got back from your trip to Denver."

I fist my free hand at my side, tortured by her response.

She's known almost as long as I have.

This poor, sweet child has been suffering as long as me. No wonder she's been acting out in school. It's a miracle she didn't earn a suspension weeks ago.

"I'm so sorry, honey," I say, offering up a broken smile. "It's not fair that you had to know that whole time—that you didn't have anyone to talk to about it. I imagine that's been pretty scary, huh?"

She drops her head.

"And maybe makes you a little mad?"

"Yeah," she whispers.

I drag my hand down the length of her hair to her back so I can rub it like I did when she was little. "Do you sometimes feel like you need to get some of the *mad* out by doing kind of crazy things?"

She glances up. The nervous look on her face assures me of what I suspected: the apple—er, *orange*—doesn't fall far from the tree.

"It's okay," I say with an understanding nod.

Fresh tears pool in her eyes, and she repositions herself so she's facing me head-on. "I'm sorry, Mom," she sputters. "I don't mean to do all this bad stuff; I just—I get so mad, and I don't know what else to do—"

She throws herself across the center console and into my arms, burrowing her face in my chest like she did as a baby. I wrap my arms tight around her narrow frame, crying, as I pull her closer to me, desperately wishing I could take away her pain. That I could give her back the life she deserves, but I can't do that. All I can say is, "I know, baby. I know you didn't mean to do it. It's okay. It's going to be okay. We'll find a different way for you to work through all that mad and hurt. It's going to be okay . . ."

We sit like that for a few minutes—crying and holding each other—before she says, "Does Auntie J know?"

I shake my head. "No, honey. Nobody else knows. And they can't, okay? We need to keep this just between us for now."

She nods. "I won't say anything."

Considering she's known for almost three months and is just now telling me, I don't doubt her sincerity.

"Are you going to get divorced?"

I wince, detesting the sound of those words coming from her lips.

"I don't know, babe. We haven't figured out what we're going to do yet. But whatever happens, we still love you just the same. You remember that, okay?" I stroke her feverish cheek, hoping it offers some sense of security. "You are the best, most important person in the world to me, and your dad, and no matter if we're married or not, that's never going to change, you understand?"

Leaning into my palm, she closes her eyes and, over a shuddery breath, says, "Don't tell him I know, okay?"

"Oh, sweetie." I pull back from her, shaking my head. "We need to tell him—"

"I know we do. I just . . ." She sighs, a heavier-sounding sigh than any twelve-year-old should ever have to release. "Can we just wait a little while? I've got a game on Saturday, and we're supposed to do banana splits and watch the Bulls on Sunday afternoon . . ."

I'm nodding in concession before the words even form on my tongue.

She wants to hang on to her safe and stable life—or at least the life she thought it was—for as long as she can.

I certainly can't blame her for that.

~

Avery's at the kitchen table doing homework while I'm wiping down the counters. Given this afternoon's developments, I decided that she should skip soccer practice and her piano lesson so we could go out for ice cream. Double scoops certainly didn't solve our problems, but they definitely eased them, for a while anyway.

At first glance, the house appears calm and restful. Soft music wafting through the speakers, the aroma of the frozen pizza we baked for dinner still tickling our noses. But if you take a closer look, you'll pick up on the heaviness in the air—the unease that comes from facing Dan for the first time, now that *we're* the ones sharing a secret.

"He's here," Avery croaks, her youthful ears tuning into the sound of the front door.

I inhale a deep breath. "Okay. Don't worry."

"What are you going to tell him?"

"Nothing," I say. "I told you we could wait a little while before we told him you knew."

"No, I mean about my suspension."

My shoulders sag. With all the "cheating father" discussion, I completely forgot about the stupid suspension. I sigh. "I'm going to have to tell him."

"Mom, no!" She pushes herself to standing, a desperate look on her face. "Please, don't say anything."

"Honey, he's still your dad. He needs to know what's going on at school. Besides, he's going to know something's up when you're home all day tomorrow."

"But he'll get mad at me. He'll take away the Bulls game."

Given her dreadful day, and her obvious distress now, I'd really like to comply, but . . . she *did* earn herself a suspension from school, and if some residual punishments follow, I'm not sure that's a bad thing.

"Mom, *please*—"

"Jane?" Dan suddenly calls from inside the house, interrupting Avery's plea.

She casts me a wary glance while I call back to him, "Yeah?"

"Can I talk to you for a minute, please!"

Even though he uses the word *please*, there's nothing remotely polite about his request.

"Be right there!" I call back to him.

"Mom . . ." Avery offers me one last pleading glance as I toss the dish towel into the sink and make my way to the laundry room, where Dan is waiting for me, jaw set, a steely look in his eyes.

"What the hell happened today?" he grouses, his tone intentionally low.

"What—uh, what do you mean?" My car isn't bugged, is it? There's no way he could have heard our conversation—

"With the fundraisers," he clarifies. "Jackie Harriman stopped by my office this afternoon and told me you weren't on the conference call. Why weren't you on the call?"

The fundraising conference call.

I exhale a relieved breath.

"Something came up with a friend of mine from the Chicago class," I start to say. "She needed my help—"

"You can't just blow those meetings off, Jane," he interrupts me, brows cinching angrily above his eyes. "Especially now, with everything that's going on with the gala. More than ever, you have to participate."

"I know," I grunt, quickly becoming annoyed with his paternal tone. I'm your wife, not your child! "I didn't just blow it off. Something really important came up—"

"What could possibly be more important than my career? Are you forgetting that everything I've worked so hard for hinges on whether or not we get that money from the Hoffstras?"

"Of course I haven't forgotten," I snap back, his arrogance grating my nerves. "But the world doesn't stop for a meeting, Dan. Someone needed my help today, so I helped her. I'm sorry that I missed the meeting, but I had to be somewhere else just then. Missing one meeting isn't the end of the freaking world."

His jaw twitches beneath my heated response. It's been a long time since I've pushed back at him.

"You *have* to be at the luncheon on Saturday," he says over a pointed look. "I don't care what kind of trouble your friends get into. You have to be there."

"I'm aware, Dan. I will be there."

He stares at me for a long, uncomfortable beat before he shakes his head and starts heading toward the kitchen.

"Be extra nice to Avery," I instruct as he passes by me. "She's having a bad day."

"Why? What happened?"

I briefly consider telling him the truth but quickly determine that after his *very* abrupt greeting, a little defiance is a much better response. I thrust my chin up and say, "She's not feeling well. It's probably nothing, but I'm going to keep her home from school tomorrow, just to be safe."

His anger gives way to a more concerned expression as he says, "Okay," then resumes his entrance into the house, calling out to Avery, "Hey, kiddo. I hear you're taking a sick day tomorrow. What's going on?"

It's definitely a poor parenting decision on my part—forcing my child to lie about her health—but I have no doubt Avery will jump at the opportunity. Lord knows the girl can sell a story when she wants to.

I make my way back into the house—acknowledging an appreciative glance from Avery as I pass through the kitchen, Dan sitting attentively at her side—then sneak down the hall and into Dan's office. He may not think helping a friend takes precedence over work, but I sure do . . . and sweet Burty still needs my help.

I round the big mahogany desk, pull open the bottom drawer, and withdraw a sheet of his letterhead. It's outdated, still adorned with the hospital's old logo with the embossed tree on the top, but it should do the job just fine.

Thank you, Dr. Osborne. You have no idea how helpful you've been.

CHAPTER 17

To whom it may concern,
   This letter serves as confirmation that Burty Bedford was seen in my office on Monday, November 29. Please excuse her absence.

Daniel A. Osborne, MD

It's about as simple as excuse notes go—and the signature doesn't come close to Dan's—but it will work.

"Who in thunder is Daniel A. Osborne?" Burty asks.

"Don't . . . worry about that . . . now," I manage over winded breaths. I had to sprint from the car to pass off the letter before class started. The plan was for Burty and Iris to meet me in the parking lot fifteen minutes ago, but a bad accident on the highway delayed me. And now we've got only a minute until class starts. "Just . . . give it to Bates," I pant, hinging forward at the waist to catch my breath. "It'll work."

"But I didn't see no doctor," she goes on, voice quaking with uncertainty. "That'd be a lie. And I don't like the idea of lyin'."

"Would you really rather tell her the truth in front of everybody?" Iris counters. "Do you want all of those women to know what you've been going through?"

"A'course not. That's my own personal, private business." And mine. And Iris's. And anyone within eyeshot of the elephant stampeding down the road. "But what if she calls this Dr. Osborne and asks him about me? Or what if she goes to his office to question him?" I glance up and see that her eyes are now wide, darting back and forth between Iris and me. "She's a cop, ya know? She's used to investigatin' things."

"She's not going to show up at anybody's office or make any phone calls," I assure her as I stand back up, oxygen finally returning to my lungs. "All she wants is a piece of paper that says you saw a doctor, and that's what you have. Now get in there and give it to her." I motion to the classroom door behind her.

"But—"

"Give her the note." Iris cuts her off with a stern look. "Even if you tell her the truth, there's no guarantee that she'll let you stay in the class. And if you don't finish the class, you'll get fined and might even end up doing some jail time. That means you'd have to leave Rosie. You don't want that to happen, do you?"

She gasps. "Lord no! I'd never leave my little girl."

"Okay then," Iris goes on. "Get in there, hand her the note, and be done with it. Go on."

With the threat of her *child* on the line, Burty accepts her instruction and heads through the door.

"You know forgery is a felony in some states," Iris snuffs under her breath.

I grin. "Only if you get caught."

And even if I do, Dan would never press charges. Not with what I have on him . . .

As instructed, Burty marches straight up to where Bates is standing at her little podium and offers her the note. "Sorry I missed class on Monday. I was feelin' real sick."

"Yeah . . . uh, that's okay," Bates mutters, not taking or even glancing at the paper. Her attention is so focused on the action going on in the corner of the room I'm surprised she even realized Burty was talking to her.

That was easy . . .

"What's wrong with Maya?" Burty asks no one in particular.

Maya, who usually sits next to me, is standing on the far side of the room facing the window, while Donna and Angel stand on either side of her; Donna is stroking her back in that comforting, maternal way I know so well.

"Her *abuela* died," Lina grunts from her usual seat.

"Aww . . ." Burty's bottom lip rolls out into a pout.

"*Abuela*'s not Spanish for *cat*, is it?" Iris mutters to me.

I fight a smile while shaking my head. "No. It means *grandmother*."

Iris winces. "That's too bad."

I nod. Yeah, that is too bad.

"Take your seats," Bates orders, her attention still focused intently on Maya.

Angel and Donna abandon their posts at Maya's side, joining the rest of us as we settle into the chairs.

My stomach twists nervously as I flip open my journal and lay it across my lap for inspection. I kept my response intentionally vague, but it's also painfully true. I wrote it Monday night, right after I stole the letterhead from Dan's office. I hadn't planned on being so honest, but something deep down inside begged me to do it. Like somehow my soul knew that getting at least *some* of those feelings out of my head—out of my heart—might make me feel a little better. And it did. But now all the good stuff is gone, and all I'm left feeling is . . . exposed.

THE HARDEST THING I DID THIS WEEK WAS . . .

Admit to my daughter that the perfect life she thought she had—the life she deserves—isn't real. And that more than any-thing I want to fix it for her, but I don't know how.

217

Bates huddles up in the corner with Maya for a few minutes before she makes her way back to her podium. "Ladies, we're going to do things a little different today. Maya's asked if she can talk to us about her grandmother, who passed away on Tuesday. Anybody got a problem with that?"

Despite the question mark trailing her words, Bates isn't really asking for our approval. Not that any of us would oppose the idea if she were. It's obvious by the mascara tears staining Maya's cheeks that she's having a hard time; it makes sense that she'd want to talk through some of her pain. I know I would . . . if I had people I could talk to.

"All right, then," Bates goes on. "Close your journals and give Maya your attention."

Despite my empathy for Maya's heartache—and my utter surprise at Bates's compassion—I'd swear I can hear a chorus of angels singing right now. I slam my notebook shut and heave a deep breath as I settle into my seat.

May you rest in peace, Abuela.

And take my journal entry with you . . .

~

"*Now* will you tell me who this Dr. Osborne is?" Burty says impatiently.

She's asked this question at least a dozen times since we were excused from class and made the three-block walk over here to Aunt B's Diner: a hole-in-the-wall place with plastic menus and cracked Formica countertops. Given its proximity to the police station, I'm not surprised that it's a hot spot for cops—there are three uniformed officers sitting at the counter to my right—but what did catch me off guard is how good their dessert is. Iris said it had won some local awards, but this peach cobbler deserves a freaking Oscar. I'm already working on my second slice.

"Come on, please?" Burty prods.

The thought of telling them anything about Dan sours the deca-
dent taste in my mouth.

Damn you, Dan.

You literally ruin everything!

I set the fork down and sigh. "Dr. Osborne is my husband."

"You're married to a doctor?" Burty chirps, eyes and jaw gaping in
wonder. I nod while casting a quick glance across the booth toward Iris.
She smirks from behind the lip of her coffee cup. "But your last name
is Holliday, isn't it? Isn't that why Bates calls you that?"

"Holliday is my maiden name. I've just been using that lately
because . . . well . . . it's a long story"—*that you're never going to hear*—
"but my married name is Osborne. Dan is my husband."

"Wow, a doctor. That's so excitin'! And he was okay writin' me an
excuse, even though he didn't see me?"

I hate the idea of lying to Burty—especially after what she's been
through this week—but knowing the truth would just upset her.
Besides, if Dan can't be a good guy in real life, he might as well be one
in make-believe.

"Yep. I told him about what happened, and he was more than
happy to help."

"Aww. What a sweetheart," Burty coos. "You sure are lucky to have
such a nice guy like that."

I force a smile.

Yeah, I'm lucky, all right.

I pick up my fork and start stabbing at a peach.

I'm real lucky . . .

"So that was quite a life Maya's grandmother lived, wasn't it?"
Iris says.

"It really was," I say, grateful for the change in subject.

Maya shared the beautiful and inspiring story of her grandmother,
Rosabel, who emigrated from El Salvador when she was just nine years
old. The woman was a powerhouse who juggled two jobs while she

earned her high school diploma, then went on to cosmetology school and eventually opened her own hair salon on the southwest side of Chicago, where she worked until the day she died. Along with her thriving career, she enjoyed an enviable sixty-three-year marriage to her high school sweetheart, Carlos, and had nine children (all daughters), twenty-one grandchildren, and six great-grandchildren. Talk about leaving behind a legacy.

"I think it was real good of Officer Bates to let her talk through all her feelin's," Burty says while loading up her fork with another hunk of pie. She's on her third slice of cherry. I don't even like cherries, and my mouth is watering just looking at it.

"I have to admit I was a little surprised by that," Iris says. "I was starting to wonder if there was a heart under all that uniform."

"You and me both." I chuckle, then pose a concern that crossed my mind during class. "You don't think Maya would use again, do you? As a way to cope with all of this?"

"What do you mean, use?" Burty says.

"You mean drugs?" Iris asks.

Their questions give me pause. I slowly set down my fork, eyeing both of them. "Well . . . yeah. She told us she was charged with possession of heroin."

Iris's brows furrow while Burty cries, *"Maya did heroin?"*

She says it loud enough that one of the cops at the counter turns and looks at us. I flash him my best nothing-to-see-here smile, then drop my head and my voice and reply, "Yeah, don't you remember on the first day, when Bates made us all stand up and say what we were charged with . . ."

"Oh, right." Iris starts to nod, recognition setting in. "Now I remember. She was the first one to talk, wasn't she?" I nod. "And there was that day in class when she said she only liked hanging out with her girlfriend when she was high. Poor kid."

"I can't believe Maya used heroin," Burty goes on, shaking her head in disbelief. "She seems so sweet and innocent."

"I know," I say. "Same with Angel. She was charged with possession of meth."

"*Shut up!*" Burty smacks the table, forcing the coffee cups to rattle in their saucers. "Angel too? I never woulda guessed that. She's so funny and is always talkin' about her mama and her baby brother. What about Donna?" Her voice suddenly takes on a concerned tone. "She's got a grandbaby. Please don't tell me she was doin' drugs too."

"No." I shake my head. "But Lina did—"

"It was crank, wasn't it?" Iris offers up, proving I'm not the only one who was paying attention that day.

I nod. "Yep. And assault."

"*Assault?*" Burty cries, palm pressed to her forehead in shock. "God bless America. That's terrifyin'!" I shift against the vinyl seat beneath me. Yes, Burty, being charged with assault *is* terrifying. "What do you think she did?"

"Probably beat up a Girl Scout for ringing the doorbell too loud," Iris mutters over a mouthful of pumpkin pie.

I burst out laughing. Guess I'm not the only one who thinks Lina is mean and scary.

"So, I guess y'all remember what I did, too, huh?" Burty asks sheepishly, a flush of pink coloring her cheeks.

Indecent exposure.

I remember it well.

"Yeah, I remember," Iris says to her. "But I bet you can't guess mine."

The redirect is obvious to me—a thoughtful gesture meant to ease Burty's embarrassment—but she doesn't notice.

Her blue eyes grow wide, and she shakes her head. "I got no clue. Jane?" She turns to me. "Do you remember what Iris got charged with?"

My chest tightens beneath Burty's question. When I met Iris a few weeks ago, she was just a stranger I was forced to sit next to: a stranger I defined by the charge filed against her. But now she's . . . well, now that I'm getting to know her . . . just the thought of pointing it out feels sort of . . .

"It was . . . petty theft, right?"

Iris rolls her eyes, aware that I'm playing dumb, while Burty gasps and says, "You stole somethin'?"

"I sure did," Iris admits over a chagrined smile. "Five fifty-milligram doses of Victonel."

"Victonel? What's that?" Burty asks, swiping the question straight from my lips.

"It's the medication my son takes to treat his prediabetes."

Iris has a son.

She's a nurse, and she has a son.

So much more than a petty thief.

"What'd you do, break into a Rite Aid?" Burty questions.

Iris chuckles. "No. Nothing like that. They were samples one of the pharmaceutical reps dropped off at the clinic a few weeks before." She inhales a long breath through her nose while settling deeper into the corner of the booth as she starts to explain. "Damon, my son, goes to college upstate and uses the student insurance they have—it's cheaper than keeping him on mine," she adds, looking directly at me. I nod. I get it. Insurance is expensive! "But there was some kind of hiccup with his coverage, so he couldn't get his prescription refilled," she goes on. "We tried calling his doctor, but his office was closed while he was on vacation, and the answering service wasn't very helpful—"

"Someone should have been covering his patient load," I interject.

"Well, apparently there was, but the doctor who was supposed to be covering contracted some weird virus and ended up in the hospital for like a month or something. I don't know exactly what happened"—she tosses a hand through the air—"but at the end of the day, nobody called us back."

I shake my head, annoyed. He may be an asshole, but Dan would never leave his patients unattended.

"Anyway, Damon had enough to get him through until a few days before the doctor was due back, but he was really scared about skipping any doses, especially being so far away from home . . ."

And now I'm nodding. Of course he was scared. Poor baby.

"So, I was at the clinic late one night and saw them sitting there in the cupboard with about a hundred other samples, and I just decided to take them." Her gaze slowly drifts down to her coffee cup. She drags her red-tipped finger along its lip and almost absently says, "The doctor gives us samples all the time. Since they're free, he just passes them out without much thought, but apparently this medication was different. They keep track of it and report into the pharmaceutical company with patient feedback or something. The office manager realized they were missing the very next day and started questioning everybody on staff. I came clean right away, but it didn't matter. The clinic has a zero-tolerance policy when it comes to stealing medication. They had no choice but to fire me."

"Oh, Iris . . . ," I mutter, my shoulders slumping sympathetically.

"Nah, don't feel sorry for me." She shakes her head firmly. "It was wrong. I deserved everything I got. And they actually cut me a break, because technically they could have charged me with a felony, but instead they just called it petty theft, so I got off with a misdemeanor."

"Does your son know what happened?" I ask.

"Huh-uh. He'd kill me. Especially after the way I've been riding him his whole life about doing the right thing and making a difference in the world. Some difference I made," she groans. "That was just flat-out stupid. I knew I shouldn't have done it, but at the time I really didn't see another way."

My heart twists at her obvious pain, but more so at the unease that's swelling in my chest. Not being able to provide for Avery is my greatest fear, and unlike Iris, I'm not so sure I'd be brave enough to take matters into my own hands to get it done.

I take a long drink of coffee, then ask hopefully, "Have you found another job?"

"Just temp work. All the hospitals and clinics around here are tight on money these days. Nobody's hiring nurses."

I blow out a frustrated breath. Chicago hospitals aren't the only ones short on money.

"Well, I think you did the right thing," Burty says over a firm nod. "It's not like you were stealin' just to be bad. You were doin' it to help yer son. And a good mom will do anything for her kid."

It's obvious that Burty's comparing Iris's situation to that of her and Rosebud, and despite the sincerity of her words, I can't help but laugh a little. She sure does love that ugly dog.

"What about you, Jane?" Burty suddenly shifts her attention to me. "What were you charged with?"

Her question slams into me as gently as a brick to the face. My eyes snap wide and I reel back, totally unprepared for how to answer her, which is completely ridiculous. We've just spent the last ten minutes talking about everyone's charges—a topic *I* stupidly brought up—so it only makes sense the tables would turn back on me.

My breath suddenly catches, though it's got nothing to do with the fear rising inside me. It's because over Burty's shoulder, I see that Chavez has just walked into the diner. And today he's not wearing his usual jeans and thermal combo; he's donned a charcoal suit that hugs every inch of his muscly frame so well Calvin Klein must have sewn him into it with his own hands.

A flutter of frustrating excitement starts rippling through my lungs.
Good grief, he is pretty—

"Oh Lordy, should I not have asked you that?" Burty suddenly reaches across the table and grabs my hand, stealing my attention.

I blink hard. "What?"

"That question. It was too personal, right?"

She clearly misread my reaction—at least the gasping part—and despite her concern, my gaze darts right back to Chavez. He's standing at the register near the front door, like he's waiting for someone.

He casts a lazy glance my way, his gaze sweeping over me, only to dart right back as he recognizes me. A true double take. My heart stammers as his dark eyes lock in on mine and his ever-present smirk slides into a warm smile.

A senseless giggle rises in my chest.

"I don't think your question is the problem, Burty," Iris chides, her neck craned over her shoulder, following my gaze.

"Huh? What do you mean?" With all the subtlety of a semi, Burty whips her head around to see what—or, rather, *who*—we're looking at.

"Son of a biscuit!" she gasps, then quickly turns back toward the table. "That's that detective guy—"

"Mmm. Yes, it is," Iris growls.

"He works with Bates," she goes on. "He must be here checkin' up on me about that note. I told y'all it was a bad idea." She braves another peek over her shoulder, then just as quickly turns back around. "Look at the way he's starin' at me. He's laughin'. He thinks this is funny. I told y'all I was gonna get caught!"

I redirect my gaze from Chavez to Burty, eager to address her misdirected panic, but Iris beats me to it, saying, "Relax, girl. He's just picking up some food."

In unison, both Burty and I turn back to Chavez. Iris is right. There's a waitress at the register now who's going over the contents of several Styrofoam to-go boxes with him.

"Well, then why was he starin' at me like that?" Burty asks.

Iris swats her arm. "He wasn't staring at *you*, you goof—he was staring at Jane."

"Jane?" She faces me again, blonde brows furrowing. "Why would he be starin' at Jane?"

Iris turns back to the table, a playful smirk on her face. "'Cause he's sweet on her."

My jaw drops.

Iris!

"He likes you?" Burty asks me.

Once again, she's just landed me with a question I have no idea how to answer. I shift against the seat. Since when is this booth made of razor blades?

"Does he?" she presses.

My gaze instinctively darts back to Chavez, as if he can somehow provide an answer that will satisfy Burty's curiosity, but he doesn't need to, even if he could. The heat that's erupting across my cheeks answers the question loud and clear.

"He does," she snips. "And you like him too."

There's a tangible disappointment dragging down Burty's statement that reclaims my attention. My heart twists when I see the disapproval filling her eyes. It's the same look she had when we rescued her on Monday: that gut-wrenching combination of anger, sadness, and betrayal.

She thinks I'm a cheater.

Just like Wade.

Just like Dan.

I shake my head while raising my hands in retreat. "No, it's not like that. It's not what you think—"

"Then what is it?" She crosses her arms over her chest.

I swallow hard beneath her accusing glare, then cast a desperate glance toward Iris. She offers me a little smile in return but understandably can't supply any backup, because as far as she knows, I *could* be just like Wade, or Dan, because neither woman knows the truth . . .

Shit.

Neither of them has any reason to believe I'm not like Dan.

Dread settles on my lungs like a wet blanket, forcing me to close my eyes and inhale a shuddery breath.

I don't want to do this.

I don't want to tell them—

Or . . . maybe I do?

Am I really going to do this?

"You okay, Jane?" Iris asks.

"Yeah, I just, um . . ." I inhale several deep, shuddery breaths, willing Dr. Deedee's soothing voice to once again penetrate my quickly building fear.

I am strong. I am capable. I can do anything I set my mind to . . .

I slowly reopen my eyes, grateful to see Chavez walking out of the diner with his to-go orders in hand.

"Jane?" Iris prompts.

I keep my gaze fixed on the door for a long beat—tears pricking my eyes, heart threatening to beat out of my chest—before I finally return my attention to them.

Burty gasps. "Oh Lordy, you're cryin'—"

"No, it's okay." I knuckle back some of the moisture from my eyes. *You can do this, Jane. You can do this.* "I'm okay. I just, um . . ." I exhale a deep breath, then look directly at Burty and almost robotically say, "I'm not cheating on my husband. He's the one cheating on me—"

"No!" she gasps, and Iris moans, "Oh, no . . ."

"—and it's with another man."

"What?" Burty's eyes practically pop out of their sockets, and despite the topic, I can't help but smile a little. My ego needed a gut reaction like that.

"My husband told me a couple of months ago that he was gay. He's been cheating on me for our entire marriage. Almost eighteen years."

"Oh god. You're kidding me," Iris groans, for once looking rattled by her surroundings.

I shake my head. Definitely not kidding.

"Aww, Jane . . ." Still looking dumbfounded, Burty reaches across the table and lays her hand on top of mine.

"Does your daughter know?" Iris asks.

I cast her a weary glance as I nod my response.

Burty makes a little whimpering sound.

"It's so hard when the kids are involved," Iris says. "On one hand, you want to protect them from everything—try to keep things as normal as possible—but on the other, you know you're not doing them any favors by letting them see you keep being taken advantage of. Kids don't want to see their moms being abused; they want to see them being strong and confident. That's how we actually protect them. But that's hard to do when you're feeling worthless. It's about the worst situation a woman can be in."

I nod again, gobsmacked by how accurately she just conveyed what I've been trying to wrap my brain around for the last two months.

"You got that," Burty adds in more of her misguided solidarity.

"So, what happens now?" Iris asks. And even though she doesn't say the word *divorce*, I know she's thinking it.

Or maybe that's just me . . .

I sigh. "I don't know. For the time being, I'm not supposed to say anything to anybody. We have to act like everything's perfectly normal between us."

"Come again?" Iris says.

I drop my head a little. "There's a lot more at stake than just my marriage."

I tell them all about Dan's job, the situation at the hospital, and how the ultra-conservative Hoffstras are the ones holding the purse strings to my entire family's future. Iris nods a lot—her own life experiences undoubtedly giving her insights as to where I'm coming from—while Burty just sort of stares at me, offering up the occasional "Lordy, Lordy" and other southern sentiments that suggest she's on my side, even though she can't necessarily relate. Neither offers a solution to my problems—not that there are any to be had—but both provide me more encouragement than I've felt in a very, very long time.

And for the first time since that fateful trip to Denver, I feel like I can breathe.

"Well, you sure seem like you're handlin' it good," Burty says when I finally finish. "If I was in yer shoes, I'd be holed up in a ball somewhere."

Despite the tears still pooling in my eyes, I bark out a laugh. "Are you kidding? I had a breakdown over all of this—in the middle of a grocery store parking lot!"

Her eyes snap wide. "You did?"

"Oh yeah. I completely lost my mind and started attacking a woman with oranges. That's why I got arrested."

"No way." Iris snorts.

"No, it's true," I say, sickeningly delighted by the surprised look on her face. "I chucked like a dozen oranges at that poor woman—"

"Why? What'd she do?" Burty cuts me off, while Iris starts to laugh. A deep, rumbly sound from way down in the pit of her belly that brings a painfully big smile to my own lips.

"She left her shopping cart in the middle of the parking lot—"

"Ugh, I hate when people do that," Burty grumbles.

"Well, first she bought way more than fifteen items," I say, correcting myself as my own amusement starts rising to the surface, memories of that night now spiraling through my mind. "But then . . . yeah, she left her cart right there next to her car, and I just sort of . . . snapped. I was screaming all kinds of horrible things at her and just throwing orange after orange at her car—"

"Oh my god, Jane!" Burty slaps her hand over her mouth, her childlike giggle seeping out from between her fingers. And now I can't help but laugh too. With a little perspective, and the right audience, it's actually pretty funny.

"So that explains the assault charge," Iris manages over sputtery breaths. "But if memory serves, you were also charged with possession—"

Burty gasps. "You do drugs too?"

From the corner of my eye, I see the same cop who eyed us earlier glance our way again, but now I'm laughing too hard to care what he thinks.

I shake my head and say, "No! Not intentionally. That night after I threw the oranges, I got back into my car and thought I was taking a Zoloft that I took from a friend, but it actually turned out to be ecstasy—"

"Shut up!" Burty shrieks.

"Yeah! I was stoned out of my mind," I go on, raking an embarrassed hand through my hair. "That's when I got arrested. The cops found me all doped up in the parking lot, licking windows and making up stupid songs . . ."

Iris is hunched up in the corner of the booth, cackling, while Burty's saying, "Lordy be, that's so embarrassin'!"

"Well, at the time I didn't know what was going on," I confess over a hearty snort, happy tears quickly replacing the scared ones of just moments ago. "But the next day was pretty bad. Especially when I realized that Chavez was the officer who arrested me."

"Oh girl." Iris comes up for air, eyes wide in disbelief. "Are you kidding me? *That's* how you guys met?"

"No. Actually, we know each other from high school. It was just a random coincidence that he was there that night."

Amusement giving way to disbelief, Iris smacks the table, saying, "Are you serious?"

"Yeah. Crazy, right?"

"Well, it definitely explains all the Bambi eyes." She smirks while batting her lashes dramatically. "What, did you two used to go out or something?"

"No." I drop my gaze a bit. "But he did tell me that he had a crush on me back in the day."

"Aww. That's so sweet." Burty presses a palm to her chest, prompting a swell of embarrassment to flood my cheeks.

"No, no, no." I shake my head. "Like I said, there's nothing going on with us. We've just been hanging out a little. Turns out we've got some . . . mutual interests." Like beating the shit out of cars. And eating pie. "We're just friends."

Iris levels me with a skeptical look.

"Well, that's a waste," Burty groans. "He's hotter than a two-dollar pistol, and Lord knows you've earned some fun, considerin' what your husband's been up to."

"She's right, you know," Iris jumps in. "Good ole Dr. Osborne shouldn't be the only one enjoying himself."

My blush deepens as an image of Chavez suddenly comes to mind. The same image I've regrettably called upon more than a few times in the last week. How sexy he looked underneath the parking lights at the impound lot. Despite the layers of clothes, they somehow still silhouetted his frame so perfectly. It was like I could see *all* his muscles—

Another frustrating flutter erupts in my chest, startling me back to the present. I quickly right my thoughts with a shake of the head. "Okay, we're done talking about me now. Somebody else's turn." I grab my fork, scoop up an obnoxiously big hunk of cobbler, and shove it in my mouth as if solidifying my statement. Jane is officially out of the hot seat.

Iris rolls her eyes at my obvious deflection while Burty says, "Well, I guess that means it's my turn."

"Oh, no, Burty—" Still chewing, I raise my fork to stop her. "I didn't mean you had to share anything."

"No, it's okay. Y'all shared your stories, so it's only fair I go next."

"Well, do tell then." Iris grins while helping herself to another bite of pie. "What did Burty Bedford do to get herself arrested for indecent exposure?"

Burty places both her palms flat on the table like she's bracing herself, then inhales a deep breath and starts. "All right, so, I'm not sure if y'all noticed it the other day, but Wade was wearin' this little elephant over his boy parts—"

I choke over the bite in my mouth.

Iris clears her throat, no doubt suffering from the same shock as me.

"Um, yeah." She winces against the pie that clearly went down her throat too soon. "Now that you mention it, I guess we did notice that. Jane, do you remember the, um . . . elephant covering?"

She launches an amused glance my way, and despite the laugh that's actively turning in my stomach, I somehow maintain my composure. I swallow hard against the half-chewed bite in my mouth, then over a slow nod say, "Oh, right. Yeah. I vaguely remember an elephant."

"Okay, well, that's called a willie warmer," Burty goes on, oblivious to our rising hysteria. "We got a whole online business where we sell those. B&W's Willies, that's what it's called. And we sell all kinds of 'em. Animals, superheroes, cars, fruit . . ." She's using her fingers to count off her inventory while horrifying visuals start infecting my brain. I quickly roll my lips over my teeth and clamp down to keep from laughing at what she obviously takes so seriously. "You name it, I can make it," she goes on. "My granny taught me how to knit and crochet when I was real little. I can make anything—"

"I bet you can," Iris mumbles against her fist. It's pressed firmly against her lips and acting as a levee to keep her own amusement secured, though based on the way her shoulders are shaking, I don't think it's going to hold up for long.

My chest starts to shudder as my own laugh threatens to give way. I quickly drop my attention away from Iris and fix it on the golden flecks adorning the laminate tabletop.

"So, anyway," Burty goes on. "A couple a months ago, we was workin' on this new product for our ladies' line, and we needed to get some pictures of it for the website. So, we went out to this kinda forest area near our house where the lightin' is real good and there are all these really pretty trees. It's where we take all our pictures," she adds, as if that makes any difference. "Anyway, there's usually nobody out there, except this day there was a bunch of little kids there on a field trip, only we didn't see them until we was already in the middle of the shoot . . ."

Her voice trails off a bit, prompting me to raise my head to check on her. My heart swells when I see that her cheeks are the same color red as the cherries in her pie. But my sympathy does little to ease the laugh that's aching to explode out of me in anticipation of whatever it is she's about to say.

"What, um . . ." Iris's laughter sputters behind her words. "What new product were you taking pictures of?"

Burty drops her head sheepishly, the slightest grin tugging on her lip. "They're called . . . kitty titties—"

Iris blows out the world's loudest snort, while I collapse against the table, howling, before she can even begin to explain what a kitty titty is.

Not that she has to.

Or should.

No explanation will *ever* be necessary.

CHAPTER 18

Twenty-four hours ago, my cheeks ached from laughing harder than I have in years, but now they just hurt from all the smiles I'm having to force out.

I never realized how much work it is to look like I'm enjoying myself.

I'm at the all-committee luncheon, where the hospital's fundraising team is revealing the plans for the Listen to Your Heart Gala. Details I would have known had I been on the conference call earlier in the week—an "egregiously bad decision" Dan refuses to let me forget.

Along with the hospital staffers and the outside consultant, there are two dozen or so local philanthropists (mostly wealthy retirees who commit ten to twenty thousand a year in exchange for party invitations and name recognition on brochures), the rest of the Second Wives Club, and, most recently, and most surprisingly, Dan. Considering he doesn't serve on the committee and has no Saturday surgeries on his docket, the only reason I can figure for him showing up at the hospital right now is to make sure that *I'm* here. Well, that and to soak up some praise from his adoring fans.

I don't need a babysitter, asshole!

"Well, look who's here! Dr. Osborne, head of our cardiothoracic department—what a treat!" Jackie Harriman, VP of fundraising, coos from where she stands at the front of the room. "Please, won't you sit down and join us."

Dan flashes one of his Ken doll smiles and says, "It would be my pleasure, Jackie. Thank you."

All eyes in the room follow him as he makes his way over to the table where the second wives and I are sitting. My jaw instinctively clenches as he grabs an empty chair and slides it into place between Brielle and me.

"Well, hey there, good-lookin'." Brielle's all chipper, southern charm as she scooches over to make room.

He extends quick greetings to the rest of the wives—each one gaping at him like he just walked on water to get here—then throws his arm around my shoulder and leans in, kissing my cheek.

"Hi, honey," he says.

My skin bristles, his words and touch grating against every nerve in my body.

"Aww . . . ," Brielle sighs while Heather groans, "Get a room, you two."

I force out yet another smile and turn to him. "I wasn't expecting to see you here."

His own plastered-on smile deepens, and with his gaze lasered in on me, he says, "Well, it's a very important meeting. I wouldn't want to miss it."

A surge of disdain starts swelling through my veins, prompting me to bury my fingernails into my palm before I hit him over the head like he's a wrecked car in the corner of the lot.

"I was just sharing with the committee our plan to invite some former patients to speak at the gala," Jackie continues, thankfully reclaiming the spotlight. All heads turn back to the front of the room. "We feel that allowing potential donors the opportunity to hear first-hand from grateful patients the impact our hospital—and our doctors, specifically—has had in their lives could be very effective. I'm sure you can speak to that fact, can't you, Dr. Osborne?"

And, once again, all attention shifts back to Dan.

Just the way he likes it.

"Absolutely," he says. "The hospital exists solely for the care it can provide the community. I can't think of a better way to convey that than bringing in actual patients so they can share their stories."

"Mmm. So true," Tamira agrees reverently.

I swallow a sigh.

"Well, we've got no shortage of grateful patients on *your* list," Jackie says wistfully. "We did the math, and you've saved more lives than Superman!"

The room erupts in a chorus of laughter, prompting Dan to do that detestable fake-humility thing he does where he shrugs his shoulders all the way up into his cheeks while smiling like a sheepish schoolboy.

I hate that look!

Fighting the urge to scream, I reach for my water glass and take a long drink while Jackie continues.

"So, along with the grateful patients, we're also going to have live music, a comedian—a really funny guy from the Comedy Stop down in Chicago. I saw him a few weeks ago; he was hysterical," she adds over an annoying, scrunched-nose smile. "And of course we'll have a silent auction. This year Heather Mills-Crosby, our resident soap opera actress and wife to Mitchell Crosby, head of general surgery, has offered up acting lessons." She motions to my tablemate, who plasters on one of her own manufactured smiles as the room turns our way. "How exciting will that be?"

"So fucking exciting," Heather mumbles under her breath.

Tamira stifles a snort while Brielle says, "Oh, how fun. I might bid on that."

I can't help but think back to the big prescription bottle stashed in Heather's bag. I'm not sure Brielle can hang with *that* much fun.

My phone suddenly vibrates from inside my bag. Dan hears the muffled buzzing, too, and gives me a stern look as if silently telling me not to check it, but there's no way I'm going to ignore it. It could be Avery, even though I'm pretty sure it's Julie. She's already sent three text messages since I've been here, each one harder to interpret than the one before, but the gist is that Mom is having a bad day, and, of course, she can't handle it on her own.

As subtly as possible, I reach down and pull the phone from my bag, and—yep, it's Julie. But she's actually calling this time, which in itself isn't that strange—she always ends up calling if I don't respond to her texts—but for some reason today feels . . . concerning.

I quickly reject the call to stop the vibration, then hide the phone on my lap and wait for the "New voice mail" notification to appear. From the corner of my eye, I can see that Dan's keeping watch on what I'm doing. I shift beneath the weight of his heavy arm, angling myself away from him for a little privacy. As soon as the notification appears, I click it open and immediately hit the "Transcribe" button, so rather than playing the message, I can just read it on the screen.

For the first time in history, one of Julie's messages comes through without one typo:

> You need to get down here. Mom's freaking out. She's saying all kinds of ridiculous things about Dan. I've tried to talk her through it like I usually do, but it's not working. And now she won't stop crying. Please come down here. I don't know what to do.

Had I actually *listened* to the message, I have no doubt that Julie's voice would've been cracking with panic—her sentences punctuated by exclamation points, not periods—but without the audio, my brain can focus on only the words in front of me.

On that one phrase: *saying all kinds of ridiculous things about Dan.*

My stomach drops.

Mom heard me.

Despite the way she was acting, some little part of her *was* there the day I confessed the truth about Dan, and now she's talking.

SHIT.

Without thought, I snatch my bag and lean into Dan, whispering, "I have to go. Mom needs me."

Still mindful of our surroundings, he maintains a pleasant expression, but the little squeeze to my shoulder assures me he's anything but happy. "I'm sure your sister can handle it until we're done here," he mutters back, jaw twitching in restraint.

I shrink out of his grasp. "No, she can't. I'm going."

I throw my bag over my shoulder and make a quick beeline for the door. I can hear the second wives murmuring curiosities as to where I'm going and can feel the attention of the room shift to me, but I keep my head down the entire time. I'm too focused on how I'm going to deal with Mom—and more importantly, Julie—than to worry about what these annoying, fake-laughing people think of me, or my cheating liar of a husband.

∽

If I'd gone the speed limit, the drive would have taken roughly an hour; I make it in thirty-eight minutes. I called Julie on the way down to let her know I was coming. As expected, her voice was quaking with fear, and it summoned that protective, big-sister instinct I have like it always does. *Dammit.* This isn't how I wanted her to find out. She shouldn't have to hear it this way.

Carol's at the front desk and greets me with a worried look when I blow into the lobby.

"I'm so glad you're here," she says, quickly scribbling out my name on a visitor's badge and handing it to me. "She's really out of sorts; I've never seen her like this."

"Well, hopefully I can calm her down a little." I peel off the plastic backing strips and slap the sticker against my chest. "They're in her room?"

"Yep. Dr. Bain is in there too."

Oh good. Now the doctor's privy to my dirty, cheating laundry too.

Pulse racing, I hustle down the hall toward Mom's suite. Her door is closed, but I can still hear someone wailing on the other side.

Dammit, Jane! Why did you tell her?

Flinching against the sound, I inhale a deep breath and open the door.

"Oh, thank god." Looking as haggard as she sounded on the phone, Julie springs up from where she's sitting at the dining table and hurries over to me for a hug. I pull her in tight while focusing my attention over her shoulder to where Mom is huddled up in a ball in the corner of the little love seat, crying. She looks more like a scared child than a sixty-four-year-old grandmother.

A pang of guilt slices straight through my heart.

I did that to her.

My lie—*Dan's lie*—did that to her.

"She's just a mess today," Julie sputters against my ear. "Nothing I say will calm her down. She just keeps prattling on with all this crazy talk about Dan and then gets so mad when I tell her they're not real memories. And I know I'm not supposed to do that," she adds over shuddery breaths. "I'm not trying to upset her, it's just—"

"No, I know you're not," I say, tightening my hold on her. Unfortunately, Alzheimer's doesn't come with a script, for patients or their families. It's impossible to get it *right* when there's no recipe to follow. "She's just having a bad day—probably didn't get any sleep last night. We'll get her through it." I glance at Dr. Bain and, despite Mom's obvious pain, still have to settle my own unease. "How long has the doctor been here?"

"She just got here a few minutes ago."

"Did Mom tell her what she told you?"

She shakes her head. "No. I told her not to say it to anyone."

I swallow a relieved breath. Thank god!

"Oh, Katherine, look. Your daughter Jane is here," Dr. Bain suddenly announces from where she's standing at the opposite end of the love seat from Mom, monitoring her with a concerned brow.

"Janie?" Mom calls out over shuddery breaths. "Janie Lou Bug, is that you?"

I release my hold on Julie and hurry across the room, saying, "Yeah, it's me, Mom. I'm here."

"Oh, Janie!" she wails, raising her head slightly while swiping at her eyes. "I don't understand what's happening! It feels so clear in my head, but Julie's telling me it's not true. I must be going crazy!"

"No, you're not going crazy, Mom," I assure her, as I have before. I drop down on the cushion beside her, surprised when she immediately unrolls from her little ball, only to collapse in a crying heap on my lap. I cast a wary glance toward Dr. Bain and say, "Do you think we could have a moment?"

"Of course. I'm just across the hall if you need anything."

The doctor gives Julie a supportive pat on her way out, then disappears into the hallway. Now it's just the three of us in the room.

The three of us and one great big damning secret.

My chest grows tight, and I instinctively start to drag my hand along Mom's mess of tangled hair. Before the disease found her, I could count on one finger the number of times I'd seen her cry—the day she learned my father had died—but now she does it a lot. Sometimes out of fear, sometimes out of frustration. Today it sounds like both. Well done, Jane.

"Everything's going to be okay," I go on, stroking her back. "You'll feel better soon—"

"But I just don't understand it!" she cries out, her thin body shuddering beneath me. "It doesn't make sense! I'm sure what I'm saying is true. I'm sure it happened. But Julie says it didn't. But it feels *so* real in my head!"

I wince against the anguish in her voice.

It feels real because it *is* real.

"I hate this!" she yells while pressing her fisted hands against my thighs.

Anger isn't uncommon in Alzheimer's patients—considering how their brains betray them, it's certainly warranted—though today it's not this damn disease that's brought her to this horrific point; it's me.

I inhale a nervous breath, then say, "Mom, why don't you tell me what you told Julie. Maybe I can help you understand it a little better."

She shakes her head. "No," she sputters against my legs. "You'll just think I'm crazy too—"

"I never said you were crazy; I just said it didn't happen," Julie snips back, the hours she's spent trying to calm her down evident in her exhausted tone.

Mom suddenly bolts upright and faces Julie, screaming, "But it felt so real!" while raking her hands through her hair in frustration. "I just don't understand why it can feel like such a real memory if it didn't actually happen."

"Mom, what was it?" I prompt again, now desperate to confirm what she's saying so I can ease her suffering. "What did you tell Julie that felt so real?"

She turns toward me and for the first time since I arrived looks at me head-on. My heart twists at the desperation pooling in her swollen, bloodshot eyes. Desperation that's quickly giving way to sadness and sympathy, because the longer she holds my gaze, the more she's assured that she was right.

She did report the truth to Julie.

She can see it in my eyes.

And now the thought of saying it aloud, with me here . . .

Her chin starts to quiver, and her teary gaze drifts away from me while she says, "I, um . . . I told her . . . I said that . . ."

"She said that Dan has been cheating on you, with another man," Julie jumps in, quickly making her way into the guest chair sitting opposite us. "But I told her that was impossible. That she must have seen it on one of her shows and somehow got it confused with real life. Like *The Love Boat* or *One Day at a Time*, or—*oh!* It was probably on *Three's Company*." Her hopeful gaze darts back and forth between Mom and me. "They always had wacky storylines on that show. It must have been something like that. Like maybe one where Jack pretends to be gay to get out of dating someone. Or maybe someone thinks Mr. Furley is gay. He was always wearing those fancy scarves around his neck. Maybe that's where the whole gay idea came from . . ."

I can tell by the way Mom's nodding that she wants to confirm that what Julie's suggesting could be true—her memory is just playing more tricks on her—but I can't let her assume that lie to spare my pride. As much as I want to keep the truth from Julie, it can't come at the expense of Mom's well-being. Good or bad, she deserves to have as many *real* memories as possible.

I intervene before Mom has a chance to respond. "It's not something she saw on TV. It really happened. I told her that."

"What?" Julie turns to me, brows furrowed. "Why would you tell her that?"

"Because it's true."

"It's what?"

"Oh, Janie. I'm so sorry," Mom sputters. "Now I remember that you told me it was a secret. I—I shouldn't have said anything. I'm so sorry."

"No, Mom." I shake my head at her unwarranted regret. "You didn't do anything wrong—"

"Wait, what are you talking about?" Julie cuts me off, now leaning forward with her forearms pressed against her thighs. "What is going on?"

I turn to her and very bluntly say, "Dan is gay."

She scoffs. "Okay."

"I'm not kidding, Julie. Dan's gay. He's been cheating on me with other men pretty much our entire marriage."

She stares blankly at me for a long beat before her eyes grow wide and she says, "You're serious, aren't you?"

I nod.

"Holy shit." She reels back, eyes now blinking hard in disbelief. "What—I mean . . . *oh my god!* How did you find out?"

"He confessed when we were on that trip to Denver."

"Denver? That was like"—she pauses to do a quick mental count—"two months ago. You've been carrying this around for two months?"

I nod again.

"Oh my god, Janie . . ." She pushes herself off the chair and quickly circles the coffee table, wedging herself into the narrow cushion space between me and the arm of the love seat. She throws her arms around my neck and pulls me in for a hug. "I'm so sorry. This is—*god*, this is horrible. Are you okay?"

Nothing about this conversation is remotely pleasing, but I still find a grateful smile tugging on my lips. I can't remember the last time someone asked me if *I* was okay.

"No, not really," I say, voice wavering with emotion.

"I'm sorry, Janie Bug," Mom joins in, giving my back a supportive rub. Another thing I haven't experienced in a very long time. As much as I hate this disease, I have to admit I enjoy how it's softened her. "I always knew he was a pompous ass, but I didn't know he was light in the loafers too."

I snort. Okay, maybe she's not *that* soft.

"Yeah, I definitely didn't see that coming," I say, sniffling over another broken laugh.

"So, what's the plan?" Julie asks, releasing me and settling down on the coffee table so we can talk eye to eye. "Have you filed for divorce? Is he moving out? Are you getting your own place—"

"Whoa, whoa, whoa." I cut her off with a raise of the hand. "Nobody's going anywhere. We haven't even talked about it—"

"What do you mean you haven't talked about it? You're not thinking of staying with him, are you?"

Mom cuts in. "No, she's not."

I'm grateful that her tears have stopped but not so sure how I feel about the authority in her voice. The answer's not quite that simple.

"Well . . . ," Julie urges.

I swallow hard, the weight of her stare suddenly making it hard to think of an appropriate response. "I—um . . . it's not—"

"*Jane!* You can't seriously be thinking of staying with him. You just said he's been cheating on you your entire marriage—"

"—with lots of men," Mom adds.

"Five," I clarify. Dan made it clear that he wasn't just out screwing around; he was always in "relationships"—not that it changes anything. Cheating is still cheating, regardless if it's with a man or a woman.

"Five, ten, gay, straight, it doesn't matter," Julie picks up where she left off. "You can't stay with a cheater. You have to leave."

I sigh. "It's not that simple—"

"How is that not simple? He cheated on you. He *lied* to you."

I swallow hard, unnerved by the accusation in her tone.

"There are a lot of things to consider," I go on. "Avery's at a very vulnerable age. We have to think about what's best for her. Plus, Dan's job is a huge factor in all of this. If this gets out, it could be devastating to his career."

"I'll give you the Avery thing," she concedes quickly. "But how would him getting divorced have any impact on his career? Doctors get divorced all the time. Hell, all of your friends are second and third wives—"

"It's not so much about a divorce; it's about him being gay—"

"So, doctors can't be gay?"

Her rebuttals are starting to grate against my nerves.

I didn't come here to be attacked. I came here to make sure you were okay. To reassure you that somehow I'd figure out a way to take care of Mom—and you!—like I always do!

"Yes, of course doctors can be gay," I go on, jaw tightening in frustration. "But if he comes out now, it could create huge problems at work; it could have a serious impact on the entire hospital."

She gasps while dramatically pressing a palm across her chest. "Wow, he really *is* the most important doctor in the world if his sex life can impact the future of the entire hospital."

She stretches out the word *entire* over the span of a mile, which is precisely how far away from her I want to be right now.

UGH!

"You know what—never mind. There's no way you could possibly get it."

I push myself off the couch and storm across the room, desperate for some space.

"Why won't I get it?" She stupidly follows up, shifting her position on the table so she's facing me. "Because I'm not married?"

"Being married has nothing to do with it. It's about being responsible; it's about taking care of other people!" I snarl back at her, enraged by her obliviousness.

"Hey, I'm responsible!" She jumps to her feet. "I take care of Avery all the time—"

"You hang out with Avery. It's not the same thing."

"Well, I take care of Mom!"

I gasp, my eyes practically popping off my face. "Since when? Last time I checked, I was the one footing the bill around here."

"Girls, come on." Mom tries to intervene, but it's too late. The resentment train has officially left the station.

Fire settles in Julie's eyes and she says, "You know there's a lot more to taking care of someone than just throwing money at them. I'm here with her all the time. I don't just show up every few weeks—I'm here *all* the time! That's more important than money."

"Says the girl whose rent I just paid," I snarl back at her.

Blood boiling, I snatch my bag off the table and head for the door. I need to get out of here before I say something I'll regret, no matter how true it might be.

"You're right, I'm not perfect," Julie calls after me. "But at least I'm smart enough to know when to ask people for help. At least I love myself enough not to suffer in a bad situation."

"Yeah, you've definitely mastered the art of taking handouts!"

I storm out of the building and into the parking lot, Julie's parting words grinding against my skin like a bad rash.

"Not smart enough to ask for help?" I mutter. "Letting myself suffer? I'll show you . . ."

I yank my phone out of my bag and send out an SOS to Chavez:

I NEED TO HIT SOMETHING. NOW.

CHAPTER 19

Despite the crisp autumn air, beads of sweat are trailing down my brow and along the hairline at the base of my neck. Breathless, I drop my bat to the asphalt, peel off my coat, and pull my hair back into a loose bun. I forgot what a workout this is.

"Water break?" Chavez hops down from the stack of wooden pallets where he's been sitting and hands me a bottle of water. He wasn't in the mood to bash cars today but was more than willing to supervise me while I did. Which is exactly what I've been doing for the last half hour, and damn if it wasn't therapeutic. Julie's selfish, misguided words are little more than a distant memory.

I'm too winded to thank him, so I just smile at the gesture, then take a long drink.

"Do I dare ask what motivated you to do that?" he jokes, pointing to the little pickup truck I just worked over. The tailgate—where I focused my attention—looks like it's been through a war.

"Not what but *who*," I pant. "My sister."

He grimaces while sucking in a deep breath over his teeth. "Been there, done that. Sisters are tricky."

"You got that right."

Truth be told, Julie hasn't been a *tricky* sister. For the most part we've always gotten along—when she doesn't need me to save her, that is.

"What'd she do?" he asks.

"Oh, she was just being her usual codependent self," I grouse over heavy breaths while swiping moisture back from my nose. "Why do anything for yourself when your big sister will swoop in and save the day?" I blow off the frustration with a shake of the head, then turn the tables on him. "What about your sister? What's her deal?"

He sighs. "She turns everything into a competition."

"How so?" I ask, then take another drink.

"Like if there's anything she can do faster or better than me, she's going to. Getting to the bus stop before me. Getting a higher GPA than me. Scoring higher on her driver's test. Who took the fastest shower—"

"The fastest shower?" I bust in, chuckling.

He levels me with a hard look and says, "She used to sit outside the bathroom with a stopwatch and time me."

"You're kidding."

He shakes his head earnestly. "She did it every night for like two months straight. It drove me freaking crazy."

"Because she was faster than you?"

"No, because I love to take showers. I can stand there for like an hour, just letting all the hot water pour over me"—he shrugs over an adorable grin—"but knowing she was out there ruined them for me for a really long time."

A naughty visual of him in the shower suddenly takes root in my mind, forcing me to raise the bottle for another drink before my flush gives me away.

"The thing is, I don't care if she beats me at any of this stuff," he goes on, oblivious to my train of thought. "I never have. But now that I'm older, I've learned to turn it around, so at least it's fun for me."

A devilish smirk I've not seen before settles in on his face.

My eyes narrow. "That sounds like trouble."

"Oh, it is. Now, whenever I get the chance, I come up with these stupid competitions just to get her wound up about beating me. In fact, the last time I did it was here." He motions to our surroundings. "I told her that I could find five Toyota hubcaps faster than she could. She tore this place apart." He chuckles at the memory. "She spent a solid hour looking for them, which made Jessie so mad. You know how he is about staying in your designated area."

I laugh and nod because I *do* know. Just like the first time we came here and were told to stick to the far-right corner of the lot, Jessie made it *very* clear that tonight we are to stay in the near-left corner. This explains why he was so wary of me when Chavez brought me here the first time. Way back when I thought he was a ladies' man.

He rolls his eyes. "She ended up collecting seven of them."

"And how many did you find?"

He grins. "None. I didn't even look."

"You're a jerk, you know that?"

"Yeah, so she's told me a time or two." He locks me in his amused gaze for a long, pulse-pounding beat before he changes gears, saying, "So, it was nice to see you yesterday."

My stomach flips as an image of him in that well-fitted suit suddenly replaces my frustrating train of thought. Grinning, I raise the bottle up and take another drink before I say, "Yeah, that was definitely nice."

"Had you been to the diner before?"

I shake my head.

"Did you try something?"

"Yeah, I had a piece of cobbler." Or three, by the time I left. But details don't matter.

"What kind?"

I grin. His curiosity is endearing and, I suspect, motivated by his own baking prowess.

"Peach."

"What'd you think?"

The lilt in his voice assures me I'm right. He's feeling self-conscious about his blackberry mess. Fighting the urge to giggle, I shrug and, as casually as possible, say, "I've had better."

"Really?" he asks hopefully.

"Oh yeah. Very recently, as a matter of fact."

He considers my response briefly before his eyes narrow and he shakes his head, saying, "You're a horrible liar."

I burst out laughing. "I'm sorry. Your pie was good, but that was just . . . I mean—"

"I know," he groans. "Everybody at the station is hooked on it. I'm in there at least three times a week, almost always for the banana cream pie. It's so good." His eyes grow wide, and he steps a bit closer, now gesticulating with his hands as he describes the pie. "She drizzles caramel and chocolate on top of the whipped cream and then adds on these big chunks of sea salt. I swear, it's the best thing I've ever eaten."

"Well, I guess I know what I'm getting next time," I say, amused by his enthusiasm.

"You know, I wanted to come over and say hi, but I was short on time," he goes on while wandering even closer, his dark eyes sparkling at me beneath the sinking sun. "I had to testify in court yesterday for this case I've been working." The sexy image reappears, bringing with it a flush to my cheeks. I drop my head. "What?" he asks.

"Nothing."

"There you go, lying to me again." He takes another step closer and tugs on my sweater sleeve, demanding my attention. I raise my head and feel my blush deepen beneath his curious grin. "What aren't you saying?"

There's a painfully flirtatious response tickling the tip of my tongue, eager to be heard but nervous to come out just the same. "Nothing. I just . . . I thought you looked really nice, that's all."

He wiggles his brows. "You had no idea Detective Sexy Pants could pull off a suit, did you?"

I gasp and quickly slap my hands over my mouth. "I actually called you that, didn't I?" I sputter through my veil of fingers. "I wasn't sure, but—"

See Jane Snap

"Oh yeah, you did," he taunts. "You called me that and a lot of things that night. And you did some things too."

Even though we've never discussed it, it's obvious he's alluding to the sloppy kiss I planted on him the night he arrested me. The kiss I've thought about more than once over the last few weeks. The kiss I can't help but think would have been amazing had I not been stoned. I shift beneath a sudden rush of heat that stirs in my lady parts.

Uh-oh.

I quickly raise the bottle and take another drink while I scour my brain for a segue into safer, less stimulating territory.

"You know, it's actually a good thing you didn't have time to come over," I go on. "One of my friends thought you were there to arrest her. She probably would've had a heart attack if you'd come and talked to us."

"Arrest her? For what?"

I give my hand a flippant wave. "Oh, it's a long, boring story."

The glint in his eye suggests he knows I'm lying to him, again (it's what I do, after all. I'm a big, fat liar!), but thankfully he doesn't pursue the issue. Instead he says, "It looked like you guys were having a pretty intense conversation. Was everything okay?"

I think back on yesterday's time at the diner and smile. "Yeah. Everything was great—"

A gust of wind suddenly kicks up, prompting me to gasp as a blanket of shivers erupts across my body, the beads of sweat stinging like icicles against my skin.

"Here, let's get this back on you before you freeze." He quickly grabs my coat off the ground and drapes it over my shoulders from behind me, his fingers grazing my neck along the way. A tremor ripples through my limbs, forcing me to inhale a deep breath through my nose while my eyelashes flutter wildly.

Good god, what was that?

"Better?" he asks, his warm breath tickling my ear.

"Y-yeah. Yes."

So much better.

I slowly glance over my shoulder to look at him. Our eyes lock for a split second before my gaze instinctively travels down to his lips. His plump, slick lips.

At least I love myself enough not to suffer—

Julie's annoying words niggle at my brain like an unreachable itch, jostling something buried deep down inside me to awaken with a jolt. *BAM!* The feral heat I felt a moment ago returns with volcanic force, erupting against all the nerves in my body.

I inhale a shuddery breath, my attention zeroing in on that mouth. That beautiful, sexy mouth.

Oh, the things he could do with that . . .

My own mouth starts to water.

"Thank you," I say, my voice unfamiliarly husky.

"You're welcome."

A desperate breath hitches in my lungs at the way his mouth moves as he forms the words. The intoxicating purse of his lips when he says *you're.* The way the tip of his tongue peeks out from behind his teeth when he hits the *L* in *welcome.*

You're welcome.

You're welcome!

God, yes, you're welcome!

Desperation steals my surroundings, muting the cold air and the stench of gasoline. All that's left is me.

And my aching loins.

And those lips.

Those fucking lips.

And the voracious need to claim them as my own—

I lunge at him, throwing my arms around his neck and planting my mouth squarely on his. My body bucks at the impact, the sudden explosion of soft, supple heat as intense as I imagined.

YES!

He responds in kind, wrapping his arms around my back and pulling me against his chest. Despite the layers of fabric between us, I feel his heart racing against mine, and I detect a smile lingering on his lips, but the sentiment is lost on me.

More.

I need more!

Moving with foreign urgency, I drag my hands down the length of his back and up under the hem of his shirt while my tongue frantically explores the nuances of his mouth. *So hot. So wet. So good.* He lets out a delicious little moan as my fingers dive under the waistband of his jeans, seeking out the tender skin of his lower back—

Oh god!

His tongue glides across my teeth, prompting a glorious ache to rumble through me.

Yes!

More.

Give me more!

Moaning at the sensation, I burrow my hands down deeper, sinking my nails into the fleshy, muscular meat of his upper thighs. His body quakes beneath my touch, stoking the needful fire inside me to burn brighter—more intensely.

Yes.

You want me!

YOU WANT ME!

And I want this—

SO BAD.

Desperation mounting, I work my way back around his waist, my fingers wantonly following the trail of soft hair that runs from his belly button down beneath his jeans. I fumble with the button, eager to reach the zipper—

"We can't do this here," he groans, his body assuring me it's not an easy statement to make.

"Then take me somewhere," I growl back.

"I don't live that far—"

"Yes!" I cry out. "Anywhere!"

Frenzied anticipation carries us as we race, hand in hand, through the impound lot, navigating our way around the battered cars and stacks of tires, before finally blowing by the check-in shed and into the parking lot.

We get to my car, but before I have a chance to open the driver's door, he presses me against the passenger door and starts kissing me again, antagonizing the animal inside me to roar to life.

I NEED THIS.

I DESERVE THIS.

IT'S MY TURN.

NO SUFFERING HERE!

I throw my arms around his neck and pull him closer, digging my fingers into the warm skin of his nape.

He moans again. That ache-inducing sound that sends another surge of desperation to rise inside me.

"I need you now," I grunt over feverish breaths.

"I know. But not here," he groans. "Just . . . follow me."

He untangles himself from my hands and hustles to his car while I climb inside mine.

Disoriented, I blink hard as I settle into the seat, then quickly slam the keys into the ignition and turn on the engine. Chavez does the same in his truck. He waves at me through the window, a delicious grin working his jaw, then quickly backs out of the space. I throw the car in reverse, catching a glimpse of my messy hair and smudgy, swollen lips in the rearview along the way.

"Dammit, girl," I mutter pridefully, gluttonously. "There's no *suffering* here tonight."

It's not quite dusk, so there's still plenty of traffic on the roads, but I manage to ride Chavez's bumper without difficulty. Despite the tint on his truck's windows, I can see him glancing back at me in his mirrors to make sure I'm still in place: a subtle gesture that keeps my cravings burning hot.

He wants me so bad.

Shifting against my seat, I force my attention onto his taillights in an effort to maintain at least some focus on the road—such a different motivation from the last time I followed a man in his car. That fateful night when I pursued Dan out to the Bone Yard and witnessed first-hand his selfishness, how he so easily conceded to his cravings without consideration for how they might affect the people around him. How they could shatter the lives of the people who cared about him—

Ohmygod!

The realization rattles me like a thunderbolt, snuffing out every desirous urge in my body.

I'm just like him.

I'm just like Dan.

Going after what I want—

Only looking to satisfy MY needs . . .

What kind of person am I—

What kind of mother am I?!

How can I just use someone—him—to satisfy myself?!

Panic and fear flood my chest, prompting me to scream out, "No!" just as Chavez makes a right turn, leading us toward the interstate. I pound the steering wheel with my fist as snapshots of the last twenty minutes start syphoning through my mind: all thoughts of me and *my* needs—*MY WANTS*—but nothing about Chavez. Not specifically. It's just moans, and aches, and urges. *He's* not a part of them at all.

Shit!

My heart wrenches as I take in his truck with clear, rational eyes for the first time.

I can't do this.
I can't do this!
Not to Avery.
Not to him.

His left turn signal starts to pulse, and his brake lights illuminate as he slows down to turn onto the southbound ramp, toward his house, while the northbound ramp, which leads back to Mount Ivy, is on the right.

Indecision nips at my bones as my finger settles on the blinker.

What do I do?
Where do I go?
At least I love myself enough not to suffer in a bad situation.

Julie's parting words suddenly explode through my brain, their intention resonating as intended for the first time.

Rage throttles my bones.

I clamp my teeth down hard.

"No more," I grit out. "It's time to stop the suffering."

I hang a hard right and head up the northbound ramp while Chavez makes the left turn heading south. In my sideview mirror I see his brake lights illuminate for a split second, but with another car behind him, he has no choice but to keep going.

"I'm so sorry," I whimper, blanching as his taillights disappear from sight.

My phone starts to ring.

Shit.

Regret twists in my gut as I stare at his name on the display.

I'm sorry.
I'm so sorry.

I tighten my grip on the wheel and inhale a deep, nervous breath before I answer.

"Hi—"

"You went the wrong way. What happened? Where are you going?"

The concern in his voice cuts like a knife. I wince, agonized by what I'm about to do. By what I have to do.

"Jane, are you okay?"

"Yes . . . I just—*god.*" I heave an excruciating breath. "I'm so sorry, but I can't do this."

"You can't—*you mean tonight?* You can't come tonight?"

"No."

"Well, that's okay. We can do it another time—"

"*No.*" I cut off his warm response with a tone so sharp it brings a chill to my skin. *Dammit.* "I can't do any of this," I go on, my voice quaking. "I'm sorry. I just—I can't do this. I'm sorry."

I disconnect from the call and quickly power down my phone. I can't talk to him right now; I can't possibly bear to hear the hurt in his voice, the disappointment that comes from being disregarded by someone you thought cared about you. I know that sound too well.

And I'll be damned if I ever hear it in my own voice again.

CHAPTER 20

Dan is in the family room in front of the TV, though I can tell by the steely look in his eyes he's not actually watching the game in front of him. He's stewing . . . because he's furious.

That would make two of us.

"What the hell were you thinking, Jane?" he growls, hammering me with a nasty glare as I walk into the room.

I slam my bag onto the kitchen table. "Where's Avery?"

"Sleeping over at Jasmine's. Answer my question."

Now that I know we don't have an audience, I have no trouble answering him honestly.

I've been waiting a long time to do this.

"I was thinking that you're an asshole."

"Excuse me?" He pushes himself off the couch and stalks across the room toward me, somehow looking about five feet taller than he is. I thrust my chin up higher. "How am *I* the asshole? You're the one who walked out of the luncheon and left me to deal with all those fundraising people and your nosy friends asking where you went—"

"They're not my friends!" I scream, which surprises me but somehow feels right. "And are you actually implying that *I'm* the asshole here?"

"I'm not *implying* anything. I'm saying it! You put my entire career on the line when you walked out of there today," he scolds while pointing an angry finger at me. "You knew how important it was for you to be there, and you still left—"

"Because my mom needed me!" I spit back, lurching toward him with fire in my eyes. He wisely drops his hand.

"Your sister could have handled it—"

"No, she couldn't—"

"Yeah, she could have! You just refuse to let her do anything because you always have to be the one in control of everything—"

"*What?*" I raise my palms, the blood in my veins starting to boil. "Have you seen my life lately? I'm not in control of anything!"

He flinches, clearly aware of the big, gay elephant I'm alluding to, but dismisses it with a flippant wave. "That's bullshit and you know it. You love taking care of her. You love coming to her rescue every time something comes up."

"*That's* bullshit. I don't *like* rescuing her; I *have* to rescue her. That's my job. She's my sister. I have to help her when she needs me—"

"And what did helpless Julie need big sister to do for her today?" he questions snidely. "Did she run out of gas money? Need help folding Mom's laundry—"

"No! She didn't know how to respond to Mom telling her that you were gay!"

He blanches. "*What?*"

"Yeah," I counter, puffing up my chest like a boxer ready for another round. "Mom told her that you've been cheating on me with other men, and when Julie said she didn't believe her, she started freaking out, thinking that somehow she'd mixed up her memories again."

"*You told your mom?*"

The fury in his eyes should probably scare me, but it just spurs my own rage.

No more suffering!

I take a step toward him and, over a determined jaw, say, "Yeah. And I told Julie too—"

"Dammit, Jane—"

"—and Iris and Burty."

"*Who?*"

"Some girls from my 'meeting.'" I air quote the word with my fingers, wishing my nails were daggers I could cut him with.

"What the hell were you thinking? You know you weren't supposed to tell anyone—"

"And I told Detective Chavez too."

"Who the hell is Detective Chavez?"

"The cop who arrested me!"

He shakes his head. "No, his name was Gunnerson."

Dan's got a thing for names—he never forgets anyone's (especially a patient's)—but because Chavez was only helping out the night I was arrested, and apparently left shortly after I was processed, he never crossed paths with Dan. In fact, Chavez's name wasn't even listed on any of my processing paperwork. All Dan ever knew about him was based on information the discharging officers gave him: he was just a nameless former classmate who offered me a get-out-of-jail-free opportunity that was too good to pass up.

"No, Gunnerson was the guy who was listed on the paperwork," I correct him. "Detective Chris Chavez is the one who actually took me into custody. He's the guy I almost had sex with tonight!"

A strange look flashes across his face before he blanches and says, "The guy you—*what?* You're seeing someone?"

"That's none of your business!"

"Like hell it isn't! Do you know what would happen if someone saw you with this guy?"

The fact that he's even asking me that makes my stomach turn and reinforces all the things I determined on my drive home tonight.

"How dare you!" I growl, my hands instinctively fisting at my sides. "You're the one who's been sneaking around, screwing other people for the last eighteen years—"

"Yeah, but I never got caught!"

"Oh my god! *What?*" I shake my hands violently through the air.

"I caught you myself out at the Bone Yard—"

"You didn't *catch* me, you *saw* me. And the only reason you did was because I told you the truth. Otherwise you never would have been suspicious of what I was doing. Nobody has ever come close to catching me but *you*," he snarls, shaking his head with disgust as he wanders deeper into the kitchen. He grabs an orange out of the fruit bowl sitting on the counter and, over a snide look, says, "Well, I think we both know you're not very good at keeping a low profile."

Oh, no you didn't.

Rage electrifies through my body, rattling my bones and prompting a familiar *snap* to echo inside me.

"*You son of a bitch!*" I grab the first thing I see—the Winnie the Pooh coffee mug I left on the counter this morning, tea bag still dangling over the edge—and throw it against the wall next to him. It shatters on impact, showering the kitchen table and floor with shards of jagged porcelain and cold chamomile.

"What the hell, Jane?" He recoils, horrified gaze shifting between me and the mess. "First oranges and now coffee mugs? What's wrong with you?"

"You're what's wrong with me!" I scream. "You've ruined my entire life! You've changed who I am! I used to be a good, happy person, but now I'm not. I'm so fucking mad, and I lie all the time! And I use people. I used Chavez! Just to make myself feel good. That's all because of you!"

"Oh, like you weren't using people to make yourself feel good before?" he counters, looking offended.

"What are you talking about?"

"This." He motions around him with big, sweeping gestures. "Me. Your sister. Your mom. All of this. You've been using all of us to get what *you* want for years! You wanted the big house with a gardener. Private schools. Exotic vacations. You wanted to be on the PTA and drive Ave to practice every day. You wanted to be able to bail your sister out when she got in trouble, and make sure your mom got the *good* suite that faced the garden. *That's* what you said you wanted, and that's what I've always given you. We've *all* been giving you that because we know how important it is for you to be in control of your little world all the time! You're just as guilty of using people to get what you want as I am."

I slam my molars together, unnerved by the way he's twisting the truth to fit his needs. Of course I *wanted* all those things. Who doesn't want their ailing mother to have the best care possible? Who doesn't want a more stable, comfortable life than the one they grew up with? Who doesn't want to help their sister when she's in trouble? But to suggest that I was *using* everyone to get it? Using the people I love . . .

"I want a divorce."

He scowls. "No."

"Yes! I'm not going to keep living like this. I deserve more than this—"

"We all deserve more than *this*," he growls back. "But life's not perfect, Jane. We have to make sacrifices."

"No, we don't! Not when it comes to loving people. I want to know that when I get into a relationship with someone, it's because of who *they* are"—my memory flashes back to Chavez—"not because of who they're not. I deserve that! I deserve to be happy too."

"Do you think *I'm* happy?" He raises his palms. "I don't like living like this either, Jane."

I snort. "Oh, please. You're as happy as a pig in shit."

"No, I'm not! I hate it. I hate lying! I've had to do it my whole life!"

On some level I can appreciate what he's saying—I have no doubt that living life in the closet isn't easy—but I'm not talking about his sexual orientation; I'm talking about us. Our marriage. The life we've built together.

"Well, I'm not doing it anymore," I say over a resolved shrug. "We can keep up with appearances until the gala's over and we get the money from the Hoffstras, but then I'm filing for divorce. And until then, you're going to move out."

He shakes his head, folding his arms over his chest. "Like hell I am."

"*Yes*, you are."

"*No*, I'm not," he counters in that maddening paternal tone of his. "There's no way I could move out without people knowing. You know how fast word travels in this town. It wouldn't work. Besides that, I need to be close to Avery."

It's ever so subtle, but I catch a little quiver in his chin when he says Avery's name that forces my chest to swell up with emotion. At least he still needs to be close to her.

I swallow hard. "You can stay in the bonus room above the garage."

"What? No." He shakes his head. "It's hardly bigger than the living room. And it doesn't have a kitchen or a bathroom."

"Not yet, but it's got all the hookups. Remember, that was part of the reason you wanted this house."

When we were house hunting twelve years ago, Dan was over the moon about turning the partially renovated attic space above the detached, three-stall garage into his office. He was just a resident then and liked the idea of having a place to stay up late, catching up on paperwork, without disrupting me and our then infant. But life soon got away from us, and the nine hundred square feet of "office space" quickly became a burial ground for Christmas decorations and old clothes that never made it to Goodwill.

"We can get it cleared out in a day or two—"

"I have a job, Jane. I have patients scheduled for surgery."

"Fine. *I'll* clear it out. And I'll get a contractor lined up. It shouldn't take them too long to put in a small bathroom and a kitchenette."

"Well, you've got it all figured out, don't you? Have you even considered what we're going to tell Avery?"

"She already knows."

All the color drains from his face.

"What?"

"She knows you've been cheating on me."

"You told her?"

I shake my head, throat growing thick as memories of that painful day in the car come screaming back to me. "No. You did."

"What? No, I didn't."

"She overheard you on the phone, talking to Julian—"

"No." He shakes his head firmly. "No way. I never talk to him at home. And definitely never when she's around."

"Well, you must have the night we got back from Denver. She said she heard you in the garage talking to someone, telling them you loved them."

He considers this for a moment before he lets out a pained *"Fuck"* while raking his hands through his hair. "The only reason I called him that night was because he was wondering how things went in Denver— with us. I had no idea she was there," he goes on, sounding as deservedly tortured as he looks. "She had just been in the house with you looking at all those souvenirs we brought back for her."

"Yeah, well, she came out to the garage, and she heard you, so . . ."

He paces aimlessly through the room, shaking his head and groaning, as if searching for a time machine he knows doesn't exist. "When did she tell you that she knew?"

"A few days ago."

"Did she tell anybody?"

I shake my head, disgusted with him—with myself—that we've even put her in a situation where we'd have to ask that question.

"And she knows that I'm . . ." He turns to me wearing a helpless look that suggests he's not only not prepared to *move* out, but he's not ready to *come* out either.

I sigh. "No. She just assumed you were talking to a woman."

"You didn't tell her the truth?"

My heart twists beneath the vulnerability in his eyes. A vulnerability that *shouldn't* get to me but, after eighteen years, still, frustratingly, does. "No," I say. "That's not my truth to tell."

He stares at me for a long beat, then says, "Thanks."

"You're welcome."

You're welcome.

The last time I heard those words, they made my heart race with excitement, but now they slice through me like a barb, bringing my intimate time with Chavez back to the forefront of my mind, and with it my disgust for the man in front of me, and the woman I've become.

∽

Eighteen hours later . . .

I drag a tote marked "Baby Clothes" across the dank carpet to the far side of the bonus room, the area I've designated the "keep" section. If I weren't so tired, I'd pop the lid and take a stroll down memory lane, admiring all the delicate, lacy outfits I used to dress Avery in, but with the way I'm feeling, that wouldn't be wise. One look at a onesie and I'd be fetaled up in the corner, sobbing for the life I used to know.

Besides being physically drained from my time at the salvage lot—the pain is starting to settle in on my muscles now—I'm emotionally spent. I managed only about three hours of sleep before the events of the day got ahold of my thoughts, replaying on the backs of my eyelids like an old filmstrip stuck on the same loop: the infuriating fight with Julie, the regretful parting with Chavez, the explosion with Dan . . . all encounters that *needed* to happen but still leave me suffocating beneath feelings I don't know how to process.

By two o'clock this morning, I couldn't take it anymore, so I came out here to the room above the garage—a.k.a. Dan's future home—and started cleaning things out. The thoughts are still finding me, but they're easier to push aside now that I've got a task in front of me. Though I suspect that will change in a few minutes when Avery gets home.

Despite my desire for the three of us to meet together, Dan said he'd like to speak to her privately. As much as I hate the thought of her having to hear his news without me, I conceded without argument. The last thing I want is for her to feel pitted between us, like she has to respond a certain way because *I'm* there. She deserves to have an honest reaction and to share that with Dan, without any outside influences, because at the end of the day, asshole or not, he's still her dad.

My phone chimes with a new text message. I work my way around the "keep" section and to the "donate" pile, where my phone sits on top of an old camping cooler. I breathe a sigh of relief when I see that it's a text from Julie and not Chavez, as I feared. He called twice last night, his messages simply requesting that I let him know I got home safely. I didn't respond until this morning, and when I did it was via text, with only three words: "I'm fine. Thanks."

If he had any doubt I was a bitch after the way I treated him last night, now he knows for sure.

I tap the screen to bring up Julie's message:

Moms good. I'm not she rebemmbrs mixed of what halfback.

Translation: Mom is good. I'm not sure she remembers much of what happened.

Grateful tears prick my eyes. Much like Chavez, I felt the need to check up on someone last night too. I wanted to call Mom directly but, given the late hour, decided it would be better to reach out to Julie instead. I sent the message just before midnight, and though I could tell it had been delivered to her phone, I had no way of knowing if she'd actually read it, and if she had, if she would answer it—

You're just as guilty of using people to get what you want as I am.

Snippets of last night's confrontation with Dan start cycling through my thoughts again, this time his horrific accusations about my relationship with Julie.

I don't use her.

I don't enable her dependence on me, do I?

No!

I shake my head, pained by the thought.

I help her.

I don't use her.

That's not what our relationship is about.

I love my sister.

I take care of my sister.

That was just Dan spouting off—that's not how she feels.

It can't be.

Can it?

Shit.

Heart twisting, I pull up her number and press the "Call" button. She answers on the first ring.

"Hey."

"Hi," I say, my greeting weighed down with as much trepidation as hers. "So . . . Mom's okay?"

"Yeah." She pauses for a long, uncomfortable beat, then says, "She was pretty wound up after you left, but then *The Love Boat* came on and she got distracted."

"That's good."

"Tony Danza was the guest star, so she was happy."

I smile sadly. "She loves him."

"Yeah."

Silence smothers our already-awkward conversation. I scrub an anxious palm across my brow, uncertain how to proceed. We've never had a fight like that before—

"I'm sorry, Janie."

Her apology catches me by surprise. "What?"

"I'm sorry—"

"No, Julie. You don't have anything to apologize for. I'm the one who lost my temper and stormed out—"

"Not just for last night—for everything." The resolve in her voice suggests I wasn't the only one up thinking last night. "You were right. I'm way too dependent on you. I need to start taking care of myself more."

I've been waiting years—a lifetime!—for her to come to this conclusion, but now that she's actually saying it, and I can hear the disappointment dragging down her words, it doesn't feel as rewarding as I imagined it would.

I drop my head and sigh. "I'm sorry too. If I've ever made you feel like you can't take care of yourself, or made you think that you weren't capable enough to be more independent—"

"What? No. You never do that."

"Well, *if* you ever do feel like that, please know that I'm sorry. That was never my intention. All I ever want to do is help you, even if sometimes it doesn't seem like that."

I hear her swallow hard before she responds. "I know."

Fighting my own emotions, I clear my throat and say, "Any chance you're available to come over tomorrow and help me do some cleaning? I'm clearing out the bonus room above the garage. Dan's moving out here."

"Really?"

The sudden lift in her voice makes me smile.

"Yeah. I actually made a few decisions last night—"

The sound of a car pulling into the driveway steals my attention. I scurry over to the window and look down to see Avery climbing out of Michelle Clark's SUV. The sleepover is officially over. Time to face real life.

"Hey, Jules, I'm sorry, but I need to go. Avery just got home, and Dan's going to fill her in on all his . . . stuff."

She makes a whimpering sound. "That poor kid. Okay. I'll see you tomorrow. Tell Avery I love her."

"I will."

"I love you too, you know?"

I smile broadly, my chest swelling beneath her endearing words and the sight of my sweet, naive little girl hopping out of the car and running toward the house.

Dear god, please let her be okay . . .

"I know," I say. "I love you too."

~

A solid forty minutes pass—all spent pacing, praying, and gnawing on my fingernails—before Avery finally emerges from the house. I try to assess her mood as she crosses the driveway and heads toward the garage, but her hair is hanging loose from its usual braid, shielding her face from my sight.

Nervousness nips at my spine as I hear her climbing up the wooden stairs, her little footfalls pounding against my heart with every step she hits.

I'm sorry, sweetie.

I'm so sorry we're putting you through this.

Hoping to appear stoic and stable in the midst of her chaos, I pull my hair back into a ponytail and blot at my cheeks and eyes with a paper towel.

The door swings open and she steps inside.

"Hey, Mom."

"Hi, honey."

I study her face, expecting to see her blue eyes bloodshot and clouded with tears, but they're not. They're as crystal clear as they always are. And there's not a hint of color on her cheeks either. She doesn't appear to have been crying at all.

Maybe he didn't tell her . . .

I take a tentative step toward her. "Are you okay?"

"Yeah," she says, surveying her surroundings with interest. "What is all this?"

"Oh, it's, um . . . just a bunch of random stuff," I say, confused by her demeanor. He must not have told her. Asshole. "These are all really old medical dictionaries," I say, motioning to the stack of boxes beside me, "and there's some camping equipment over there, and some old dishes and pots and pans, and there's a big container of all your old baby clothes back there—"

"My old baby clothes?" She glances toward the corner where I'm pointing. "You kept those?"

"Mm-hmm."

"Why?"

I shrug. "They're fun to look at sometimes—to see how much you've grown."

She rolls her eyes. "You're so weird."

She wanders through the stacks and piles, dragging her fingers along their dusty lids, still no evidence that she's just had a difficult, life-changing conversation with her father.

Thanks a lot, Dan.

Now I have to explain what I'm doing up here.

"So, how was the sleepover?" I ask.

"Fine. We didn't really do anything—just watched movies and played on our phones. So, Dad's really going to move up here, huh?"

I blink hard, startled by her frankness.

"Um . . . yeah. He is. I guess he told you the plan, huh?"

Still eyeing the room, she nods.

I take a tentative step toward her and say, "How do you feel about that?"

She shrugs. "I don't know."

Not exactly the heart-wrenched response I was bracing for, but it's probably the truth. I imagine it will take some time for her to figure out how she feels about all this. Dan and me too.

"Did he tell you anything else?"

She must tune into the apprehension in my voice because her lip pulls up into a strange little smirk before she turns to me and says, "You mean about him being gay?"

My eyes spring wide, another blunt question catching me by surprise. I nod.

"Yeah. He told me."

"And how do you feel about *that*?"

She shrugs again, her gaze slowly wandering away from me down to the floor. "I don't know. There are some kids at school whose parents are gay. Parker's got two moms; they seem pretty cool whenever they volunteer, so I guess it'll be okay."

Despite her optimistic response, there's a heaviness weighing down her words. A kind of bulky sadness that suggests she's doubting everything she's ever known about her father: whether any of the lifetime of memories they've made together have any meaning at all, or if they were just another facet of his lie. At least, that's how it felt when I first heard that same tone in my voice.

Blinking back a tear, I close the distance between us, gently pressing my palm against the back of her head.

"It will take some time to get used to," I offer, stroking her golden hair. "But it will all be okay. The most important thing is you know that it doesn't change the way he feels about you. He still loves you and thinks that you're the best thing in the whole world."

"I know," she mutters. "He told me that like a thousand times."

She inhales a deep breath while easing closer. I wrap my arms tight around her petite frame and hold her against my chest, savoring the warmth of her skin beneath my fingers: so soft and delicate, just like when she was a baby.

"I sort of feel like I don't know him," she says quietly.

My heart twists at the sadness in her voice, and despite my disdain for the man in question, I suddenly feel compelled to sing his praises.

"I know, honey," I say, nuzzling my nose against her hair. "But I promise he's still going to be the same old Dad he's always been. He'll still be the guy who likes to help you with your science projects, and who sings along with every contestant on *The Voice*, even when he doesn't know the words—"

She laughs a little.

"He'll still make that annoying humming sound while he brushes his teeth, and even though it looks stupid, he'll always eat his pizza with a fork—"

"He's such a freak," she chuckles.

My throat starts to ache as I nod in agreement. "Yeah, he is," I say, eighteen years' worth of memories weighing down my voice. "And he'll still be the guy who wants to watch the Bulls with you while you eat banana splits."

She glances up at me. "So maybe it won't be so different after all . . ."

My heart wrenches at the naive hopefulness in her eyes: the same hopefulness I once saw in my own reflection. I offer up my most encouraging smile, then lean down and kiss her forehead. "Yeah," I say. "Maybe it won't be so different."

CHAPTER 21

I ditch my Monday meeting in the city—grateful that Dr. Daniel A. Osborne, MD, was generous enough to provide me an excuse note nearly identical to Burty's (considering Bates never even glanced at Burty's note and knows me only as *Holliday*, there's no way it will be an issue)—and instead spend the morning clearing out the bonus room with Julie and the afternoon interviewing potential contractors.

Contrary to Dan's insistence that no one would be available to take on our job for at least a few months, I land a guy who's willing to start our little renovation immediately and has assured me the space will be move-in ready by next week. Of course, he's charging me double his normal rate to make it happen—triple time over the weekend—but money's not a concern when my sanity is on the line. Despite the front we're putting on for Avery, the tension between Dan and me is on the rise. Now that we've finally aired our *true* feelings, neither of us can stand the sight of the other. The sooner he moves out, the better for everyone.

Iris calls later that night, concerned because I wasn't in class. It's no surprise that the gory details of my weekend don't rattle her. She's supportive and encouraging through them all, even when it comes to telling her about the things I did to Chavez. Which, along with the regretful incident at the salvage yard and my abandonment of him on the highway, now also includes ignoring the text message he sent yesterday afternoon in response to the curt one I left him yesterday morning:

I'm fine. Thanks.

That's all you're going to give me? I was worried, Jane.

We need to talk about this.

"Well, that explains why he was hanging out in the lobby before *and* after class today," Iris says over a heavy sigh.

My heart sinks to the floor. "He was?"

"Yep. And you could tell he was on the lookout too. He was just standing in the corner with his arms folded in front of him, staring at the door. You know he's going to be waiting for you again on Friday, and you *have* to go on Friday, Jane; it's the last class. Bates will fail you if you miss more than one."

"I know," I say over a pained breath. "But what am I supposed to say to him? How can I possibly rationalize what I did?"

"Just tell him the truth. Tell him that your life is a shit show and you have to get your own head on straight before you can even think about getting involved with someone."

Just tell him the truth.

It sounds so easy when Iris says it. And considering how much lying I've been forced to do over the last few months, you'd think I'd jump at the opportunity to be honest for once. Unfortunately, though, this is one instance when I'm pretty sure that telling another lie would be a whole lot easier than coming clean.

~

"My life's a shit show. I can't get involved with someone right now. It wouldn't be fair. My life's a shit show . . ."

For the last four days, I've been reciting the explanation that Iris so bluntly, and astutely, provided like a mantra, hoping it will boost my confidence when I undoubtedly face Chavez this morning. Up until this moment, it's been doing a decent job of settling my nerves, but now, as I pull into the police station parking lot, it's not doing me a damn bit of good. My palms are slick with sweat—sliding all over the steering wheel—and my stomach is wrenching like I swallowed a jackhammer.

I don't want to do this.

I don't know how to explain this!

Dread building, I climb out of the car and head for the station.

The day fits my mood. Dark, heavy clouds hang low in the sky, making it feel more like dusk than morning, and the air is so crisp there's almost an edge to it, like little barbs are riding the wind, nipping at my nose and cheeks.

I nestle down deeper into the folds of my wool coat. The weatherman said our first snowfall of the season would likely roll out later this weekend, but I'm thinking more like this afternoon—it's freezing!

Unfortunately, my homeless friend still isn't back on his corner. It's been a full week since I've seen him. Hopefully that means he's safe and warm in one of the area's many shelters, though I must admit I'm more than a little disappointed he's not here. Of all the days I could benefit from one of his toothless smiles or funny signs, it's today.

I make my way across the street and up to the building. My heart thunders hard as I lay my purse, phone, and keys down on the conveyor belt and walk through the metal detector, eyes nervously searching the lobby for Chavez. He's not in the back corner by the elevators, where he usually is, and he's not leaning up against the information desk either.

Maybe he didn't come.

Maybe he realized the only truth he needed to know was that I'm a bitch.

A cold, unfeeling bitch—

"You're all set, ma'am." The officer at the security line motions for me to pick up my things at the end of the belt.

I grab my stuff and quickly head for the stairs. I manage to get a foot on the first step when I see Chavez emerging through a door behind the information desk, my toothless friend following close behind. Startled, I stop dead in my tracks.

He brought him into the police station?

Is he okay?

"It's Reggie's birthday," Chavez, clearly unaware of me, says to the female officer behind the desk. "I told him we'd get him a change of clothes from the lost and found. Maybe hook him up with something to eat?"

"Absolutely," the officer says.

"All right, Reggie. You have yourself a great birthday, okay?" Chavez says, giving the man a gentle pat on the shoulder. "And I don't want to see you outside anymore. It's too cold. You need to head down to the shelter on Riverford."

"Yeah, okay. I will. Thankth, Detective," Reggie agrees over a gummy grin before his dark eyes shift my way and he says, "Oh, hello, pretty lady."

My breath catches as all three of them turn to look at me, Chavez's expression instantly transitioning from festive to something much less happy.

Shit.

My brain begs me to kick it into high gear and disappear up the stairs, but my heart knows better. I need to have this conversation, no matter how desperately I don't want to.

"Jane, can we talk for a minute, please?" Chavez says as he circles around the side of the desk to the foot of the stairs.

His tone is as rigid as his demeanor, forcing my breath to get cinched up in my lungs. I hike my bag a little higher on my shoulder. "Yes, of course."

My life's a shit show.

I can't get involved with anyone right now.

Not until I know it's for the right reasons.

Nerves rattling, I mentally recite my mantra as I follow him around the stairwell and to a small alcove that sits in the far corner of the lobby.

He settles in beside a tall potted plant, his back to the lobby, and in a restrained voice says, "What the hell happened to you?"

Though almost verbatim to the question Dan greeted me with the other night, Chavez's tone isn't angry; he sounds . . . concerned.

Regret swells in my chest, forcing me to clear my throat before I can answer.

"I'm sorry. I didn't mean to worry you—"

"Well, you did. It was obvious you were upset. I didn't like you driving in that frame of mind. And then when you didn't call me back . . . you just sent that short text . . ." His voice trails off beneath a pained expression that instantly magnifies my guilt. "Is everything okay at home?"

Things are far from okay at home, but I still say, "Yes, everything's fine," because I know that right now he's asking that question as a concerned cop, not as the guy I almost had sex with.

"So, what happened?" he presses. "Did I come on too strong? Did I make you feel uncomfortable—"

"Oh god, no!" I quickly grab his forearm, hoping to stifle his unwarranted concerns. "It wasn't you at all. I was the one who started everything." His gaze travels down to my hand, and despite how good his skin feels beneath mine, I pull it away, dropping my head in the process. "You didn't do anything wrong," I finish quietly.

"Then what was it? What happened?"

Just tell him the truth, Jane.

Just be honest.

I heave a deep breath and slowly raise my head to look at him. The explanation I spent hours rehearsing flits through my thoughts but doesn't land anywhere. It can't. The confusion in his eyes makes it impossible.

"I—um. I wasn't myself the other night," I bumble weakly. "I . . . I shouldn't have done that with you."

He stares at me for a long beat before a big knot slides down his throat. "Why not?"

"It's complicated."

"Because you're still married?"

I shake my head, pained by the answer I know I need to give but don't want to.

"Then what is it?" he asks again.

My stomach churns with regret, forcing me to shift my stance as I scour my brain for Iris's sage words. "My life is, um—it's . . . shit—I'm shit. I'm a shit show," I sputter. "And even though I like being with you and spending time with you, I'm not sure that"—I swallow hard, fisting my nervous knuckle at my side—"I just . . . I don't know if what I'm feeling for you is—"

From over his shoulder, I see Officer Bates suddenly emerge from behind the information desk. Our eyes lock for a split second before she turns away from me and heads up the stairs, a scowl working her jaw.

Dammit.

Now she's going to be primed to give me more hell than usual. Especially if I'm late—

"If what you're feeling for me is what?" he prods.

I turn back to him, desperately wishing the words I'm about to say will make sense to him but fully aware that they won't—because they hardly make sense to me. "I'm just . . . I'm not sure if what I'm feeling for you is real, or if I'm just using you because you're something different—"

"Oh." His shoulders sag, and he drops his head.

"That's not to say I don't like being with you," I quickly add. "I do. It's just . . . *god.*" I scrub an anguished hand through my hair. *Think, Jane. THINK!* "I hardly know which way is up right now. I don't trust myself with anything, and I don't want to get involved with you if I'm not sure—"

"Nah, I get it." He cuts me off with a raised palm.

"What?" I reel back, startled by the insistence in his voice. "No. There's more to it. There's a lot more about my life you don't know. My husband is a very important doctor. All kinds of people are relying on him—"

"I don't need to know," he says, now raising his other palm so his hands are splayed out in a very definitive *stop* gesture in front of him. A stark contradiction to the position his hands took with me on Saturday. "I know how divorce works. And I know how *important* doctors are. One saved my life, remember?"

"Yes, of course I remember. But there's so much more to it for me," I counter, pained by the resolve in his voice. He's writing me off without knowing all the facts. I at least want him to know why I'm in such a tough position. "In a few months, I'll be able to file for divorce and I think—well . . . I mean, I hope that by then I'll have a better idea of where I am—how I feel about you—"

"Jane, it's fine." He locks his cold gaze onto mine. "I understand that you need time to work through your stuff, and I seriously hope that you can because what your husband is doing to you is pretty messed up, but I'm not going to wait around while you figure things out."

Now my shoulders sag.

That's not what I was suggesting.

Was it?

"But—"

"No, it's all good," he repeats, sounding anything but *good*. "I wish you all the best. I really do. But I learned a long time ago—when I almost died—that our time here is too short to wait around for anything or anybody. If something feels right to me, I go for it. If I want to try something new, I do it. I trust myself enough to make those kinds of decisions, but if you don't, then . . ." He shrugs. "Well, then there's nothing more to say. You better get upstairs, or you'll be late for class."

He storms off, disappearing down the long hallway, while I stand in the corner watching him, wishing I could undo what I just did.

Wishing I'd told him more. That I'd made him understand that over a hundred jobs are depending on Dan—on us!—and our big fat shit show of a marriage.

With heavy, regretful steps, I climb the stairs and find Iris and Burty waiting for me outside the classroom.

"Did you see him?" Iris asks.

I nod weakly.

"How'd it go?" Burty asks.

I sigh. "Horrible. I really hurt him. He doesn't want anything to do with me."

Burty's bottom lip rolls out into a pout. "I'm sorry, Janie," she says, and then gives me a hug.

"It was the right thing to do," Iris says over one of her stoic smiles.

"I know," I sniffle. "It was just hard."

"The truth usually is. Come on." She motions toward the door. "Let's get this over with."

I follow my friends inside, not surprised to see that a very perturbed-looking Bates is standing at her podium with her eyes zeroed in on me, like she's been waiting for me.

Shit.

"Come here, Holliday," she instructs with a crook of her finger.

Iris casts me a wary glance while Burty mutters, "I'm sure she just wants to see your doctor's note."

"Yeah, I'm sure," I reply, wishing that were the case.

Nerves racing, I make my way over to the podium, Bates tracking each of my steps along the way.

"You weren't here on Monday," she says gruffly.

I swallow hard. "I was sick."

Her eyes narrow like she knows I'm lying. I shift beneath the weight of my coat.

"Got a note?"

"Yes. Here." I pull the letter from my bag and hand it to her.

She stares at it for a long, nerve-racking beat and then mumbles, "Where's your journal?"

My journal?

Crap!

My stomach flops to the floor.

My latest journal entry was the most honest and gut-wrenching response I've ever written, but unfortunately it won't meet Bates's criteria, as it was limited to only one word. I meant to add on to it—to beef it up to at least a full paragraph—but completely forgot, given everything else I've been dealing with this week.

A kind, compassionate person would accept it for what it is—trusting that writing that word was one of the hardest things I've ever done—but this is Officer Bates we're talking about. She hasn't liked me from day one, and after what just happened with Chavez—when it was obvious I was making him upset—*shit!* She's going to kick me out of the class—

"Come on, Holliday," she urges, pulling me back to the present.

With nervous hands, I pull the notebook from my bag and hand it off to her. She takes it with a grunt, then says, "Find a seat."

Today, the metal folding chairs are aligned in a straight row instead of their usual circle. I settle into the empty chair between Burty and Iris, clutching my bag against my chest for support.

"You okay?" Iris asks.

I shrug and mutter, "I don't know."

"All right, ladies," Bates says to the group. "We're going to do something a little different today, since it's our last class—"

"Woo!" Angel chirps from a few chairs down, prompting Donna to chuckle over her gravelly lungs while Lina mutters, "Halle-fucking-lujah."

There's no way Bates doesn't hear them, but she continues without acknowledgment.

"—I've asked a former student to stop by and talk to you about her experience in this class and how it's impacted her life now that she's moved on."

Still holding my notebook firmly in her hands, Bates lumbers across the room—boots squeaking louder than usual—and leans out into the hallway, returning a moment later with a dark-haired woman following along behind her.

"This is Stephanie." Bates motions to the woman. She's dressed in a black cashmere turtleneck, with her dark denim jeans tucked into her over-the-calf riding boots, and I half wonder if she was arrested for stealing from my closet. "She was arrested three years ago for possession of cocaine, but I'm happy to report she's been clean ever since."

Stephanie smiles with deserved pride as Maya calls out, "You go, girl!" while the rest of my classmates clap and "woot woot" their support. I join in with a smile and an encouraging nod of my own, but it's not as heartfelt as it should be. Despite this woman's great accomplishment, my attention is solely focused on my stupid notebook, and whether it's going to be the catalyst that earns me a dismissal from the class, promptly followed by a stint behind bars.

Dammit, Jane!

A one-word journal entry? You know better than that!

"Well, I'm really glad I can be here to talk to you today," Stephanie starts. "Like Officer Bates said, I was given the opportunity to participate in this class after I was arrested for possession. I wish I could say that my story is unique, but I've been talking to a lot of women over the last couple of years, and unfortunately, it's not." She assumes a confident but comfortable stance against the podium, suggesting that she's delivered this message more than a few times. "At the time I was arrested, I'd been married for thirteen years, had two kids—seven and nine then—and spent pretty much every waking hour taking care of them and about a million other things that came with it. I served on every PTA committee ever created; was room mom for both kids' classes; played chauffeur to baseball, soccer, piano, cooking class—"

Her comments catch my attention.

Is she talking about her life or mine?

"I was living the stereotypical life of a stay-at-home mom," she goes on. "And it was great. But it was also exhausting, and more than a little stressful." I feel myself nod. I can relate to that. "I was in the midst of a particularly bad week: my period was raging, my husband was out of town for work, both kids had huge projects due that they hadn't even started, and I had stupidly agreed to head up the wrapping paper fundraiser at school, which, if you know anything about school fundraisers, is the worst of them all."

I can't help the little chuckle that crosses my lips. That *is* the worst fundraiser, quickly followed by the one for See's chocolates.

"I was basically at my breaking point," she goes on. "And then one of the other moms pulled me aside and offered me a little pick-me-up to help get me through." She shakes her head over a sardonic laugh. "I knew I shouldn't do it. I could actually see that little 'Just Say No' stop sign flashing in my mind"—she wiggles her fingers in front of her, emulating twinkling lights—"but everything just felt too big in that moment, so I did it. I went into the students' bathroom with that woman, ducked down beneath one of the three-foot-tall stalls, and took my first hit of cocaine. And that was all it took. Next thing I knew, while the other moms were going to yoga after the morning carpool run, I was hiding out in parking lots, snorting coke in the back seat of my car." She chuckles despite the weight of her confession, which allows the rest of us to laugh a little too. Not because it's funny but because . . . wow.

"Bless her heart," Burty mutters.

"Nobody in my family had a clue I was using. My husband was working crazy hours back then, so he wasn't around a lot to notice, and my kids were, well . . ." She smirks. "They pretty much ignored me—"

"Sounds about right," Iris murmurs. I grin.

"—so it was like this private little thing I had that got me through all the craziness of life, and I loved it. I did," she admits over an unapologetic shrug. "I felt like Wonder Woman, you guys. I had so much energy, my house was insanely clean, I finally hit my goal weight . . ." She sighs. "I'm telling you, for the few months I was using, it was great. Until it wasn't." She pauses and offers a thoughtful look around the room. "The night I got arrested, I had overdosed. The cops found me unconscious in the back seat of my minivan in a Trader Joe's parking lot."

Someone down the way—Maya, I think—gasps, "Oh my god," while I shift uneasily in my seat.

Apparently, a lot of life-changing events take place in grocery store parking lots.

"Of course, I don't remember anything about it," she continues. "I woke up in the hospital the next day with tubes in my arms, hooked up to machines, completely clueless. I thought I'd been in a car accident, until my husband told me what happened. I can still remember the look on his face . . ." Her voice starts to waver a bit, and she gives her head a regretful shake. "He was scared, obviously, and mad, and confused, and worried and all the things you'd imagine someone would be feeling in that moment, but what really stuck with me was how disappointed he looked . . ."

Disappointed.

That bravely spoken word sends a shudder of unease rattling through my bones. It's similar to the one I wrote (I even thought of using it myself), but it didn't convey exactly what I was trying to say.

I cast a wary glance toward Bates, to my notebook, which she's clutching in her hands.

"And it didn't stop with him," she goes on. "My kids looked at me like that too. And my parents—*god*, they were the worst. Even though they were all supportive of me and got me into rehab and cheered me on every step of the way, there was always this underlying disappointment in their eyes." Her gaze drops down to the podium. "I think that was the hardest part of it all—even harder than kicking the addiction, which wasn't easy," she confesses, refacing us wearing an earnest expression. "I felt like I'd let all of them down, and I didn't know how I was ever going to make that up to them, or even go on living with myself, for having made them feel that way—"

I swallow hard, my throat growing thick beneath the similarity of our thoughts.

"—but then I came to this class, and everything changed." A smile slowly starts to spread across her cheeks. "I remember how scared I was on the first day," she says, eyeing the room nostalgically. "My plan was to come in, do my time, and get out without talking to anybody, but then somebody made us stand up and say our names and what we were charged with . . ." She casts an amused glance toward Bates.

"I still do that," Bates replies, grinning.

"Yeah she does," Lina grunts, and everyone laughs. Including me.

"Well, believe it or not, that was the game changer for me," Stephanie goes on. "Up until that moment, everyone in my life had been disappointed by me for what I'd done to them. Me"—she pats her chest with her palm—"Stephanie. The wife who had been sneaking money out of the vacation fund to pay for her habit. The mom who had been showing up to her kids' games stoned out of her mind. The daughter who lied and said she'd joined Weight Watchers to explain her sudden weight loss. I did all those things to them. But the women in my class . . ." She shrugs over a reminiscent smile. "I hadn't let them down at all. They weren't mad at me for anything. To them, I was just Stephanie, the lady who was charged with possession, no better or worse than any of them, and that was the most liberating feeling in the world."

My chest starts to swell beneath the succinctness of her words. They're so honest and familiar somehow. Like my brain's been reciting them, but they've never actually crossed my lips.

"Now, I'm not going to stand here and tell you that I enjoyed coming to this class," she goes on, casting a sheepish glance toward Bates, who smirks in response. "I hated talking about my personal life with a bunch of strangers, but looking back, I think it actually helped me. I can't tell you how many times I've been faced with a hard choice, and my mind inevitably wanders back to one of the conversations I had here. When someone called me out for the choices I made. At the time, it felt like a personal attack, but looking back I can see it was just them being brutally honest with me. And I needed that, because the people in my life were too busy being disappointed by me to tell me what I needed to hear in a way that I could hear it. Sometimes brutal honesty is the only way to be heard."

"Yeah, it is," Lina mutters, as if she's aware she's the most *brutally* honest of us all.

"And then there was that damn journal," Stephanie goes on over a heavy eye roll that makes my classmates laugh again, but I don't. I shift my attention back to Bates, and my notebook. "I hated that thing," she admits. "It felt like the biggest waste of time in the middle of my busy day, but I'll be damned if I don't pull it out every now and then, just to be reminded of how far I've come. Crazy as it probably sounds to you right now, there's a lot of good stuff in those journals."

"Which is exactly why we do them," Bates replies over a firm nod. She turns her attention out to the class and raises my notebook into the air while saying, "There's a wealth of wisdom in these pages, ladies—wisdom that came straight from you—but you have to be willing to put in the time to find it." Her gaze lands directly on me as she says the words.

Shit.

That's it.

She's going to fail me.

She's going to kick me out of the class.

I'll be formally charged, and then everyone in Mount Ivy will know, and the last month will have been for nothing!

"She's right," Stephanie says. "All the tools you need to get to a better place are in your hands; you just have to know how to use them. For me that means regular NA meetings, counseling, phone calls with my friends from this class who *actually* get me . . ."

I cast a quick glance toward Iris and see her nodding along.

"Whatever *your* tools are, you owe it to yourself to find them and use them, because without them you'll never be okay with yourself, and then you're no good to anybody else."

"I couldn't agree more," Bates affirms. She hoists herself out of her seat and strides over toward the podium while the rest of us clap in appreciation for Stephanie's testimony.

"Dang, that was powerful," a misty-eyed Burty says as Bates gives Stephanie a hug and then sends her on her way. "I swear, she could be one of them motivational speakers. Like we used to have at school assemblies."

I nod. Yes, she's definitely motivating. Unfortunately, though, her attagirl speech can't magically make more words appear in my journal.

"Okay, ladies." Bates reassumes her position at the podium. "I've got one last journal entry I'd like you to complete, in class, before I send you back into the world. And while I'm not going to review it, I want you to put some serious thought into it. Like Stephanie said, you may need it someday."

Whether it's the inspiration still lingering in the air or the promise of impending liberation, my classmates quickly whip out their notebooks while I squirm, empty handed, in my chair.

She's dragging this out.

She's intentionally making me suffer.

Waiting until the very last moment to tell me I didn't pass before she drops the ax—it's payback for Chavez!

"The prompt is: What I am most looking forward to doing after this class . . ."

I see Iris and Burty scribbling down the prompt and can hear the pens and pencils of the rest of the class gliding across their papers, but I can't do anything—

"Holliday."

My breath catches beneath the terse sound of Bates calling my name. In my periphery, I see Iris's hand stop mid-pen-stroke.

"It's gonna be okay," she whispers.

On wobbly legs, I make my way up to the podium, where Bates is waiting for me with a flat, unreadable expression on her face.

Shit.

This is it.

Shit.shit.shit.

She stares at me for a painfully long and uncomfortable beat—brown eyes boring straight into my soul—before she says, "You know, Stephanie wasn't kidding when she said there's a lot of good stuff in here."

I blink hard, confused.

"I'm . . . sorry?"

She hands me my notebook. "There's good stuff in here," she repeats, her expression still as deadpan as it was a moment ago. "Now get to work and use it."

I stare down at the book, brows burrowing into my forehead.

Wait—

What?

"So, does this mean . . . did I pass—"

"Sit down and respond to the prompt, Holliday. It's the only way you're going to pass the class."

"Oh . . . okay." I nod quickly, scared if I don't shut up she might change her mind.

"And make it more than *one* word," she adds, confirming that she *did* read my journal.

"Yes. I will."

Heart hammering, I hustle back to my seat and flip open my notebook.

PROMPT: WHAT I AM MOST AFRAID OF IS . . .
ANSWER:

Me

My heart wrenches as I stare down at my most recent journal entry.

Me.

The twenty-two-year-old waitress who still wonders if sacrificing her happiness for stability is the better choice.

Me.

The thirty-nine-year-old mother who questions whether joint custody can ever be the right answer.

Me.

The big sister who shudders at the thought of not solving her little sister's problems.

Me.

The daughter who can't let go of a lifetime of resentments.

Me.

The woman who treated someone she cared about like an afterthought.

Me.

The terrified soon-to-be divorcée who wonders if she can actually do this on her own.

Through blurry eyes, I see an impression of blue ink pushing up on the back of the page, like someone's written on the other side.

Confused, I turn it over.

You can't be scared of someone you don't know, Holliday.

Take the time to figure out who you are.

You'll be glad you did.

And so will the people you've hurt.

CHAPTER 22

Eight weeks later . . .

"So, how did Avery respond to Dan's big question last week?" Dr. Deangelo asks. I level her with a hard look that makes her grin. "That good, huh?"

"She told him that she'd rather get eaten by a shark than meet his boyfriend."

She winces. "How did Dan take it?"

I sigh. "The same way he seems to respond to everything these days: he played it off like it didn't bother him, but I could tell it hurt his feelings."

"And how did that make you feel?"

I drop my head, ashamed by the answer that's tickling my lips.

"Jane," she prompts. "Remember, feelings aren't wrong. You're entitled to have them, whatever they are."

"I know."

It's not the first time she's told me that.

I stare down at the crocheted goat that's attached to the tip of my pointer finger—a therapy puppet, Burty calls it—and tug on his little horn. Just like the rubber band, he provides my brain a necessary redirect when I'm feeling stressed or uneasy about something. I relied pretty heavily on him when I first started seeing Dr. Deangelo seven weeks ago (poor guy, he used to have *two* horns), but now he serves more as a reminder of the cheering section I've got outside these walls. An unexpected smirk tugs on my lip as I think back on the first time I saw one of Burty's creations. That poor elephant . . .

Grateful for the memory, I inhale a deep breath, then raise my head and get back to the topic at hand. "It made me feel good," I admit. "Validated, if that makes sense?"

"It does."

"Not that I like Avery being in a position to have to feel that way. I hate that we've done this to her," I continue, shaking my head with the same regret I do every Thursday between 10:00 and 11:00 a.m. "It just seems like he cares more about what she thinks than anybody else, which sort of feels like a slap in the face, considering *I'm* the one he cheated on, and I'm now covering his lying ass, but I don't know . . ." I sigh. "I guess so long as someone can make him feel bad about what he's done, that's a good thing, right?"

She does that psychiatrist thing where she doesn't actually answer my question; she just stares at me in that contemplative way of hers while she waits for me to come to the conclusion myself. Which I do. Yes, it's a good thing that Dan feels some guilt for what he's done to our family. Lord knows I can't bear that burden on my own—something Dr. Deangelo has helped me realize.

"Does Avery ever talk to you about Dan and his relationship?"

I shake my head. "Not much. She'll say little things in passing, but we don't have any deep conversations about either of them. I think she saves all of that for Dr. Tidwell."

Dr. Tidwell is the child psychologist Avery's been talking to. She sees him once a week to help her deal with all the changes, but mostly they seem to be focusing on her anger issues (like mother, like daughter), and thankfully it's working. Rather than acting out at school, she's learning to convey her feelings through her words: like telling her father she'd rather be chewed apart by a vicious animal than meet his special someone.

"Well, that's still good," she says. "So long as she's talking to someone, and working through all those feelings, that's the important part. We just want to keep her talking."

Yes. Just keep her talking.

"And you've got the big gala coming up soon, right?"

"Tomorrow night," I say with some trepidation.

"That's a big day for you."

"Yeah."

"Are you ready?"

I sigh. "I don't know. Part of me is terrified, because there's so much riding on this and we still don't know how it's going to play out"— the Hoffstras have confirmed they will give *something* to the hospital, but they've yet to announce the actual amount; they'll be making the announcement at the gala—"but then there's this other part of me that's . . . excited. Is that wrong?"

"Not at all. The gala doesn't just have an impact on the hospital; it's also the starting point for your new life. It makes sense that you'd be excited for that."

I nod. I am definitely excited for the next chapter.

I've already spoken to an attorney in the city, who is more than happy to take on our case when the time is right, and thankfully Dan's conceded to the plan. He's as eager to put some distance between us as I am.

"How does Avery feel about you getting divorced?"

"She's okay with it," I say with a surprising amount of confidence. "I mean, she knows things are going to change again, but she seems ready for it. Like she's eager to get on with life, whatever it looks like."

"I think a more permanent routine will be good for both of you." She nods encouragingly, then takes a sip of her tea and says, "And how about your journal?"

She's referring to my notebook from the first-offenders group and the last prompt—what I'm most looking forward to—which I've still yet to answer beyond the pathetic placeholder I scribbled down that day: *To be determined.* Thankfully, Dr. Deangelo doesn't incorporate journals and writing prompts into *her* treatment plans, but she is really big on "tying up loose ends so you can move forward," so she's been encouraging me to respond to it ever since our first appointment. Despite my many attempts, I've yet to come up with a more thoughtful answer.

I shake my head.

"That's okay. The answer will be there when you're ready." I sigh. We'll see . . . "Any luck finding a shelter?" she asks, which unsurprisingly brings a smile to my face.

"Yes, actually there's one down in Cannon Park just a couple of miles from my mom. I'm going to serve lunch there on the weekends when Avery's with Dan, and then stop in and visit with her and Julie after."

Even though I know that Reggie, my toothless friend from the city, is safe under Chavez's watchful eye, I still find myself thinking about him, and feeling grateful for the little rays of sunshine he brought to my life on those dark and unsettling days. In the grand scheme of things, serving up macaroni twice a month isn't going to change the world, but my hope is that it will bring a smidge of that same kind of "Reggie light" to someone else's life, and maybe give me a sense of purpose along the way.

"It sounds like a perfect fit," Dr. Deangelo says. "I'm really proud of you for looking into that." I nod, feeling a little proud myself, as she takes another sip of tea, and then she finally poses the question I've been dreading ever since I got here. "And how about the detective? Last time we spoke, you said you had an apology text ready to go; you just had to hit the 'Send' button."

I sigh. "No."

"How come?" She tips her head thoughtfully. "You've been talking about doing it for a couple of weeks now. What do you think is holding you back?"

"I don't know." I return my attention to the goat and start tugging on his lone horn again. "I guess I'm . . ."

"What?"

"I'm not sure exactly." I give my head a frustrated shake. "Scared, maybe?"

"What is there to be scared of?"

More than a few responses come to mind:

That he's moved on.

That he hates me.

That I snuffed out any spark there was between us.

But I end up saying the one that weighs heaviest on my heart. "Rejection."

"You think he'll reject your apology?"

Along with her belief in tying up loose ends, Dr. Deangelo also encourages patients to right wrongs when the patient feels it's necessary. And I do. Even though I know it was the right thing to do, I still haven't forgiven myself for the way I treated Chavez.

"Or is it possible there might be more to the conversation?" she astutely wonders.

My cheeks flush with heat, prompting a nervous laugh to feather my lungs. "I don't know." I tug a little harder on the horn. "Lately I've been missing him, I guess."

"The physical intimacy?"

"That, yes," I admit. "But also, the way I felt when I was with him."

"How was that?"

I smile a little. "At ease. Special. Happy. I laughed a lot."

"So, you think you might be interested in reconnecting on a more personal level?"

"Maybe. I . . . I don't know." I tug the goat off my finger and set him down on the leather cushion beside me. "I'd like to see where it could go—if there was more to our connection than just high school memories and our shared love for smashing things—but I'm not sure I can run the risk of getting rejected. I don't think I could handle that right now."

"Why are you so sure he'd reject you?"

I raise my head. "You didn't see the look on his face when I broke things off with him. He was so upset."

She shrugs. "People get upset all the time; it doesn't always mean their feelings change."

I'd like to believe that what she's saying is true—that hurt feelings don't always equate to a change of heart—but in this case, I can't.

I shake my head. "If he still felt the same way, he would have called me by now, and he hasn't."

"But you haven't called him either," she reminds me over a pointed look.

"Yeah, but my feelings *have* changed," I counter. "And that's the problem."

∿

"Whoo-wee! Somebody's lookin' good tonight!"

Julie ogles me from the corner of the sectional as I walk into the room. I roll my eyes.

"You do look really pretty, Mom," Avery adds over a sweet grin.

"Well, thank you." Despite my mood, I grab the hem of my glittery midnight-blue cocktail dress and give a little curtsy.

Julie laughs while Avery turns back to the TV, groaning.

"So, big night tonight." Julie climbs off the couch and joins me in the kitchen, where I'm grabbing a glass from the cupboard and filling it up at the sink. "Are you ready?"

I sigh. "No, but I don't have much of a choice, do I?"

I take a quick sip of water to wet my tongue, then tuck a little white pill into my mouth and swallow it back with a big gulp. Seventy-five milligrams of Paxil once a day—not Zoloft, and most definitely *not* ecstasy. "Just enough," according to Dr. Deangelo, "to take the edge off." And she's right. It's been a tremendous help.

"It'll all be okay," Julie reassures me over a sympathetic smile. "Even if they don't give the hospital the money, it'll work out. Dan may be a dick, but he's still a good doctor. He'll find a job somewhere else if he has to."

I nod in agreement, though just the thought makes my heart ache. The last thing I want is to make Avery earn air miles traveling from one parent's house to the other's. Across town is one thing, but different cities are a different ball game.

"Speaking of the dick . . . ," Julie mumbles, her gaze darting over my shoulder.

I turn and see Dan striding into the house through the side door, something he does from time to time, though usually when I'm not home. Of course he looks runway ready in his tuxedo, like the Marlboro Man decided to snuff out his cigarette and join the party.

"Hello, everyone," he says.

"Wow, Dad, you look really good," Avery calls out.

"Thanks, sweetie. You think this monkey suit will land me some big bucks?" He waggles his brows and tugs on the edges of his bow tie.

"Eww, not if you do that."

He chuckles in that unnerving way of his, then turns to me and says, "You look very nice, Jane."

The compliment is for Avery's benefit, not mine. Even though she's aware of our animosity for each other, we still try hard to be civil.

I force a smile. "Thanks. So do you."

"Well, isn't this fun," Julie mutters under her breath.

I cast her a knowing glance as I empty my glass in the sink, then set it on the drying pad.

Yeah. This is fun, all right.

"We should probably get going," Dan offers. "Jackie's got us on a tight schedule."

"Yeah, I know," I groan.

Besides having us dine at the head table with the Hoffstras and some other hospital bigwigs, Jackie has also mapped out some other potential donors she'd like us to woo at the predinner cocktail reception. I grab my little clutch from the counter, then head over to the couch to say good night to Avery.

"Love you, sweetie." I plant a kiss on the top of her head.

"You too," she mutters back.

I turn to Julie. "Hopefully it won't be too late." A look passes between us. Over the past few weeks, my sister has become my emotional backbone, supporting me in ways I never would have imagined. And only she knows my plan for the night: As soon as the Hoffstras announce their gift, I'll be feigning a headache and catching the first Uber off the premises. My time pretending to be Dan's devoted wife— his devoted *anything*—will officially be done. "I'm guessing by ten thirty at the latest. I'll text you if I get hung up."

"Yeah, no worries," she says. "We're just going to eat ice cream and watch *Footloose*—"

"No, we're not," Avery cuts in. "I told you I don't want to watch that. It's old and looks stupid."

"Fine, you can pick," she says back over a chuckle, then turns to me and with an encouraging nod whispers, "You've got this. Just try and focus on what comes at the *end* of this charade."

I smile wearily, grateful for the reminder. "I will. Thanks."

"Good night, kiddo," Dan calls out to Avery, then turns to Julie and says, "Thanks for watching her."

"Uh . . . you're welcome." Julie's puzzled expression mirrors my own confusion. Since when has Dan ever thanked Julie for watching Avery? Or . . . anything?

"Shall we?" He motions toward the door.

Perplexed by his atypically thoughtful behavior, I sigh and say, "I guess so."

I take the lead and head through the living room—grabbing my floor-length wool coat from the closet along the way—and out the front door. I wince as the frigid February air slams into me, prompting goose bumps to rise across my skin and my warm breath to hang, ghostlike, in front of me.

It's been a week since our last snowfall, and while the roads have long been cleared, mountains of dirty, frozen snow still erupt from the ground like weatherworn tepees. I nuzzle deeper into my coat's collar and cautiously navigate my way down the slick flagstone pavers toward the driveway. In another shockingly courteous display, Dan takes my elbow as if worried I'll slip.

Why is he being so nice?

What is he up to?

His touch sends a frosty tickle down my spine, but thankfully he's already got his car running, so it's warm when I climb inside, melting away my annoyance and giving me back my perspective: it doesn't matter what he wants. I'm not giving him anything else. *Ever.*

Because there's valet parking at the event, we decided beforehand that it would be better to ride together—so we're seen getting out of the same vehicle—but as I buckle myself in, I'm suddenly wishing we were going separately. I haven't been this close to Dan in months. I shift against the leather seat, my skin suddenly feeling a bit itchy.

Oh, the things that have happened in this seat . . .

"The news says we're supposed to get another storm as early as Sunday," he says as we take off down the road.

"Uh-huh," I mumble, keeping my gaze fixed out the window.

"Hopefully we won't get too much snow. I planned to take Avery into the city to watch a game Tuesday night."

He told me this information last week, so I don't feel the need to respond.

That and I don't want to.

I'm not in the mood for small talk.

I scooch closer toward the door.

Since when is this car so small?

"I'm sure the freeways will be open, though," he carries on, his voice quickly getting under my skin. "But just to be safe, we'll leave a little earlier. Maybe we'll stop for dinner beforehand."

I nod but don't say anything.

Fine.

Stop for dinner.

Leave early.

Whatever you want, Dan. So long as it doesn't involve me.

"You know, your dress reminds me a lot of the one you wore that night we got lost in London," he goes on. "Remember we were supposed to see that show on the West End, and we could never find the theater? What were we trying to see? Was it *Evita*—"

"Would you just stop, *please*," I snip, turning toward him.

Even though it's dark, the dashboard provides enough light that I can see his eyes narrow.

"Stop what?"

"Stop pretending you enjoy talking to me! Your voice is just—" I grit my teeth, searching for the words. "It's like nails on a chalkboard right now."

Two months ago, I would have swallowed my annoyance and let it fester inside me until I snapped, but thanks to Dr. Deangelo, I've learned it's better for me to say what I'm feeling when I'm feeling it.

"Fine," he grunts, shifting his gaze back to the road. "I was just trying to be polite."

Trying to be polite?

Since when?!

We ride in uncomfortable silence for a few more minutes before he stupidly starts in again. "I'm sure you're not aware, but there's been a change to tonight's schedule."

The condescension in his tone grates against every nerve in my body.

I'm sure you're not aware.

As if he's the all-powerful Oz, and I'm just some brainless fool wandering down the yellow brick road waiting for directions.

You're such a self-centered ass!

"Okay. Whatever," I grumble, disinterested and annoyed.

Thankfully, the hospital's philanthropy staff has been on top of every detail of the gala. In the last two months, the only demands placed on the committee members were to assist with the seating chart and offer input on the wine selection. And even though I received an email with the schedule of events, I hardly even glanced at it—because I don't care! I don't care when the first course is served or what time the freaking comedian takes the stage. All I care about is that the second Dan gets his precious donation, I'm leaving. And I'm never going to have to lie about my life again!

"Well, I thought it might interest you to know that at the last minute, I decided to invite one more grateful patient to come and speak—"

"*Ugh!*" I cut him off over a disgusted grunt. "You really are the most selfish person on the planet, aren't you?" I turn to him, scowling. "One grateful patient wasn't enough, so you had to invite *two?*"

He reels back. "No. That's not why I—"

"Do you really think I care about this, Dan? Seriously?" I raise my palms, and while there are question marks trailing my words, I'm not looking for an answer. And he knows it. "I couldn't care less about who you invited to come and talk about what a great doctor you are. I mean, I'm glad you're good at your job and that you were able to help these people, but if they knew the *real* you, they wouldn't be coming tonight. Anyone that knows the real you would never sing your praises."

My words are harsh and prick my tongue like little needles, but they needed to be said.

"Well, excuse me for trying to help you out," he says snidely, making an intentionally hard right turn into the hotel's parking lot.

"Help *me* out? How are you helping me?"

"It's obvious you're wound up about tonight. I just thought you might like to know there's been a change so you can better prepare yourself—"

"*Better prepare myself?*" Despite the antianxiety meds pumping through my veins, my blood starts to run hot. "Are you kidding me? What do you think I've been doing for the last three months? I've been preparing myself for *this* night. The night when I have to put on a show for two hundred and fifty people—"

"You make it sound like everybody's going to be watching *you*," he grouses back, bringing the car to a stop behind a Jaguar, where an older, tuxedo-clad gentleman is taking a ticket from the valet. "I'm the one who has to get onstage in front of everyone."

"Yeah, but *I'm* the one who has to talk you up all night. I'm the one who has to pretend like the person I'm married to *isn't* an asshole."

He flinches. "Yeah, well, it's not easy for me either. Don't forget, I've been pretending my whole life."

My stomach wrenches beneath the anguish in his voice, no doubt reflective of how hard that must have been for him. As a kid—a teenager—never being able to be honest with his parents or his friends. With *anyone*. It must have been awful. No wonder he's such a good liar. But that doesn't mean it's okay to turn me into one too.

"Dan, I'm sorry you had to live like that. I am. But you *chose* the lies you told; I didn't. I just want to live an honest, genuine life, but because of you I can't. And that's not fair," I go on, recounting some of the revelations I've made with Dr. Deangelo. "You've put me in a horrible, *shameful* position where I'm forced to lie to everyone I know. I don't get to be *myself* because you're too scared to be *yourself*, and that's just wrong."

He blinks hard, and his lips part like he's about to say something—

"Save it!" I cut him off before he has the chance. "Whatever it is you're about to say, don't. In fact, don't talk to me for the rest of the night! When we're around other people, we can do all the bullshitting we have to, but when it's just you and me, don't say anything. After everything you've done to me, you at least owe me that."

CHAPTER 23

I'm all forced smiles and fake laughs as Jackie Harriman parades us through the cocktail reception like the show ponies we are. First, we make small talk with Stan and Irma Vandersloot—potential donors from Grand Rapids who made their small fortune selling farm equipment at their chain of thirty-eight stores that "serve the entire Midwest at our best!"—then we're herded over to Marcia Greenbaum, a Chicago widow with no heirs and an estate worth nearly two hundred million. Jackie tells us privately that should the Hoffstras not come through with a substantial gift, we may have an opportunity with Marcia, in a year or so, though it will take some extra schmoozing from the two of us.

My stomach sours at the mere suggestion.

A year or so?

No way.

Thankfully, Dan minds my demand and doesn't talk to me about anything outside our fronted conversations. In fact, he's quieter than usual—almost subdued—which a few months ago would have worried me . . . made me wonder if what I'd said in the car had hurt his feelings. But today it doesn't bother me at all. If his feelings are hurt, so be it. He'll get over it soon enough. And in the meantime, I'm just grateful he's leaving me alone.

I exchange a "You look gorgeous" over a cheek kiss with Heather when I pick up a glass of chardonnay from the bar—she's sipping something over ice, her eyes already a bit glassy—then wander into the auction area, where I bid on things I don't want and will never use.

The overhead lights flicker, like the end of intermission at the theater, and the huge ballroom doors swing open, indicating that it's time to transition to the next phase of the evening.

I blanch as Dan takes my elbow and ushers me through the crowd toward our table in the center of the ballroom. With soft-lit crystal chandeliers dangling from the ceiling and gold-plated utensils adorning the tabletops, you'd think we were attending an event at Buckingham Palace rather than the Mount Ivy Hilton.

Our tablemates are already in their seats when we arrive. Along with the Hoffstras are midlevel donors Jim and Patty Demers (Jim is a retired banker who now sits on the hospital's board of directors), and Diane Porter (the hospital's COO) and her husband, Mason, I think. Or maybe it's Tom—

"Well, look who's here." Mr. Hoffstra stands, greeting Dan and me with a smile so sincere it makes me feel guilty about mine. "Nice to see you again, Dan. Jane."

"Phil, very nice to see you." Dan offers him a hearty handshake over one of his million-watt grins, but there's something off about the delivery of his greeting. It's a little flat.

The pressure of the night must finally be getting to him.

Now that we're here in front of the Hoffstras, everything that's riding on this event is starting to feel very real.

I swallow through my own unease and say, "Nice to see you again," to Mr. Hoffstra, then turn to Mrs. Hoffstra, who's looking up at me with a kind smile of her own. "Hello. How are you?" I ask, dropping down into the empty seat beside her.

"Oh, we're doing just fine, dear," she reports while giving my hand a tender pat. "How are you? And how's your daughter?"

My heart twists at the sincerity behind her question.

I hate that I have to lie to her.

Damn you, Dan!

"We're all doing great. Avery's busy as always, which keeps me hopping, but, yeah, we're all doing really, really well."

To me, the lies are obvious—clanging like cymbals against my ears—but thankfully Mrs. Hoffstra's none the wiser.

Just get through the next couple of hours, Jane.

Just get through this night, and then you're free . . .

From my seat, I offer up softly spoken "Good evenings" and "Nice to see you's" while Dan glad-hands his way around the table before settling into the empty seat on my right. He immediately assumes the attentive-husband position by throwing his arm around me. Thankfully his hand only grazes my shoulder before coming to rest on the back of my chair.

"Good evening, everyone"—Jackie's voice suddenly erupts through the room—"and welcome to the Mount Ivy General's Listen to Your Heart Gala. I'm Jackie Harriman, vice president of fundraising, and I'm thrilled to be here with all of you at this very important event." She pauses, allowing the room to break into a round of obligatory applause before she continues. "As you know, Mount Ivy General has been providing exceptional health care to the residents of this and surrounding communities for nearly forty years, and now it's time to bring our service to the next level, and that starts with the addition of a state-of-the-art cardiothoracic wing that will put Mount Ivy General on the map, where it belongs!"

"Hear! Hear!" someone yells just as the crowd breaks into another round of applause.

"Of course, you all know this is a fundraising event," she goes on, her tone taking on a more playful tone, "so we'd love if you'd participate in the silent auction taking place in the foyer. I hear that Dr. Brahman is generously offering up his car-washing services—"

"No SUVs!" someone, Dr. Brahman, I assume, calls out from the back corner of the room.

Everyone laughs.

I take a cautious sip of wine, mindful that too much in combination with my meds tends to wind me up. The last thing I need is to have a bad reaction and start throwing dinner rolls across the room.

"Okay, no SUVs for Dr. Brahman," Jackie goes on, chuckling. "But more than that, tonight is about introducing you to our hospital family. We're a small, tight-knit group who support and encourage each other through the good, the bad, and everything in between, and we'd love if you'd consider joining that family, because together we can do amazing things for this community."

"We sure can," Diane Porter mutters over an enthusiastic nod.

I take another sip.

"To kick things off, I'd like to invite comedian Rizzo Biggs to the stage," Jackie says, prompting a tall, gangly man with Gallagher-style hair to saunter out to the center of the stage. Thankfully, he doesn't have any mallets or watermelons.

"I sure hope he's funny," Mrs. Hoffstra says to me. "I love a good comedian."

For her sake, I hope he *is* funny. But my only care is that he'll be sparing me fifteen minutes of Dan-praising chitchat. Speaking of Dan, in my periphery I notice that he's not looking at the stage like everyone else is; rather, he's staring off toward the far corner of the room. I try to follow his gaze to see what—or who—is so interesting, but there are too many people to distinguish one person out of the crowd. Not that it matters. His attention needs to be focused on the people at *this* table. The Hoffstras in particular!

I give him a kick to grab his attention, then level him with a hard look that says exactly what I'm feeling: *Pay attention! We've still got work to do!*

He reads me loud and clear, quickly shifting his gaze back to the stage, where it belongs.

Get with the program, Dan!

We're here because of you, after all!

Though some of his material is a bit dated, the comedian delivers a good set, keeping everyone laughing as we work our way through the first course of roasted beet and sliced tomato salad. As expected, though, the painful conversations I've been dreading start the moment he departs the stage and the entrées are served.

"So, Dan, I read an interesting article about you in *Physicians Monthly* not too long ago," Diane Porter's husband, what's his name, says to Dan, referring to the fluffy piece the magazine wrote about him last summer. "It said you recently won a big award?"

"Is that so?" Mr. Hoffstra inquires before Dan even has a chance to respond.

"Yes, that's true," Dan answers over a modest-looking grin. "The Council on Cardiac Excellency awarded me their physician of the year award."

"Oh my, isn't that wonderful," Mrs. Hoffstra utters reverently.

I pause from picking at my braised ribs long enough to offer her my first earnest smile of the night.

Why do you have to be so nice?

"It was quite the coup for the hospital," Diane chimes in.

"Yes, I imagine it would be," Mr. Hoffstra says, clearly impressed.

"And, Jane, you were quoted in the article, too, weren't you?" what's his name asks, now dragging me into the conversation.

My cheeks flush as all eyes turn my way. *Here we go, Janie. It's showtime!* I lay my fork down on the plate and after a quick clear of the throat say, "Yes, they asked me what it's like to be married to a successful surgeon."

"Stressful, I imagine," Jim Demers offers up, prompting everyone to laugh.

I push out another smile as I think back on that interview: *Being married to a surgeon has its challenges; he's very busy and often puts his work before us, but at the end of the day it's a sacrifice I'm glad to make. Knowing how many lives he saves makes it all worthwhile. I can't imagine a better life than being a surgeon's wife.*

I swallow a heartsick whimper. What a naive fool I was . . .

"So, what was your response?" Patty Demers wonders, her blue eyes growing wide with curiosity.

A thousand different answers flit through my mind—none of them the response my heart wants to provide—but as I take in the hopefulness on Mrs. Hoffstra's face, I'm quickly reminded that this night is not about my current discomfort; it's about my future. Avery's future. Mom's future.

Mustering up every ounce of courage in my body, I raise my chin and say, "I told them it was a pleasure. That knowing how many lives he's impacting makes all of our sacrifices worthwhile."

I can feel my bones rattling beneath my skin, but my words somehow come out as smooth as custard on a warm summer night.

"Well said." Jim Demers raises his wineglass in my direction, then Dan's.

From the corner of my eye, I see that Dan's smiling stoically.

Asshole.

"I couldn't agree more," Mr. Hoffstra adds, raising his glass of iced tea into the air.

The rest of the table joins in, each raising their glass in salute to me and Dan. My gut wrenches. "To Dr. Dan Osborne and his wonderful wife, Jane."

"To Dan and Jane," they chant back.

Dan and I exchange a seemingly loving glance before we both assume our adopted smiles and then grab our own glasses. I raise mine up, then, despite the self-loathing burning my soul, press the crystal to my lips and take a long drink.

I did it.

I sold him the way I was supposed to.

Just like I said I would.

And the Hoffstras bought every bit of it.

"Well, I hate to leave such a festive group, but I'm up next," Dan says a moment later, motioning to the stage.

"Making you work after hours, huh?" Mr. Hoffstra chides.

Dan chuckles. "No rest for the weary." He backs his chair away from the table, and just as he starts to stand, he leans in close to me. My skin bristles as his lips graze my ear, but for our audience's sake, I maintain my warm expression.

"I'm sorry," he whispers.

I'm sorry?

I blink hard, confused. I wasn't expecting him to say anything. I just assumed it was more Ward and June fodder for the crowd, but *I'm sorry?* For what exactly—

"Should you be heading to the stage too?" Mrs. Hoffstra asks her husband.

"No, no. I've got plenty of time," he answers.

I think back on the email that outlined tonight's schedule of events. I peeked at it for only a minute, but I do remember that Mr. Hoffstra is scheduled to announce their gift sometime after the doctors introduce their grateful patients.

My heart starts to beat a little faster.

This is actually happening.

Mr. Hoffstra will make his announcement, and then I'll get my headache and leave. I'll be done.

I'll be free.

Finally!

"Hello again, everyone." Jackie thunks the microphone with her finger to grab our attention. "I trust you all enjoyed your dinner—"

"Mm-hmm," Mrs. Hoffstra mutters, then glances back at me and winks.

My heart twists despite my budding happiness.

I'm so sorry.

I wish I could be honest with you.
You don't deserve to be lied to.

"As much as I hate to interrupt your conversations," Jackie goes on, "we've reached a very special point in the evening. As I said earlier, Mount Ivy General has treated countless patients over the years—some with very unique and inspiring stories—so tonight we've invited a few of them back to share their experiences with you. And who better to introduce them than the doctors who treated them? So, without further ado, please welcome Dr. Daniel Osborne to the stage."

The entire ballroom erupts in a round of applause while my table-mates and others nearby turn my way, as if paying homage to the woman behind the great man. I slap on my most supportive smile yet, just as a surge of bile starts churning in my stomach.

You're almost free, Jane.
Just hang on a little bit longer.
Don't lose it now . . .

"Thank you so much," Dan says into a handheld microphone as he makes his way out from behind the long velvet curtains to the center of the stage. With his gleaming smile and confident stride, he looks every bit the superhero the crowd thinks he is. I fight the urge to roll my eyes. "It's a real pleasure to be here with you tonight. As Jackie said, my name is Dan Osborne, and along with being the head of the cardiothoracic division, I'm also the chief of surgery at Mount Ivy—a role I've had the privilege of holding for the last five years now. As we were just discussing at my table, one of the greatest joys of being a surgeon is the impact we have on the lives of our patients—"

I'd be lying if I said Dan didn't still have the natural charisma that drew me to him all those years ago. That kind of relatable charm that grabbed me from the first word he spoke. And as I take in the faces of those in the crowd, I can see he still has that effect on people. But, again, he seems a bit stiff somehow. He's not quite himself.

I'd like to think that standing up there on his foundation of lies is as hard on him as it is on me, but I know better. Stiff or not, that's not Dan. He lives to be worshipped.

"Several years ago, I was prepping for a routine surgery when I got an urgent page from the emergency room that two police officers had just been admitted with multiple gunshot wounds to the chest—"

His story catches my ear.

"Unfortunately, one officer's injuries were fatal, claiming his life before we were able to get him into the operating room," Dan goes on, now fully grabbing my attention. This sounds *very* familiar. "But the other officer was stable enough that we were able to perform surgery, and I'm happy to report that after twelve long hours, he came through, and he's here tonight to speak to all of you—"

My lungs start to cinch around my breath, as if my body is aware of something my brain hasn't quite figured out yet, or won't allow itself to, because it seems utterly impossible—

"Please join me in welcoming Detective Christopher Chavez."

"Oh my god," I gasp.

"Are you all right, dear?" Mrs. Hoffstra turns to me as the room explodes in applause.

My hand is plastered so tightly over my mouth that I can't respond to her with words, so I nod instead. But the truth is, I'm not okay. Not by a long shot.

Dan is the doctor who saved his life?

Eyes wide, heart hammering, I shift my gaze toward the left corner of the stage—to the crimson drape that shielded Dan just moments ago—and watch as he—Chavez, *my Chavez!*—emerges onto the stage.

Oh my god.

He's here.

He's here right now.

Flutters of nervous disbelief thrum through my body as he strides to the center of the stage, where Dan is waiting for him.

Does Chavez know who Dr. Osborne is to me?

Does he have any idea that the man who destroyed my life is the one who saved his?

My blood turns to concrete, limbs stiffening like boards, as I brace for the moment when I see the two of them together.

My worlds colliding in front of me.

Each one assumes a smile as Chavez grows nearer. Dan's is as sincere as any I've ever seen, while Chavez's is . . . nervous.

An empathetic whimper tickles my lips.

Poor Chavez.

They shake hands, and then Dan takes it a step further, giving Chavez a hearty pat on the arm, like he does with his father when he visits.

I clutch the edge of the table, confusion once again claiming my emotions.

How can this be happening?

Dan has to know this is the same Detective Chavez I was involved with.

A flashback of that volatile night in the kitchen suddenly spins through my mind.

Dan didn't know Chavez was the arresting officer. He didn't even know his name until I told him. And when I did, he—*oh god!* He flinched. I remember that. He must've recognized his name as a former patient right then. All these weeks he's known Chavez was *my* Chavez, and he didn't say anything!

Why would he bring him here?

What point is he trying to make?

"Isn't this just wonderful?" Mrs. Hoffstra mutters.

Part of me agrees with her. This *is* wonderful. I wasn't sure if I'd ever see Chavez again. But here he is, looking as handsome as ever in his sleek black tuxedo, his mile-deep dimples on full display. But another part of me—the part that's now inciting my fingers to tremble—thinks this is terrible. What if he doesn't know that I'm Dan's wife? What if we run into each other in the foyer and he sees me, and all the hatred he has for me comes rushing back? We'll make a spectacle. People will start to question how we know each other, and then all this will have been for nothing—

"Thank you all so much." The familiar sound of Chavez's smooth timbre pulls me back to the moment, settling my worries a bit. "I'm glad to be here tonight, but you should know that I'm not really one for public speaking, so I'll probably keep this short."

A hushed chuckle wafts through the ballroom while Dan says, "That's okay," from where he stands a few feet behind.

My heart twists at Chavez's obvious unease.

It's so unlike him.

I've never seen him nervous before.

Chavez raises the mic back up to his mouth. "Well, like Dr. Osborne said, it was just about eight years ago when my partner and I got tangled up in a bad situation while we were undercover. The drug dealer we'd been surveilling somehow got wind of who we were a couple of days before our planned bust and went on a shooting spree we weren't prepared for. Unfortunately, neither of us were wearing our vests—"

"Oh, good heavens," I hear Patty mutter from across the table.

"Just awful," Mrs. Hoffstra adds, sounding equally shocked.

"—so we were pretty much sitting ducks. My partner, Jay, took the shots first," he goes on, voice wavering a bit, "and then I got hit when I went in to try and help him. Thankfully, our backup was nearby and able to take the shooter out before he could hit anyone else, but by that point the damage had been done. Jay died in the ambulance on the way to the hospital, and I was in surgery for . . ." His brows crinkle in that adorable way they do when he's thinking. He glances back at Dan. "How long did you say it was?"

"Twelve hours," Dan confirms.

"Wow." Chavez turns back to us, shaking his head in disbelief. "I didn't realize I was in there that long. I guess time flies when you're having fun, huh?"

His unplanned joke provides a little levity to the room, but unlike my tablemates, I don't laugh. Instead, I swallow through the desperate ache that's quickly swelling in my throat.

Any doubts I had . . .

Any fear I felt about being rejected . . .

I don't care.

I just need to see him.

I need to talk to him—

"Anyway, it was a really hard time for me. Besides the physical recovery, I had some tough personal things to deal with too." He sighs. "Even though everyone else was happy I was alive, I wasn't. I couldn't figure out why I got to live when my partner didn't—"

"Survivor's guilt," what's his name mumbles, and then Jim Demers adds, "I've known servicemen that had that."

"—but eventually I worked through it," he continues, "with a lot of help from my family and my fellow officers. And you know what?" He shakes his head like he can't believe what he's about to say. "I think I'm actually better for it. A lot of really good things came from that experience."

My breath catches as his gaze suddenly lands on mine. He's not actually looking at *me*, of course. With the spotlight shining directly on him, he probably can't even see the edge of the stage, let alone a specific person seated at a table in the middle of the ballroom, but it still feels like he is, or like he might be. And that makes me feel good. Like there might be some hope.

"And now I can honestly say that I'm happy to be alive," Chavez goes on, turning back to the crowd and sounding a lot more like the cocky and confident guy I know. "I feel like I've been given a second chance at life, and I intend to live it to the fullest every day—not just for me, but also for Jay. And thanks to you"—he glances back at Dan—"I have the opportunity to do that."

A prideful smile stretches across Dan's face while the room erupts in a symphony of noise—applause, cheers, whistles—but none can compete with the violent pounding of my heart.

I need to see him.

I have to talk to him before he leaves!

Moving with unfamiliar urgency, I say a rushed "Excuse me" to Mrs. Hoffstra and then scramble out of my seat and hurry toward the exit at the back of the ballroom. Thankfully, most everyone's attention is still fixed on the stage ahead—where Dan is now saying something about who the real heroes in life are—but I'm too focused on my destination to pay any attention.

Just get to him.

Find him before he leaves.

"How do I get to the stage?" I call out to a busboy who's cleaning up the remains of our cocktail reception in the foyer.

He glances up from his tub of dirty glasses, looking unimpressed with my very important request. "Down at the end of that hall." He motions over my shoulder with his dishrag. "You'll see a door on your right."

I follow his terse instructions and hurry down the marble-floored hallway, teetering like a drunk in my heels the entire way.

Please still be here.

Please still be here . . .

I skidder to a stop when I come upon the door with the STAGE ENTRANCE sign plastered across its front. Winded, I pull it open to find a short flight of stairs in front of me and the sound of Dan's voice reverberating off the concrete walls around me. He's introducing a woman now. Someone named Mary Crosby. That must be his other grateful patient. The one who *isn't* a sexy detective.

Despite my hurried state, I'm aware that Jackie and the rest of her fundraising crew are nearby, so I take off my shoes and climb the steps barefoot, not wanting to draw any unnecessary attention to myself while I look for Chavez.

Heels dangling from my left hand, I make it to the landing, which is stage level. Much like when I earned extra credit painting sets for our sophomore class production of *Grease*, the backstage area is dimly lit and cluttered with scaffolding, props, and whatever other kinds of equipment they keep stored in those big black chests.

Moving on tiptoes, I creep deeper inside, coming to a stop when the stage lights start to break through the darkness. My heart beats fast as I peek around a tower of boxes to my right for a better look. From here, I can see the back of the stage—the hardwood floor gleaming beneath the spotlights—and the small audience waiting in the wings behind the floor-to-ceiling curtains. Jackie's there, of course, along with one of her staffers, as well as Harold Dixon, Brielle's plastic-surgeon husband, and there's also a middle-aged woman, who, I assume, is the grateful patient Harold is going to introduce. But no Chavez.

Dammit.

My shoulders slump.

I missed him—

"Jane?"

The sudden touch to my shoulder amplifies the sound of his voice. Breath suddenly shallowing, I turn to face him.

"Hi," I say, unable to mask the smile that's tugging on my lips.

"Hi," he replies over a budding smile of his own.

"I, um—" I swallow hard, trying to prioritize my thoughts. Before tonight, I had a laundry list of things I wanted to say to him—most importantly, *I'm sorry*—but with what just transpired, I'm not even sure where to begin.

"I'm sorry I didn't tell you I would be here," he says, unknowingly squashing my burden. "I thought about texting you, so I wouldn't upset

Bethany Crandell

you on your big night, but your husband specifically asked me not to say anything. And I, um . . . well," he sighs over a pained expression, "I honestly wasn't sure you'd even care if I was coming—"

"*What?* No." I step closer, gaze fixed squarely on his. "Of course I care. I'm *so* glad you're here."

"You are?"

"Yes. I mean, I was *really* surprised, but . . . yeah. I'm happy to see you."

"Well, that's good to hear." He blows out a relieved breath, suggesting that the nervousness I saw onstage had nothing to do with him speaking in front of a large crowd but rather with facing one person within that crowd, uncertain how she might receive him. "I was worried you'd never want to talk to me again after the way I treated you, and then to show up here on your important night—"

"Wait, what do you mean, the way you treated *me?*" I cut in, eyes narrowing. "*I'm* the one who was horrible to you. I'm the one who should be apologizing."

"No, you shouldn't. You were just trying to be honest with me, but I let my stupid, bruised ego get in the way of hearing you out. And now that I know what you've been going through, I completely understand why you did it."

I know what you've been going through.

A flicker of vulnerability nips at my nerves, forcing me to inhale a deep breath before I look up at him and say, "What all did he tell you?"

His smile sags. "Pretty much everything. He told me about this event and how important it is to the hospital, and about the older couple who would never give the money if they knew the truth about him." *The truth about him.* As if Dan even knows what the truth is anymore. "He said that he used your mom as leverage, and that he basically forced you into going along with all of it, even though he knew how much you didn't want to—"

"He told you that? He said he *forced* me?"

He nods.

My shoulders droop and I sigh, dumbfounded. Never in my life would I have imagined Dan would see this situation through my eyes, but apparently, he did.

"I know I should kick his ass for what he's done to you," he goes on, "and believe me, there's part of me that wants to; it's just that he . . . well, he's . . ."

"No, no. I get it." I grab his wrist with my free hand, silencing his unnecessary worry. Just as it did three months ago, the heat from his skin warms me from the top of my head all the way to my bare toes. I swallow hard and slowly pull it away. "He saved your life. I understand why you care about him." I drop my head. "I used to too."

Recognizing my sadness, he gently nudges my chin with his finger, prompting me to raise my gaze to him. The kindness pooling in his eyes nearly steals my breath.

"Believe it or not, he still cares about you. That's why he called me last night and invited me to this thing. He said he felt really bad about what he's been doing to you and wanted to make amends."

My jaw drops. "Huh?"

He smirks. "He wants to make amends with you," he repeats, even though we both know I heard him the first time. "He feels bad about what he's done, so he's trying to make it right. I guess he thought bringing me here would help do that."

Startled, I stagger back a step.

Ohmygod.

Dan feels bad?

He wants to make amends?

I scrub a hand across my brow.

I can't believe this.

He wants to do right by me, so he confessed the truth to the one person I needed to hear it the most.

That's why he was acting strange—why he seemed so off tonight.

317

He was putting my feelings before his own!

"Hey, are you okay?" Chavez reclaims my attention with a tug to my hand.

I shrug over a tepid laugh. "I don't know. My head is sort of spinning right now."

"Yeah, I bet. That's a lot to take in."

Our eyes meet, and that familiar flutter I've been craving returns to my chest, bringing with it all the things I've been wanting to say to him. The things I've been hoping to clarify but wasn't sure I'd ever get the chance to. The things I didn't know I'd be brave enough to say if I *did* get the chance.

I'm sorry was always first on my list, but what comes out is, "I've missed you."

He smiles softly. "I've missed you too."

The flutter expands from my chest through my entire body, snuffing out any flicker of fear I had about being rejected. "Really?"

"Nobody else wants to smash cars with me."

I snort out an unexpected laugh, then, without thought, twine my fingers through his and say, "Maybe we can do that again sometime?"

"Yeah. I'd like that," he says, then leans forward and presses a warm, soft kiss against my cheek—

"Mrs. Osborne?"

A deep, unsettlingly familiar voice cuts through the air, slicing our intimacy like a blade.

I jerk away from Chavez to find Mr. Hoffstra staring at me, his dark eyes wide in disbelief.

I gasp.

Oh no.

My stomach drops.

No.

No, no, no.

This isn't what it looks like.

I quickly snatch my hand back from Chavez and hurry across the stage toward him, desperation fueling my movements.

My damn barefooted movements!

"This isn't what it looks like," I spit out, tucking my shoes behind my back.

Mr. Hoffstra blinks hard but doesn't say anything.

Shit.

Agonized by the ramifications this will have, I press my free hand against my heart and in a panicked voice say, "*Please*, you have to believe me. This isn't what it looks like. There's more to this than you know—"

"*Oh!* Mr. Hoffstra! There you are! We thought we lost you." Jackie Harriman suddenly appears, crowing like a rooster at dawn. "We need to get you in place so you're ready to go on when he calls you." Oblivious to the surrounding tension, she loops her arm through Mr. Hoffstra's and quickly ushers him toward the "on-deck" area, where the other lookie-loos are spying on Dan from behind the curtain. "Jane, you and the detective can watch the announcement with me," she calls out over her shoulder.

"Is that the money guy?" Chavez asks warily. A wave of bile swirls through my gut as I nod in response. "What do we do?"

I raise my palms, a desperate wail rising in my chest. "I don't know. I—*shit*." I press a palm against my forehead, desperate for a plan that will fix what I've just done, but there isn't one. *There isn't one!*

Nothing can fix what I've just done.

All these months spent pretending.

SPENT LYING!

They were all for nothing.

I just ruined everything!

"Jane!" Jackie whisper-yells, calling me onward with a wave of her hand.

SHIT!

Stomach reeling, I slide my shoes back onto my feet and, with Chavez following stoically behind, make my way up to the curtain area, where everyone is gathered and listening to Dan finish up his conversation with Mary Crosby before he transitions to the all-important Hoffstra announcement.

". . . there just aren't enough words to say how grateful I am for what you did for me," Mary says, her voice wrought with emotion. "If not for you, I never would have seen my daughter get married," she sniffles, "or have met my beautiful granddaughters. It's all because of you. I owe my life to you, Dr. Osborne."

My heart twists as the crowd erupts in applause, and even though I can't see what's happening onstage from our vantage point at the back of the little crowd, I have no doubt that Dan is hugging his grateful patient right now, because that's the kind of doctor he is. He's a gifted, loving surgeon who deserves to have this new hospital wing, but now because of my foolish, reckless behavior, he won't get it.

At least, not from the Hoffstras.

Dear god, what have I done?

A fleeting thought suddenly crosses my mind: Maybe he'll overlook what he just saw. Maybe Mr. Hoffstra has some tawdry experiences of his own that will make him turn a blind eye to what he just witnessed.

I cast a ridiculously hopeful glance toward the man in question—standing just a few feet in front of me—and wince when I take in the simple gold wedding band wrapped around his finger. The same band he's worn for more than sixty years and undoubtedly has never forsaken.

He glances up and frowns in my direction. Tears well in my eyes as the reality of what's about to happen settles in: Dan's going to stand in front of this crowd of people and tell them how kind and generous Mr. Hoffstra and his wife are (and they are), and then he'll invite Mr. Hoffstra to join him onstage, where Dan'll be expectantly waiting for him to reveal his wonderful news. But he won't. Of course he'll donate *something*—twenty-five, fifty thousand, if we're lucky—but it won't come close to what we need. Certainly not the twenty-five million we were hoping for. And then Dan will be left to put on a brave face and pretend that his entire world hasn't just crashed around him.

An hour ago, I would have called that karma.

Now, I just call it regret.

How could I have been so careless?

After everything we've done . . .

After all the effort Dan put into bringing Chavez here tonight, I turned his peace offering into a sacrificial lamb.

"Well, thank you, Mrs. Crosby—"

Dan's deep voice once again emits through the microphone, but now it's bogged down with a very distinct waver that to other people probably sounds like sentimentality, but I know better. That's his nervous voice. And though I've heard it only a few times in my life, I'd know it anywhere.

Even on an "off" night, Dan is never nervous.

"It's almost time," Jackie chirps excitedly to Mr. Hoffstra.

I raise my fist up to my mouth and start nibbling on my knuckle.

"Hang in there," Chavez mutters.

"I certainly do appreciate the praise," Dan goes on, "but I'm sorry to say that I don't deserve it."

"He's so modest," Jackie titters to the staffer beside her.

"You see, while I may be a good surgeon, I'm afraid . . ." His voice trails off for a brief moment before he swallows so hard the microphone picks up the sound. "I'm afraid I'm not a very good man. Or a very good father. And I'm most certainly not a good husband . . ."

"What is he talking about?" Jackie mutters, casting a perplexed glance back at me.

My heart starts to beat harder.

What *is* he talking about?

"For the past few months, I've been asking my wife to lie about our relationship because I thought it would help us ensure the hospital gets the money it needs for the cardio wing—to ensure the stability of the hospital and all of our jobs—but the truth is, I've been asking her to lie because I've been too scared to face who I really am, and I can't ask her to do that anymore—"

His voice starts to crack with the nervousness I heard moments ago, prompting my chest to swell with an ache so deep I can feel my ribs starting to buckle.

I press my palm over my mouth, stifling the gasp that's rising inside me.

He's doing this.

He's actually doing this . . .

"I can't ask her to live her life as a lie because I'm too scared to live mine honestly," he goes on, the presence of tears now evident in his tone. "And if that costs us the funding we need, then so be it, but I'm not about to accept any money that was earned under false pretenses—"

"What on earth is he talking about?" Jackie snips, clearly growing agitated.

Fighting back my own tears, I glance toward Mr. Hoffstra, curious if he's feeling equally as perturbed, but his expression is unreadable.

Chavez squeezes my shoulder, a silent confirmation of his support.

"Contrary to what we've been telling all of you, my wife and I are not happily married. In fact, we'll be filing for divorce very soon because I recently revealed to her that . . ." He stalls and clears his throat as I wrestle with the knot in my own. "I am gay. And while I'm hoping that won't impact my career itself, it certainly has had a devastating impact on her, and our daughter, and for that I am truly sorry."

A hush of disbelief falls over the crowd while tears begin to rain down my cheeks.

You did it, Dan.

You did it!

Overcome with unexpected pride, I skirt my way around the crowd and look out onto the stage. My heart wrenches when I find him standing alone beneath the spotlights—exposed and on display for everyone's judgment—while a shell-shocked Mary Crosby looks on from just a few feet away.

As if sensing my presence, Dan turns, his blue eyes finding me in an instant.

My chin starts to quiver as a lifetime of memories and shared adventures pass between us. I offer him a broken smile. A smile that says *I'm proud of you* and *In some way, I'll always be your family.* He nods in response, then sets the mic down on the stage and heads for Mr. Hoffstra.

Though understandably curious, Jackie and the rest of the lookie-loos are still respectful enough to back out of the way, offering the men a bit of privacy, though Dan urges Chavez and me closer with a wave of his hand.

Blotting at my eyes, we clear the distance between us just as a lone soul in the audience breaks the silence with a very slow and intentional clap.

"Sir, I need to apologize for misleading you." Dan blinks back tears as he addresses Mr. Hoffstra. "You and your wife have been nothing but kind to us, and we betrayed that kindness—well, *I* did," he clarifies, glancing at me. "It was wrong, and I'm terribly sorry. I completely understand if you want to leave now."

"Leave?" Mr. Hoffstra snuffs. "I thought it was my turn to speak?"

Dan blinks hard. "Well, yes, sir, it is. But I just assumed after what I confessed—"

"Young man," Mr. Hoffstra cuts him off while laying a hand on his shoulder. "Do you hear that person clapping out there?"

Dan nods, and so do I. Even though he wasn't asking me the question.

"That's my wife," he says. I peek around Dan for a look. Just as I suspected earlier, you can't make out one face in the crowd through all the lights. "I'd know that clap anywhere. That's the same clap she gave when our daughter finally came out to us a few years ago. Of course, she did it at the dinner table and not in front of three hundred people." He chuckles, eyes almost smiling. "But mark my words, that's her. And by the time I get out on that stage and announce that you're going to get your new wing, the rest of those people will be clapping too. They just need a few minutes for the dust to settle and to be reminded that your personal life has nothing to do with your excellent skills as a surgeon. Now, if you'll excuse me, I've got a speech to give."

He gives each of us a parting handshake—even Chavez—then sets off for the stage. And just as predicted, Mrs. Hoffstra's solo support is soon drowned out by the rest of the crowd's.

Jaw hanging, Dan turns to me. "I can't believe that just happened."

"Neither can I," I chuckle while sniffling back tears.

He stares at me for a long beat, his amusement quickly settling into a sincerity I haven't seen in a very, very long time.

"You know, it's okay if you guys want to get out of here," he says, shifting his gaze between me and Chavez. "You've been through enough tonight, and I imagine it's going to get pretty intense around here."

I know what my answer would have been thirty minutes ago, but everything's different now. I turn to Chavez to make sure he's on the same page.

He offers me one of his adorable smirks, then turns to Dan and says, "Nah. I think we'll stick around. I've been trying to get a first dance with this one for almost thirty years. I think I better take advantage of the dance floor while I can."

My cheeks flush beneath his playful banter, while Dan looks on with a glint of approval in his eye.

"I think a first dance sounds like a great idea," he says. "I hope you have a good time."

A flood of contentment washes over me as he heads off to deal with Jackie and the rest of the backstage audience, leaving me with Chavez.

"Shall we?" He extends his hand to me.

"Absolutely." And even though I know his intent is to lead me to the dance floor, I can't help but feel like I'm about to take the first step of my brand-new life.

I drop my hand in his, and we set off across the stage.

"You do know how to dance, don't you?" I ask.

He offers me a sexy little smirk. "Almost as well as I can swing a bat."

His reference to the salvage lot brings back a flood of delicious memories, inciting my own smirk to emerge.

Just a few steps in, and this new life is already looking very promising.

EPILOGUE

WHAT I AM MOST LOOKING FORWARD TO DOING AFTER THIS CLASS IS . . .

Living MY life.

ACKNOWLEDGMENTS

All glory to God for steadily supplying me with fresh ideas, the tenacity to explore them, and most importantly the talents and support of the following folks, who have helped transform them into something worthwhile (and to whom I owe much more than a few kind words. Next round is on me):

My phenomenal editors, Maria Gomez and Selina McLemore. Your enthusiasm for my words is as delightfully overwhelming as your ability to make me laugh.

From cover design to copy edits, the entire team at Montlake and Amazon Publishing for your professionalism and timeliness. You're this schedule-freak's dream!

My very patient and wise agent, Amy Moore-Benson. Your confidence in my abilities is astounding.

Anita Howard, my incomparable critique partner. Your name should be on the cover of this book too. (Smaller, but still there.) Thank you for navigating the ledges with me.

Heather Love King and A. S. Youngless for faithfully retweeting, even when the GIFs are bad.

Bonnie Carnow for your thoughtful insights on the pain of loving someone with Alzheimer's.

Kelly Grimando and Shelly Munson for always thinking I'm cool, even though you know the truth.

The Goat Posse for your endless support.

Terry, Gracie, and Becca for ensuring my humility.

My parents and sisters for the consistent reminders that I'm not in control, and that's okay.

And to all the women hanging on by a thread, I hope Jane's story brought you a momentary reprieve from the chaos. Or at the very least, that your grocery store is stocked with oranges.

ABOUT THE AUTHOR

Bethany Crandell is the author of *The Jake Ryan Complex*. She lives in San Diego with her husband, teenage daughters, and two destructive puppies. Bethany loves guacamole, afternoon naps, and eye rolls. You can visit her online at www.bethanycrandell.com.